The Poison Bed

E.C. Fremantle holds a First for her BA in English and an MA in Creative Writing from Birkbeck. As Elizabeth Fremantle she is the critically acclaimed author of four Tudor historical novels: *Queen's Gambit*, *Sisters of Treason*, *Watch the Lady* and *The Girl in the Glass Tower*. She lives in London and Norfolk.

The Poison Bed

E.C. FREMANTLE

MICHAEL JOSEPH
an imprint of
PENGUIN BOOKS

MICHAEL JOSEPH

UK | USA | Canada | Ireland | Australia
India | New Zealand | South Africa

Michael Joseph is part of the Penguin Random House group of companies
whose addresses can be found at global.penguinrandomhouse.com.

First published 2018
001

Copyright © E.C. Fremantle, 2018

The moral right of the author has been asserted

Set in 13.5/16 pt Garamond MT Std
Typeset by Jouve (UK), Milton Keynes
Printed in Great Britain by Clays Ltd, St Ives plc

A CIP catalogue record for this book is available from the British Library

HARDBACK ISBN: 978–0–718–18048–5
TRADE PAPERBACK ISBN: 978–1–405–92008–7

www.greenpenguin.co.uk

For Alice and Raphael

Whether we fall by ambition, blood, or lust,
Like diamonds, we are cut with our own dust.

The Duchess of Malfi, John Webster

Her

She was ready when they came, the three men. They smelt of damp wool and resisted staring but stole furtive glances instead. She walked to the door. Her sister sobbed, folding her into a wet embrace, while the nurse, bawling child in her arms, watched with a blunt glare.

Outside, the wind slapped hard in bitter gusts of mizzle. She felt eyes at the windows on her but refused to adopt a posture of shame. Shame is ravenous. If it is allowed in, it will eat away at you, to the bone.

They followed the route towards the river, over slick cobbles.

'Must we go by water?' she asked. But they had orders to obey.

She became aware of a clamour, a frenzy of chanting and bellowing, and once through the gates she saw the crowd: red faces, bared teeth. Were it not for her armed escort she might have been torn limb from limb. The thought tightened her gut like a drawstring and she forced her mind off it for fear of losing her composure. But neither could she think of the river's beckoning fingers and wondered which was worse: the crowd, a quick, savage battering, or those icy fingers about her throat?

A shadow broke from the throng, snarling. It spat. She lost her footing, skidded down the river steps, but was caught by one of the men and as good as carried the rest of the way down, into the waiting boat.

'Hope you fall in and drown, bitch,' someone shouted.

She took her handkerchief from her cuff to wipe away the trail of mucus, discarding it over the side. It floated away, bobbing, like a small white bird. The vessel jolted and her head cracked hard against a wooden strut. The pain was sharp, but she maintained her poise. She would not give her escort the satisfaction of seeing her suffer.

One of them seemed familiar. She racked her brain for his name, thinking it might give her some small advantage if she could use it. Again, the boat rocked, oars slapping, and she was thrown back in time: a vast hand pressing down on her head, the wet shock, the tide of panic and the quiet menace of his voice, *You must learn to trust me – to resist weakness.* Her breath stuttered, the guard looked over and she coughed, pretending irritation in her throat.

Approaching the bridge, she could feel the force of the rapids sucking them into the shadows. She shut her eyes, holding her breath, until they emerged on the other side where the tower loomed. Her husband was there, somewhere behind those sheer walls. She wondered if he watched her approach and could picture him, like a carved angel, gilded by the low winter sun. But she mustn't think of him, mustn't be distracted from what she was about to face.

The boat slid into the tunnel that ran beneath the outer ramparts, where torches reflecting on to the rippled surface made it seem in flames. She half expected to encounter Cerberus when they reached the other side. But they found instead a small man, starched with deference, who took her hand to help her from the barge. She imagined his, beneath its glove, as a pink paw with sharp claws to go with his rodent's face.

He led the way up a flight of steps. Wind whipped around the walls, tugging at her clothing as she waited for him to unlock a heavy door, which fell open with a shriek. Within, the chamber had small windows on both sides and an unlit hearth from which a foul stench emanated, as if a pigeon had died in the flue. One wall glistened with damp and the chill made her shiver despite her thick cloak.

'The attorney general will be here shortly,' he said, without looking at her, and Bacon arrived as if on cue, blowing in through the door, like a demon, on a blast of wind.

'Why is the fire not lit?' he said, even before making his greeting. 'I can't be expected to carry out my business in this cold . . .' he paused to cast a look her way that pricked the nape of her neck '. . . can I?'

A boy was sent for. He set down his bucket of hot coals on the flagstones with a clang and began laying the hearth while Bacon silently dissected her. His eyes hadn't an ounce of kindness in them. She had no use for kindness, anyway.

But she was accustomed to men responding to her appearance. In Bacon she couldn't discern even so much as a dilated pupil, and that disarmed her. Perhaps she was not quite as immune to fear as she liked to believe.

'I haven't seen you since you hosted the celebration for my wedding.' She wanted to remind him who she was.

'Three years ago,' he stated, seeming to imply that things had changed since then, and she regretted bringing it up. Her wedding and the circumstances that had brought her to this place were inextricably linked. His expression remained indecipherable.

With a pair of tongs the boy plucked a red-hot coal from his bucket, which caught the kindling instantly, flaring up.

They became aware of heavy footfall mounting the steps and turned simultaneously towards the door. Her breath faltered.

'This must be the lord chief justice now. He will be joining us.'

Coke lumbered in, wheezing. He smelt strongly of sweat, as if the steps had been a mountain, and ran his gaze slowly over her. She saw the hungry spark in Coke's eye, lacking in Bacon's. A young man, ledger tucked beneath his arm, slid quietly in behind him.

She took back control and offered them a seat, as if it was a social visit, noticing that Bacon wiped the bench before he sat, slapping his palms together to remove the dust.

The fire was smoking, stinging her eyes. The servant opened a window to help it draw, and Bacon snapped, 'What do you think you're doing, idiot? In this weather.' The boy flinched as if he feared a beating and she suggested he look in the chimney for blockages. He prodded about with a long broom, and the half-rotted carcass of a bird dropped into the flames. They watched it burn. The smell turned her stomach.

'So,' said Bacon, once the boy had gone, clasping his hands together and stretching them out, palms turned forward until his knuckles cracked. 'I suppose you intend to deny the charges.'

'No.' She met his gaze. 'I'm guilty.' His posture crumpled almost imperceptibly. It was clear she had surprised him, even disappointed him perhaps. 'I wanted him dead.'

The clerk held his pen aloft, eyes wide. Bacon sighed. Regret, or something like it, began to wrench at her. But it was too late to turn back.

'You *are* aware of the inevitable outcome of such a confession?'

She nodded. 'I know I must accept the consequences. It *is* the whole truth.'

'The whole truth – is that so?' Bacon's look penetrated her, as if he could see into her bones. 'You may be clever,' he narrowed his eyes slightly, 'for a *woman*. But don't think you can outfox me.'

'I don't know what you mean.'

'No?' He continued to scrutinize her, making her feel like the subject of one of his philosophical enquiries.

They fell quiet, the only sound the scratch of the clerk's pen and the draught whistling through the ill-fitting windows.

It was Coke who spoke eventually, firing off a volley of questions.

'Is it not enough that I confess but you must know how?'

He carried on, asking about things and people that seemed to bear no relation to the case, seeking links where they didn't exist. Bacon seemed irritated by Coke's line of query, thrumming his fingers on the table.

Eventually he interrupted: 'And your husband? What was *his* part?'

'He had no hand in it.' The words exploded from her too loud and too fast.

Bacon spat out a caustic laugh but said nothing.

'He's innocent.' She knew she sounded rattled and wondered if repeating herself made the declaration sound less credible.

And that was it.

They stood, the clerk clapped his ledger shut, and she was left alone, wondering if her husband had also confessed.

Him

I sit alone in the gloom. A shaft of thin light leaks through a single window. The other is covered. I cannot bear the view it offers.

I line up the few relics I have of her, among them a small pearl, a square of unwashed linen and a package of letters tied with a ribbon that once held her undergarments together. I hold it to my nose but her smell is gone, leaving me with the memory of untying it, her clothes falling away to expose the landscape of her flesh. Heat surges through my body. Tears burn the back of my eyes.

I must find a way to make sense of my situation, find believable answers to all the questions I am asked over and over again. But fear coils itself round my throat until I think I will choke. So, I think of her.

The first time I set eyes on her was almost five years ago. She was in Henry Stuart's apartments at the heart of a cluster of women. One of them – a girl – was holding out her hand, palm upward, and Frances had taken it, was examining it with studied concentration. I thought at first the girl had a splinter but there seemed more to it – all the group gazing at Frances intently, waiting for her to speak. I couldn't help but eavesdrop.

'I see love.' She spoke softly. I later heard it said that her quiet voice was an affectation, designed to draw people into her thrall. But Frances had no need for such tricks. 'Yes, it is quite clear in the intersection of these two lines.'

The girl blurted an embarrassed laugh. 'Is it someone I

already know?' Red blotches appeared from nowhere on her throat.

Frances closed her eyes for several moments, as if waiting for some kind of celestial intervention, before saying firmly, 'No, he's a stranger.' She dropped the hand, moving away towards where the men were gathered around Henry, inspecting a small bronze statue.

The court was filled with striking women, all of them marble goddesses. I barely noticed them – mine was not a world of women. But she was different. There was nothing cold and dead about Frances. No, she was undeniably human, life pulsing beneath her surface. She reminded me, in some curious way, of a beautiful boy. It was the fact she went unpainted. Her skin was fresh and clean, making me think if I dared move close enough that she would smell of laundered linen. But it was also the lithe ranginess of her body, the unusual directness of her gaze. There was no artifice to Frances Howard.

When I say it was the first time I set eyes on her, it is not quite the truth. Seven years before I had seen her wedding procession from a distance. She was flanked by her father and great-uncle, yet despite their combined magnificence they failed to diminish the effect of her. Though she was only fourteen she seemed older, steeped in self-possession. I found myself gaping. I was a nobody then, just the orphaned son of minor Scottish gentry who had been taken in as a page to someone on the fringes of court.

'They won't be consummating it yet,' said an onlooker to his neighbour. I found myself stirred at the thought of that. It shocked me: I had felt such things only for men. 'He's to travel Europe and she'll be sent back to her parents until she's old enough.'

I was on tiptoe, hoping for another glimpse of her bright

brown hair. It fell gleaming almost to the floor – everyone talked of her hair – and that mouth, which seemed, even at rest, to be set in a slight smile that suggested a kept secret.

'She looks old enough to me.' The other man snorted, almost salivating. I was caught in a muddle of feelings, and despite my own burning arousal, I found myself incensed by his disrespect. To speak of something so pure and untouchable in such a way seemed sacrilege. I could have punched him, knew I had the strength to knock him cold. Those with no family learn early in life how to look after themselves.

In the intervening years, she'd become a woman. I watched her with Henry, laughing about something, their heads flung back, mouths open, but she stopped suddenly, turning away from him, her gaze locking on me, as if she were a hawk and I a hare. I like to imagine it was the force of my desire that drew her attention. I had never seen such eyes, dark glossy ovals. Just a square of white in each, a reflection of the window behind me, and my own tiny form etched there. She said nothing, just smiled, displaying teeth as neat as a string of pearls.

Only then did I notice Henry was watching me watching her. 'Come to spy on us, Carr? Or is it Rochester, these days?' he said, with a scowl. 'Didn't my father ennoble you recently?'

A few of his friends stared at me in disapproval, but not her. She smiled my way again and I saw Henry's hackles rise.

'I suppose he's sent you to persuade me to take that Catholic child as a wife. Well, you can tell him my answer is no.' He was pulling on a pair of articulated gauntlets and didn't look at me. 'What would I want with a nine-year-old papist?'

I felt Frances's eyes still on me. 'She comes with a substantial –'

'A *substantial* dowry,' Henry interrupted me. A page was holding out several fencing foils for him. He picked one, slicing it through the air. 'To pay off my father's *substantial* debts?'

As I searched for a response that wouldn't give offence, the foils slipped from the page's grip, clattering to the floor. The boy blushed and crouched, retrieving them to a hail of sniggering. As he was reaching for the last, a foot kicked it out of his range, causing a renewed eruption of laughter.

'That's uncalled for.' I glared at the perpetrator and stooped to pick up the foil, handing it to the page, patting his shoulder, giving him a few words of encouragement.

Someone said, 'You tell him, Carr.' And I sensed I had gained a little ground.

My adversary was annoyed, his mouth set in a thin snarl – 'For a man who's come from nowhere you haven't done badly, have you?' – then, under his breath, 'In the King's bedchamber, like a woman.' Southampton had never liked me and the feeling was mutual. He was puffed up and wore the swagger of someone who didn't realize he'd lost his looks to age. I held my ground, keeping a steady gaze on him, but didn't react. 'No answer to that, Carr?'

'Some things don't dignify a response.'

He didn't like that, and wasn't meant to. 'Where did *you* learn about dignity? Not in the gutter you came from.'

I half smiled. 'One thing I did learn in the gutter is that a prize ram, butchered and cooked, is indistinguishable from ordinary mutton.' She beamed at me, meeting my eye.

Henry glowered and placed a proprietorial hand on her arm. I recognized jealousy when I saw it. He was four years her junior, still a boy. It seemed an absurd pairing. But the attraction of power should never be underestimated. 'Ordinary mutton,' Henry spoke directly to her, 'can get stuck in your teeth.'

Rage flared beneath my surface. The thought of silencing him flitted through my mind – I imagined my hands about his throat, thumbs pressing into the soft flesh, could hear his choked pleas for mercy.

Henry was addressing me: 'Pick a rapier, Carr. Let's see what you're made of.' The air was tight, everyone waiting for the clap of thunder after lightning. I hesitated. 'Winner takes that.' He pointed towards Frances. I was momentarily appalled and might have reacted had I not then realized he hadn't meant Frances but the little bronze shepherd beside her.

I nodded my assent. A breastplate was produced and fitted on to me. I chose a foil. They were all blunted, just practice weapons. The only thing that risked damage was someone's vanity. The doors to the courtyard were opened and out we went, followed by the entire company, waiting to see if Robert Carr would have the gall to out-manoeuvre the heir to the throne.

We danced back and forth, the occasional steel scrape ringing out as our blades touched. Prince Henry was good, elegant and skilled, but I had complete control, though made it look otherwise, sensing the importance of putting on a show. I knew well enough that audacity would win me the crowd. I may have lacked his refinement but I was older – twenty-four and in my prime – and I knew I was better, faster, more aggressive. I'd learned to fight rough, with my fists, and I wasn't going to lose, not in front of her. No matter what trouble it might cause me.

His foil whistled close by my cheek. I ducked.

'Mind your pretty face, Carr,' Southampton called scornfully.

Pretending not to hear, I saw my chance. In a moment's hesitation from Henry I made my lunge, the tip of my weapon landing on the side of his neck, where a great blood vessel runs. Had it been a real fight our shoes would have been drenched red with Stuart blood.

'You've made your point.' Southampton was tugging at my sword arm and added, under his breath, 'You'd better watch yourself.'

'What did you say?' It was clear he'd have liked to pick a proper fight. Despite his years, he was battle-hardened and I knew he wouldn't be so easily beaten. 'Is that a challenge?' A ripple ran through the company. I shrugged my arm from his grip and looked him full in the eye. 'Is it?'

I had the King behind me. I had his ear, I had his trust, I had his love, and ill-bred or not, I had a great deal more influence than Southampton. But still he pushed his face up tight to mine, like a rutting stag. I spat out a laugh. 'I thought you were hopeful of a place on the Privy Council?'

He pulled back, flushed, half turning away, and I couldn't help whispering, 'I knew you didn't have the balls.'

Henry stepped between us, slapping a hand on my shoulder. 'I'm grateful to you, actually, Carr. I shan't develop my fencing skills by being allowed to win.' His generosity of spirit made me forget a moment that we were rivals for the attention of Frances Howard, who was watching us carefully as we walked back inside together. 'Here,' he said, taking the bronze shepherd from its plinth and handing it to me.

It was heavier than I'd expected, a dead weight, and it crossed my mind that it would have made an effective weapon, but I returned it to its place. 'It's better off here, where it will be appreciated.'

If I'm honest, the little sculpture seemed to me quite ordinary but Frances was transfixed. 'The lines are exquisite,' she was saying, in her low voice. 'See here, the way his weight seems to fall into his staff — and that backward glance. He is perfectly balanced.' She paused, giving a small sigh. 'Why is it when we see things of beauty we want to possess them?' She was running a finger over the curve of the bronze thigh.

Henry watched her, head cocked. We must both have been imagining ourselves as that tiny man beneath her finger.

The doors opened, breaking the spell, and Northampton appeared. 'Uncle,' she said, moving towards him, her voice velvet smooth. 'Where have you been? You've missed all the excitement.' I saw a rare glimpse of girlishness about her beside her great-uncle. He wasn't particularly tall, though he carried himself as if he were, with the poise of a much younger man that belied his grizzled appearance. I noticed, seeing them together, the extent to which they were alike. They shared the same high forehead and arched brows, giving them the patrician air that came with centuries of good breeding.

But there was a trace of menace beneath his elegant surface. It made the atmosphere in the room shift, everyone seeming to shrink back a little. Even the prince's close companions vibrated with begrudged respect and Northampton seemed to expand under their attention.

'I have a rather pressing private matter to discuss with Your Highness ...' He and Henry moved away together towards the window alcove.

'Come with me.' She beckoned. Like a dog, I followed at her heel as she walked to the far end of the room. I was close enough to hear the whisper of her dress as she moved.

'I enjoyed that.' She had come to a halt. She was tall, as tall as I, her eyes level with my own. 'The swordplay.' I searched for a response but my wit had deserted me. She lifted a finger, inspecting it. 'Look, it's broken.' She held it out so I could see the nail, which she then pinched tightly, ripping it away with a little wince, tossing the fragment to the floor. I followed it with my eyes, and when I looked up again she was pulling her finger from her mouth.

'Give me your hand.' She took it – 'Strong hands' – unfurling my fist to examine the lines of my palm, running that damp finger across it. 'Shall I tell you what I see?'

Desire had near paralysed me. All I could manage was a nod.

'I see love.'

Remembering what she'd said to the girl earlier, I found my voice: 'I suppose you say that to everyone.'

'I only say what I see.' One of her eyebrows rose minutely.

'You're teasing.' I smiled – but she didn't.

'You think this is a game?' Her grip was firm. 'There,' she prodded the mound below my thumb, 'I see death and . . .' She shook her head slightly.

'And what?'

'No,' she whispered.

Northampton was calling her over. 'I'm coming.' As she turned she caught me with a look, a smile – that smile – so secretive, so knowing, I felt she'd had a glimpse of my soul. I belonged entirely to her.

Her

A male scream echoes through the saturated air, and another, then silence.

'At least that hellish racket's stopped,' says Nelly, who sits opposite Frances, unlacing her bodice. In a single movement she pulls out her breast, positioning the baby to feed. She's such a scrap of a girl, with a pinched face and dull hair the colour of hay, Frances can hardly believe she is able to sustain the voracious baby.

Through the quiet Frances can hear the lap and glug of water, reminding her that just below, on the other side of the wall, the river slides by. There is a patch of mildewed damp blossoming near the window and she imagines the water rising, soaking through the stones as if they are made of sponge.

Sometimes in the dark she believes she is floating, that her bed has become a boat and the objects around her – a gown hanging from a peg, the high-backed chair, the wicker cradle – are the ghosts of the room's previous inhabitants. The bed is heavy and carved with hideous winged creatures. Frances hates it, and the ugly set of German bed-curtains conceived with a grander space in mind than the room above the watergate. But at least she is no longer alone.

'Watch this!' With her free hand, Nelly picks up a playing card, flipping it, making it dance from finger to finger, like a butterfly. Then, with a smirk, she flicks it, so it flits through the air landing on Frances's lap. She gives a whoop of laughter, exposing a muddle of teeth. Over the last few days,

Frances has come to rather like Nelly's audacity and her apparent obliviousness to the deference expected of her.

'*Please* tell us,' the girl implores. 'Just a few snippets. I only want to know how it can happen that a person like you,' she looks straight at Frances, 'that's been so kind to me, listened to me grumbling about my problems and – well – treated me as a human being, when most would barely look at me, can –' She stops, as if unsure how to put it.

'Can fall from grace?' Frances says. 'You must know.' The pamphleteers have published every detail of the scandal and much more, so she must have a good idea. Nelly won't know of her confession, though, and Frances is determined to remain evasive.

'I have the gist but I'm sure you're not what they say you are.'

'What do they say I am?' Frances is anxious to know exactly what the girl has heard.

'That you're a witch and talk with demons. Some even say you've had . . .' she looks at the other woman to see if she's gone too far, but Frances tells her to continue '. . . relations with the devil,' she mouths.

'Yes, I heard that too.' Frances laughs tightly, making light of it. It occurs to her, not for the first time, that the girl may have been planted here to milk her for incriminating information.

'I knew a cunning woman. She was our neighbour. People went to her for remedies but I know she would sometimes cast spells.'

'Spells?' Frances raises her eyebrows. She is remembering how she got on the wrong side of such a woman once. Her suspicion flickers: is the girl deliberately trying to draw her into a conversation about witchcraft, hoping something will spill? 'I expect she was nothing but a swindler.'

'She cast a spell on a man and he was found dead in his bed within the hour.'

15

'Sounds more like murder to me.' As Frances says it she wishes she hadn't.

'They found her guilty. She hanged for it.'

The girl's green eyes are drilling into her. Who are you? Frances asks silently. 'Who taught you?' She points at the cards, changing the subject.

'My pa. Soon as I was old enough he used to take me out with him. Card tricks was his living, see.' She manoeuvres the baby on to her other breast, 'Besides, you're not the only one round here to have taken a *fall*.' She stresses the final word, as if she means the fall from Eden.

Frances is tempted to shut down the conversation, berate the girl for her insolence, but she senses she must tread carefully. 'Is that so?'

'I got myself in the family way without a husband and birthed a dead baby.'

'I know that, Nelly. That is how you came to be here.' Beneath the girl's hard shell Frances thinks she can discern a well of sadness, making her question her earlier misgivings, thinking it unlikely that Bacon or Coke would come into the orbit of a creature like her. Some well-born young woman, with a grudge, sent to report back perhaps, but a girl like Nelly, she doubts it. God knows, it must have been hard enough finding someone for the job of wet-nurse to a murderess's infant.

'But what you don't know is who fathered my baby.'

She has pricked Frances's interest. 'So, who was he?'

Nelly looks at her lap. 'My father.'

Frances hadn't expected that. She is well aware such things go on but nonetheless she's shocked. In her world virginity is too valuable an asset to be adulterated. But this girl has nothing of value about her except her wits.

'You don't believe me? That's no surprise. People like you

never do believe people like me.' Nelly seems not to have an ounce of self-pity.

Frances feels a burst of compassion. 'You must have –' She stops herself before suggesting that Nelly must have wished the next-door witch had cast a spell on her father. It would be unwise to turn the conversation back to witchcraft. Instead she says, 'You must not have known whom in the world you could trust. Is that why your mother cast you out?'

Nelly is nodding. 'Some things can't be changed, can they?'

'That's true.' Frances is impressed by the girl's stoicism. It is a quality she admires.

'Stupid, really, but I used to wish I'd been born into a family like yours, have a marriage all set up with some rich . . .' Her words trail off. 'What was it like?'

Despite herself, Frances begins to open up. 'I expect you already know that I was married to the young Earl of Essex when I was a girl.' It strikes her now that a dozen years have passed since that wedding. 'The union was designed to mend an old rift between my family and his.' There is something comforting about sharing her story after all those secrets to be kept. 'We lived separately at first. He went abroad for his education. I was still very slight, you see, and my mother thought I'd struggle with a birth. The trouble didn't begin until much later, once we'd set up house together.'

∞

I pulled the short straw. Uncle took his silk handkerchief and wrapped it around my eyes. We were all playing: my two maids; Uncle and his man; my favourite brother Harry; Essex's three gentlemen; even the chaplain wanted to join in.

17

Only Essex refused and sat in a nearby chair, stiff as if he'd been cut from card. He'd barely said a word since we arrived that afternoon.

His house, Chartley, was remote. We'd been five days on the road before we saw the great ruined castle perched on a ridge and the house tucked behind it. I can't pretend I wasn't disappointed on arriving: although it was vast it smelt of dust and was gloomy, the windows too small to light the rooms properly. The whole place was sullen – it creaked and groaned at night as if ghosts were trapped beneath the floors, and it was crooked: if you put a bead at one end of the hall it would roll all the way to the other. When you are accustomed to houses like the ones I grew up in – new and splendid with their acres of glass and sleek cool marble, splashed with sun, looking out over gently rolling vistas, places filled to the brim with life – it spoils you.

Uncle, Harry and I waited in the hall for Essex to appear and I tried to imagine what kind of man he had become after all his years away. An old clock ticked loudly and his painted relatives glowered at me from the walls, reminding me that I'd been raised to think of them as Howard adversaries. His father, the old Earl of Essex, was silk clad and smug, as if he owned the world.

'He was insufferably cocksure,' said Uncle, pointing up at the picture. 'Glad he's out of the way.' He made a chopping motion against his neck. 'Shame his faction of bloody Protestant fanatics endures.' A disingenuous smile spread over his face. 'Ah, but we're all supposed to be friends now.'

'Thanks to me.' I couldn't hide my bitterness. I was inwardly cursing the marriage that had put me in this gloomy place.

His response was cold: 'You're twenty now, quite old enough to understand the importance of diplomacy.'

Of course I'd grown up with my own set of painted relatives hanging on the walls. My grandfather and great-grandfather had been executed too, long before. It occurred to me that decapitated antecedents were all Essex and I had in common.

A prickling at my back, the sensation I was being watched, made me turn to see Essex standing in the gallery above. 'I hope your journey wasn't too arduous.' He began to descend the stairs and I wondered if he'd overheard us.

Once he was closer I could see that he was no longer the fresh-faced boy I remembered from the altar six years before. I tried to conceal my shock behind a smile. I was aware that he'd suffered a bad bout of the smallpox – it had put him out of action for a good eighteen months and delayed our reunion. I expected him to have a few pocks and scars, but nothing could have prepared me for the angry-looking craters that covered his cheeks and the way the skin around his right eye was swollen and pulled out of shape, as if he'd been badly burned.

'You find me monstrous,' he said. He did look monstrous next to Harry, who was younger but taller, with unblemished skin and sleek dark hair. Harry was like me.

'No.' My smile had become rigid. 'But does it give you pain?' I willed myself not to stare.

'I don't seek your sympathy.' He had shrugged, changing the subject, asking one of the servants to show us to our rooms.

The blindfold was tightly tied, leaving me in absolute darkness. Unidentified hands began to spin me and I was left, arms outstretched in the middle of the floor. I could hear laughter and the shuffling of feet as I took a few tentative steps. They began to taunt me, scuttling about calling, 'Over here,' as I flailed, finally catching a shoulder. I realized it was Essex when he said, 'Not me,' pushing me away harder than was necessary so I stumbled and nearly lost my footing. After what seemed an interminable chase I finally caught the edge of someone's garment in my fist.

'Who can it be?' I ran my hands over clothes I recognized instantly as Uncle's. I pretended otherwise, walking my fingers up his neck and over his face, through his hair, deliberately poking and prodding, saying, 'I know only one person with hair growing from his ears.'

'You little minx,' Uncle guffawed. He lifted my blindfold. 'For that you will have to be punished.' He began to tickle me. 'Say you are sorry.'

I collapsed to the floor, helpless with laughter, gasping for breath, begging him to stop. He wanted an apology. It was an old ritual: I would never give in. I would have held out until I went blue and fainted if I'd had to, but somewhere through my hysteria I heard my husband say, 'I'm not staying to watch this indecent display.'

The room fell silent. Uncle let me go and we watched as Essex marched from the room.

'It's only a bit of harmless fun,' I called after him. 'Oh dear.' I felt suddenly at a loss. 'It seems I've married a killjoy.' I attempted a laugh but it rang hollow.

'Well, *he* didn't live up to his early promise, did he?' said Harry. He was right. I remembered the bright, keen boy I'd married and this one didn't match up. 'Did someone put a poker up his backside on his travels round Europe?'

One of the maids snorted behind her hand and Uncle said, quietly, so the others couldn't hear, 'Don't worry, Frances, he'll soon change his tune when he's had the pleasure . . .'

I slapped his hand and told him not to be so crude.

Later I thought it wise to pay a visit to Essex's rooms to make amends and found him on his bed, half undressed. He was not alone.

He glared at me. 'What in Hell's name are you doing in here uninvited?' He was shouting. 'Get out, you stupid girl.'

I would have turned and run, but was rooted to the spot and, not knowing what else to do, stood blankly waiting for the pair of them to untangle. She was still half behind the bed curtains, fumbling to get her stockings on. They were expensive ones, fine silk, embroidered with a pattern of roses, and I wondered if they'd been a gift from him. He stood up and we faced each other as if primed for a fight.

'Just go!' His spit landed on my face. I didn't move. He collapsed back on to the bed, dropping his face into his hands, reminding me of an infant who hides its face, thinking it can't be seen.

The woman emerged, finally in her clothes, and was not what I'd expected at all. She was compact with a round face and lovely wavy auburn hair that made her seem prettier than she was. But she was old, perhaps even old enough to be his mother.

She slid by me with a little curtsy and out of the door, leaving the two of us alone.

'Look,' I said, at last finding my voice. 'Shall we start again – imagine I never saw her?' I went to perch on the bed beside him. The covers smelt musty, as if they hadn't been aired in months. We sat in silence. One of his dogs, curled up by the fire, started twitching in its sleep. He was folding and unfolding his hands, which were long and fine. I'd noticed them at our wedding and thought them quite lovely, imagined him strumming a lute with those fingers and singing me love songs, silly girl that I was. I reached over to touch them.

'Get off!' He pulled away, his face blurred with tears. That shocked me. Weeping was scorned in our household, even for the girls, and in childhood I'd developed strategies to control myself. If I bit the inside of my cheek until I could taste blood, it helped.

'I don't mind.' I *didn't* mind. Uncle had warned me on the journey up that my husband might have mistresses. I made my voice soft. 'We barely know each other yet. But we have to, you know, do what married couples do.'

He still refused to look at me, so I undid the tie of my nightgown, slid it over my head and lay down on the bed. Some girls were shy of nakedness, but not me. I wasn't ashamed of my body. It didn't make sense to me that God had given us bodies yet insisted we take no pleasure in them.

He turned to me, seething. 'You brazen little whore.' His hands were fisted, knuckles white.

'But I'm your wife.' As I said it, the thought struck me that I was not really his wife, not until we consummated our marriage.

He didn't respond, just threw my nightgown at me and I fumbled my way back into it. 'Now, get out of here.' His silent anger abraded me as I scrabbled on the floor for my slippers, finding them eventually and slinking from the room, wishing myself invisible.

The mistress was skulking in the shadows outside. If I'd had more confidence I would have said something to her, shown her I wasn't cowed, but I crept by in silence as if I were the impostor.

I made my way straight to Uncle's rooms, where he was still up, playing dice with Harry. Uncle bellowed with laughter as I told them what had happened. '*You* can work out what to do with a man surely, Frances. It's not so difficult.'

I was grateful for his lightness, for it had been so awkward and heavy. 'I tried my best.'

'I'm sure you did – lad must need his head examining.' He patted my hand and reassured me that we'd become accustomed to each other in time.

'He called me a brazen whore,' I said.

Uncle snorted. '*He* should be so lucky.'

'Bastard,' growled Harry. 'I should run my sword through him for that.' It was just like Harry to jump to my defence. He was a hothead, whereas I had learned the value of appearing calm, whatever the circumstances.

'No trouble! Do you hear?' said Uncle, with a daunting firmness.

I asked him what I should do about the mistress. He advised me to do nothing, adding, 'She'll disappear eventually. They all do.' He shook the dice in his fist and rolled them on to the table. 'And if she doesn't, she can be made to disappear.'

My stomach shrank, and I met Harry's eye. We were both thinking of our childhood chaplain. Harry and I had found him suspended from a beam in the stables, his dangling shoes dripping urine. He had crossed Uncle. It was called suicide.

When I left them, instead of going to bed I went to the chapel where I knelt in the gloom, silently pleading with God to make my husband love me.

Him

'Tell me what happened in the Prince's rooms.' The tic in James's eye was pronounced, which usually meant he was tired or worried or both.

'He refused the proposal.' I forced myself to concentrate, to stop for a moment my obsessive mulling over how to make Frances Howard my mistress.

'I didn't expect him to accept, if I'm honest.' He lifted his arms so I could undo his jacket, which was too tight, straining against the fastenings. 'It's all very well Henry wanting a Protestant bride but none of those German girls has two pennies to rub together. He's so brimming with principles. He'll understand *one day* that things are not so straightforward.'

I knew what he meant by 'one day': the day Prince Henry became King. 'It won't come soon. Plenty of life in you yet. You Stuarts are robust as they come.'

'If an assassin doesn't get me,' he said bitterly, shrugging himself out of the garment, releasing a musky waft.

We fell silent. The talk had riled me, and my mind began to churn on the fact that if James died my own position would be precarious, unless I found a way to shore myself up. I was painfully aware of my lack of powerful relations. I rinsed a cloth in a basin of water and began to wipe it over his chest. His body had lost some of its tautness, but for a man in his mid-forties he was still sinewy and strong. He always said I made him feel young again but I wondered if one day the twenty-two years between us would have the opposite effect.

'Doubtless Southampton and all the rest of the Essex crowd, who cluster about my boy like flies on shite, pray nightly that I'll drop dead and leave them with a young king in their pocket. They'd help me into my grave if they could get away with it. And they'd be at war with Spain before my body was cold.'

His knee began to jig. I gently placed my hand to steady it, stroking back and forth, still unable to shake off thoughts about my own future.

'They all *think* they want a soldier king who'll seek glory by going to war. But if they had what they wished for they'd see that war is a beastly business. If you learn a single thing from me, Robbie, let it be that diplomacy is a far greater weapon.' He paused, as if deep in thought.

'Why not get rid of Southampton?'

He gave me a wry look. 'Trying to play them at their own game? That's not like you.' I wanted to qualify what I'd said, tell him I hadn't been serious. I didn't want him to think of me like that, but he continued talking. 'Was young Essex there?'

'No, but his wife was.' Her smile flashed through my mind.

'Frances Howard – she's wasted on that charmless pup. He's been a disappointment, that one. Nothing like the spirit of his father.'

I combed his hair and rubbed ointment into his dry skin. It was worse than usual, raised and sore in patches. I preferred him peeled back to his human self with all its frailties, the king set aside, because in those moments of intimacy we were just two ordinary men and, in some strange way, we were equal – it was an illusion, of course.

'Henry challenged me to a fight. I accepted.' I replaced the lid on the ointment, watching his frown take hold.

'For God's sake, Robbie, you can't go –'

'Just a fencing match.' Taking out my pipe, I pressed a pinch of tobacco into its bowl.

His expression softened. 'I thought . . .'

'What do you take me for?'

'I suppose you let him win?'

'Actually, no.' I grinned, lighting my pipe, inhaling deeply and expelling a stream of smoke.

'I bet Henry didn't like that.' He laughed, and I knew I had him in my clutches. There's power in humour. Just ask the playwrights.

'In fact, your son was perfectly chivalrous. It was Southampton who didn't like it. Should've seen his face – like a monkey's arse.'

'Oh, Robbie,' he spluttered, pulling me towards him. 'What would I do without you to cheer me up?' He wrapped his arms around me, trapping me, pressing his mouth over mine. The pungent ointment, with his smell beneath it, made me suddenly nauseous.

I had a momentary vision of Frances's black eyes boring through my surface and was glad James didn't have sight of my face as I feared my disgust was spelled out on it.

I pulled away slightly, taking another draw on my pipe but it had gone out. 'Northampton arrived for a private conversation with Henry. He asked to see me later. I don't know why. He's never shown any interest in me before.'

'Watch him,' James said. 'He's bound to want something but it will be well disguised. Likely he wants to get to me through you. So, bear that in mind when he flatters you, which he will.' He caressed the side of my face with rough fingers.

'But he has your favour anyway, doesn't he? Don't all the Howards?'

'At present, yes – but Northampton knows better than most that favour needs to be kept warm.' James stifled a yawn.

'You're tired. You've been up since dawn. Why don't you rest?' Really, I wanted to be free of him for a while and left alone to unpick the morning's events. I patted the bed.

He sat. 'Lie down with me, Robbie. Take this off.' He was pulling at my sleeve, looking at me with heavy eyes.

As I stroked his hair, his free hand wandered to my crotch and his breath deepened. 'Take it off. I want to look at you.' He was more insistent. 'Since when were you so coy?' He was losing his patience, still tugging at my jacket.

A vivid image of Frances, her finger in her mouth, distracted me and I knew he'd misinterpret my arousal.

But he pulled his hand away, drawing something, a fold of paper, from my sleeve. 'What's this?'

I snatched it back. 'Nothing.'

'Nothing?'

'Just some powders the doctor advised I take for my sore throat.'

He looked at me, head tilted. 'I wasn't aware you were unwell.'

I couldn't tell if he believed my lie. 'It's nothing, really.' I stashed the fold back in my sleeve. It contained Frances's discarded broken nail.

Just then, thankfully, a servant knocked. We hastily pulled ourselves back together and I went to open the door. He'd come to conduct me to Northampton House. James complained as I gathered my things. 'The wretch! What the hell does he want with you anyway?'

We needed each other, James and I, in our own way. I lacked a father and he . . . Well, I cannot speak for him. The love between a mature man and a youth was the purest kind there was, he'd always maintained. 'You see, Robbie,' he'd said of it, 'women are inherently deceitful with their primping and preening and face paint. You never know what they really are, while a man shows his true self to the world.' Now it made me think of Frances's clean scrubbed face.

Evening had fallen by the time I arrived at Northampton House. The place was designed to impress, making even Whitehall seem tawdry. Its polished surfaces gleamed and its ceiling was high, high enough to accommodate the grand sweep of two staircases, which rose on either side of the hall, coming together at the top in a balcony. Having climbed, I stood a moment to marvel at the inlaid pattern of the floor below, before entering the gallery.

Northampton was at the far end, framed in a doorway, inviting me in. His study was more intimate, lit by several lamps. On the desk was an abandoned game of chess but no sign of an opponent, just a dog, flat out on the floor, lifting its head to inspect the visitor.

'Good of you to come.' Something in the directness of his gaze reminded me of his great-niece, though his eyes were set in a bed of creases and were sharper, less warm certainly. Given his reputation, I was surprised by his friendliness, if a little wary.

He poured wine. 'I was told about your fencing match with the prince. Sounded most impressive.' His manner teetered on the edge of ingratiating and I assumed he was buttering me up to petition James about a promotion, so I didn't say much, hoping to draw him out. It couldn't do me any harm to have a favour owed by a man like him.

But no petition was mentioned. He talked about a tilt he was organizing, wondered whether I would participate. I showed some interest but remained equivocal. 'Though don't go falling off and break your leg, like you did once.' He snorted with laughter. 'Didn't do you any harm, did it?' He slapped me on the back. He was referring to the accident that had first drawn the King's attention to me. Even before my bones had knitted together, I was in his bed.

'I'm a better horseman, these days.' I laughed too. The awful humiliation of that fall had long gone, smoothed over by the royal attention and my rapid elevation, other favourites booted aside to accommodate me.

He explained the theme of the tilt and how he imagined it would be, how many horses, who would participate. 'The Howards'll make the Essex crowd look like a bunch of incompetents. Southampton and Pembroke think they're fighters but we'll put them in their place.'

I knew where I stood in those court factions. I was part of neither. I belonged to the King. Perhaps I was like the Fool in the cards, blithely walking off the cliff while looking at the sky.

'There's no doubt, if you join us, you'll outshine young Essex,' he said.

I knew he was appealing to my vanity but the prospect was tempting of having the opportunity to knock Frances's husband off his horse, so I agreed to participate.

He couldn't hide his delight and repeated his statement about crushing the Essex crowd. It occurred to me that James might enjoy me taking sides for once too.

'Have you read it?'

I didn't understand what Northampton was asking, until he pointed at a book on the table that I'd been absently running my fingers over. I picked it up. Tooled into the spine were the words *Troilus and Criseyde*. 'I'm not really interested in poetry.'

'You should be. Everyone speaks of the value of reading

political tracts but I've learned some of my greatest lessons from poetry. And this' – he snatched the book from under my hand – 'this is majestic. It's about a warrior destroyed by his passion for a woman – poisoned by love.' He looked at me. 'See, I've ignited your fascination.'

I laughed, admitting he had.

'Women!' he said. 'Cause of all problems, but wouldn't the world be a poorer place without them?'

'I'm not sure I agree with that. I'd say pride and greed were a greater source of problems than women.'

He cocked his head, seeming surprised. Perhaps he was unaccustomed to being contradicted. 'Well, *this* would suggest otherwise.' He tapped the book. 'You see, love can take you by surprise and make you its captive without your permission.' He gave a snort of laughter. 'Talking of women,' he held the book up to his nose and inhaled deeply, 'have you considered marriage?'

I hadn't expected that. 'No, I suppose I haven't,' It was true. The idea had never crossed my mind. I was more concerned with finding my place in the world.

'If you want my advice, pick a girl from an old family – good blood is always an asset.'

'I'm very taken up with my duties to the King.' One of the lamps began to flicker and smoke, dying, making half the room fall into darkness.

'Of course you are, of course, but the King won't want to see you without offspring, I'm sure.' He refilled my cup. 'I have a proposition.' He looked at me, head tipped to one side, a congenial smile on his lips. I sensed that at last we had come to the true reason he had called for me. 'A Howard girl might do the job. You and I could be very helpful to each other. We Howards have a good deal of influence.' He paused. 'And I like you.' He patted my shoulder. 'Now, I have a great-niece –'

I cursed the blood rushing to my cheeks, as Frances had sprung uninvited to my mind, when I was well aware he couldn't have meant her. I knew she had more than one unmarried sister. He didn't seem to notice my embarrassment and began to rummage on his desk.

'I have a picture of the girl somewhere.' He finally passed me a miniature of a surprised-looking woman. I'd hoped for more of a similarity with her sister, at least a glimmer of that unquantifiable spirit. My disappointment must have shown, for he said, 'I know she's a little plain, but that's not the point. The point is that through her you could become part of our family.' He took a taper and relit the extinguished lamp, having snipped off the blackened end of its wick. 'Will you consider it?'

I wasn't utterly devoid of sense. I realized that he, too, might gain a good deal by connecting himself to me, given my proximity to the King. But the advantage wasn't his alone. My mind whirred. An alliance with the great Howard tribe would prevent my downfall, should anything to happen to James.

'I'll certainly give it some thought,' I said, returning the portrait to him as I made to leave.

He smiled and held out the book. 'Here, why don't you borrow this? I think you'll enjoy it.'

I took it, thanking him. 'Poisoned by love, you say?'

He was still wearing that smile, and nodded slightly, raising his eyebrows, as if he knew something I didn't.

Her

It is dark outside with rain driving at the windows, which at least masks the night chorus of inhuman sounds that threaten to drive Frances out of her mind. Damp has seeped into everything. She begins to uncoil her hair in the hope of drying it a little by the fire, pulling out the pins with numb fingers.

The baby sighs in its sleep. Nelly, who seems strangely impervious to the cold, is shuffling her cards, making them appear to flow magically from one hand to the other in an uninterrupted stream. She has been teaching Frances one of her tricks but progress is slow. Frances wonders about Nelly's tricks: there is something inscrutable about the girl, despite her willingness to talk about even the most intimate aspects of her life.

'Let me help you.' Nelly puts the cards down and goes to stand behind Frances, who hands her the comb. 'The length of it.' Nelly holds a half-unravelled plait carefully by the end, as if it might take her by surprise and bite her.

Frances is remembering how as a child her great-uncle used to make her take her hair down for him to comb while he recounted the Howard stories for her, teaching her about power, how it is hard won and easy to lose. 'You have to learn resilience,' he used to tell her, twisting a hank around his fist and pulling hard. If she didn't make a sound, not even allow her breath to tremble, he would stop.

'So thick, so beautiful.' Nelly wields the comb carefully. 'Mine won't grow below my waist and it's all rats' tails at the ends.'

Frances looks down at her hands: she has bent a hairpin out of shape. 'I should cut it all off for comfort.' Nelly is aghast but Frances doesn't mean it. She'd be afraid to lose her strength, like Samson.

Nelly returns to the table, suggesting a game of cards, and they play without speaking for a while. Frances watches how Nelly holds her hand in a tight fan, ordering and reordering it with precision.

Eventually Nelly looks up to say, 'But I don't understand why you had to marry a man you didn't like. I thought your sort had the right to refuse a match?'

Frances wonders what has made the girl think of that. 'Normally it should be so,' she explains, 'but we were very young when the wedding took place. We couldn't have possibly known how the marriage would turn out. Besides, I'd never have dared disobey my great-uncle and he was determined to tie the Howards and the Essex crowd together.' She picks up the ace of diamonds, which gives her a run: knave, queen, king, ace. She places them face up on the table.

Nelly sniffs, reordering her hand again. 'The Essex crowd?'

'They were all the friends of the old Earl of Essex, who would have been my father-in-law if he'd still been alive.'

'How did he die?'

Frances is astonished. The girl seems not to have heard of the earl and his disastrous attempt to unseat Elizabeth Tudor. But Nelly would have been a baby at the time. She is reminded of that portrait at Chartley. How she'd loathed the way he glowered down at her.

'Executed,' Frances says bluntly. 'On the old Queen's orders. But his supporters came into favour again because they'd helped King James to the throne. They made up the Protestant faction – had a good deal of influence back then.' She can see Nelly is confused. It is no wonder. The court's fluctuating allegiances are as complicated as the pattern in a Turkish carpet. 'My great-uncle wanted their prestige to rub off on the Howards and it did. But the Essex crowd fell from favour. Essentially it's all about power and proximity to the King.' Nelly picks up a card and discards another.

Frances simplifies it, saying, 'Imagine the King is a lit candle. The closer you stand the more light you have. But too close and you're burned. My great-uncle wanted power more than anything, you see.' She stops, suddenly worried that she might have revealed too much, and pretends to focus all her attention on the game.

Nelly's expression ruffles with what appears to be genuine sympathy, allaying Frances's concerns a little. 'But why were they enemies in the first place?'

Frances is becoming familiar with the girl's direct style of questioning and she wishes there were an equally direct way to explain the old political rivalry between her family and the Essex crowd; the way her great-uncle had clawed himself back to royal favour from the wilderness after his own brother had been executed for treason decades before. She simply says, 'They stood for different things.' It is an unsatisfactory explanation, reduced to its bare bones.

'I see,' responds Nelly and, with a flourish, snaps all her cards down. 'I've won!'

A window bangs open, making them jump. It flaps, crashing back and forth, and rain gusts into the room. The candles stutter. Nelly gets to her feet to close it, saying, 'The catch is broken.' Frances passes her an old hair ribbon to tie it shut, and Nelly drags a stool over, clambering on to it, as the windows on the river side are set high. 'Something's happening. Look.'

Frances steps up to peer out. Freezing rain batters at her face but she can make out a small boat, lit by a single lantern, tossing and bucking below them and dark figures aboard, hauling something heavy out of the water.

'What in Heaven's name are they doing?' Frances can't make out what it is. 'Can you see?' A large pale shape tumbles into the vessel.

Nelly gasps, grabbing Frances's shoulder. 'Jesus, it's a body.'

Frances steps down before she falls. She cannot tell if the room is spinning or her head.

'Oh, no,' says Nelly, turning, laughing.

'*It's not funny.*' Frances has no idea if she's speaking aloud or not.

'But it's only a pig.' A dark puddle is spreading over the floor. 'I thought it was a –'

Frances feels her throat tightening but manages to spit out, 'For God's sake, tie up the window.'

Nelly does as she is told and the storm is shut out. It's only when the girl asks, 'What's wrong?' that Frances realizes she is standing like a lunatic with her head in her hands.

'Nothing. I'm quite all right.' She pulls herself together. 'I saw a woman drown once, that's all.'

∞

Uncle and Harry left Chartley and I was abandoned in a place where time stood still. Essex made no effort to disguise his contempt for me, and if I tried to engage him in conversation or speak of our situation, he would demand my silence. We would dine together under the watchful eye of his painted relatives, with a handful of hushed servants, listening to the tick of the iron clock. Neither of us had anything to say to the other, beyond bland comments about the weather and requests to pass the bread.

As soon as the meals were over I would return to my own rooms at the other end of the house, where he rarely ventured. Occasionally I would see his mistress lurking, a flash of embroidered ankle slipping out of sight as I approached. He never mentioned her and I never asked. I was unused to such a quiet existence, and sometimes I would go down to the kitchens, on some pretext to do with the running of the household, just so I could experience the warmth and bustle.

Several weeks later Essex paid a visit to my rooms. I woke, disoriented in the pitch dark, to the sound of someone moving about. I asked who it was, assuming it was one of the maids up early to light the fire. But the bed curtain was swiped back sharply, causing me to gasp. 'It's your husband,' he slurred and, slumping down beside me, lunged beneath the covers, tugging my nightdress up roughly.

I heard the thin fabric tear. 'Your hands are freezing,' I said into the darkness. It was an attempt to create some small line of affinity with him, but I received no response, just the continued grappling.

He manoeuvred himself out of his clothes, puffing and heaving, stinking of ale. Despite his fumbled efforts, and mine, his body refused to respond.

I feared it was my lack of experience that was causing his frustration. 'Tell me what it is you like,' I whispered, tenderly running my fingers over the cratered surface of his face.

He grabbed me tight by the throat, choking the breath out of me and muttering, 'Shut that mouth of yours, you shameless piece of work.'

Those visits became a regular occurrence. On hearing his footsteps, I would steel myself, but every encounter ended in failure and his angry outbursts made me increasingly wary of him. My reserves of stoicism were wearing thin and I greatly missed Uncle's advice – he would have known what to do. I wrote to him often, unloading my woes and begging for snippets of gossip from court.

The seasons eked by in this way, interminably, each day much like its predecessor. My married life had been staked out and I had no choice but to live within its confines. Occasionally family members, both his and mine, would visit to break the monotony and I would have to fend off questions about when we would produce a child. I learned to respond, 'When God wills it.' But, short of a miracle, even God's will would have been insufficient in our case.

The anniversary of my arrival at Chartley was nearing when I found a group of maids in a huddle, babbling about a fair that was coming to the village. Everyone had permission to go, I learned. They were teasing each other about the boys they liked and what they might dare do with them, emitting peals of red-faced giggles. For several weeks, there was talk of nothing else. I imagined the festivities, the music and dancing and the little intrigues, despondent in the knowledge that I would be left to rattle around the house alone with my husband for the day.

On the eve of the fair, anticipation among the servants had built to a crescendo and I sat with Essex, as usual, in the heavy silence of our evening meal, broken only by the interminable tick of the clock. I was beset by an overwhelming sense of hopelessness, a vision of my life stretched out before me, empty and meaningless. But rather than submit to wretchedness I became filled with a determination to resist my husband's dull tyranny and suggested to him that we might profit from a little joy in our lives.

He was puzzled. 'Whatever do you mean?'

'Perhaps we might go to the fair tomorrow. A change of scene would do us good.' I couldn't look at him and fixed my eyes on a drip of wax that was running down the candlestick, pooling on the table.

I noticed one of the servants whisper something behind his hand to another. We all waited for Essex's response as he slowly finished his mouthful. I absently picked at the warm wax, rolling it between my fingers. He took a swig of wine, then another, finally saying, 'I don't see why not.'

His transformation was a mystery to me, but on the following morning he even took my arm and helped me into the carriage, rather than leaving it to the groom. I felt a tentative sense of optimism as we drove along the lanes, while he pointed out the places he had liked to ride as a child and told me about the hound that used to follow him everywhere he went. His habitual bitterness seemed forgotten but I didn't ask the reason for his bright mood, for fear of bursting my hope.

We slowed to a crawl at the edge of the village in a line of carts and riders, making way for groups of people walking, bright with eagerness. A dog was barking manically – someone was trying to catch it but it kept darting away. There was music playing up ahead, the rhythmic beat of a drum, and the scent of roast hog filled the air, making my mouth water. A crowd had gathered around the pond, jostling and cheering at something. We came to a halt and I opened the carriage door so we could stand side by side on the step to see over the heads to what was causing the stir.

A woman was being pulled from the river by two men. Water poured from her gaping mouth, her pale shift sticking to her body to outline her shape beneath. Her skin, where it was visible, was blotched purple and grey, like a bruise. She was dropped heavily on to the bank and lay there, twisted at an angle. We were too distant to make out her features but it was possible to see that her head had been roughly shaved, the scalp patchy and tufted.

'Is she dead?' It was a stupid thing to ask, given the ghoulish colour of her skin and the fact that the vicar was standing over her muttering prayers.

'Witch,' said Essex. 'That's what happens to women who don't do as they're told.' I'd assumed it a warning but he nudged me with a smirk. He was joking.

'Is that right?' I watched in horror as her body, like any old carcass, was flung over the back of a donkey and crudely tied in place. 'And what about men who don't do as they're told?'

'Men are not witches.' He puffed out a laugh and sat down inside the carriage, asking me to do the same.

But a whip cracked and the donkey began to move slowly towards us with its grim cargo. I couldn't prise my eyes away. As it passed close by I saw, where her shift had ridden up, an ankle embroidered with a pattern of roses.

'Oh, God.' I clapped my hand to my throat, thinking of Uncle – *she can be made to disappear* – but refusing to accept that he could have taken such drastic measures.

Essex pulled me down on to the seat. He was still laughing, oblivious to the dead woman's identity, and seemed not to notice my distress, as he said, 'The bitch got what she deserved, I'm sure.'

The next day he ordered the house to be packed up – we were to leave Chartley for London. He wouldn't speak to me, couldn't look at me, but I saw the devastation threaded through him, in his hunched posture, in his barren eyes. He was curdled with grief. I never mentioned it to Uncle. Perhaps I was afraid to know the truth.

Him

When I arrived, a boy levered himself from the tangle of bed sheets, pulling on his clothes as he slid out of the door. Thomas stood shirtless on the threshold, unsmiling, arms crossed. Squeezing past him into the room, I could smell the feral scent of the boy on his skin.

The space was cramped and stuffy, with only the most rudimentary of furniture. I threw the sheaf of papers I'd brought on to a small table that was wedged into an alcove. I was there to ask for an opinion on some business. James had begun to trust me with increasingly sensitive state matters and, strictly speaking, the papers were for my eyes only, but Thomas was astute – sometimes ruthlessly so – and I wanted his advice.

'This place isn't fit for a dog.' I was annoyed, as it was I who had asked the steward to house him and it seemed a personal slight.

'I don't mind. It's not for long and I'm better off here than being fleeced by one of those boarding-house landladies at the Greenwich docks. You've become too used to luxury, Robin. There was a time when you were happy just to have a roof over your head.' He picked up the papers, looked briefly at the heading and glowered at me. 'It's not the lodgings I mind, it's seeing so little of you. We've been here almost a week and I've only seen you at a distance. When you *do* come it's because you want something.'

I leaned on the corner of the table and muttered some excuses about the King leaving me no time to myself, but I couldn't control my petulant tone. Guilt powered my snappish mood.

'It's intolerable' – I could see the hurt scored through him – 'knowing you're up there with *him*.'

'What do you expect?'

'I expect loyalty.' He turned his back, began to make the bed, violently banging the pillows into shape.

'You got what you wanted.'

'I didn't mean it to go so –' He emitted a pitiful sigh and didn't need to finish what he was saying. It was a conversation we'd had a thousand times over, how all he'd intended was for me to turn the King's head for a while, so we could gain a little influence. I remembered his delight when James first noticed me. But neither of us could have anticipated that I would climb so high, almost beyond his reach, or that I would grow truly fond of James. 'You were mine once.' He turned back to me, stepping close to run his hand slowly over my cheek.

I ducked away from his caress. 'Don't.' His upset touched me but, since that encounter in the prince's rooms, Frances had become a mania that left no space in me for other intimacies. 'Look, you're my friend. That's all we've ever been – friends.' I was being disingenuous, which made him remind me acerbically, as he often did, how coarse and green I'd been when he'd plucked me from obscurity and that he'd taught me all I knew. 'How often must I voice my gratitude? I'm grateful, you know I am.' I might have listed the opportunities he'd gained through me but I knew when to hold my tongue with him. He was a decade my senior, liked to think he'd made me from scratch, and sometimes it was easier to let him believe it.

'I do everything and you take the credit.' Rather than confront the resentment in his eyes, I looked at his mouth – his straight white teeth. He was very proud of his teeth and looked after them meticulously. 'Then I have to wait patiently like a good dog for your scraps.' A vein throbbed in his temple.

'You're suffocating me – I can't breathe. You don't own me.' I took him by the forearms. 'Look, we're together *now*. Let's not fight – please.'

He apologized then, and I suggested we leave the paperwork for the time being and take some air. 'Lucky I'm so fond of you.' He gave me a playful push, his bad mood forgotten. 'What's this?' He reached inside my jacket, pulling out the slender book that was tucked inside. '*Troilus and Criseyde*? I've never known you to read poetry.'

'It was –' I stopped myself before I revealed how the book had come to me. He was unequivocal about his dislike of Northampton and I didn't want to have to field a series of probing questions. 'It's just for pleasure.' I tried to sound insouciant but those verses, like the encounter with Frances Howard, had transformed my inner world beyond recognition.

He laughed. 'As long as you don't get the wrong kind of ideas about women.' He was being ironic and couldn't have known what was percolating beneath my surface.

I felt a flush of heat and pretended to tie my shoe so he couldn't see my expression as I said, 'Women? Hardly!'

As I looked up again he threw me one of his rare, flashing smiles. When Thomas Overbury gave you one of his gold-dust smiles you'd do almost anything for him.

I lay back on the bed to watch him dress. I never tired of watching him. There was a particular kind of grace in the sleek musculature of his body and the way the different parts of his face – the straight nose, the sculpted cheekbones – conspired to create perfect harmony. In moments like that I often considered what our lives might have been had the King not come across me – but not on that day. Not ever again.

'Here, help me with these.' He held out his sleeves for me to tie, the amusement in his grey eyes telling me he was enjoying seeing me do the job of a servant for a change. I let him take his pleasure: it salved my guilt. I even crouched to help him with his boots.

It was a perfect June morning, bright and verdant, the hedges twitching with little birds, and it felt good to be away from the grime and noise of London. The river slunk by lazily, watched over by the palace windows, blinking in the early sun, and we walked along the bank where the tall reeds rustled with invisible life.

We stopped for a while to watch Prince Henry at a distance, bathing. It was a daily ritual of his, the morning swim. You wouldn't have caught me dead swimming at Greenwich, downriver from the city, with all the filth the Thames carried, but the prince seemed to imagine he was immune to it. A few of his men were seated on the little pier, chatting easily, bootless legs dangling, with a pair of guards watching.

The prince stood at the edge of the jetty, circling his arms. Despite his athleticism, he still carried a little of the awkwardness of youth, as if his limbs had grown faster than his body. 'We're looking at the future,' said Thomas. 'He has the makings of a good king.' What he really meant was a resolutely *Protestant* king. That was what Thomas wanted.

'It might be a long wait,' I said.

'You're perfectly positioned . . .'

I looked at him. 'What are you getting at?'

He must have seen the suspicion written over me as he said, 'I just meant, couldn't you persuade *your* James to be less tolerant towards the Catholics? People don't like it.'

I paused. 'He's not open to persuasion.'

'Then what in Hell's name do you think you're doing in his bed if you can't at least –' He expelled a peeved snort. 'The Essex crowd are beginning to doubt where you stand. I've heard Southampton say it – and Pembroke.'

'What *Southampton* says means nothing,' I snapped, remembering my spat with the man. 'Besides, that lot –' I was about to say that Thomas believed himself better friends than he was with the Essex crowd. Once I'd overheard Southampton refer to him as 'Sir Thomas Overbearing', but hadn't the heart to tell him.

It would have never occurred to Thomas that, though he shared their Protestant politics, they disliked him as a person. He was neither well born enough nor sufficiently deferent for their taste, and he brandished his brains and principles too much for some. But, whatever others thought, and no matter how exasperating he could be, *I* could never have contemplated not liking Thomas. Our friendship went too far back.

The prince plunged in and began to swim against the current, shoulders rising and falling, hands slicing through the surface. Water seemed his natural element as if he might be half fish. We watched silently, engrossed in the sight, and the way the early-morning light caught the froth in his wake, making it seem as if he was trailed by cascades of diamonds.

The memory of his eyes sliding after Frances a few days before crept through my mind, and I pictured a stray oar meeting with his skull, could hear the sharp crack and the sound of him half shouting, gasping for breath, panicked hands grappling at the air as the current tugged him under. In my trance, I saw his bright blood leak into the water, a crimson pool, flowering, spreading, beautiful.

'You've heard about Lady Essex.'

I turned, with an abrupt intake of breath, to Thomas, shocked, fearing he had read my thoughts.

'What about her?' I tilted slightly away from him so my hair obscured my eyes.

'She's carrying on with the prince.'

'I doubt it. Surely he has better taste.' I was deliberately putting him off the scent. If Thomas got wind of my developing obsession with Frances Howard he'd be appalled. Guilt slithered through my gut. Thomas knew me better than anyone. There had been a time when we'd shared everything, but now I had secrets that were seeping into our friendship – polluting it.

The prince had circled round and reached the pier. We watched him climb up the ladder and vault on to the boards, shaking the water from his hair like a dog.

'It makes sense,' said Thomas. 'If he's to take a mistress then it'll have to be *someone*'s wife and I hear there's trouble in the Essex marriage. Hardly surprising. The young earl's misery personified and she looks like a fistful of trouble to me.'

His words sent a pang of jealousy through me as I imagined her already Prince Henry's mistress, and suddenly she was in my head again, whispering about love and death: *I only say what I see.* If she would be anyone's mistress she would be *mine*.

He didn't let up. 'None of the Howards can be trusted but she's thick as thieves with that great-uncle of hers. He's the worst of them.'

'The King likes him,' I said, with a noncommittal shrug. Thomas didn't need to know of my new-fledged friendship with Northampton. He'd have been horrified to know I was considering his offer of the hand of one of the Howard girls – even in the face of my desire for Frances. I could see my life veering in a new direction and Thomas becoming a thorn in my flesh. The thought pulled me up, made me feel uncharacteristically hard-hearted.

'Believe me, Robin, there's nothing good about that man.' He stopped to look around, seeming to make sure there was no one in earshot, and came in close. 'You and I, we could do something about him – set him up.'

'What in Hell's name are you getting at?' There was a spark in his grey eyes that I'd never seen before.

He slid his gaze to meet mine. 'Come on, Robin, don't play dumb.'

I turned, without responding, walking towards the long grass in the direction of the palace gardens. He followed, catching up, slinging an arm over my shoulders and picking a burr off my sleeve. 'I get the impression that the King would like to see the Howards and the Essex crowd fight it to the death. Do you suppose it's a strategy of divide and rule?'

'He never talks of it as such.' It was often hard to interpret the King's intentions but he had mentioned recently that the Howards might see off the Essex faction. It was not something I was going to divulge to Thomas.

'Doesn't like sharing his power. He's showing himself to be a weak leader. Needs more integrity. Needs to learn to curb his extravagance, or people will turn on him.'

'Think *you* could do better?'

'You know perfectly well what I think.' He squeezed my arm. 'And with you so well placed . . .'

'Stop!' I pointed towards a labourer digging nearby, thankful for an excuse not to continue the conversation. I knew Thomas could read me too easily.

We had reached the barns to the back of the stables and took the path that ran behind them. It smelt dank and loamy and was shaded by a row of chestnut trees. The only sounds were the soft tread of our footfall and the occasional call of a bird. We walked in silence, the air thick with what wasn't being said.

'What's that?' He put up a hand to halt me, listening, and I heard it too, a crack, like the snap of a branch, followed by a moan of pain. We followed the source of the sound to a small yard scattered with new-cut logs. A man, big and barrel-chested, clutching a whip in his raised fist, didn't see us. Wedged in a corner on the ground in front of him was a grubby shirtless boy. He couldn't have been older than about twelve, still carrying the yielding plumpness of childhood. His back was slashed to ribbons. He was begging for mercy.

Thomas and I exchanged a look, and as he snatched the whip from the man's hand, I grabbed him, pulling his arms behind his back and pinning them there. He struggled, kicking out and hurling abuse, shouting that the 'wretch deserved it'.

'That's punishment enough. You might have killed him.' Thomas helped the boy to his feet and sent him to the safety of the stables.

The man spat on the ground, calling after him, 'Next time, I'll have your guts.'

Possessed by a sudden rage, I smashed the brute hard in the face, feeling my knuckles crunch into the gristle of his nose. He staggered and fell. I pulled him up by his collar, swinging my fist again, but Thomas got between us, pushing me away. 'What are you doing? Don't meet anger with anger.' The man slunk away, and Thomas dragged me by the sleeve back out on to the path. 'What's the matter with you?'

'I can't bear to see that.'

'Nor me – but there's a proper way of dealing with things.'

I was annoyed with him because he was right. My breath was heavy. But I was annoyed with myself too. It had been a long time since I'd boiled over like that and I was struggling to control my rage.

I calmed as we made our way through the gardens towards Thomas's lodgings. And thankfully so, because unbeknown to us we were being watched. We became aware of it only as we passed close by the palace walls and saw the Queen with one of her women framed in a window just above.

'There goes *Rochester*' – she said it as if she patently didn't believe I merited my new title – 'and his puppet master.' She spoke to her companion but her words, articulated as if from a stage balcony, were clearly designed to reach our ears.

My fist throbbed, reminding me to keep cool. Managing to make my tone light and jocular, I countered, 'Do you mean to imply I have no mind of my own, madam?'

'Mindless – yes, that describes you rather well.' She seemed pleased with her insult.

Thomas blurted, 'The pot calls the kettle black,' with a burst of spiteful laughter. There had been nothing light about *his* tone. I knew he disliked the Queen, thought her shallow and despised her Catholicism, but I was shocked that he dared be so openly rude to her. Perhaps he was still charged by our rescue of the boy. Something had got into him as he continued laughing loudly, seeming not to see her bitter expression.

I should have said something to mollify her, insist he apologize at the very least but, without thinking, I took his arm and led him firmly away.

'You can talk – telling me there's a proper way of dealing with things,' I said, once we were out of earshot. 'She'll take it as a great insult. We'll be in trouble for it.'

He was suddenly serious. 'But I won't have her belittle you in that way.'

I reminded him that she had a right to feel aggrieved towards me, given our situation, but he wouldn't have it. 'She doesn't dislike you because of the King. She was perfectly accepting of your predecessor. It's your low birth that offends her and I won't have it.' That was Thomas all over, standing up to small injustices. 'Oh dear.' His expression changed to one of worry, as if he'd just grasped the consequences of his outburst. 'We *will* be in trouble, won't we?'

'I'll talk to James. He'll make sure nothing comes of it.'

'*You*'ll be fine, Robin. But the King's affection doesn't stretch to me.'

'I'll make sure of it.' I tried to bolster him as he began to list all the promises I had made him recently that I hadn't kept.

'She's right. I *am* your puppet master. You can barely sneeze without asking me whether you should or not.'

He knew how to get under my skin and my temper escalated once more. 'You, the King, you both seem to think I'm not a person in my own right.'

'You'd never have been noticed by anyone, never mind the King, if it hadn't been for my guidance.'

'Not this again, Tom.' I was bristling and it was taking all my will-power not to give him the slap he deserved. 'At least I genuinely care for James.' I knew by his taut expression that my comment had hit its mark and regretted it instantly.

'Just like you' – his eyes were clamped on to me – 'always trying to take the moral high ground, but you forget how well I know you. You want to be seen as a good person because you believe the opposite of yourself.' He walked away, calling over his shoulder, 'So go to him if you care for him so much.'

Still smarting I made my way to James's rooms, where I found him seated at his desk amid a stack of paperwork.

'Ah, Robbie! Come to cheer me up?' He looked tired, his eyes baggy and bloodshot. I could hear the prince and his party still out on the pier below, larking about.

'What's all this?' I pointed at the contents of the desk. 'Shouldn't your secretary of state be dealing with it?' I perched on the corner, facing him, and he brought a hand to rest on my thigh. My mind flashed an image of a female hand there in its place, a spot of blood where its nail had been torn off. I felt myself begin to harden and forced my mind away from the gush of thoughts that followed the image.

'Salisbury's still unwell, so it falls to me.' The weariness in his voice was evident.

'Give it to someone else until he's better.' I knew Thomas would have jumped at the chance to fill the role. I heard a loud splash, then laughter, and assumed someone had been thrown into the river.

'These matters are delicate. I can't trust anyone to be discreet. Everyone in this place serves themselves. At least Salisbury serves *me* first.'

'*I* serve you first.'

'I know that.' He took my hand and planted a wet kiss on it. 'You take offence so easily. You know how I rely on you. If I had my way I'd have you with me day and night – every night.' He went on, damning the duty rota that dictated the nights each of his gentlemen slept in his chamber. 'Can't we do away with it and leave them all to their wives?'

'You know it's impossible. Imagine the gossip. It would harm you, and I couldn't bear that.' It was true. I couldn't have borne the idea of bringing harm to his door, when he'd been nothing but good to me. But it was convenient too, as I feared he might notice the diminishing of my desire for him. I might be thought insincere, given the secret fetish I'd begun to harbour for Frances, but the love I felt for the King was of a particular kind and is difficult to explain.

'If I am thought of as your favourite it is one thing but quite another if we are thought of as –'

'I know, I know.' He stood with a sigh. 'Come here.' His arms opened and I was drawn into his embrace. *I only say what I see*, she whispered.

'Perhaps if I were to find a suitable wife it would help.' My voice was muffled in the folds of his shirt. He was stroking my hair. I knew he would happily have seen me married, in the ordinary way, to a girl I didn't care for.

'It's an idea,' he said, but suddenly the thought of marrying Frances's sister – Howard or not – was abhorrent.

'Let's not think of it just yet,' I said, and felt his arms squeeze about me.

'I hear you've upset the Queen.'

I pulled back to meet his eye, puzzled as to how he already knew this.

'News travels quickly in this place.'

I began to explain what had happened.

'She's insisting on Thomas Overbury's dismissal.' He studied my expression.

All those secrets I was keeping from Thomas were weighing me down and it occurred to me that, with him out of the way, I might find a little freedom to woo Frances on the sly. I don't know where I truly thought it could go at that stage. But all who succumb to desire can understand that there is no logic to the way in which its force can drag you back and forth between joy and misery, and how believing the impossible possible is the very thing that sustains its victims.

'You must give your wife what she wants,' I said, suppressing the twinge of shame that caught me.

He looked puzzled. 'I expected you to defend your friend – you usually do.'

'All I want is what's best for you.' I tucked my hand around his neck and pulled him towards me. 'If it makes your life easier, then my sacrifice is a small one.'

'You always were kind, Robbie.' The King pressed the palm of his hand to my heart, holding it there. 'Kindness is a rare commodity. It sets you apart from all the others.'

My prevailing thought was that I wasn't being kind to Thomas.

'I'll send Overbury away, then.' He paused, as if waiting for me to protest, but I remained silent.

It hadn't occurred to Thomas that he might no longer be pulling my strings.

Her

Frances wakes in a sweat. The storm is still blowing hard and the broken catch knocks repeatedly against the windowsill. A shadowy figure looms. In her half-sleep, she thinks it is Death come to claim her, rendering her paralysed in the sodden sheets. Something, a rope, a serpent, is twisted about her throat. She struggles for breath. Fingers brush her cheek.

'You're having a nightmare. Wake up. It's me, Nelly. Let me light a candle.'

She comes back haloed in a yellow glow. 'Your hair's come unpinned. Might've strangled yourself.' She unwinds the long plait from around Frances's neck. Frances would never admit it but she is profoundly thankful for the girl's presence, though neither can she bear that she has come to depend on her. Sometimes she thinks Nelly is all that stands between her and a pit of madness. As if the waif of a girl is a pin fixing her to a still point in a world spinning out of control.

'You were talking in your sleep.'

Frances feels disturbed, wondering what she might have revealed. 'What did I say?'

'All sorts.' Nelly opens a pot of lavender salve and begins to rub it into Frances's temples. 'A right chatterbox, you are.' The scent fills the room with summer, but summer feels hopelessly distant to Frances. Perhaps it will never come: she will be tried before then.

'What did I say?' Frances repeats, her reedy tone betraying her.

'You were mostly on about Essex.'

Frances is trying to remember her dream and is sure he didn't appear in it. If Nelly wants to find out more about her time with him then she will be disappointed.

'There's not much to say about him.' She feels her composure return. 'Uncle had other plans for me.'

∞

We were invited to St James's soon after our return to the capital but Essex, still steeped in melancholia, refused to join me. I knew the place well and, as I passed through the bustling panelled corridors, I felt the old grip of anticipation that I had missed in my year at Chartley. At court, you never knew who might appear or what might occur.

The hall was a large bright space with smooth chequered flagstones, looking out over a cobbled courtyard where a fountain danced prettily. Familiar faces were gathered into groups, a rowdy corner of dice-players, a colourful gaggle of women and a number of men around the prince, helping him into his fencing armour.

He looked up as I entered and I spotted the delight plastered over his features. Before my departure, the prince and I had become close. It was a friendship that was entirely innocent, a youthful infatuation on the prince's part, but had provoked a good deal of gossip, for which the court had an insatiable appetite.

I joined the women, one or two of whom I knew quite well. I felt their appraisal, seeking outward clues as to the state of my marriage – a marriage that hadn't produced a child would always be a source of speculation – and responded vaguely to their interrogations about my condition.

'You never know what lies ahead,' I said.

'But I thought you could tell the future.' A young girl I'd never seen before said this. I wondered how she knew, remembering the impossibility of keeping secrets at court.

'I'm no expert,' I told her. 'It's just something my childhood nurse taught me.' But glad for an excuse to deflect the attention away from my own situation I said I'd read her palm. She tentatively offered me her hand. It was fragile and trembled slightly.

'I wouldn't do that in *public*,' said a po-faced woman, who was known for her sanctimony.

'She's hardly making spells,' laughed someone in my defence.

'It's only a bit of harmless fun,' added another, and the woman moved away, with a roll of the eyes, while the rest gathered in a tight circle to listen.

The girl looked at me, credulous, asking, 'Will I be wed soon?'

It was then I became aware of Robert Carr standing in the doorway, surveying the room. He had changed in the time I'd been away, seemed instilled with a new confidence. He'd always been beautiful, with his chiselled pout and pale eyes, intense beneath the sullen, knitted brow, which gave him his beguiling anguished air. But there was something different, a kind of feral physicality that threatened to burst out from his clothes, and his gaze had taken on a cryptic edge that, when it alighted on me, made me wonder what sort of thoughts were brewing in him.

I sensed a ripple run through my companions when they, too, noticed Carr, as if they were sending out invisible shoots to wrap about him and draw him in. He wasn't interested in the women, though, and strode eventually to the group around the prince. I noticed a tense exchange take place between him and Henry so, once finished with the girl's palm, I moved towards them, eager to know what it was about.

A sudden loud clatter caused the room to turn. A page had dropped half a dozen fencing foils on to the stone floor and was on his knees recovering them. Southampton kicked one out of his reach. A few bursts of laughter came from the onlookers. The boy crawled to fetch it. 'Good dog,' said Southampton, kicking the foil away again. The laughter escalated and the boy looked mortified.

'Leave him be.' It was Carr who spoke, crouching to pick up the stray weapon, handing it to the boy with a few words of encouragement. The support in the room shifted and I felt my curiosity swell.

The air was charged and nobody spoke, waiting to see how Southampton would react. He was huffy and red-faced, stamping about. Prince Henry, sensing trouble, suggested that he and Carr spar in the courtyard, leading the way out, Southampton muttering insults in their wake.

We crowded on to the steps to watch. I found my sympathies secretly with Carr, whom I'd never so much as spoken to, rather than Henry, who was my friend. Henry was a fine fencer but Carr was by far the stronger and merciless, forcing his opponent into a corner until his dignity was in shreds. I, feeling contrite for not having supported my friend, rushed over to help unbuckle his armour, making light of the situation. But the altercation started up once more between Carr and Southampton.

'He's trouble, that one,' said Henry. I didn't know which of them he meant, until he said, 'Though my father thinks he can do no wrong.' He glowered at Carr who, in response to some whispered insult from Southampton, made a lunge. He grabbed the older man by the collar and, pressing his forehead right up close, spat out a threat, then released his grip.

'What did he say?' asked Henry. I hadn't heard either, though the comment must have hit its mark as Southampton skulked off, visibly cowed. 'Whatever it was Southampton won't let that go.'

The whole thing made me think of a pack of dogs establishing a new hierarchy. It was plain to see Carr was on the rise and keen to make clear that he wasn't afraid to assert his power.

Uncle arrived then to speak to Prince Henry, and Carr sidled up to me in the hiatus. 'Will you read *my* fortune?' He beamed at me and winked, I was sure he winked, pulling me to one side away from my friends. I saw Henry shoot a hostile glare our way but was more concerned with how Uncle might react, as it was he who had encouraged me to cultivate Henry. A *prince in our pocket might one day serve our needs*, he'd said, when he'd schooled me to befriend the boy.

I couldn't help but be a little thrilled by Carr's audacity and turned away from Uncle, taking Carr's hand, turning it palm up. 'Do you see love?' His slight Scots burr softened the edges of his words.

'That's what they all ask.' I still felt Henry's annoyance bristling at my back. I wanted to break away but Carr's hand was warm and his eyes bored into me, making me think things I shouldn't.

'But *do* you?'

'There's love in everyone's future – and death.' I pulled myself together, refusing to be drawn into his game, adding primly: 'I'm a married woman.' Dropping his hand, I marched off to the relative safety of Uncle's side.

It crossed my mind, as I traversed the room, that I still wasn't quite a married woman, though perhaps I soon would be. Essex had begun to impose himself on me at night with a sickening new vigour and I suspected our marriage might soon be sealed. I couldn't let myself think about what had caused the change in him, that poor dead woman – a wasted life. I should have been pleased, for a pregnancy would mean he'd leave me alone. It would be my success. But it felt like a trap. The price had been too great.

Soon after I arrived back at Essex House Uncle appeared. I assumed he had come to admonish me for upsetting the prince but he seemed in a surprisingly ebullient mood, dismissing my two maids and striding about the place, taking it all in.

'Rather lovely here!' he exclaimed.

It was true. Evening sun poured through the four large, west-facing windows, pooling on the polished boards and casting the vast room in a warm glow. High above, the moulded ceiling was like the sugar work on a celebration cake, and a frieze, depicting a series of mythological scenes, ran all the way round just beneath. We stood for a moment looking out over the courtyard where the grooms were brushing down the horses and a boy was lighting lamps, which cast wavering patterns on the walls. Beyond we could see the Strand, with its constant stream of humanity, people trudging home from their work, and others, more sprightly, venturing out to explore the city at night. Children buzzed about them, begging for coins or touting themselves as guides, hoping to find a stranger foolish enough to trust them.

Despite the mild weather, a chill set in once the sun was gone, so we moved closer to the fire. Ribbons of flame danced, making the bare-breasted marble dryads on either side of the hearth flicker with life. 'You must be glad to be away from that gloomy old house. This place is so much more suitable.' He sat near the fire and pulled me on to his knee. 'And it's within spitting distance of court, so all the better.'

'I'm too old for this.' I got up, wrenching myself out of his reach and almost knocking over the candle that burned on the small table beside him.

He was running a hand back and forth over the carvings, caressing those marble breasts as if they were flesh. 'You'll break an old man's heart.' He grabbed my arm pulling me back towards him. I resisted but he held me tight, so my wrist was suspended a hair's breadth from the candle flame. My skin seared but I kept my gaze steady on his cold eyes. The fine hairs on my forearm fizzled, releasing an acrid smell as the heat intensified. I clamped my inner cheek between my teeth, slowing and deepening my breath. In and out. In and out. He let go first.

'What have you come for?' I asked, stepping away. Heat still pulsed through my wrist.

He responded with a question of his own, uttered almost under his breath. 'Where's Essex?'

'I've no idea.'

He went to the door, opened it and looked each way before returning to his seat and asking, 'How are things in the bedroom, Frances?'

I wondered if he took a prurient pleasure from imagining his favourite great-niece between the sheets and gave him a blunt response: 'Still nothing happening there.' Expecting his annoyance, I said, 'But his mistress is no more, so . . .' I scrutinized him for signs that he already knew about the fate of the poor woman but his face might as well have been wrought in stone '. . . it seems all of that will be resolved soon.' I didn't want to satisfy him by going into details.

He looked at me strangely then. 'I've had a change of heart –' He stopped. 'You're sure we can't be overheard?'

It was I who went to the door then, listening out into the silent corridor for footfall. Forgetting our earlier tussle, I returned to draw in close, eager to know the cause of his furtiveness. 'The King's beginning to alienate the Essex crowd. He's started to suspect they'd like to see him overthrown in favour of Prince Henry. Consequently, your husband and his friends are fast losing their influence.' He gave me a hard stare. 'I don't think your marriage is serving us well any longer.'

'But what do you mean? There's nothing *I* can do about it. I'm wed to Essex, "till death us do part".' Despite the heat still throbbing through my wrist, I was suddenly chilled to the core. 'You can't want . . . ?' I couldn't say it but he knew what I meant. My hands had begun to shake. I tucked them into the folds of my skirt and felt pressure on the back of my head, the cold splash into my face knocking the breath out of me. Uncle couldn't bear a coward.

'No, of course not. Don't be silly. It may take a little time, but I think we can have your marriage undone – particularly if he hasn't performed his duty yet.'

'Undone!' I couldn't help my raised voice.

He shushed me. 'You mustn't breathe a word of this to anyone, not your mother, not your sisters, your maids, *no one*, unless I sanction it.'

A thousand thoughts were circulating my mind, and the idea of being somehow freed from my wretched husband was blowing about me, like a fresh breeze.

'I want you free to wed someone who can be of more use to us.'

I opened my palm, inspecting the familiar lines, finding, as I well knew, only a single line to indicate a single marriage at the root of my little finger. But I hadn't noticed before that a fine yet definite crease intersected it, indicating a disruption, filling me with a sense of foreboding. It was as if something had drawn it there without my knowledge.

'Whatever's the matter?' asked Uncle.

'Just a paper-cut.' I hid my hand. 'Who would you have me wed?'

'Robert Carr.'

The memory of my encounter with Carr only hours before sent something slinking through me. I tried to keep it at bay, but when I spoke my voice cracked slightly. 'The King's favourite?'

'Exactly.' Uncle seemed very pleased with himself, running a hand over his chin. 'The King is increasingly giving Carr greater authority. He's become rather influential, and looks set to become more so. That's what matters to us.' He paused, as if considering what else he wanted to say about Robert Carr.

Uncle always weighed people up in such a manner, calculating their exact worth to him. 'I suspect he's loyal – blindly probably. And the King trusts him above all others, even above Lord Salisbury, and anyway, I happen to know that Salisbury is ailing. He's past his prime. Once *he* goes everything will shift. And, with the Essex crowd being slowly frozen out, if we can extract you and wed you to Carr it will place us perfectly in the inner circle.'

'I don't understand.' I did understand. I understood exactly but the whole idea seemed so far-fetched.

'It came to me this afternoon when I saw Carr with you. It was obvious to me then that he could be convinced. I've already started working on it. I got him over to Northampton House, offered him your sister's hand, just to introduce him to the idea of an alliance with us. This'll be a long game, Frances, but I'm convinced we can pull it off.' He simmered with suppressed excitement. 'Think of it – what it will do for us if we can get our claws on the King's favourite. The Howards will be untouchable.'

I wanted to ask him what it was that continued to drive his ambition, for he was surely too old to reap the benefits of it. But I knew what his answer would be: *It's all for you, Frances. When I'm gone you will be my legacy.* He'd said it before. He'd said it when he persuaded me to marry a sworn enemy. But I suspected a deeper force at play, born of a desire to right the ancient wrong perpetrated on his executed brother, the fall from which he'd had to claw his way back over decades.

'But how?' I couldn't fathom the way in which he believed he could achieve his ends.

'For the present, all you need do is what you do best. Work a little of your magic on pretty Robert Carr.' He rubbed my cheek with his knuckles. 'You know what I mean. Make him fall for you – the spark is already lit. But be discreet, keep your distance . . .' his hand slid round to my throat, encircling it, squeezing slightly '. . . won't you?'

I cannot lie, I was exhilarated by the thought of escaping my grim marriage, and if Uncle wanted me wed to the disturbingly beautiful Robert Carr then I would do as I was told. I often ask myself why I never questioned Uncle and did his bidding no matter what. But I suppose I didn't dare do otherwise.

'And for goodness' sake,' he added, 'don't let Essex get you with child. Make sure you don't lie with him. We'll have to prove your marriage was never sealed if we are to undo it, and if it is the truth, then all the better.'

'But if he insists?' I felt weakness invade me.

He cut me with a razor look. 'Don't you want this? Isn't it what I raised you to want?'

He waited for my assent, which I gave him with a slow nod.

'I'm sure you can find a way to keep that dull boy at bay.'

'Perhaps he'll solve the problem of his own accord. With

his temper, it's only a matter of time before he visits trouble on himself.' I said it to satisfy Uncle, really. Despite everything, I didn't wish Essex any ill: he was as much a victim of circumstance as I was.

'That's more like it, Frances.' He laughed. 'I've always known it. You and I are more alike than anyone could ever imagine.'

It was an unsettling thought and I would have contradicted him if I'd had the courage.

'They all want you, Frances. I've seen the way they look at you. And perhaps, as you say, your inconvenient husband will find someone challenges him to a duel' – he held an arm out horizontally, two fingers pointed forward to mime the shooting of a pistol – 'and save us all a good deal of bother.'

I turned away. 'And what about Robert Carr? Surely the King –'

'All you have to do is turn his head. I'll see to the rest. The King seems unable to refuse the boy anything, and it may also be convenient to him if his favourite is wed. It might shut up the gossips.' He tugged me in for a kiss. His moustache chafed but I didn't resist. I knew there was little point in resisting Uncle. He was strong as the devil himself.

When he'd gone, I stared into the fire for some time in a tangle of thoughts. I felt porous, as if something had breached my boundaries. Carr had burrowed his way into my head and wouldn't be ousted. The bare bones of Uncle's plan – a simple shift of family allegiance – seemed straightforward. But I felt the prod of danger, not from anything outward but from a weakness in me, of which even Uncle wasn't aware.

Voices below drew me to the window and I saw Uncle in the yard, deep in conversation with a woman. She was in the shadows making it impossible to see her features. I watched them, noticing how they broke apart when the groom arrived with his horse. He made to mount, one foot in the stirrup, but stopped a moment, glancing up as if he'd sensed my gaze on him. I ducked to one side, out of sight but still able to watch as she mounted the steps to the door.

There was something familiar about the way she carried herself but I still couldn't see her face, so I opened the window to lean out for a better view. A sudden vertiginous sensation came over me, of someone pushing at my back, urging me over the sill. I lurched away from the edge, leaning for a moment against the wall. My breath was shallow and, despite the reassuring solidity behind me, I felt as if the wall might open and swallow me. Paralysed, I could hear the faint echo of her footsteps beyond the door. She was mounting the stairs, closer and closer.

Moments later she arrived.

'Good God! Anne Turner! I thought you were dead.' I hadn't meant to be so blunt but felt an idiot for my earlier frenzy. It was the furtive exchange in the courtyard that had unsettled me.

She placed a large bag beside her on the floor and held her arms open, smiling like a siren in a painting, her face a perfect oval, her eyes big and blue and beatific. 'I was very unwell, you must have heard, but my husband passed away and I recovered.' She laughed then. 'You look as if you've seen a ghost.'

I found my voice. 'The last time I saw you, you were leaving to marry.' A distant memory flitted through my mind of lying in bed as a child in the grip of a fever, Anne Turner hovering over me, straightening my covers. I'd thought her an angel, truly believed I could see wings sprouting at her back. She said it was the delirium but that angelic image endured. Uncle had employed Anne Turner as my nursemaid, just for me, causing some envy among my siblings, who remained in the care of the family nurse, a harridan with a vicious streak.

Forgetting formalities, we fell into an embrace. 'It's hard to believe,' she said. 'Me a widow and you a married woman. It seems only yesterday you were still a child.'

We sat by the fire, she in the seat Uncle had just vacated. My mind kept returning to their conversation below. 'I'm sorry for your husband's death.'

'He went quite suddenly – painlessly. I'm glad of that. Though, to be honest, we were estranged by the time –' She stopped, looking into the flames and lowering her voice: 'There's someone else.'

In that moment, I understood that I was no longer a child to her and that we were talking woman to woman. 'Who?'

'Arthur Mannery – you don't know him.' Her smile couldn't disguise the twist of pain in her eyes. I asked what the matter was.

'You were always so perceptive, Frances. Do you remember when I taught you to read palms? I could see then that you had the touch.' She said the word 'touch' as if it were a secret between us. 'Arthur won't marry me and my husband left me with almost nothing to live on.'

'How do you manage?' Mine was a world of abundance, and it was hard to imagine her straitened circumstances. But she seemed well dressed, her clothes beautifully tailored from good fabric, and her fingers were free from callouses. 'Do you take in sewing?'

She laughed and, though we were entirely alone, leaned forward to cup a hand to my ear. 'I introduce fallen girls to gentlemen seeking a little comfort.'

It took a moment for the truth of what she was telling me to sink in. 'You mean . . . ?'

She nodded, raising her brows. 'Many think ill of me for

it, but the girls I help have already been ruined. They have nothing left but their bodies, and my intervention keeps them from the stews. The gentlemen often set them up with a roof and board, and some are of very high standing, like your –' She stopped herself.

'Like my what?'

'No – no . . . I didn't mean . . .' She was clearly flustered, her hands squabbling like pigeons.

'One of my brothers, my father?'

'Yes, one of your brothers.' She responded too quickly and I knew it to be a lie because two red spots had blossomed on her cheeks. It was a tell-tale sign I remembered from when she used to cheat at cards. I was suddenly convinced it was my great-uncle's name she was refusing to say, which would have explained their surreptitious exchange.

'And that provides you with a living?'

She nodded. 'To a degree. But I'd like your opinion on another endeavour.' She picked up her bag, unbuckling it.

'If you need money, Anne –'

'Goodness, no!' She seemed mortified and then, like a magician, produced a great circle of golden lace from the bag. 'Look. Isn't it a wonder?' She held it up to her throat.

It was a ruff, but unlike any ruff I'd seen before. It shimmered in the candlelight, seeming dipped in gold. 'It must be worth a fortune. How did you come by it?' I was trying to calculate the cost of so much precious thread and the thought crossed my mind that she might have stolen it.

'Convincing, isn't it?' She tossed it to me.

Something wasn't quite right about it: it hadn't the cold feel of metal. 'It's dyed linen?' I felt tricked.

Her eyes flared. 'All the ladies wear them at the French court. It's a starching technique with saffron – a secret formula I managed to get my hands on. I have wristbands too.'

66

She thrust her hand into the depths of her bag once more, pulling out several cuffs.

The lace was fine and the colour remarkable. 'Do you intend to sell them?'

'Well,' she trained her gaze on me, 'I was hoping you might wear a ruff to court. If you're seen in it everyone will want one. With your connections, we can make a good business out of these.' She broke into the angelic dimpled smile I remembered from childhood.

I couldn't help but laugh. Anne enthralled me. She had a boldness and an ingenuity that made me glad she had returned to my orbit. 'What harm can come of it? I'm sure you're right. They'll all want to get their hands on one.'

'I was hoping you'd agree.' Her excitement was contagious and caught hold of me, making me forget my earlier unease.

'Ingenious – you'll hardly need your Arthur Mannery to marry you.'

Anne laughed. 'I'll be a wealthy widow – the best of all worlds: able to own property, make a will, answer to no one, have none of the suffocating ties of marriage.' Her excitement was replaced with a look of fervent determination. 'But I *want* him. Sometimes when you want something enough you will do anything to have it.'

I knew what she meant, know it all the more now – that the wanting is a force more powerful than the having.

She was talking at a whisper again. 'Dr Forman is making me a love potion.'

'A love potion?' I remembered then that Anne's fascination with the occult didn't stop at fortune-telling games. When I was very small she used to tell strange and terrifying stories of demons and magic. They gave my sisters nightmares, but not me. 'You don't really believe in such things, do you?' I don't know why I asked, for I knew she did and she wasn't the only one. Dozens of women at court consulted Dr Forman.

'Just you wait and see.' She tapped the side of her nose with a finger. 'But what about you, Frances?'

'What do you mean?'

'Listen,' she said, shifting closer, seeming conspiratorial. 'I know things are on the change for you.'

'What are you talking about?' The thought struck me that she had delved into my mind and read my secrets. 'What change?'

'I can help you.' She stroked a hand down my arm to my burned wrist. I snatched it away, wincing. 'I know you must keep your husband at bay.'

'How do you know that?' I sounded perturbed, my voice high-pitched, but I hadn't needed to ask because now I understood the scene I had witnessed in the yard. 'He told you?'

'I know only that the plan is to have your marriage annulled. He thought I'd be able to help you.' She threaded her fingers through mine. 'I'm not meant to have told you I know but you needn't face this alone, Frances.'

It was a relief, I suppose, to have someone with whom to share my secret. Uncle must have had my interests at heart when he involved Anne but, nonetheless, his clandestine behaviour chafed me. 'I'm not meant to know that you know?'

She shrugged with a smile. 'He moves in mysterious ways. But that doesn't matter.' I was wondering if perhaps it *did* matter as she continued, 'You must come to Dr Forman. He'll know exactly what's needed to keep your husband from – you know.'

'Perhaps.' I was noncommittal, as Dr Forman reeked, to me, of trouble and I had no intention of paying him a visit.

Him

I had discovered that unspoken love can capture its victims until they no longer recognize themselves. That summer I was reborn, existing only in the context of Frances Howard. I became Troilus, subsumed by sweet suffering, propelled towards her by some enigmatic force beyond my control. Love makes prowlers of us all, does it not?

I indulged my obsession, watching her from the shadows, making the feeblest excuses to find myself in the places where she might be. I invented reasons for my barge to drift slowly past Essex House, in the hope of a brief sighting, and I'd offer my services for errands that would take me to the Queen's house where she sometimes was. I felt unhinged, stalking the prince for signs she had been near him, once even waiting for him to remove his coat so I could sniff it, seeking her scent. I courted Northampton, ingratiating myself with him, and befriended her brother, whose similarity to her struck me like a slap each time he smiled.

Once I came upon her with a group of women and concealed myself to watch, riveted by the scene of female ritual that unfolded. She, her face fixed in concentration, pinched a hair from her head, tugging sharply before drawing the invisible thread carefully away.

A woman lay flat on the floor with the others kneeling about her and removed her wedding ring. Frances threaded the hair through it, letting the ring hang down. Holding the makeshift pendulum over the woman's belly, she closed her eyes, appearing to fall into a trance, her head gently rocking.

The ring began to swing slightly, then circle, eventually making great loops in the air. I was transfixed.

'It's a girl,' she uttered, coming out of her daze, looking up, then casting those black eyes in my direction, as if she had the power to see right through the hanging I lurked behind. She returned the ring to its owner, allowing the hair to drift to the floor. I waited and, when the women were gone, searched on my hands and knees in the dust by the skirting for that hair. Unable to find it, I stood, turned, and there she was, as if she'd floated there soundlessly, those eyes on me. My breath lurched.

'What on earth are you doing?' She wasn't so much smiling, as smirking.

Thinking fast, I held out my hand to show her a ring I wore that had lost a stone. 'I'm looking for this.' It seemed impossible that she couldn't hear the loud thump of my heart.

'I'm sure it's easily replaced.' She touched the empty setting lightly with the tip of her finger, and I was on the brink of declaring myself, when one of her friends came to the door, calling her name, and she spun away, back into her world.

I became bolder and followed her in late summer, like a spy, stealing in the shadows as she walked with a companion through the city. She wore a golden ruff, like a slipped halo, barely visible beneath her outer garments. They left Essex House, walking with purpose along the Strand, stopping for a drink, she wiping the wet from her lips with the back of her hand. The pair of them continued, past St Paul's and down to Thames Street, past the bridge, shrugging off the hawkers, and on in the direction of the Tower. Eventually they stopped at an address near the Billingsgate dock, where a vast ship was berthed, its great masts towering above the roofs of the houses.

The two women disappeared inside. I loitered nearby, watching, as the ship was unloaded to the shouts of the men and the shriek of the winch. The dock was a mayhem of activity and a fellow approached me with a caged parrot, brightly plumed and big as a goshawk, asking me to make an offer for it.

'He can speak three languages,' he assured me, demonstrating by saying a few words, which the parrot mimicked.

It struck me that I was much like that parrot, in my fine feathers, repeating things that others put into my mouth. It was only my secret love that was truly my own. 'I'm not in the market for a parrot,' I replied. 'But I wonder, do you know whose house that is?' I pointed towards the door where the women had entered.

'Strange sort lives there. A Dr Forman.' He looked at me with narrowed eyes. 'Not an ordinary doctor. I wouldn't think you'd be wanting to consult one such as he.'

'What do you mean by that?'

He seemed to have no answer, only shrugged, saying, 'Like I said, strange sort.'

The women emerged some time later, reversing their tracks, back through the city towards the Strand, but instead of turning into the gates of Essex House they continued westward to where the houses gave way to fields. The thought lodged in my mind – and with it a rising sense of agitation – that they were heading for St James's Palace and a tryst with the prince. But my fears were allayed when they disappeared into the church of St Martin.

I followed them in, lurking in the dark at the back. They walked all the way down the aisle, stopping eventually close to the altar, where they knelt side by side and began to pray. I wondered why, since there was a chaplain at Essex House, she would choose to make her prayers at St Martin's. The enigma deepened when they stood, approaching a passing verger to exchange a few words and he disappeared, returning a short while later with a package that Frances's companion cached beneath her cloak. Aware of the rumours surrounding the Howards and their papist sympathies, it occurred to me that the mysterious package might contain religious paraphernalia.

I felt a shiver of fear for, though James's policy was of tolerance for both faiths, families with Catholic leanings had to tread with great care. The Gunpowder Treason, six years before, had left a grim shadow.

Only once they had left the church did I emerge from the gloom, walking down the aisle to the place where Frances had been minutes before. I sank my knees into the very hollows where hers had rested, thinking of the fine silk of her stockings, all that lay between her skin and the tapestry surface where my own knees were nestled. The thought wound me tightly. I shut my eyes, feigning prayer. The place echoed with the intense silence particular to places of worship, interrupted only by the soft slap of the verger's slippers as he moved about, lighting candles. Then I saw it, lodged in a corner of the prayer stand, a pearl that must have dropped from her sleeve.

I plucked it from its niche, bringing it to my lips, touching my tongue to its surface. Bliss made me lightheaded. To me it was another fragment of her to add to the collection of relics I was amassing.

Her

'No, like this.' Nelly is jigging the baby on her hip as she demonstrates how to hold two cards together but make them appear to be one. 'The edges must be lined up perfect.'

Frances's fingers are all thumbs and she drops the cards in exasperation. 'It'd take real magic for me to be able to do it as well as you.'

'I know a fair bit about real magic.' Nelly bends down to whisper, 'I made a spell once. I wanted rid of my baby cos – Well, you know why.'

'I'd watch what you say.' Frances is disarmed by her frankness. 'They could burn you for that – making spells.'

'But I trust you.' The baby has picked up a card in its sticky fist and Nelly gently prises it away. '*You* wouldn't say anything. We trust each other, don't we?' Her words seem weighted with something. Frances isn't sure what.

'Of course.' She nods, adding, 'I don't know much about such things. It was Anne Turner, not me, who was fascinated by the occult. She was involved with a Dr Forman.' Frances is on the brink of launching into a description of her ill-advised appointment at Dr Forman's house but thinks better of it. Though it was entirely innocent, and she had gone there only because Anne had been so dogged about it, she fears it may give Nelly the opposite impression.

The thought drags her back to that day with disturbing force. She had taken care to dress plainly and cover her face with a scarf, so as not to be recognized. She and Anne had made slow progress weaving their way through the city.

Frances rarely had opportunity to mingle with the myriad life on the streets, so it was a thrill of sorts to be incognito among it all. They stopped where a woman was selling ass's milk straight from the animal and shared a single cup, lifting their scarves to drink. It was still warm and she relished the pleasure of it, laughing at Anne's milky moustache and wiping it away with her thumb.

Anne was elated. Just as she'd predicted, her fortunes had turned since Frances had worn one of her gold ruffs in the Queen's chambers. From one week to the next everyone was wearing them. 'Once it gets about that they're being worn at court, every goodwife this side of Chelmsford will be after a set,' Anne was saying. 'Who says a woman needs a man to survive?' She was bubbling over with it, but once they arrived at Forman's house her chatter subsided.

A hideous fellow, with a russet bush of beard and a nose half eaten away by the pox, opened the door.

'Ah, Franklin, we have an appointment with the doctor.' Anne seemed unperturbed by the man's gruesome presence. He greeted her in return by name and led the way inside. His gait was awkward: either one of his legs was considerably shorter than the other or one shoulder considerably higher. The two women were left to wait in a room at the back of the house.

Although it was midday, the place was gloomy and silent as a tomb, with a pervading smell of dust and something sweet and rancid, like fruit forgotten in a corner and left to rot. Every surface was stacked with books and curiosities. The shed skin of a gigantic snake, fine as a spider's web, lay across the mantel, weighed down at one end by the shell of a tortoise and at the other by a large glass jar containing an organ of sorts preserved in liquid, a heart perhaps. Spread over the table was a map of the heavens, the stars picked out in gold on a bed of black bordered with indecipherable text. Beside it lay a dish containing a fistful of bright stones. Frances picked one up, holding it to the window, seeing how it cast its rosy colour on to her skin.

She had a suspicion that cunning men, such as Dr Forman, were charlatans, who staged an atmosphere to squeeze money out of those who knew no better. And it crossed her mind that the servant, with his grisly appearance, might have been employed as part of the ruse. But, nevertheless, she had to admit Dr Forman's rooms, arranged by design or not, were morbidly captivating. Noticing a skull perched on a stack of papers, Frances nudged Anne. 'Do you suppose that's human?' She stretched out a hand to touch it when something shrieked loudly, making her gasp and grab her friend's arm. The sound came again, seeming to originate from behind a screen in a corner. Frances took a step towards it and, breath held, pulled back the screen to reveal a caged monkey. It was whiskered and fanged, standing upright, clinging to its bars with miniature old-man's hands.

It emitted a bloodcurdling sound. Frances jumped back, as if scalded, and someone behind her said, 'I see you've met Diabolo.' She turned sharply with a cry, to see a creature, spotted like a leopard with a wild frizz of orange hair and glazed amber eyes. 'I'm so sorry. I seem to have frightened you.' She realized then that what she'd momentarily feared was a demon was nothing more sinister than a diminutive freckled man with a magnetic gaze.

'I don't know what came over me.' She pulled herself together and offered her hand as Anne introduced the doctor. He opened the cage and the monkey jumped on to his shoulder, from which it examined the visitors with disturbing fascination.

Once they were seated Forman picked an apple from a

dish and produced a paring knife to cut slices for Diabolo. Not wanting to watch its munching yellow fangs, Frances returned her gaze to rest on that skull, wondering to whom it might have belonged.

'To remind me of the vanities of the world,' Forman said, apparently noting her fascination.

'Whose was it?'

He didn't answer, just tapped the side of his nose, a gesture she'd always thought peculiar to Anne. 'Now to business.' He produced a phial, which Frances assumed to be the purported love potion, as Anne reached for it impatiently.

'I can't impress on you enough the strength of this.' He moved his hand out of her reach. 'Use it sparingly. A mere drop in his wine before he retires each night.' He began to shake the phial while murmuring some verse in a language Frances didn't recognize, then handed it to Anne.

She held it very carefully between the tip of her thumb and forefinger, as if it might burn her. 'And he will want to marry me?'

'Dear Anne,' he said, taking her other hand, in a manner that seemed strangely intimate, as if they knew one another better than Anne had intimated. 'These things rest with the spirits but I have done what I can to make sure that they help you achieve the desired outcome.'

Frances watched, fascinated, wondering if what he said was for effect or if he truly did commune with the spirits. A bristling sensation ran up and down her spine, and despite her scepticism, she felt drawn by some invisible force into the world of this odd man and his potions. She *wanted* to believe in him.

'Mind you take care,' he warned. 'It's a potent mixture. You wouldn't welcome any undesired effects, now, would you?'

Frances tried to imagine what those undesired effects might be but dared not ask. Then he trained those strange eyes on her, asking what it was she required, and when she told him, he pondered on it for several moments. Eventually he said, 'That's an unusual request. Are you absolutely sure?' She nodded tentatively. 'Once it is set in motion it cannot be reversed.'

His ominous tone made her tense. 'I'm sure it's what I want.'

Even now, after everything, Frances wonders, against her own better judgement, if he might have had the power to see into her future. He seemed to know something no one could have known.

'Absolutely sure,' she reiterated. It felt impossible to refuse, as if some compulsion had her in its grip.

He simply shrugged, saying, 'As you wish,' then stood, handing the monkey to Anne. It clung to her collar with its small hands as she fed it pieces of apple. Her ease with the animal gave Frances the impression that her friend had fed it many times before.

Forman took a large book from a shelf, placing it on the table. Frances shifted her chair closer for a better look. It appeared to be a Bible bound in almost translucent leather, as fine as human skin and embossed with a filigree pattern. She wondered what on earth a man like Forman might do with a Bible under such circumstances but was reassured to think it was the force of good he sought to invoke.

'See this.' He fondled the leather before flicking open the ornate clasp that held the book shut. Then, rather than laying it flat on the table, he stood it upright, opening its cover like a door. She leaned in closer to see, catching a sulphurous stench.

It was not a Bible at all, or once had been but was now

defaced for a new purpose. The sacrilege disturbed her, and she would have moved back but felt some otherworldly force rooting her to the spot. Its pages had been cut away to secrete a cabinet of little drawers, each labelled and furnished with a minute handle, carved from a glassy black substance.

A green bottle the height of her index finger was strapped by a leather thong into a niche. It contained a dark liquid. On the inside of the cover was an ink drawing of a skeleton leaning on a staff, its head thrown back in despair. Fascination drew her to read the labels on the drawers: *Hyoscyamus niger*; *Papaver somniferous*; *Aconitum napellus* . . .

'But they are poisons,' she murmured. Instinct was telling her to run from that place before it was too late. But she was immobilized, as if victim to some nefarious spell. Anne, though, seemed entirely unconcerned and continued petting the monkey that was sitting on her lap like a baby. She cooed at it and scratched its belly until it cackled, exposing its fangs.

'Please don't be afraid.' Forman's voice was velvet smooth. He held Frances momentarily with a limpid gaze that seemed profoundly benevolent, which, instead of reassuring, bewildered her.

'And, yes,' he added, opening one of the drawers to scoop, with a small ivory spatula, a little powder from it into a fold of paper. 'If the dose is sufficient, any of these will kill a man, but if correctly administered they have great healing powers. They must be harnessed, that is all.' He continued spooning small amounts of different powders into the sachet. She leaned in closer but he told her to back away: for those unaccustomed, he said, even the scent could cause giddiness or worse. He sealed the sachet, then repeated the process.

'Where do you get them?' she asked, transfixed.

'From all sorts of places.' He looked at her once more. 'But I cultivate some myself, with the help of Master

Franklin. He has wonderfully green fingers and can distil like a wizard. Distillation takes patience, you see – like alchemy.' He gave a cough of laughter but she couldn't see what was funny. 'Would you like me to show you outside?'

He didn't wait for an answer and led the way out through a door that opened on to a walled garden at the back of the house. She stopped on the doorstep, temporarily blinded by the sun, and had to lean on the jamb to steady herself. She took a deep inhalation, but the air was thick and made her breathless. A harsh inner voice told her to pull herself together. Anne squeezed past and Frances grasped her arm, walking with her down the path behind the doctor. As she became accustomed to the brightness, her senses settled, leaving her feeling silly for having allowed herself to become so addled.

Forman came to a halt, saying, 'Here it is, my little physic bed.'

It was a racket of colour. Blushing foxgloves and purple larkspur towered over wavering black-hearted poppies. Blue monkshood sprouted in and around fronds of rue the colour of ripe lemons, and nearby grew a bush that dripped with clusters of waxy crimson berries. Intoxicated bees purred lazily from bloom to bloom, and an almost unbearably pungent scent hung in the air. Franklin was there, crouched over the bed wearing a big pair of leather gloves, rendered more grotesque than ever surrounded by all that splendour.

'It's all so beautiful,' Anne was saying.

Frances knew well enough that if she picked a bunch of that pretty rue her skin would show raised welts within the hour.

'Beautiful, yes,' Forman said, 'and these plants will heal most ills, but you are wondering how it is,' he turned his eyes on Frances once more and echoed exactly the thought that had crossed her own mind, 'that God makes deadly things so alluring.'

She refused to submit to fear, saying brightly, 'It hadn't crossed my mind.' But she was sure he could see it was a lie.

Once back inside, Forman found a small silk pouch into which he put one of the sealed sachets. He hung it round her neck, instructing her to wear it next to her skin for the full duration of a moon's cycle. The other he told her to place beneath Essex's pillow, promising that her problems would be solved, then told her what she owed for his services.

She took out her purse, as he continued, 'I recommend also you design a figure in wax, a little man with the correct anatomy.' Frances was taken aback to see him point towards the monkey's genitals. 'That detail is most important for it is there you must thrust a needle daily to douse any residual ardour in your husband.' He spoke in a prosaic manner, as if giving her a recipe for a fruit cake. 'It is crucial the wax comes from candles that have been blessed. We must call on the power of Godly spirits, rather than the dark arts.'

As she counted out the coins to pay him, she stepped out of herself for a moment and the sceptic in her returned, making her wonder if she had fallen for an elaborate hoax. But she had no other means to deal with Essex, and chose to believe in Dr Forman and his peculiar methods.

'You will find his anger abates, also.' His tone remained matter-of-fact but she was unsettled once more. She felt certain she hadn't mentioned Essex's temper to him.

As the two women made to leave, he took Anne to one side, saying, 'It is unlikely I will be able to see you many times more.'

'I don't understand.' She looked distressed, like a rejected lover.

'The date of my passing is near and I must prepare myself.'

He was expressionless, standing there with his monkey on his shoulder, its tail curled about his wrist, as if he'd been telling them nothing more extraordinary than the time of day. Frances wanted to say he'd gone too far with his deception, that only God knew when someone's time was up, but something stilled her tongue.

'What do you mean?' Anne was aghast.

'I've seen it in a vision, the manner and moment of my death.' He gave a date in early autumn, a mere few weeks away.

Anne was muttering, 'It can't be true. It's not possible.' Her eyes were wet and her face twisted in distress. But Forman hustled the women out, saying if they were to need anything, 'anything at all', they were to consult Master Franklin, who, Frances noticed then, was looming in the bright opening to the garden, watching them.

As the door shut she turned on her friend, angry with her for luring her to such a place. 'What is he to you?' Anne was in a dither on the step, white as a ghost, unable to answer. 'He said it for effect. There's not a soul alive can predict their own death. It's against the order of things.' Frances didn't temper her harsh tone and Anne refused to look at her, so she took her roughly by the shoulders repeating, 'What is he to you?'

Anne looked at her then, with red eyes, and gave her head a little shake.

Him

The hot days sloped by, eventually giving way to autumn, and I was to accompany the King to his hunting lodge. Royston was a modest place and I knew James was at his happiest there, where he could imagine himself an ordinary man without the burdens of his status. In many ways that was the version of him I preferred and I usually enjoyed those visits to Royston too. But this time I feared that, when I was alone with him, James would strip me back and discover evidence of my secret passion engraved in me.

On the eve of our departure Northampton invited me to visit. As I arrived at his house I held the hope that I might encounter Frances there, though I never yet had. I found him alone in the vast gallery. He guided me to a window niche looking over the busy sprawl of Whitehall.

'I'm pleased you're here,' he said, as we sat, explaining that the niece he'd suggested for me had received an offer of marriage.

'It's a good proposition – very suitable. Obviously, I'd prefer to see her married to you but she's not getting any younger.' He gave me a stringent look. 'And I'm not entirely convinced by your enthusiasm.' I inspected him for signs of what might lie behind his firm tone but he was indecipherable. He continued: 'I'm afraid I've decided to accept. And her father's keen.' Convinced that he was cutting me loose, I admonished myself inwardly for allowing my obsession with Frances to interfere with my good sense. But then he added, 'I'm sure we can find someone else for you – a cousin, younger, prettier.' He gave me a conspiratorial nudge.

I made my enthusiasm clear and he apologized for not having spoken to me sooner. He'd been distracted, so he said, 'by other pressing family problems'. He was fidgeting, rearranging the objects on his desk, seemed perturbed. 'You must be familiar with another of my great-nieces, I'm sure. Frances. Wed to Essex. All sorts of difficulties there. The boy's not even managed to consummate –' He stopped abruptly, thrusting a hand over his mouth. 'Forgive me – I shouldn't have . . . It's not something I ought to talk about. Can we pretend you didn't hear that?'

I nodded, smiling. 'Hear what?'

He matched my smile and continued talking about other matters, oblivious to the fact that his blurted confidence had opened a fissure in my imagination into which ideas of Frances were pouring. When I left the room, my head was filled to the brim with her, and as I descended the grand sweep of staircase to the hall, my heart sprang to see her there, being helped out of her coat. I stopped halfway down, waiting for her to see me.

'Robert Carr.' She began to mount the stairs. 'Again! Any-one might think you were spying on me.'

'Perhaps I am.' I trained my eyes on her. She flushed slightly and I leaned back against the banister to watch her climb. 'Actually, I've been with your great-uncle. We were talking about marriage. He'd like me to wed one of your cousins.' She'd reached me and I looked for signs of disap-pointment in her face but found none.

'I have several cousins.' Her tone was playful and she came close to my ear, almost touching, and whispered, 'I'd be very jealous.'

It took a superhuman effort to keep my voice even. 'But you're married.'

'So are *you* – as good as.' And then she tripped on up the

stairs away from me. I stood a moment, gathering myself, and at the top she called back, 'I hope I'll see you at the entertainments later. I'm performing.'

I floated on air back towards Whitehall but Thomas blew into my mind out of nowhere, like a cold breeze, registering his disapproval. I don't know why. I'd barely thought of him lately.

I was crushed. Frances hadn't looked my way all evening. It was as if I didn't exist. The banqueting hall was alive with dancers and filled with the grating jangle of cheerful tunes. I sat beside James, frayed, watching her, unable to disguise my dark mood.

Across the room, she peeled away from her family and slunk towards Prince Henry, engaging him in a whispered conversation. Then, to my horror, she took his hand and, finger by finger, removed his glove, before – as she had once done with me – unfolding his palm to examine its lines. Though it was torture I was unable to drag my eyes away. I could have stormed over and snapped his head off with my bare hands. James watched them, too, his suspicious gaze shifting back and forth from them to me. At once she dropped his hand, a look of alarm passing over her face. 'What?' he appeared to ask, her distress catching like a flame in his eyes too. 'What have you seen?' But then she broke into a smile and said something with an insouciant little shrug. The idea of leaving her to go to Royston was tormenting me.

'The little hussy,' James said.

Without thinking I spat out, 'Leave her be.'

'Why are you jumping to *her* defence?' James's bloodhound look fixed on me.

'I'm not defending anyone.' I tugged my eyes away and stretched out a placatory hand to James's arm.

84

'Whatever's the matter with you?' He swilled back his drink. 'You're so tetchy this evening. For goodness' sake, cheer up.'

'I'm not feeling very well.' I dared a glance, to see Frances had settled in to sit beside the prince.

'The fresh air at Royston will do you good.'

'Perhaps . . .' I hesitated. 'Perhaps I should stay here and join you in a few days, when I'm feeling better.'

'You were perfectly well an hour ago.' His scrutiny fizzed under my collar. '*Why* do you want to stay? What's keeping you? You've been so distant lately anyone would think . . .' He drained his glass, holding it out to be refilled and didn't finish what he was saying.

'Of course I want to come. I love Royston.' I hated myself for my deceit.

'You love *Royston*?' He spat out a bitter laugh and drained his glass again. I knew I should have said I loved him.

People were taking turns to perform, each with a song or a poem. Princess Elizabeth, delicate as a moth, skipped through a few dance steps, to a clamour of applause. James glowered beside me. When Frances stood to recite 'The Folly of Love', a spellbound hush fell over the room. I sat stiff as a corpse, watching my adversary's eyes devour her.

'Come outside.' James got up, stumbling slightly. 'Come on. Come outside.' He was slurring and pulling at my arm.

The music stopped and everybody rushed to stand, wood scraping against wood. He left the room, and I followed as he zigzagged along the passage towards the gardens. Once outside he pressed me up against the wall. The brick was cold and damp. A low full moon cast a pallid glow over his features, illuminating his annoyance. 'My favour isn't limitless, you know. I saw you looking. I saw you.' He prodded a finger in my face. I tried to calm him: he was much drunker than I'd realized. 'There are no guarantees, Robbie.' The stink of his breath made my stomach turn. 'Everyone's replaceable.'

The thought flashed through my mind that some accident might befall him: he might stumble, hit his head on a stone, making him unable to travel. I should have taken him to his rooms then, to sleep it off, but I couldn't bear the idea of leaving without at least trying to speak to Frances, so I took his arm and guided him back to the melee.

We stood a moment in the entrance, and I saw through the throng that Henry had taken his father's seat. He must have assumed we'd gone to bed. James hadn't noticed and I distracted him by pointing out the dancers. I knew how he would feel to have such a bald vision of the future: that new-minted boy sitting on *his* throne, the hated Southampton and Pembroke at his side with a fawning host of followers. Frances wasn't with him. I scanned the room, unable to find her, supposing her with the clutch of Howards at the far end.

People began to realize the King had returned and got to their feet, those nearest first, parting to allow us to pass. Henry, chatting with his friends, was still lounging in his father's place. As we approached I felt James wind tight as a bowstring. It was only when we were a yard from him that Henry saw us and sprang up, appearing genuinely mortified. He offered profuse apologies, while his cronies slunk away to the edges of the room.

'Wouldn't be so quick in my grave,' James snapped. He looked drab and worn beside that fresh boy. One eyelid flickered and his jaw gritted as he watched his son sidle off. 'He'd take every last thing that is mine, given half a chance – even you.'

I wanted to laugh out loud in relief to hear that it was Henry, and not Frances, whom James suspected was taking

86

my attention from him. 'Not me – he won't take me from you,' I said. 'You can't possibly think such a thing.'

I must have sounded convincing – after all, it was the truth – for he chose to believe me, apologizing for his suspicion. His mood transformed instantly, as he claimed his seat and called for more wine. I knew he would stay until the bitter end to make his point. But as the crowd began to thin and the Howards dispersed there was still no sign of Frances. Despair bit into me and, desperate to be alone, I begged leave to go to bed on the pretext of sleeping off my feigned illness before the following day's journey.

As I trudged away to mount the stairs, the muffled hubbub from the hall became more distant. I stopped at the large window on the landing, and stood to look at the moon, contemplating, like a lover in a poem, the tyranny of desire. Thinking of Troilus pulled back and forth by love, I basked in the frigid light, rolling her pearl between my fingers.

I heard a door sigh below. Air riffled over my skin. Then came the soft patter of footfall. I made to leave, reluctant to nod a greeting to whoever it might be. A touch, light as a feather, caressed my shoulder. Turning, I heard my name whispered, the sound bringing with it a trembling stupor, as if I'd been drugged.

'I've been looking for you. Why do I always find you on the stairs? As if you only exist in the space between floors.' She took my hand. 'You're cold as death.'

I feared I would wake and find I had dreamed her. She began to rub my hands between hers, bringing them up to her mouth, blowing hot breath on to them, as a mother would to a child.

'Look at the moon,' I said, willing myself to think of something less banal to say. I watched her gazing out, the sinuous curve of her neck and how the silver glow caught on the edges of her golden lace, reflecting a pattern like frost on her cheek. I remember, with a clarity that is undimmed by the five years that have passed since, the way that the moon was mirrored in her eyes, two bright spots in a sea of gleaming black, making my breath catch in my throat. She was talking, telling me how the poem she had recited earlier had made her feel a hypocrite.

'It was a celebration of wedded bliss and I have found no contentment there.' Her voice wound around me like smoke. 'And there I was,' she continued, 'for all to see, reciting on the foolishness of lovers and celebrating the soundness of marriage. They are not *my* words.'

'Not long ago I was offered a parrot at Billingsgate docks,' I found myself saying. 'A great beauty.'

'A parrot?' She seemed thoughtful, as if something sad had settled over her.

'It spoke three languages, or so the vendor told me. But it didn't have any words of its own, only mimicked those of others.'

'Go on,' she breathed.

'I felt an affinity with that bird, dressed in its fine feathers spouting sentiments it didn't understand.' I looked at her fingers woven through mine. 'I sometimes feel I am not my own person.'

Regret spilled into me: my confession made me seem horribly weak and I was desperate to think of a way to retract it when she said, 'You see,' so quietly I had to lean tight in, close enough to know she smelt clean, like a new book, 'we are the same, you and I, just beautiful puppets.'

We stood in silence for a time. I was rejoicing – fireworks exploding in my head. She still cradled my hands in hers. The moon had moved slightly so the dark outline of a tree's branches disrupted its perfect edge. I listened to the rhythm of her breath, matched my inhalation to her exhalation so I could imagine drawing invisible fragments of her into my body.

'I had a parrot once,' she said. 'I have never loved anything as I loved Troilus.'

'Troilus?' I believed it an omen, good fortune.

'He was dandelion yellow, with a crimson-hooped neck, and was small enough to sit on my hand. He was always with me, even perched on my bedhead while I slept. He used to incense Father by pecking at the plaster mouldings but I wouldn't have him caged. I taught him to say, "I love you, Frances."'

'Where is he now?' I asked, afraid the story wasn't a happy one.

'When I was seven, he died.' Her breath shuddered. 'I killed him. It was –'

I held her tight to me, like a shipwrecked man clutching a piece of driftwood.

After a few moments she pulled out of my embrace and began to speak, her eyes cast to the floor. 'I had almost finished a panel of embroidery. It had taken me four months, was to be presented to the Queen – the old Queen Elizabeth. I'd used gold thread, so precious not an inch could be wasted, and . . . It doesn't matter really what I was making, only that it was the finest thing I had ever made. While I slept one afternoon Troilus pecked it all apart, shredded it beyond repair. Uncle – I mean Northampton – found me surrounded by the tattered remains crying my heart out.' She looked at me then. I had never imagined sadness could be so beautiful and took my handkerchief to dab at her eyes, an act that felt more intimate than any kiss.

'He told me there was a lesson to be learned. "A lesson that will make you strong." He made me catch Troilus, watched me as I called him down from the ceiling. I'd had Uncle's lessons before and –' her breathing was jagged, as if something was stuck in her throat '– and once he was perched, almost weightless, his little claws clutched around my finger,' she was shaking her head, shoulders hunched and holding out a hand as if remembering the bird there, 'Uncle said, "Your embroidery was for the Queen. By destroying it your bird has committed treason." Oh, God!' She looked up then and I saw terror scored through her.

'Stop,' I said. 'You don't have to –'

'No, I *do* have to. I do have to. I've never told a soul and I can't bear it any more.' She stood straight, seeming to gird herself. 'And he said, "What is the punishment for treason, Frances?"'

She placed a hand over her mouth, talking through her fingers. 'He forced me. "Now break its neck," he said. Troilus watched me with his little trusting eye, thinking it a gesture of affection as I brought my hands about his throat. His pulse quickened – he must have sensed a change in me. "Go on!" His wings opened, flapping. Uncle was going to tell me to stop, to tell me it was just one of his tests. I waited, struggling to hold my grip. Troilus writhed. Uncle watched, saying nothing.'

She hid her face in her hands, her breath coming in gusts. 'He said – he said that to kill something I loved would make me invincible. He said that I would hate him for it, but that one day I would understand. He said that to overcome love was the greatest lesson of all. He said I'd proved I was special, proved I was strong.'

I couldn't speak.

'I sat for hours with Troilus in my hands until he grew stiff and cold. I grew stiff and cold with him. It broke me. I'm still broken.'

'But how did you – your uncle . . .' I had an image of them together, tight as father and daughter. 'You seem so fond . . .'

'You don't know him.' She looked at me. 'Nobody really knows him – only me. He genuinely believed he was doing something good. He wanted me strong, so I would survive.' She fell silent, immersed in her own thoughts. 'And doesn't God ask us to forgive?'

'But even so.'

'No one knew. I lied about it. I was eaten away by it. I was so far under Uncle's influence I had no will of my own. You see, we Howards are taught never to show weakness. Some of us are better at it than others.'

'But you were so young.'

She turned away from me for a moment, then back, grabbing me with those eyes. 'Not too young to know I'd committed an act of murder.'

'You were a child. He *made* you do it.' I was appalled, couldn't equate such an act with the affable man I knew.

'I could have refused. I live with the shame. I pray every day that the Lord will cleanse my soul.'

The fervour of her piety dilated my heart. 'It's not *your* shame –'

She stopped my words by placing two cool fingers over my lips. 'But some things will not be shaken off or rationalized.'

We fell to silence once more. The moon had travelled and was half obscured by a filigree of branches. She shivered and said she must go. 'They'll be wondering where I am.'

That small yellow bird was planted in my breast, where it pulsated, forcing life to throb through me, whetting me, making me sharp and ready. She had shown me her broken self and it had become my mission to mend her.

Her

Frances's fingers are white with cold. She reaches her hands over the fire attempting to warm them. 'Anne Turner was devastated by the doctor's death.' Frances treads carefully, talking of Dr Forman. It had been that gruesome assistant of his, Franklin, who had come to give Anne the news. 'He correctly predicted the time and manner of his own end. Imagine that!'

'Really?' Nelly seems thrilled by the idea, her eyes sparkling. 'Sounds like the dark arts, I'd say.'

'Don't be silly. I expect it was just coincidence. Why –' Frances stops herself saying what she is thinking: Why the pretence, Nelly? You must have heard of the doctor's death – all London knew about it.

'My ma thinks there's no such thing as a coincidence. Either God's plan or the devil's, she says.'

'That's what Anne said of it too.'

'I know what *I* think.' Nelly seems so very sure of herself, leaning back in her seat with her hands behind her head.

'If you anticipate something greatly, you can bring it on yourself.' Frances pauses, then adds as an afterthought: 'Despite God's plan.'

The girl looks at her with a puzzled expression, suddenly seeming not sure of herself at all but naive, making Frances's suspicion that she is a spy seem preposterous.

'Anne was inconsolable,' Frances continues, remembering clearly how her companion had become hysterical, white as a sheet, ranting and crying, as if the dead man had been her father or lover. 'I hadn't known she was so close to him. She'd never spoken of him in those terms to me. She insisted Franklin return all her correspondence with the doctor. I can't imagine what she wanted to hide.'

'Sounds like you were better off not knowing.' A whimpering starts up from the cradle. 'Are you upset, little love?' Nelly's voice is singsong as she addresses the baby, taking it in her arms, but then she turns to Frances, asking bluntly, 'So, how did the doctor die?'

'I don't know much about it. I expect he was drunk and fell into the river.' Frances will not be drawn to talk about another drowning. The mere thought reminds her of the water lapping beneath, seeping up through the stone. She can feel it in her lungs, blue mould growing there, clogging her vital organs, rotting her heart. 'We left that day for Chartley. My great-uncle wanted me away from court by the time the King returned from Royston. He said it would inflame Robert Carr's desire all the more if I were to disappear for a few months.'

'Didn't you ever think of defying him?' The baby begins to howl. The sound gets under Frances's skin.

'Nobody ever defied Uncle.'

Nelly positions the baby to feed and the noise subsides. It has grown fat and round and dimpled. Frances wonders how it is possible for someone as slight as Nelly to produce so much milk.

'Besides, what Uncle didn't know was that I was falling for Robert Carr. I wasn't meant to. Uncle believed love was a weakness. So in a way – a very small way – I *was* defying him.'

Him

We rode to Royston on one of those early-autumn days, balmy and blue-skied, when summer seems to have returned to collect something forgotten. My high spirits didn't go unnoticed, and James claimed he'd been right in thinking all I needed was fresh air. He was in good spirits too, urging his horse on and singing a filthy ballad that was doing the rounds, guffawing at its obscenities. But we were barely there, not even in the door, when a dispatch arrived to dampen our spirits.

James crumpled the letter with a sigh. 'It's the French. They've got wind of my' – his voice lowered – 'Spanish plans. They need placating, and with Salisbury out of action . . .' He dragged a hand over his brow. The secretary of state was still unwell and his absence was taking its toll on him. 'No peace for the wicked.'

'Here.' I prised the paper from his fist. 'Let me deal with it.'

A smile broke over his face. 'What would I do without you, Robbie?'

'You'd be lost,' I teased, making him laugh, feeling deceitful.

Inside the scent of lavender hung in the air, bunches of it suspended from the low beams, and a fire blazed in the hearth. The rooms were small and warm, without the neck-cricking draughts that blew about the vast spaces of Whitehall. Royston reminded me, though my memories of it were vague, of the house I'd lived in as an infant before my parents died.

Scanning the letter, I was dismayed to see it was written in French. I had only the most rudimentary knowledge of the language. In the past I'd always relied on Thomas to translate any French papers. It was a risk, but rather than admit to James the linguistic failings I'd always managed to conceal from him, I sent for my friend.

Since his exile our contact had been sparse, but as a lure I suggested I might be able to twist the King's arm into revoking his punishment. *I'm sure he'll agree that you've stayed away long enough*, I wrote, with details of how to take the back stairs directly to my room. *No one will be any the wiser.* As an afterthought, I added, *I miss you, Tom.* It was the truth. I sealed the note in haste and sent it with a trusted messenger, under strictest confidence.

Perhaps I was foolish to have gone down such a path but I had James's best interests at heart. Without Salisbury, he was so burdened with responsibilities and desperately in need of a rest. I was aware that to carry some of his load would be of benefit not only to him but to England. The matter was pressing and calling on Thomas seemed the most efficient way of achieving such an end.

Upstairs the house smelt of fresh whitewash, and the brilliance of the walls contrasted sharply with the black struts and beams crisscrossing them. I had been allotted my usual room. It was a square space, vaulted into the roof with a door on three of its sides. One led, via a couple of steps, to James's quarters, another to the main landing. I unlatched the third and, taking the pot of grease I kept for cleaning my pistols, ducked under its low lintel on to a tightly spiralled stone staircase that led to a quiet corner of the stables. I descended in the gloom to the door at the bottom and, finding the key on the cobwebby lintel, unlocked it. The hinges rasped loudly, as I'd suspected, so I doused them with grease, ensuring they were silent, and returned to my room to prepare for supper.

The following morning the fine weather broke and rain was slashing against the window. I woke feeling the worse for wear after the rowdy evening to find that James had joined me in my bed. He was always concerned that gossip about his private life would undermine his authority – perhaps, if I'd been another kind of man, I might have tried to turn that to my advantage – and in my room we were less likely to be interrupted.

It was cosy under the covers, warm and intimate. We began, in our half sleep, to indulge in the pleasures of each other. Some might think the acts we performed monstrous, certainly they contravened the law, but human desire can take many forms and something born of great fondness does not seem so sinful. Are we not all sinners in one way or another?

He had me in a tight grip, giving me no choice but to submit to his rhythm, his urgent breath heating my skin, the sheets flung back. My eyes were screwed shut, my thoughts running wild around Frances, casting her naked in the bed in his place. He reached a hand round to grab me. But it was her cool clasp that sent me juddering and he with me.

We were drifting in our post-coital daze, when, like a shot, James sprang out of the bed with a cry, to stand in the centre of the room.

I sat up to see Thomas in the dark opening of the door to the steps. He observed us, his body rigid. He was soaked, water dripping from the wide brim of his hat. His face was cast in shadow but I could imagine his expression. He must have been there for some time, as there was a puddle on the floor at his feet.

'What in Hell's name are you doing here? Explain your-self.' The force of James's rage was like a blow to the head, and I remember being glad that there were no weapons within his reach, noticing my sword propped in a far corner. He stood there naked, his member shrivelled in the cold, the tic in his eye flickering.

For a moment we were suspended in time, the air crack-ling with acrimony, until I sprang up to put myself between them and the blade. *'I* sent for him. It's my fault.'

James slowly swivelled his eyes to me and back to Thomas, who was crouched into a half-bow, still dripping water on to the floor. He was trembling, I noticed, but not with fear.

Neither man moved. I snatched up the sword, skidding it out of reach under the bed, then flung a blanket around James's shoulders and pulled on a pair of breeches, fumbling to fasten them.

'What's going on, Robbie?' James's face crumpled and I saw he'd misread the situation. He'd thought Thomas my lover. It was certainly how it appeared.

I stumbled out an explanation. 'It's not what you think. I needed his help with the French problem. You see – you see, my French isn't up to scratch. I worried you'd think less of me. I was ashamed of it.' A shot of tenderness crossed James's features. 'I wanted to save you from anxiety.'

He said softly, 'Oh, Robbie, you can be so very naive.'

To Thomas, he was not so gentle. He strode up to him, swathed in his blanket like a togaed Caesar. 'Breathe of this to a soul and I will find a reason to strike your head from its shoulders.' Menace rattled in his voice. 'Is that understood, Overbury?'

Thomas seemed to shrink. 'I swear to it, Your Majesty. It is my solemn vow.' He backed into the doorway slowly. 'I humbly beg your pardon.'

James turned his back. 'Just get out.'

As Thomas disappeared into the dark stairwell, James trained a look my way, direct as a cosh. I knew what he was thinking. He fell into a barbed silence as I helped him into his clothes.

Crouched on the floor, lacing his boots for him, I dared speak. 'I know him. He's trustworthy. I will vouch for his silence.' I stood to stroke my hand over his hair. 'James, please –'

He slapped my arm away. 'Don't call me that. You are my subject. To you I am "Your Majesty".'

I dared not remind him that he'd often said how much he loved to hear his given name on my lips.

He began to prod the air with a finger as he fired words at me. 'Don't assume you know Overbury better than I. I should never have knighted him. He's been hanging around court for years waiting for opportunities. I know a man on the make when I see one. God knows, there are enough of them about.' He was seething. 'People like him don't have my interests at heart. If they see a chink in my armour they will prise it open and –'

'He would never speak ill of Your Majesty. He loves you as a true subject.' I was back on the floor at his feet.

'You cannot know that.' He sounded calmer but his face remained tight, his leg jigging frantically.

'But I do – no one knows Thomas as I do. He's been like a brother to me.'

'And no one knows human nature as *I* do. And he's *not* your brother, is he?' He sounded exhausted, resigned. 'I've lived two decades more than you and I know that an ambitious man – you cannot deny your friend is that – will go to any lengths to gain a little ground.'

'But there is so much gossip anyway about what might go on between you and me.'

And he repeated what he'd said earlier: 'Oh, Robbie, you can be so very naive. Don't you see? Mere supposition is groundless. Now we have a hostile eyewitness to our – to our –' It was as if he couldn't name it out loud. 'You have given Overbury the means to destroy me.'

He made for the door, still not looking my way. 'Something will have to be done about him.' Those final words thudded, like an axe into wood.

'He would *never* betray you,' I said, repeating it, as he didn't seem to be listening. The rain hadn't let up: it was driving at the panes and I imagined Thomas soaked and buffeted as he galloped away. I wondered if our friendship could ever be salvaged. The idea of losing him seemed suddenly very real and unbearable.

I went after James, curling a hand about his neck to kiss him. 'Please believe me.' He kissed me back, hard, as if to suck the life from me, then turned away abruptly. 'You may well be my downfall yet.'

With a sigh, he wiped a palm over his eyes and left.

Her

Frances is sure she can hear whispering outside the door. She presses her ear to the wood but can't make out what is said and jumps back as Nelly enters, followed by the maid, who is carrying a tray. She has brought bread and soup and places it on the table. Frances is sure she sees a furtive look pass between the two girls as the maid leaves. The soup is lukewarm with a film on its surface. She has no appetite anyway, and walks back and forth like a caged cat. 'What were you two whispering about?'

Nelly seems to falter slightly. 'Daft girl's sweet on someone. But he's married.'

Frances doesn't know whether to believe her. From the window she sees the maid cross the yard, stopping to watch as a man is dragged over the cobbles with a sack over his head. He trips and one of the guards kicks him in the kidneys. The maid spits on him before disappearing into a doorway.

Frances feels like a dead weight, as if her bones are filled with lead. Pouring herself a cup of wine, she returns to sit by the fire away from the window.

Nelly wolfs her food as if it is her last meal, talking between mouthfuls. 'There was a laundrywoman lived near us who used to starch them yellow ruffs. Her arms were stained with it, up to the elbows.'

Frances takes a gulp of wine. It is sharp, unpleasant on the tongue, but she keeps swallowing until the heavy feeling is gone. She is reminded of the fine French wines she used to drink.

∞

Chartley was frigid. It had snowed. Not the thick blanket that makes you want to dive into its arms but a sparse covering over hard black ground, dusting the trees with sadness and hanging dull icicles from the eaves. Anne and I languished in the gloom of my quarters, barely venturing out, awaiting word from Uncle to bring us back to court.

She was throwing papers into the fire. Each sheaf flared up for a moment, then died back. She had waited months, fretting, for those papers, and as soon as they were in her hands she'd spent hours combing them, like a mother searching for nits.

'There,' she said, 'all traces gone.' Fine black flakes floated, twisting upwards into the flue. She looked pale and upset. Dr Forman's death had distressed her, more than seemed normal. I'd seen her once or twice rocking to and fro on her knees on the floor, incanting his name as if it was a spell. I didn't ask her about it. It seemed like the kind of trouble it was best to stay out of. Once all the papers were gone, she prodded the embers with a poker. 'No one will be any the wiser.

'I thought there might have been mention of *that*.' Anne pointed at the little homunculus on the table. 'But there wasn't.' She had procured the wax from the verger at St Martin's and insisted on making the thing, on my behalf, then mutilated it daily with her embroidery needle. I'd allowed it, more to humour her than anything else. The ritual was absurd but Anne took it with deadly seriousness and was gleeful that my husband's attempts between the sheets had been reduced to the occasional impotent tussle, in which he would become frustrated and sometimes violent. She was convinced it was her doing but I was certain it had less to do with her wax figurine than with my encouraging him to drink heavily in the evenings. He lacked the head for it and often collapsed in a stupor, having to be hauled to his bed by a servant.

We had been at Chartley by then for the entire dead winter. The only thing alive was my secret passion. The absence, designed to inflame Robert Carr, had caught in me too, surprising me. Like any woman, I had known the fixations of youthful desire. But this was different. This was like possession. I had believed myself incapable of such feelings, that Uncle had trained the possibility out of me. My siblings always told me I was too unemotional, too flinty, to be susceptible to the whims of love. But even flint will cause a spark if rubbed in the right way, and in the wake of our moonlit conversation on the Whitehall staircase I had begun to smoulder. Love is like that, I suppose. It takes you by stealth. In the back of my mind I imagined Uncle's disdain: *That was not part of our plan – you've weakened yourself with it.*

That encounter with Carr was never far from my thoughts. His honesty had disarmed me; his guileless self-revelation had made me forget Uncle's orders and allow my own true self to appear. We were, both of us, peeled back. He was nothing like the swaggering courtier I'd assumed him to be and wore his undeniable magnetism with a surprising tenderness. But still I regretted so readily spilling my darkest shame to him. I feared he would like me less for it. What man could love a woman who was capable of murdering a beloved pet? Only Uncle, and Robert Carr was nothing like Uncle. I was unused to self-doubt. Uncle had trained me well, but perhaps not well enough.

Anne tugged me from my thoughts. 'Why are you so sceptical of Forman?' She couldn't hide her annoyance. 'His methods are working on your husband. He hasn't succeeded in,' she made a crude gesture with her finger, 'has he?'

'That has nothing to do with it.' Infuriated, I pointed to

the wax figure. 'And you *still* haven't had your marriage proposal, have you? If Forman was as gifted as you think . . . All you did was line his pockets.'

'Don't speak ill of the dead.'

I noticed she was almost in tears and felt guilty for being so insensitive. Charlatan or not, Dr Forman had meant something to her. 'I'm sorry, Anne. I don't mean to argue. It's just this situation is becoming too much for me. We're rotting away here and I'm beginning to wonder if Uncle really means to get me out of this infernal marriage.' I had begun to suspect it was just another of his power plays, that he wanted the King's favourite in his pocket and I was the lure to achieve his ends, just as I had been with the prince.

Anne apologized too but looked at me strangely as if something had struck her. 'If you really want to escape your marriage there are ways. Franklin could –'

'What – that great ghoul who came to tell you of Forman's death? I don't want that creature doing anything for me.'

She looked hurt. 'I only meant –'

'Enough!' I snapped. 'I've had enough of your mystical nonsense. I've had enough of this waiting.' I sank on to a chair, deflated.

'This place is getting to you,' she soothed, her own upset seeming forgotten. 'I'm sure there'll be word from your great-uncle soon.'

She was right. A few days later a letter arrived.

I scanned the page. 'It's beginning, Anne!' She stood, looking over my shoulder. 'He wants me to talk to Essex. I'm to convince him that we should seek an annulment, say that it's in both our interests. He's going to make sure I am ordered back to court.' I felt suddenly daunted by the thought of confronting my husband.

103

'At last.' Anne was smiling. My doubts must have crept to the surface, as she added, 'But what's the matter?'

'He's so unpredictable.' She tried to reassure me with platitudes. 'If you want to help,' I said brusquely, gathering my fortitude, 'you can make sure his pistols are out of the way before I go to him.' Alarm scudded over her face. 'Just a precaution.'

I picked up the wax figure and flung it on to the fire. Anne clapped a hand over her mouth in outrage. 'It's only a toy.' Watching the wax succumb to the flames, I wished my marriage could be undone as easily. I left for the chapel.

The place vibrated with silence; a lonely candle burning on the altar cast a vague light that made the shadows shift, as if people were hiding in the corners. The single crucifix hung behind, stark against the pale wall, Christ slumped forward, hanging from nails. A faint whiff of sandalwood hung in the air. The prayer stands had been stacked to one side, so I got down on the bare flagstones, kneeling in penitence. The cold bit in, prowling up through my body until my extremities were numb. My sins pressed, like hands about my throat. I begged forgiveness and protection again and again, until my prayers dried up.

As I got to my feet the candle snuffed itself out and I rushed in a panic, stumbling through the dark, out of the chapel to face my husband.

Him

I noticed a slight withdrawal of James's affection, a new guardedness, and felt sure, though he never mentioned it, that the embers of the incident with Thomas smouldered in him. Thomas had gone to ground. I had never felt his absence so keenly and it made me understand that he was the only friend who saw beneath my surface and cared for me, despite the failings he found there. A part of me had been ripped away – I even missed our quarrels – and I was determined to find a way to make amends, though I questioned how it would be possible when my being was so subsumed by Frances of whom he disapproved so greatly.

On the journey back to Whitehall I thought endlessly of her, anticipating our next encounter. But when we arrived I was crushed to discover that she had left for her husband's house in Staffordshire.

I don't know what I'd expected – a note, a message, a letter, some kind of sign, but there was nothing. Christmas came and went – still nothing – and winter gave way to spring, but even the bright buds unfurling brought me no joy. Each day crawled by as I waited for news of her return, indulging in my lover's misery, like a pining sonneteer, and seeking out the company of Harry Howard just for his resemblance to his sister.

Summer was almost upon us when news came that the secretary of state had finally succumbed to his illness. I was alone with James in his rooms, just a single guard by the door, stifling yawns in his heavy uniform. Sun danced across the floorboards, filtered through the trembling leaves of a horse chestnut, where a magpie cackled. A messenger arrived, disrupting the peace, and I watched James's demeanour crumple as he took the letter, inspecting the seal, recognizing it as Salisbury's. He slumped forlorn and wordless at his desk.

Cark, cark, cark, went the magpie, laughing at his sorrow. James seemed, in an instant, a decade older. I thought perhaps he was remembering that he and the dead man were close in age and felt a step closer to death himself.

'It was the sickness that did for him, not his age,' I said, with that in mind. 'Forty-nine is not old.' The bird cackled on.

'That damned creature.' James screwed up his face, as if in pain. 'Can't you do something?'

The guard on the door was almost dozing, lolling against the wall, and before he realized what was happening I'd whipped the loaded pistol from his belt and fired it into the tree. The kickback jarred my arm and the sound, a blast of shattering intensity, boomed round the walls and through my head, as I watched the startled bird take to the sky. James, his hands clamped over his ears, shouted something at me but I was temporarily deafened, as if under water. A consignment of guards burst into the room, at the ready, taking hold of me, disarming me with ruthless efficiency, and James was obliged to explain that it wasn't an attempt on his life.

'What's the matter with you?' he said, when they'd gone. 'It would have been enough to shut the window.' He began to laugh, wildly, as if determined to shake off his grief. Once calmed, he turned to me, rearranging his features in seriousness. 'Now to business. I must decide what to do with Salisbury's offices. I've a mind to make Northampton lord treasurer. What do you think of that?'

I imagined the Essex crowd enraged to see their adversary

promoted. 'I think he's a steady pair of hands. A sound choice.' I recognized the potential advantage to me of Northampton's promotion. I had grown to respect the man, with his firm grasp on the nuances of politics. He had none of Thomas's fervent righteousness; he was measured and realistic – a good statesman. I had chosen to set aside the lingering menace of Frances's story. It was from the distant past and people change, don't they?

'If Northampton is treasurer then the Essex crowd will want one of theirs as secretary.' I understood that the ship of state needed ballast on both sides to keep it buoyant. 'I won't give it to them.' James looked defiant. 'I don't trust them. Do you know what I think, Robbie? I think we, you and I together, can cover the duties of state. I won't have that lot sneaking about making trouble abroad, poisoning the alliances I seek and pushing for a German bride for my son. I won't have it.' He looked at me then and I knew I was firmly back in the fold.

'As you wish.' I should have tried to convince him not to pursue such a one-sided policy, but an idea was taking shape in me, a way to facilitate Thomas's return.

A servant arrived with a suit of black mourning clothes. I dismissed him and dressed James myself, carefully stroking the nap of the velvet over his shoulders. 'Do you think,' I tendered, 'it might be wise to invite Thomas Overbury back to court?'

He inhaled sharply. '*That* man?'

Very quietly I said, 'Keep your enemies close.'

And his expression transformed to that of a proud father who has witnessed his son shoot his first roebuck.

Her

The baby has been crying for a good hour with colic. It's fraying Frances's temper, making the walls encroach on her, as if the space is shrinking. Nelly, though, appears unperturbed as she balances the infant upright on her knee, deftly lifting its chin with one hand and patting its back to wind it with the other. 'Weren't you afraid of your great-uncle?'

Frances answers with a question. 'Were you afraid of your father?' She cannot find the words to explain how Uncle, even when he had to punish her, made her feel special. She suspects Nelly must have felt the same about her father.

'I was terrified of him!' The girl looks defiant.

Frances is taken aback. She can't imagine hard-nosed Nelly frightened of anything.

'And if I could have got away with it, I would have caved his head in.'

∞

Essex, puce with rage, shouted a string of obscenities and hurled his glass across the chamber, narrowly missing me. It shattered against the panelling, leaving a deep gash in the wood. 'I'll be assumed impotent. You think I'll tolerate public humiliation just so you can be free?'

I cursed Uncle for forcing the task on me. He could have convinced Essex to sue for an annulment – it was business between men, after all.

I spoke very quietly, trying to keep my voice steady. 'To

set us *both* free. We're neither of us happy.' I took a step towards him but he backed off as if I was contagious. 'Think of it. You could marry someone else – start again, choose your own bride this time.'

He turned away, staring at my feet where a large shard of glass lay. 'No one will accept me if they suspect I can't –' He wasn't able even to name his impotence and, despite everything, I felt compassion for him.

'Your peace of mind is as important to me as my own.'

His demeanour tightened. 'Do you really expect me to believe *that*? You're one of the most selfish people I have ever had the misery to know. You gad about court like a whore in your yellow lace, making eyes at Prince Henry, drawing attention to yourself, not considering for a moment that you make a fool of me.'

I wanted to shout at him that he didn't know me, but held my tongue and set my foot so it covered the glass shard.

He slumped on to the edge of the bed with a defeated exhalation. 'I'll be a laughing stock – did you think of that? Of course not. *You* only ever think of Frances Howard.'

I refrained from pointing out that I also risked ridicule for not having the power to arouse my husband, that it would be equally humiliating for me. 'You can say the fault lies at *my* door.'

'Not a soul alive will believe *that* – oh, God!' He began to hit his forehead repeatedly with the heel of his hand, like a lunatic. 'Only death can release me from this prison of a marriage. You know what, Frances?' He looked up and his expression softened, so I thought at last he was going to say something kind. 'I have wished you dead every day since we first –' He didn't finish.

A dense silence hung over us until he spoke again. 'Everybody thinks you're Prince Henry's mistress. Are you?'

'You shouldn't listen to gossip. The prince is nothing but an infatuated boy.'

'You have many faults, but I suppose stupidity isn't one of them.'

'You're right. I wouldn't be so stupid. But I *will* be labelled a whore nonetheless.' I was thinking that it might be the longest conversation we had ever had.

'If you're a whore, that makes me a cuckold. You won't get any sympathy from me.'

'I don't want sympathy.' I wondered what had made him the way he was. I'd blamed his overreaching father, hanging in the hall with his white satin clothes and self-satisfied expression, the man Uncle called an Icarus. 'What fool,' he'd once commented, 'would raise an army to overthrow his monarch when there are far more effective means to gain power?'

'Please.' I sat beside Essex. The scars on his face were taut and sore. 'Please. We are both so very unhappy. Can we not give each other our freedom?'

'I've had other women, you know. It is only you who renders me –' He still couldn't name it. 'You're poison.' He prodded a finger at me with a grimace. 'Some say only a spell can render a man impotent in such a way. There are rumours about you – your fortune-telling. You pretend it's just a game but they say it is only a step from there to befriending the devil.' His eyes dug into me. 'If you were found to be a witch I'd gain my freedom, wouldn't I?'

His words froze me. 'Is that a threat?'

He didn't answer, just kept his bitter gaze on me until I slunk from the room.

Him

I arrived unannounced at Thomas's lodgings, two rooms behind Newgate Market. Much of the neighbourhood was run down. Few wanted to live so close to the prison. The houses leaned against one another like drunks, their beams laced with woodworm. Thomas's building was sturdy, though, made of stone, and his rooms were large and high enough up to let in the light and offer a good view over the square, with the prison and the church beyond.

I found Ralph Winwood there. I hadn't seen him since Thomas and I had lived for a time in his London house, long before I came into the King's orbit. It was where my friendship with Thomas had begun. I was a page in Winwood's household and Thomas was employed to help with his legal matters. They were simple days with few responsibilities and I felt lucky to have landed on my feet.

Thomas became a surrogate older brother of sorts and initiated me into the quiet ruthlessness of the court. He said he saw potential in me and recommended me for the post of household clerk, tallying the accounts. I never quite got to the bottom of how Winwood had amassed his wealth, but wealthy he was and liked everyone to know it. More recently he'd been in the Low Countries, serving as a diplomat, as far as I knew.

'Here he is,' said Winwood, as if I had been the recent topic of conversation. He was a small man, a good foot shorter than I, but broad and with an air of self-satisfaction. He looked me up and down, as if to assess the worth of everything I wore, saying, 'Good fortune really has alighted on you, hasn't it? I'd like nothing more than to hear your news but I have an appointment and I'm already late.' He took something from his pocket and must have noticed I was staring, as he said, 'For all your fine clothes I'd wager you've never seen anything like this before.' He handed it to me. 'Largest emerald the gem dealer had ever seen – bigger than anything in the King's jewels.'

It was the size of a bantam's egg with a lid on a pivot and he was right: I'd never seen the like of it. I twisted the lid open to find a timepiece of exquisitely detailed enamel work on gold, beneath which a metal heart pulsed.

Winwood smiled and held out a stubby hand to recover his treasure, pocketing it. 'We must arrange to see one another. That is, if you have time. I should think His Majesty keeps you busy.' His smile was a leer and then he was gone, leaving me alone with Thomas.

'He's as ostentatious as ever,' I said.

'He's a decent man, and very generous.' Thomas was clearly not pleased to see me. His jaw was set rigid. 'What are you doing here anyway? I don't know how you have the gall.' He launched into a tirade about how I had not adequately defended his case with the King and that I only ever contacted him when I wanted his help. 'This situation, my disgrace, is all your doing.' He turned his back to look out of the window. 'You haven't been a good friend, Robin. After everything I've done for you – I feel betrayed.'

In that moment, I wished myself back in that carefree time at Winwood's house and had the stinging sense of innocence having been irretrievably lost. 'I've come to make amends.' I knew as I said it that my betrayal continued – my heart belonged to Frances. I stood beside him but he wouldn't look at me and we silently watched some labourers dismantling a gibbet in the prison courtyard opposite.

Eventually he spoke. 'How do you think I felt seeing you and him like that?'

'It was never my intention.' I would have reminded him that we were friends now, not lovers, but couldn't tolerate the thought of upsetting him further. 'I won't try to defend myself, I just want you to know I'm sorry. I truly am.' I put a hand out to touch him but he flinched away.

'I think you should leave.' His tone was brusque and unforgiving.

'I'm not abandoning our friendship, Tom. You matter too much to me.' I meant it but feared it sounded trite and suspected he doubted my sincerity. 'And I have good news. James wants you back at court.' He turned then, looking as if he didn't believe me. I nodded. 'Really.'

I saw that he was trying to suppress a smile. 'Really?'

I nodded again. 'You haven't told anyone what you saw at Royston, have you?'

'What do you take me for?' He pushed at my chest. 'Don't you trust me?'

'Of course I do. You above all people.' His posture relaxed slightly and I reached out to stroke back a lock of his hair that had fallen over his eye.

He grabbed my wrist. 'You – Whatever will I do with you?' We were close, so close our foreheads almost touched. A bystander might have thought we were about to fight. There is always a sense of intimacy with those you have loved and with it the bittersweet understanding of time having passed, of no longer being who you once were. It seals a friendship. But what I had once felt for Thomas seemed insubstantial, a youthful indulgence, in the face of my feelings for Frances.

'I've brought you something,' I said. 'Remember that bay gelding you liked so much?' He looked at me with incredulity.

'Outside with the groom.' And there was that smile, catching like fire. 'Why don't you put him through his paces?'

Soon we were out in the fields to the north of the city, riding side by side as we always used to and I felt a building elation. It was a balmy afternoon, one of those perfect days that belong in a painting with fat white clouds and pale golden light. It was a year, almost to the day, that I had first met Frances in the prince's chambers. Time for me was marked out from that day – before Frances and after Frances – as if it was the moment I'd been born. And she was on her way back from Chartley.

I knew this because I'd been with her brother Harry on the previous evening, drinking, finding ways to turn the conversation to her, when he whispered quite unexpectedly, 'You like her, don't you?' I didn't answer and he looked at me, amused, with black eyes stolen from her. 'She's on her way back.' The door behind me had opened. Harry looked up. 'Isn't that right?'

I turned to see Northampton. 'Isn't what right?' he said.

I scrutinized his face for signs of the cruel streak Frances had revealed to me but all I could see was the genial old man I'd come to know.

'That Frances is on her way back to court.' Harry exchanged a look with his great-uncle, as if they were sharing a secret.

'It *is* true,' said Northampton. 'You must meet her properly. I have a feeling the two of you will like one another.'

She's on her way back, she's on her way back. The words ran round my head in rhythm with the thrum of hoofs. In my mind, she was not on her way back to court, she was on her way back to me.

Thomas had ridden ahead, getting the feel of his new horse. He looked fine in the saddle. He was a skilled horseman and the bay was highly strung, but Thomas had him completely under control. Watching his firm but gentle handling of that skittish gelding, I understood that I needed his friendship to keep me rooted. Perhaps I was asking for too much in wanting both Thomas's friendship and Frances's love.

We arrived eventually at a stream in a light-speckled glade, where we stopped to let the horses drink. It was a place we knew well. We used to go there, years before, to swim and I was surprised to see the little dam, which caused the water to pool, still intact. Thomas and I had built it together.

I dismounted, watching the dragonflies hover over the water in their metallic coats, glad we'd found ourselves at that secret place. The water was high and lapped at the grass, which was long and bright lush green. I lay back in it, spread-eagled. Thomas came to sit beside me.

'What did Winwood want?' I asked.

'He's got his eye on the position of secretary. He was hoping I could get you to put in a word with the King. I told him I hadn't seen you and then you appeared, like a blessed mirage, on the doorstep. Just like you, Robin. What do you think about Winwood? You could give him a leg up.'

'I'm not sure.' The King had sworn me to secrecy about his plans for the post.

'You owe me, Robin, and this would be a way . . .' His words trailed off.

I felt a twinge of suspicion that he might have been trying to manipulate me for his own ends but dismissed it – not Thomas, he wasn't like that. I *did* owe him and could see why he wanted a friend in high office, given I'd proved so unreliable. 'He's offering a large sum. He'd be good in the job – solid, dependable, someone we know, a proper Protestant.'

A Painted Lady landed on his knee. We watched it in

silence, opening and closing its brilliant wings, until it dithered away. 'How much is a large sum?'

'Two thousand.'

'Good God.' I was thinking it was the King, rather than I, who could have done with such an amount, given the state of the coffers. 'Well, you shall have to tell him to keep his money.' I saw Thomas's good mood slide. 'The King intends to keep the post open. You mustn't repeat this. I'm not supposed to tell.'

He batted away a fly. 'What do you mean? He's not appointing anyone? Why?'

I wasn't about to tell him the King's reasons. He already knew far too much, so I merely shrugged, saying I didn't know.

'Who'll take on all those duties? The running of the country depends on a secretary.'

'I'm to share the duties with the King.'

'*You?*'

I chose to rise above his condescending tone, saying, 'Look, we both know I haven't the education.'

'It's not that,' he cut in. 'You're sharper than most of those inbreds on the Privy Council. But it's the job of an experienced statesman.'

I sat up. I wanted to see his face. '*You* will help me.'

'Me?' He looked as if he'd just learned of a very large and unexpected inheritance. 'Is this what the King wants?'

'Not officially, no. But it is what *I* want.' He seemed to deflate infinitesimally. 'No one must know.' I had a sudden misgiving about having told him, wished I'd waited until things were settled. 'I *can* trust you, can't I?'

'For God's sake! It's the second time today you've doubted my loyalty.' His eyes narrowed and I saw his fists clench, knuckles blanching. 'Perhaps you're judging me by *your* standards.'

I'd forgotten quite how quick to anger he could be. Things were different now, though, and I wasn't going to allow a quarrel. 'I won't be able to do it without you, Tom.' I put a hand on his knee and his fists released. 'It'll be our secret.'

I'd said the right thing: his smile was testimony. I pulled off my boots and began unlacing my breeches. 'Come on, let's swim.' Running towards the water's edge, I flung off my clothes, discarding them like shadows on the grass. 'Come on.'

I threw myself into the water, embraced in the shock of its cool splash, and swam a few strokes. He was watching me from the bank where he sat with his feet hanging. I knew that look, knew he couldn't help but forgive me. I swam over to him, tugging at his leg. 'Come in.'

He pushed me away with his foot. 'I don't feel like it.'

I'd forgotten he was a weak swimmer, never went out of his depth and must have been put off by the height of the water that day. Holding my breath, I plunged down, disappearing. Gliding along near the bottom, where the dark shapes of fish darted, my heartbeat throbbed in my ears and I felt an overwhelming sense of joy to know that Thomas was back in my life. After all, he was the closest thing I had to a brother.

I resurfaced and heaved myself on to the bank where I lay face down in a patch of sun. 'You should've come in. The water's glorious.' I rolled on to my back feeling the heat soak into my skin.

He was smiling at me. 'You always loved the water.'

We stayed there a while, reminiscing, until a bank of clouds blotted out the sun. I dressed, my clothes sticky against damp skin.

'You've dropped something.' He was crouched in the grass and had plucked up a small object between finger and thumb. 'What's this?' He held it out to me.

'Oh, God! Frances's pearl.' I snatched it from him, without thinking.

'Who's Francis, and why do you have his pearl cached away?'

'*Her* pearl,' I corrected him, realizing my mistake even before he'd understood.

'*Her* pearl,' he echoed back at me, and I watched his face screw into contempt as realization settled in. 'Tell me it doesn't belong to Frances Howard. Any other Frances but that one.'

I would have lied, or brushed it off with a quip, but I found myself unable to deny her, felt it would be a betrayal, so said nothing.

Thomas's forehead corrugated into a frown. 'Have you lost your mind? Please tell me this is a joke.' He was standing with one boot on, the other hanging forgotten from his hand.

'If you knew her, you'd think differently. She's not what she seems.'

He hurled the boot to the ground. 'She's a Howard, for Christ's sake.'

'It's you who insists the Howards are your enemies, not me.'

'You can't have a foot in both camps.' He stooped to pull on his boot in silence, then vaulted on to his horse, girding it into a canter, calling back, 'It won't end well.'

It sounded like a warning.

Her

Someone has been weeping for hours in the adjacent chamber, the sound worming its way beneath her skin, so Frances is relieved when the guard comes to take her out for air. She is glad it's William today – the only one who doesn't treat her warily.

Once outside, the brightness of the day lifts her but they have only gone halfway across the walled yard when the sky darkens and a sudden chilled squall lashes them with rain. There is no immediate shelter and they stand for a moment, not knowing whether to go back or forward. Water runs down her face. It is fresh, exhilarating, not like the dark, moving mass of river water. William looks embarrassed as if the weather is his fault.

A laugh escapes her as she runs towards a shallow arch. It offers little protection but she is already soaked, right through to her underwear. He is big and handsome, eager as a puppy, and is laughing too now, pink-cheeked, pressed up against the wall beside her. She feels alive for the first time since she came to this place, and the way he can't quite look at her sets her thoughts to the vague possibility of escape. She might convince him to help her. Looking up at him through her lashes, she sees the sharp little intake of breath that signals his ignition. With careful planning it might be achievable – if it comes to the worst.

The rain stops as swiftly as it began. 'I hope you have a spare uniform.' She smiles at him, imagining him shirtless, feeling a quick gush of desire. 'Or you'll catch a chill.'

They stay for a few minutes, listening to the drip and

gurgle of the gutters before he says, 'We'd better,' and stands aside for her to walk in front.

The room is fuggy. It smells of baby and the windows have misted. At least the weeping has stopped. Nelly smirks at William. Frances stiffens and sends him packing, then stands by the fire to take off her wet clothes.

Nelly begins to unravel her damp hair, saying, 'It'll take hours to dry.'

Frances has a sudden memory of the moment Robert first saw her with her hair down, how he'd felt she'd been keeping a secret from him.

'Robert loved my hair.' She is surprised by how wistful she sounds.

'What was he like?' Nelly's eyes are gleaming, hungry for the next instalment – too hungry, perhaps – and Frances realizes they've been talking about Robert in the past tense, as if he is already dead.

∞

There is a way of getting from Whitehall to Northampton House almost without having to set foot outside, by passing through the tangle of dark, little-used corridors that link the sprawl of buildings. I was in one of those corridors on my way to see Uncle when I heard footsteps in my wake.

There was an urgent stealth to the tread that made me uneasy. I slowed. They slowed. I speeded up. They did the same. I broke into a run but my follower was with me, on my shoulder, tying my throat in a tight knot. Stopping abruptly, I turned and, before I had a chance to catch my breath, was pressed up against the wall. My cry was stopped with the clap of a hand over my mouth. His face was covered, save for a pair of scornfully probing eyes.

Ripping my purse from my waist I held it up to him, willing my hand not to shake.

'Keep your coins.' His voice was a low growl. I kicked out, trying to bite his hand, and somehow managed to knock the bridge of my nose sharply against his forearm. It smarted painfully. *Never show your fear.* His face was an inch from mine. He smelt of bergamot, a scent of women and courtiers. He wasn't some ordinary cutpurse, then. 'Stay away from Robert Carr. I'm warning you.'

He released me with a push, running off as I stumbled back, calling into the darkness. 'Who are you?' All I could hear was his departing footfall. 'Who sent you?'

I stayed against the wall for a while, waiting for the clamour of my heart to subside before continuing. Uncle was at the entrance when I arrived.

I must have been visibly shaken, as he said, 'Whatever's happened to you? You're white as ash. Are you hurt?' He seemed concerned, putting an arm round me, gently guiding me to a chair.

'No – no, not hurt.' There was a quiver in my voice, which I struggled to hide. 'But some man just accosted me and warned me off Robert Carr.'

'Who have you told about Carr?' His tone was caustic, all his sympathy drained away in an instant.

'No one. Only Anne Turner. No one but her. And she already knew.'

'If Anne Turner's been speaking out of turn, she'll have me to answer to.' I was glad Anne wasn't there to be on the receiving end of his malice. I tried my best to defend her but he seemed more interested in identifying my assailant, firing questions at me about what he'd been wearing, the colour of his eyes, what kind of weapon he carried. 'Didn't you think to unmask him, Frances?'

He hustled me upstairs to where my parents were waiting in the gallery. They had come to discuss the undoing of my marriage. I noticed that Uncle omitted to mention the incident in the Whitehall corridor, which made me wonder what else they kept from each other.

Father was dressed for his portrait, sword, spurs, boots all polished to a sheen and an ostrich feather the size of a hearth brush in his hat. Master Larkin was painting us all that year, and Northampton House smelt permanently of linseed oil and turpentine. The likenesses were lined up at the far end of the room, none quite finished, though mine had been started months ago, before I left for Chartley.

On a table to one side was an array of equipment: a palette wrapped in a damp cloth to keep the paints from drying out, a set of brushes fanned out in a jar, a stack of preliminary sketches trembling in the draught from the open window. Beside a pestle and mortar stood bottles of unknown liquid and coloured powders, like a sorcerer's concoctions.

We all sat, except Father, who paced. He was formidable enough but always seemed diminished beside Uncle, and I wondered if he remained on his feet to feel superior. He took charge of the conversation, probably for the same reason. 'You spoke to Essex, then?'

Uncle, who was leaning back in his chair, appraising us all as if we were actors in his play, nodded at me to respond.

'He's as keen as I to find a way out of his vows. Though I don't think he'll –'

'Don't think he'll what?' Father rapped his knuckles against the back of my chair. 'He's not going to be stubborn about testifying, is he? You'll have to *make* him, Frances.' Father was defined by his impatience and rarely let anyone else finish a sentence.

'Can't you sit down?' snapped Uncle, who sounded as

irritated as I by Father's pacing. 'What *exactly* did Essex say?' He looked at me.

'He's concerned about public ridicule. Said one of us would have to die before –'

'What utter nonsense,' Father interjected.

In contrast Uncle's tone was measured. 'The sooner we get you out of that marriage the better. And if the boy's unable to do his duty it's not a marriage at all. I've already touched on it with the King.'

'What did *he* say?' This was the first time Mother had spoken all afternoon. She was being painted, too, and was in her best jewel-laden gown. She was still a handsome woman, with the kind of sharp bone structure that gave definition to her features, and pale colouring that disguised the grey in her hair. I didn't take after her.

I was darker, like Harry and like Uncle. Seeing our portraits side by side brought our similarity home to me, made sense of the hushed speculation that my brother and I were the result of one of the misdemeanours Mother thought no one knew about. It wasn't impossible. The Howards were tangled in secrets, kept even from each other.

'The King didn't say anything we don't already know,' replied Uncle. 'He insists that Essex swear to his impotence at a hearing. And, given what Frances says, I don't know yet how we'll achieve this. It might help if we arranged to bring him and his people here so we can discuss it face to face.' He put his hand over mine on the table. It was large and mottled, like a piece of dead wood. 'In the meantime, I need you to keep working on the favourite.'

'I think Carr's hooked.' I smiled at him. He'd always told me that nothing alive could resist my smile. 'Mind you, I haven't seen him in months.' I had only encountered him in public since my return but I knew he was captivated – it was scribbled all over him, in the furtive glances and his unexpected appearance wherever I was. I neglected to mention that I was as much caught on Robert Carr's hook as he was on mine.

'Have you given yourself to him yet?' Father was to the point.

'For goodness' sake.' Mother clearly thought he had probed too far, but I waved her aside, saying there was no point in being coy about it and that of course I hadn't.

Uncle said, 'Well, *don't*. Not *yet*, anyway.'

I wanted to shout: *I'm in love with him*. But I imagined Uncle's horror, Father snorting with laughter and Mother saying: *You, in love? I doubt that.*

'You're a good girl, Frances.' Father oozed insincerity. 'Your mother and I are very proud of you.'

'I thought you couldn't stand Carr,' I said. 'You used to call him "that ill-bred Scots cur".'

'Things have changed – he's become useful.' Father didn't like being challenged, particularly by his least favourite daughter.

'We certainly *are* proud of you,' said Uncle, always the peacekeeper. 'Between us we'll bring more power to the Howards than they have ever had.' He leaned in close, murmuring, 'I knew you were up to the task.' He gripped my waist tightly, as if I were a glove puppet. 'Even when you were an infant I knew you had something the others didn't.'

I soaked up his praise. My great-uncle's approval had been all I'd sought for as long as I could remember. And if his approval could be gained by repudiating a husband who loathed me and winning a man I thought I loved already, then being Uncle's creature was a blessing. Or so I believed.

He took my chin and turned my face to his, speaking as if we were alone in the room. 'But you need to prepare yourself. There will be a good deal of mud-slinging and most of it will be directed at you. They will attack you and you must not retaliate.'

'Attack me how?'

'They will say you bewitched the prince, then set your eye on the favourite, and most likely that you have seduced every other man who has ever cast his eye over you. You know how people are. You must hold your head high and ignore it all.'

'People can think what they like.' I knew well enough that the plan had more chance of success if I was as cold-hearted as they all believed.

'That's my girl.' He looked over at the clock. 'Carr should be here soon.'

'He's coming?' My nerves jostled. Uncle knew me too well and I wasn't sure if I would be able to hide what I truly felt if Robert Carr was in the room.

'This must be him now,' said Father, in response to some noise outside.

And there he was, in the doorway. I noticed him glance at the row of paintings, then at me. I was embarrassed by his beauty, or by the effect it was having on me. He seemed amused, pointing to his jacket, and I saw that it was made from the identical deep red damask of my dress.

Uncle said brightly, 'If you two were in a play you'd be assumed to be husband and wife in those matching outfits.'

Quick as a whip, Carr said, 'If we were in a play, she'd be a boy,' making us all laugh, even Father.

Mother was simpering and I knew that the favourite's charm had worked on her too. But all at once her amusement dropped away and she cried out my name, her face contorting. The room fell silent, everyone staring at me.

Something warm trickled over my upper lip and, touching

my fingers to it, I found them bloody. A splash had fallen on my dress turning the deep red deeper still. Carr held out his handkerchief, which Mother snatched, pressing it over my face, and I was hustled to a chair to sit with my head tipped back. Someone was sent for ice. Only then did I remember the violent knock I'd suffered earlier.

Uncle took Carr to one side and I could hear them discussing poetry. Carr was quoting a few lines of something, his soft voice lingering like music. Father continued to march impatiently, as if I'd deliberately inconvenienced him with my nosebleed. I was enjoying the obvious camaraderie between Uncle and Carr. Essex had always been sullen and ungracious with him, and when I heard those two chatting easily like old friends, I seemed to glimpse a better future.

Once the bleeding had stopped, Mother suggested I go and lie down. I refused, not wanting to seem weak, and sat stalwart, using all my will-power to resist turning my gaze on Carr. I felt soft and warm and tender, and wanted to fold myself into his red damask arms. I imagined myself invisible against him, in my matching dress, disappearing, like a magician's illusion.

Eventually Uncle said, 'I gathered us all here with an ulterior motive.'

He looked at Father, who cleared his throat before saying directly to Carr, 'We want to offer you our daughter's hand.'

Carr looked puzzled, asking if he had heard correctly, and adding, 'But Lady Essex is already wed.'

'Lady *Frances*,' Mother corrected. 'We call her Lady Frances.'

'I'm not properly married, you see.' He stared at me then in silent scrutiny. 'My marriage has never been fully sealed.'

'It's true, then.' His look of euphoria set my nape tingling. I wondered what he'd heard and from whom.

'The pair of you seem well matched,' said Uncle, 'and I want to see Frances settled happily. She's the closest thing to a daughter I have.' He took my hand in ownership and went on, talking about his regret at never having known the married life and what a lonely fate it made for an old man. 'The annulment may take some time to achieve. There are one or two obstacles – nothing insurmountable.' Uncle gave Carr an avuncular pat on the arm. 'I'm sure you can impress upon the King the benefits of such a match – benefits to *him*. He doesn't refuse you much.'

I could see the machinations of Uncle's mind. He had thought of everything. He knew that the King would see the advantage of his favourite marrying and that this would also make the Essex crowd think they were getting what they wanted: the son of their dead hero freed from a bad marriage. It would lull them into a false sense of security.

The plan, seen in its entirety, was impressive. But there was a single lurking defect: Essex. I suspected it would take more than ordinary persuasion to make him testify, but Uncle's conviction was contagious. We were all blithely buoyed up by it while the details of my dowry were discussed. Our eyes met for an instant and I had the sense Robert Carr would have taken me in my petticoats without a penny.

'I think it goes without saying that the pair of you must proceed with the utmost discretion,' said Uncle. 'And what we have discussed today must not leave this room.' Carr swore agreement. Then Uncle added, with a lascivious grin, 'I think you two might seal your promise with a kiss.'

I could hear Uncle's breath, rasping slightly, close at my shoulder as Carr and I leaned across the table towards each other.

He was perfect, like one of the prince's bronzes, formed by the hand of a master craftsman, and I wanted him then, wanted to possess him, to distil his essence and wear him on me always. The swell of his mouth, slightly open, and his golden-lashed eyes drew me closer but Uncle's doggish gaze was adulterating the moment so I lifted my hand to disrupt his view. Our lips touched, flesh pressing firmly on flesh. I could have eaten him alive. We broke apart eventually. He seemed intoxicated, eyes half-mast, mouth turned up.

But, suddenly, his blissful expression fell away as he said under his breath, almost as if talking to himself, 'Thomas won't be happy.'

'Thomas?' Father jumped on it. 'Thomas who?'

'It's nothing.' Carr waved a hand, as if to erase his words.

'You don't mean your friend Sir Thomas Overbearing, do you?' Father gave a scathing laugh. 'I shouldn't worry about *him*. He's nobody.'

I noticed Carr's dark look. 'Don't speak of him like that.' He was staunch. 'Overbury's like family to me.' I was impressed.

I wanted to ask why he thought his friend would object and why it even mattered. There was something Carr wasn't saying, something that didn't quite fit.

'If you want my advice you should cast Overbury aside.' Father was brim-full of disdain. 'Don't know why you'd want base friends like him.'

Uncle, who had been observing the scene, spoke up then. 'If he objects, come to me. I'll talk him round. There's nothing that can't be dealt with.' His tone was reasonable, but the knowing look he flashed briefly my way made me shrivel.

At the time, I didn't know that person, the thought of whom had provoked such unfathomable doubt in Carr.

Him

A ribbon of river looped almost back on itself, as if to shrug off Greenwich, clinging to its outer edge. The weather was cold and brisk and clear – the best kind of autumn day, rendering vivid the redbrick palace and its straggle of outbuildings far below. Once magnificent, it seemed neglected and cowed, as if weighed down by all the history it had witnessed: the birth of three Tudor monarchs, royal weddings, the arrest of a queen, dark secrets whispered into its walls.

We had crunched up to the high point through drifts of fallen leaves, the dogs singing as they flushed pheasants from the undergrowth. A bonfire below sent up a blue billow, and traces of wood smoke drifted to us, mingling with the dank smell of autumn undergrowth.

I felt restored to be out in nature and glad to see that James, too, seemed renewed. He was sparked up with life, more like the man I had known before – all those tics and twitches stilled. I was reminded of the tenderness I had once felt for him. During the previous five months without an official secretary of state, the constant press of work had worn him down, diminished him.

Artemis, my kestrel, sat on my arm, quiet beneath her hood, while James's goshawk strained at his jesses. Hannibal was a great grey beauty the size of a small dog, with long speckled breeches. James adored that bird, liked to hold a morsel of meat between his teeth so the hawk could pluck it directly from his mouth. Whenever he did so the falconers winced, imagining, I suppose, the royal lips shredded and themselves blamed.

In comparison Artemis was small and tame. Hannibal's restlessness began to disturb her and she gripped my glove, sinews tight, instinct telling her that under other circumstances she might well be prey for a goshawk. She had flickering jet-black eyes, rimmed in yellow, the colour of Frances's ruffs. Everything reminded me of Frances. I spilled over with thoughts of her. All those empty months of waiting were forgotten, replaced with a new, more tangible, desire.

With James's cheerful mood it seemed the perfect moment to broach the subject of my marriage. He had talked of finding a match for me, more than once, but had never followed it up and I was unsure of how he might respond. I sidled around the topic, talking of a recent wedding at court and turning the conversation to parenthood, asking him how he had felt on becoming a father.

I hoped he might take the bait and raise the subject himself but he didn't and, in the end, I said, 'I, too, would like to enjoy the experience of fatherhood.'

'It would be a crime for you not to reproduce, with your looks.' He nudged me, and seemed to be half joking. Hannibal batted his wings with impatience.

'I would need to be wed to do that.'

'Not necessarily,' he teased, making me feel I was getting nowhere with my tactful approach. He was distracted, stroking and cooing to his hawk in a bid to settle him. But then his tone sharpened: 'Seeking to replace me?'

'Don't be silly.' I slapped a jovial hand to his shoulder but felt disheartened as the conversation had effectively been closed. Inside my glove, I could feel the familiar small, hard sphere of Frances's pearl. And tucked inside my shirt, next to my skin, was my newest relic: a bloodstained handkerchief, her blood.

He flicked a wry look at me and we fell to silence as he

untied the hawk and slipped off its hood. The creature leaped up, unfolding the vast span of his wings, soaring into the crisp air. James watched him rise with a look of wonder, as if he were up there too, unencumbered by the responsibilities of his position.

I waited until Hannibal was almost out of sight before sending Artemis up. The unfinished conversation prodded at me as I followed her path with my gaze, until I had to speak. 'It would stop the wagging tongues if I married and it would make the Queen happy. She'll assume you've cooled towards me.' Artemis was wheeling above. 'Make your life easier.'

He was silent for some time. 'Salisbury suggested it to me before he died. "Find the boy a wife, Your Majesty."' He was doing a passable impression of his old chief minister. 'Salisbury always had a knack for burying a scandal. Whenever I've gone against his word I've regretted it – seems he controls me from the grave now.'

Artemis was making low circles on outstretched wings, tips spread like fingers. Hannibal was further afield, a speck floating in blue, but then turned and began to skim back towards us. Artemis hung oblivious, her eye fast on the ground. I whistled to warn her but she ignored me.

'So, who do you want for a bride?'

I hadn't expected his question and doubted his sincerity, but didn't want to take my eyes off my bird to study his expression. Hannibal changed direction, away from us once more. Relief buoyed me. 'I want Lady Essex.'

He guffawed with laughter. 'You *do* like to court controversy. Are you absolutely sure?'

'I am.' I felt a traitor, as thoughts of Frances assailed me, my broken Frances, her golden ruff discarded on the floor, her unstinting dark stare.

Artemis had spotted something in the undergrowth and

began her dive, body drawn tight, sleek as a bullet, speeding earthwards.

'Her annulment won't be straightforward. She's been wed to Essex for some years, though Northampton swore on the Bible that she was still a maid. God knows what's wrong with the husband. Even *I* can see the appeal of Lady Essex.'

'A little controversy might provide a distraction from your Spanish dealings.' I felt pleased with myself for coming up with this. He was well aware that his secret diplomacy with the old enemy might be the catalyst for rebellion, were it to come out.

'You sound just like Salisbury.' He looked impressed, seemed to be weighing up the idea. 'And there's another advantage. If you wed *her*' – the thought seemed to have just occurred to him – 'it might stop my son's fantasies getting out of control. He's developed a fascination for the girl. Don't want any inconvenient little Stuart bastards, do we?' He let out another bark of laughter. My gut tightened. I didn't want him thinking of Frances in that way. I wanted to set him right about her, tell him she wasn't like that. 'Think of the beautiful infants you will make with *her*, Robbie.'

Artemis was returning, carrying something that looked at a distance like a piece of rope but as she approached I saw it was a snake, flailing. She opened out, fanning her wings, landing nearby in a furious tussle with her prey.

'I wager you a crown the adder wins,' James said.

I felt inexplicably choked at the idea of losing Artemis. They grappled and thrashed, on and on, until she lifted up and away from the ground, high as the top of a nearby oak. The snake slipped towards cover but Artemis dropped at speed, talons first, to meet with the reptile's head. It writhed on hopelessly, its movements decreasing in force until it was still.

We walked over, curious. 'I owe you a crown.' He tossed me a coin.

I caught it and threw it back. 'But I didn't accept the bet.'

'You're much more honest than you need be.' He was smiling, appraising me.

'I'm not like the others.' I saw everyone trying to bleed him dry, taking and giving nothing in return. I was determined not to be one of them.

I held out my gloved hand. Artemis came to me for her reward. Her beak and face were smeared crimson, black eyes quivering as she reined in the wild part of her.

'Do you mean it, about me marrying?' My question hung in the air. He was watching Hannibal.

'My jealousy doesn't extend to women, if that's what you're asking.' The hawk swooped near and away again. 'And the advantages do seem numerous. If it's Lady Essex you want, then Lady Essex you shall have. We'd better set proceedings in motion to undo her ties.' He paused, smiling – 'I look forward to being godfather' – and gave my cheek a sharp little slap. 'You'd better not fall for her.' The smile had gone from his face.

Her

Nelly plants the sleeping bundle on Frances's lap. 'She's an easy little thing – not like some.'

The baby's sour-milk smell makes Frances nauseous. There is a small blister on its lip, created by the force of its suckling, and the little swollen mouth still pumps minutely. Its entire existence is an eternal cycle of feeding, dreaming of feeding and demanding to be fed. 'Like a tick,' she murmurs.

'What?' says Nelly.

'Nothing.'

Envy drip-drips into Frances, uninvited. She would steal the baby's contented oblivion, if she could. Every night worries flit into her shallow dreams, spiralling round her exhausted mind. The hours are punctuated by half-human sounds, yelps and moans and whimpers, coming from the bowels of the building. The trial looms and the outcome she once felt quite sure of now seems uncertain, as if some malevolent god has her fate in his fist.

Nelly is standing over her, gazing at the infant. Frances wonders if the girl is thinking of her own stillborn baby but there is nothing wistful about her expression. 'She's the spit of you.'

Frances looks again and sees then what she hadn't yet noticed. There is nothing of Robert Carr in his daughter. The baby stretches, yawning, and in the most fleeting glimpse she can see Uncle. It is as if they made this child with bits of themselves. A well of emptiness opens in her and she realizes, for the first time since his death, the extent to which she misses him. It surprises her. *I am only half myself without him.*

She hands back the baby abruptly.

Thoughts of Uncle give way to thoughts of Robert and she is thrown, with unexpected vividness, to a bright afternoon almost four years before, the sun falling through the window in stripes over their skin, the peal of cathedral bells, their bodies hot, the smell of him on her and her on him. She had felt as if he saw into her soul and loved her despite what he found there – because of what he found there even, perhaps.

The memory of it is vivid in her mind, the heat that day and his lilting voice: *I've never known a woman.* The idea had engorged her desire. She feasted on the sight of him, his burrowing eyes, the curve of his mouth, the way his hair gathered into golden whorls at his temples. He drew on his pipe and puffed out a ring of white smoke. She put a finger through it and it disappeared. She wanted to consume him, absorb him into her, imprison him in her body until they were a single entity, a monster of desire.

Never? she'd murmured in disbelief.

Never, he'd echoed.

She could hear laughter beyond the thin walls. Someone strummed lazily at an instrument, singing a lewd song. He had unfastened her ruff, casting it off, and brought his fingers to her bared throat, pressing slightly with a sigh. They began to tear at each other's clothes, feverishly unpinning and undoing until they found the warm accommodation of each other's flesh. *I was always waiting for you,* he was saying. *I didn't know it but now it is all clear. Do you believe in destiny?*

She felt him stiff, pushing at her pubic bone. *I don't know.* She didn't know. Everything in her life had been so carefully planned. She had never thought about destiny. Everything was as it was – Uncle always there to make things happen.

The cathedral bells reminded her she was being watched. *Will God punish us for this?*

No. He seemed so sure. *We are promised to each other.*

But he hesitated then, halting the exploration of her body, shifting away minutely, enough for her to feel a sense of departure: *But —*

She was beset with a sudden fear that he had changed his mind, not just about that afternoon but about everything, about her, having seen her unwrapped, with her banal thoughts and ordinary female body, all the mystery gone. She felt herself caving in, a fault line opening in her. *But what?* The bells had got inside her head and she couldn't hear her own thoughts.

I'm afraid it will hurt you — you so soft and me so . . .

She wanted to laugh. Relief made her solid again and she sensed that a person can be pared back to their bones yet retain their enigma. Her appetite, the need to consume him, possess all of him, was renewed in force. She rolled, lifting herself, until she was lying flat along his body, her face so close as to transform his two eyes into one. The coarse maleness of his smell intoxicated her to a point at which she couldn't be held responsible for her actions.

Frances. Precious Frances, he murmured. *I couldn't bear you to suffer even the smallest hurt.*

Hurt me, she said. She wanted to feel something, wanted to feel the sting of his palm against her skin, to feel the hard press of his thumbs in her flesh, nails digging, leaving marks to prove she was alive. He looked horror-struck.

No, you don't understand. It'll be the sweetest pain — make me feel as if I exist.

His smile flashed.

Him

My boat slid through the oily water, heading home from the playhouse. I'd invited Thomas there in a bid to soften him before I announced my plans. It was cold on board but we drew the hangings around us, huddling over the burner in the dark.

'I have some news.'

'I assume by your conciliatory tone that you think I won't like it.'

'Don't be daft!' I made it sound light. 'I'm to be married.' I sensed a charge of tension between us and added, 'Just for convenience's sake.'

'Whose convenience?' There was an edge to his voice, before I'd even mentioned Frances.

'Come on, don't be like that.'

'Like what?' He sat back, arms splayed, in pretend insouciance.

There was no good way to tell him so I simply gave him the bald fact of it. 'The bride is Frances Howard. I have James's blessing.'

'Well, you won't have mine.' He was simmering but kept his voice low because the oarsmen were so close. The vague light obscured the detail of his expression but the air had grown thick with resentment.

'It's the King's wish.' It was partly true.

Thomas changed the subject, began to talk of the play we'd just seen, about a king of Scotland sowing the seeds of his own demise. 'Through his own weakness,' he said pointedly, and I saw he hadn't changed the subject at all. 'At the hands of his own wife.'

'And you imagine such a fate for me. You can be so dramatic, Tom.'

'I do – *I do* imagine such a fate for you, if you must insist on pursuing your folly. Every tragic hero has a flaw and she is yours.'

'But you don't know her.'

'I know she's a *Howard*.'

'Meaning what, exactly? James sees advantage in having the Howards kept close.'

'I don't have to tell you how corrupt her family is. They're dangerous, Robin.'

'Only according to *your* so-called friends.' This was an old argument and I could feel a storm brewing. 'The Howards seek only to serve the King, not like *some*.' He knew exactly whom I meant. 'There's not a bad bone in Frances Howard's body.'

He gave a burst of sour laughter. 'What was it Cicero said – "Only a fool persists in error"?'

'You always think there's an answer in something someone said a thousand years ago.' I felt belittled by his learning, unable to counter his comment with an apt quotation of my own.

'She's to be *divorced* – been married for years. I won't see you ruin yourself for a *divorced* woman.'

'Annulled, not divorced – annulled!' Frances was paying a high price for her freedom. All the Howard enemies were doing everything in their power to destroy her reputation, spreading it round that she'd bewitched Essex and caused his impotence. Court was a cacophony of lewd gossip spread by those Thomas believed were his friends. But I realized that in his mind this was not about court factions or who took whose part – it was about him and me.

'Annulled! She's no virgin.'

'You don't know that.'

'Oh, but I do – Essex himself told me, described it in explicit detail, blow by blow.'

'He's lying.' My thoughts were tangling. Since when was Thomas so close to Essex as to discuss such a thing? 'I don't believe you had any conversation with Essex.' I wanted to knock the deceit out of him.

'I've never known a husband loathe his wife so much.' He paused, leaning in closer. 'I could repeat the things he said about her – filthy things.'

His words catapulted me back to Caritas House where I was untying her shoes, unrolling her stockings, peeling her like a fruit, finding her soft flesh within – my beautiful broken Frances, whom I would put back together. 'You are the first to have my heart,' she had whispered. She had told me of her husband's cruelty, his terrifying temper, how sometimes she feared for her life.

I wanted to shout at Thomas that it was true she was no virgin for *I'd* taken her virginity and see what he thought of *that*. But it was deeply secret – even Northampton knew nothing of our tryst.

'For pity's sake, when are you going to wake up and see she's a base whore and her family are pimps?'

Without thinking, I slapped him hard across the cheek, shocked by the power of my strike. My palm stung and, even in the gloom, I could see a mark where my ring had caught him. A cloud of impenetrable silence engulfed us. I opened the curtain to look out at the river.

The oarsmen were laughing and exchanging jokes, passing a bottle round. I took it, swallowing. It seared my throat. 'You want to be careful with that. It could knock out a bull,' said one of the men. I took another swig and another, until my head felt comfortingly muffled, then slouched back on the bench. I offered the bottle to Thomas, slinging an arm over his unyielding shoulders.

He leaned forward to swipe the curtain shut again, taking a gulp of the drink, then turning to me. 'I care too much for you to stand back and watch you ruin yourself on that witch.'

'Why do you hate women so much?' The drink had made my anger seem distant.

'I don't.' He was offended. 'Just that one. God, Robin, I can't let you do it – *won't* let you.'

'How do you plan to stop me?' My head was swimming and my diplomacy had floated out of reach.

'I'll testify – prevent the annulment. Tell of what Essex confided – all the sordid details.'

I sobered in an instant. 'Essex was lying. Besides, you wouldn't dare. You'd find yourself at the sharp end of a sword, kicked quietly into the gutter – murder made to look like robbery. You think they are your friends but they don't care about you. Any one of them would happily see it done. Essex's lot want this annulment as much as everyone else – apart from *you*, it seems.'

'It's a risk worth taking – for *your* sake, Robin. Can't you see? It's for *you*.' He was pleading, had taken my hand tight in his. The mark on his cheek had deepened. 'Can't you see I'm the only one who truly loves you?' He drew me to him, as if to kiss me, but whispered, 'Don't you remember?' His eyes were wet. I couldn't bear to see that. But then he pulled away. 'I'll do anything to stop you.'

'You wouldn't dare,' I repeated. 'I know you, Tom. I know you don't have the guts. You'd make a hundred enemies in a single morning. At best, you'd be an outcast – lose everything you've worked your whole life for.'

We sat in silence for some time and I thought that was the end of it, but then he said, very quietly, 'I know a good deal about the King's state affairs. I have been party to all sorts of details that he wouldn't want leaked.'

'Are you threatening me – the King?' I snatched my hand out of his. I was thinking of all the confidential state papers he'd helped me with and suddenly my gut felt heavy, as if filled with a ballast of gravel.

'I'm not threatening anyone. I'm trying to save you. You don't understand – you're nothing but an object to her, something to collect, like one of the prince's bronze figures.' He held his forehead in his hands and let out a groan of frustration. 'You'll thank me for it one day.'

'You wouldn't do it.'

He had begun to list the things he knew in a murmured growl: 'Most people wouldn't be pleased to hear of the King's flirtation with Spain, his desire to broker a marriage for his son with a Catholic infanta just for the dowry she'd bring. You see, Robin, I also know the truth about the depleted coffers – England is bankrupt – *and* I know . . .' He hesitated. 'Oh, never mind.'

'What? *What* else do you know?' Alarm was gushing through me. I couldn't look at him, focused on a spot of grease on my glove, trying to settle my thoughts.

'What I came upon at Royston.'

An insistent pulse beat in my temple. 'The King would *force* you to keep your silence.'

'He won't need to' – I had never seen this calm, ruthless Thomas before: he was a complete stranger to me – 'because you will let go of that Howard girl and find another woman to wed.'

I could sense the resolve scored into him as I flailed for a response, a way to make him change his mind.

'I'll do whatever it takes to protect you.' He sounded absolutely rigid.

'Don't make me choose.' His breath was the loudest sound in that enclosed space. 'You'll regret it.'

A dark thought washed through my mind.

A little provocation and Thomas would be on his feet, dragging me up by my collar. He knew me better than anyone, but the reverse was also true. My right arm would swing round, fist exploding into his jaw. Stunned, his grip would release and a firm push would send him toppling backwards into the black water.

He was a weak swimmer, even without the drink. The oarsmen would stand witness to the fact that I was defending myself. They would try to save him, shouting at him to cling to an oar, but the cold and the panic and the alcohol would have crept through his body, along his limbs to his fingers, making his grip weak. And he would slip under, down, into the dark.

I could never *do* that, of course.

Her

A thick March fog is pressing at the windows, as if the building has been wrapped up, with them in it. Frances wonders if they are slowly suffocating. Not for the first time she is profoundly grateful for Nelly's presence, whatever the reason she is here – she needs the girl. It is an unfamiliar feeling that she is compelled to nurture for the sake of her sanity.

'Want to hear a secret?' she asks, watching as Nelly's eyes glitter with intrigue. People like it when you trust them with a secret. It makes them feel special.

'I slept with Robert Carr once before we were married.'

Nelly looks as if she has been given a fistful of sovereigns. 'How did you do it without being caught? Where?'

'At Caritas House.'

'Caritas House?'

'It was what Anne Turner called her place in Paternoster Row – Charity House.'

'What?' Nelly smirks. 'Where her girls would meet their gentlemen? Sounds more like a bawdy house to me.'

Frances snorts with laughter, they both do, forgetting, for a moment, where they are. Frances likes Nelly more for her apparent inability to be shocked, though she suspects the girl *would* be shocked to know that she'd confessed to the murder.

'You're right,' Frances says. 'All sorts of things went on at *Caritas* House.'

'But . . .' Nelly is counting on her fingers, then lifts the baby slightly '. . . this one wasn't made then, was she?' It is

143

not a question. 'You didn't have her till a while after you were wed, did you?' She burrows into Frances with her green eyes.

'What exactly are you suggesting?' says Frances. 'If you mean to question her paternity . . .' She was well aware of the slanders – after all, when you're labelled a whore people assume things.

Nelly laughs, loudly enough to startle the baby in her sleep, the little arms lifting, hands spreading open. 'No need to sound so suspicious. I'm not here to interrogate you! I'm only interested in this little poppet' – she strokes a finger fondly over the baby's cheek – 'aren't I?'

Frances feels exposed. 'It was all a secret for so long. I'm not used to sharing it.' She tries to keep her tone playful, as if they are just two women swapping confidences.

'The whole of London was talking of you and him, waiting to see if you already had one in the oven at your wedding.'

It is easy for Frances to forget the extent to which her private life was a source of public fascination. But no one knew of that first time at Caritas House, not even Uncle, and she wonders if she will regret having divulged that particular fact.

'Did you do it just the once?'

'Yes. Something happened then, you see. It all changed.'

∞

A dense crowd had gathered outside St Paul's under a fine haze of drizzle. The mass of the cathedral, its perpendicular walls reaching up to the thick sky, blocked out the light, casting the path in gloom. I had to force my way through the press of people into the narrow entrance of Paternoster Row and was thankful to enter the warm quiet of Caritas House.

Anne was waiting in the chamber at the top. The one Robert and I had used before, a small square room made smaller by a vast bed, which was dressed with fresh linen and plump pillows. She told me Robert was on his way: Weston had been sent to fetch him.

I never could work out exactly what Weston was to Anne. He was a kind of henchman, I suppose, to ensure there was no trouble at Caritas House. I'd seen him before once or twice. He was a great big coarse fellow, with square shoulders and a neat white scar, like a line of cross-stitch, running from his cheekbone to the corner of his mouth. He seemed the sort who had never lost a fight, and even his smart clothes couldn't quite smooth his rough edges.

I shook off my cloak, glad of the roaring fire, and settled into a chair, lulled by the soft lamplight and the heady fragrance wafting from an oil burner. 'You've gone to a lot of trouble.'

'You know me, I never can resist a romantic intrigue.' Something didn't quite add up about Anne. There were things she was keeping from me. I had seen her earlier in a corner of the yard at Northampton House in a heated conversation with Uncle and that strange man Franklin – the one who'd come to tell her of Dr Forman's death; his was not a face you'd forget. The sight of them had unsettled me and I was on the brink of asking her about it when we were interrupted.

A maid, very young, with pale skin and a thick skein of dark hair, put a plate of sweetmeats and a heavy pitcher of wine on the table. The liquid slopped over its lip. Anne reprimanded her. She was cowed, dabbing at the spill timorously with the edge of her apron. I noticed something familiar about her, wondering where we might have met, and found myself captivated by the pale sheen of her skin and the way her hair came alive with copper highlights under the light. I hadn't met her before but she looked rather like me.

Once the girl had left, I said, quite firmly, 'I saw you this morning, Anne.'

'Saw me? Where?' She was fidgeting with her bracelet.

'In the yard at Northampton House.' Those tell-tale spots of red had appeared on her cheeks.

I was hoping she'd have a perfectly ordinary explanation but she said, 'I thought you went to visit the prince this morning.' Unease burrowed its way into me.

'I came back early.'

'How is the poor boy?' She was changing the subject: she knew Henry was dangerously ill. Everybody did. That was the reason for the crowds at St Paul's: they were there to pray for him. Another great congregation had amassed at the gates of St James's for the same purpose. The court was in a state of suspension, holding its breath, awaiting news.

'I wasn't admitted. No visitors.'

'He must be unwell if they wouldn't even let *you* see him.' She had relaxed, stopped fidgeting.

'You were talking to Uncle and that man Franklin.' She couldn't look at me and started twisting her bracelet again. 'It seemed a heated exchange.'

She hesitated slightly, but then met my eye. 'Your great-uncle needs a new gardener and I thought of Franklin.'

'Surely that's a matter for Uncle's steward.'

'It should be, but you know what he's like. Wants to take charge of everything.' That was the truth, if nothing else. 'And Franklin did so well with Forman's garden. Never seen such well-cared-for beds. Such an abundance,' she went on. I didn't wholly believe her, but chose not to pursue it. It was unlikely she would give me a straight reply.

I thought there might be other ways of finding out the truth.

Sipping my drink, I inspected the glass. It was fine,

Venetian probably, very expensive, and it struck me that all the furnishings in that room were more lavish than I might have expected. I had no experience of other such places but I doubted them as well appointed. I began to speculate whether Anne was in Uncle's pay for some reason, reminding myself it was he who had first employed her as my nurse all those years ago.

'Exquisite glassware.' I held it up. It was delicately etched with a pattern of vines.

'I know,' she replied, with a conspiratorial tone. 'Courtesy of a customer. They're always so grateful.'

The drink was delicious, spiced and heady, and I could feel it taking its hold as the evensong bell rang. We stood at the window to watch the crowds entering the cathedral. I stumbled, feeling unsteady on my feet, and was struck by the fleeting thought that she'd charged my drink with something.

'It's strong stuff,' I said.

'Only the best for you.' She smiled, draining her own glass. I set mine aside, opening the window to take a sobering breath of cold air. Anne was chattering beside me, in the normal way, and I felt a fool for allowing my imagination to run away, putting it down to the anticipation of seeing my lover again.

The drizzle had let up and evening had closed in so some churchgoers carried lanterns on rods throwing out pools of dim light. I remembered the summer afternoon I'd spent in that room, how hot it had been, even with the windows thrown wide and the sound of that bell deafening.

'He's at least an hour late,' said Anne. 'I can't imagine what he's up to.'

'Perhaps it's something to do with the prince,' I said. I wondered, with a jolt, if Henry had died. But he was robust:

we all knew he'd pull through one way or another. It occurred to me that if the King was lying in his sickbed there wouldn't have been such a multitude praying for *his* soul. I wondered if it irked him that he enjoyed nothing like the popularity of his son. He certainly lacked his boy's charisma. Much was made of his intelligence but, in my mind, he didn't have the presence of a king. People care so much about how things seem.

The bells died down and we could faintly hear the incantations begin. A rhythmic creaking started in the chamber downstairs and the sound of a woman's moaning. I felt like one of Anne's whores, waiting there. The thought excited me, made me impatient for Robert's arrival, thinking of his body, his smell, my skin under his hands. Anne left the room and I heard her bang on the door below, calling for them to keep the noise down.

It didn't seem long before the bell was ringing again to mark the end of the service and the jabber of conversation rose up to us from the departing crowds.

Eventually we heard a heavy footfall on the stairs: a man's tread. My heart began to pound. Anne looked at me, nodding. We both made for the door. I was lightheaded with wine and anticipation. She opened it to reveal the hulking Weston with a letter.

I ripped it open.

My most beloved Frances,

I wish beyond anything that I could come in person and tell you of the bad circumstances I find myself in that explain my absence.

Sir Thomas Overbury is making threats. He intends to spill dark secrets, to which he is party, which would greatly damage His Majesty. I cannot describe to you my devastation, as the condition for

Overbury's silence is that I give you up. I have no choice but to do his bidding or cause great danger to the King and the country.

I implore you to find it in your being to forgive me and believe me when I say that my suffering knows no bounds. I will hold you in my heart above all others as long as I have breath in my body . . .

'God must want to punish me.' I thought of all my sins, running far back to childhood, gathering into a vast and putrid pile, and collapsed to my knees, dropping the letter. Anne swooped in to pick it up.

I sat on the floor trying to understand what was happening. Since Robert had mentioned Thomas Overbury at Northampton House, his name had come up with increasing regularity. He wasn't liked. I recalled Father referring to him as 'nobody', and I'd recently overheard the Queen say he was guilty of poisoning her beloved son. But the Queen often took against people.

I'd never met the man, only knew he was some kind of childhood connection of Robert's. I was aware he'd been slandering me, though. People had delighted in telling me so. One man I barely knew, Sir David Forest, who liked to hang around the women at court, even offered to pick a duel with him on my behalf. 'I'll give you a gold crown for it,' I'd joked.

The slanders I'd been prepared for, but threats against the King were a different kind of attack – the sort that could get someone killed.

'Oh, God!' Anne exclaimed. 'Oh, dear God, my poor darling.' She reached down to embrace me but I pushed her off. I couldn't bear the idea of anyone touching me, of anyone's pity, even hers. 'I thought we could get him here before –'

'Before what? Did you know about this, Anne?'

'Of course not. How could I? But I feared there might be problems – that someone might try to dissuade him from you . . . you know, with all the gossip, and the King.' She was waffling again. 'I thought if he could see you once more, it would stiffen his resolve.' A high-pitched laugh came out of her. 'Stiffen! Oh dear, I didn't mean . . .'

'What are you talking about, Anne?'

'Well, I know what men are like.' Her forehead was slick with perspiration.

'I'm going to see Uncle about this.' I waved the letter. I'd had enough of Anne's odd behaviour. 'Come or stay, as you wish.' She chose to come.

The ride was only a few minutes but the cold was biting, and by the time we arrived my hands were blue. Uncle was in his study with one of his men, discussing the prince's condition. 'Things have taken a turn for the worse,' he was saying. 'That quack Mayerne has bled the poor boy almost dry, used all sorts of outlandish cures.' He looked towards me then. 'What is it, Frances? You look as if you've seen a ghost.' His impatience was almost palpable but he must have grasped that my news was important because he sent his man out of the room.

I gave him the note. He picked up a magnifying glass to read it, his features hardening, and despair leached into me.

'I had my suspicions that Overbury might cause problems. He's a difficult character and too close for comfort with Carr.' He didn't look at me as he spoke.

'Is that what you were talking about in the yard this morning with her and that Master Franklin?' I pointed to Anne.

Uncle looked straight at me, then towards her. 'Yes, the fellow seemed to think he'd heard Overbury making threats. He wanted to warn us. Isn't that right, Anne?' She had apparently been struck dumb and gave a vague nod but kept her eyes down.

'Why didn't you tell me?' My tone was terse. One of them

150

was lying and, judging by Anne's nervous hand shuffling, it looked to be her.

'Frances' – he was smooth as butter – 'we're all trying to ensure you are freed from Essex.' His smile was a grimace.

Then he dashed his fist hard on his desk. I imagined it was me he'd hit, felt somewhere deep down that I deserved it. 'That scab's mouth will have to be shut. Your marriage to Carr is our unbreakable link to the King. It *must* be salvaged. I need to think.' His voice seethed with rage, rage towards Overbury, but also, I suspected, as a knot tightened in my gut, towards me.

'I'll go to Carr. If I see him, I can convince him. I know I can.'

'Carr's shut up with the King. You'll never get to him, not with the prince in such a bad way.' I was about to speak, to suggest that Uncle himself talk to Overbury, but he continued, 'All you had to do was keep Carr in play. You've failed, Frances.' He pinched my chin hard, forcing my face up to meet his granite stare. '*You* must find a way to rekindle his desire. I don't care how you do it, I don't even want to know – but do it.'

He was completely calm and all the more menacing for it. He swept his hand in the direction of the door to indicate that we were dismissed. 'I'll deal with the scab.'

The betrayal stung. 'You lied to me,' I muttered, as Anne and I hurried away. 'You said Uncle wanted a gardener.'

'I didn't want to upset you. I hoped we could repair the situation without causing you any distress.' It was a thin excuse and my trust had been so far bent out of shape as to be unrecognizable but I chose to accept her word. I had no one else to help me unpick the knot in which I'd become entangled.

I have often wondered what my true crime was but foolhardiness must come near the top of the list.

I walked away towards my rooms. Anne had stopped to speak with Weston. I should have listened in, but I'd had enough of Anne and her scheming. Uncle's parting words rang ominously in my head – *I'll deal with the scab.* I knew I must urgently win Robert back, not only for selfish reasons but to prevent more of Uncle's 'dealings' on my behalf. My strength of spirit had worn thin. I would have sought out my brother's advice, but Harry was in the country, and so was my closest sister, Lizzie. The extent to which Uncle had secured my isolation began to dawn on me and I had to fight the wretchedness that threatened to sap my resolve.

Anne arrived soon, wearing a feverish look, closing the door, leaning against it. 'Weston says he might be able to help.' She looked me in the eye. Her pupils had dilated disconcertingly.

Who are you? I thought. 'Your servant, Weston? Whatever does *he* think he can do?'

'He knows of a woman. She has certain powers.' She took my hand. There was only a single lamp lit and the fire was almost dead. Her fingers, clutching me, seemed like claws.

I stepped sharply away. 'Not this again, Anne.'

'She's not a witch. Nothing like that. She just has the power of prophecy. It would help, don't you think?'

'No, I don't – there's no good to be had from some woman's fakery.' I was thinking of my own silly palm-reading games, done more for amusement than anything else.

'But she has a gift. She located a cousin of Weston's who had disappeared. Saw exactly, in her mind's eye, where he was.'

There were a few sticks and some kindling in the log basket. I threw them on to the embers, blowing until they flared. 'For God's sake, I don't even know Weston.'

'But *I* do. He's been in my employ for a decade. I trust his judgement.'

My reason was being wrenched apart. It was Anne's trust I questioned, more than that brute of a henchman. 'I won't do it.'

She came up close to me, too close. Those vortex-like pupils made her seem inhuman. 'You have no choice.' Then she smiled. 'And it can't hurt.' In an instant, she was back to the Anne I knew.

I went along with it for lack of any other path of action, I suppose. The idea of doing nothing seemed worse and I was fuelled by desperation, not only to have Robert returned to me but also by my fear of what Uncle might do, were I to fail.

If only I had gone instead to the chapel to ask the Lord's help rather than taking the path I did, but I wonder, with hindsight, if I had somehow been bewitched by Anne into discarding my judgement.

Just after dawn we were up, cloaked and hooded, following Weston on foot along the Strand. We walked eastward, to where the great gated mansions gave way to tall, ramshackle buildings, their upper floors leaning in to their opposite neighbours as if sharing guilty secrets. We stopped at a cook shop. A woman was topping a tray of pies with pastry. 'These won't be ready for a good hour,' she said, thinking us customers. 'I've some from yesterday, if you're in a rush.' Beside her a tear-stained girl chopped onions, periodically wiping her eyes on her sleeve.

A few people milled in the street: a woman selling eggs, another heaving a handcart full of grain, and some boys were playing knuckles close by. One threw a look at me. He couldn't have seen my face, covered as it was, but I felt suddenly exposed and shifted into the shadows, glad of Weston's solid presence.

He explained we were not after pies but had come to see

Mary Woods. The woman looked him slowly up and down, taking in the scar and the coarse features, teamed with the good wool suit. She indicated a narrow staircase in the semi-darkness at the back of the place, saying, 'All the way up.'

We walked past lumpen sacks of vegetables and hanging poultry into the depths of the shop, where a boy was pluck-ing a goose in a corner, feathers floating everywhere, like snow. We mounted in single file, up and up the creaking staircase, six flights, then along a corridor and up a further flight, to the very top of the building. There were two doors. One hung open and a young man was leaning against the jamb, smoking a pipe. A woman was calling to him from inside for help with something, but he ignored her as he eyed us silently. Weston knocked on the other door.

A female voice answered, 'Who is it?' Weston mentioned a name she must have known, for a series of bolts shot back, the door opened and we were hustled inside.

Mary Woods was younger than I'd expected, in her mid-dle twenties, neatly put together with a crisp white apron over a blue dress, and lazy-lidded, bovine eyes. Her very ordinariness seemed all wrong. She didn't ask who we were, just said, with an efficient smile, that there was no need for names.

The lodgings were small, lit only by a single mean square of window and the few flames flickering in a diminutive hearth. There was a box bed in the corner, a shelf holding a few jars, and a small table with two chairs and a three-legged stool. Despite the crudeness of the place, everything was impeccably tidy and well swept. A cat was perched on the shelf, watching us, which put me on edge. I wasn't fond of cats.

I took off my cloak, provoking a whistling intake of breath from Mary Woods. 'That's the finest satin these walls have ever seen, I wouldn't doubt.'

I thought it a lie: Weston had told me on the way there that Mary Woods had read the future for several courtiers that he knew of. It didn't surprise me – people resorted to women like her all the time in the hope of resolving their romantic worries. I'd always thought them foolish, but there I was.

'And look at this.' She had my ruff between her thumb and forefinger. 'Have you ever seen the like?'

Anne began to explain about her special starch. Mary Woods still had hold of my lace, saying, 'I'd love to wear a confection like this.' She let go, smiling strangely, as if she knew something we didn't. 'But in my line of work it's best to be inconspicuous.'

'Why so?' I asked. 'There's no law against prophesying.'

She didn't answer, just made a strange little snort, and unease crawled over me.

'What can I do for you, then?' She offered the two chairs to Anne and me while she remained on her feet. Weston stood at the door like a sentry. He seemed too big for the space, his head almost touching the ceiling.

Anne began to speak. 'My mistress needs to ensure a man's love is kept alive. He must love her so deeply he'll do anything to have her.'

'What are you saying, Anne?' I shot a frown her way. 'We're here to know what the future holds for me.'

But Mary Woods responded directly to Anne, as if I hadn't spoken: 'Anything?' Her long-lashed gaze turned to me then, curiously beguiling. 'I can get her in the family way.'

'No,' I said. 'This is not –'

Anne interrupted: 'They're not sharing a bed, you see.'

Weston shuffled from one foot to the other. The cat began to wind about my ankles. I shoved it away, provoking a sharp glare from Mary Woods.

'I could make a spell, but it'll cost you.'

'Absolutely not!' I stood, angry now, and grabbed my cloak from the hook. 'I'm not having this. We're going.' I found myself standing in front of the great immobile bulk of Weston. 'Come on!' Anne didn't move.

'Will this do?' Anne produced something from her pocket: a ring. It was mine – a diamond that Essex had given me.

'What are you doing with that?' I grabbed her wrist but Mary Woods, quick as a flash, had plucked up the ring and was scrutinizing it by the window.

'You hate that ring,' said Anne. 'Didn't you once say you thought it brought you bad luck? I'm only trying to help.'

'If you wanted to help you wouldn't have hoodwinked me into coming!' I was shouting in rage, and it was all I could do to stop myself slapping Anne.

'I wouldn't make a scene,' said Mary Woods, firmly. 'My neighbours can't be trusted not to gossip.'

I knew I was trapped. 'I wanted only to help.' Anne sounded tearful.

'The road to Hell is paved with good intentions,' I barked. 'Give me the ring.' I held out my hand. It was quaking.

'I only mean to use it to make your prophecy. A diamond can work as a conduit and one you've worn makes the vision so much clearer.' With her cow's eyes, Mary Woods was inspecting the shank where it was engraved with Essex's and my entwined initials. 'That's what you came for, isn't it, a prophecy?' I felt, suddenly, that I'd made a fool of myself, misinterpreting the situation, and sat, handing a handkerchief to Anne. The cat began to rub itself against my skirts, purring, like a mill. We sat in a moment's heavy silence.

Mary Woods was the next to speak: 'This is not a gift from the man in question, is it?'

Anne nudged me. 'See? She knows.'

'That's no matter of your concern, Mistress Woods,' I said.

'But I'm right.' She bored through me with a look. 'I only say so to prove to you that I have the gift. It's clear you think me dishonest.'

I assumed that she'd seen the initials and put two and two together. Though the combination of letters could have belonged to a hundred couples and, really, I could have been any lady from court. I hadn't even given her my name.

'So, this is a gift from the husband. Not the man in question.' She held up the ring.

Her accuracy disturbed me. I had not mentioned a husband but she could have surmised that any woman of my rank and age must have a husband, or at least be a widow.

'I can get rid of him, if you so wish it.' She let out a small riff of laughter.

I was appalled by her suggestion, couldn't tell if she meant it or not. Anne looked alarmed.

'But you *don't* wish it, do you?'

I spoke bluntly: 'As I said before, what I require, Mistress Woods, is to know what future awaits me. That is all.'

'All?' She looked as if she didn't believe me.

'Yes, all.'

'He loves you but a strong force prevents him being yours.' I began to wonder if she was reading my mind. But Uncle was in my head, saying, *Don't believe that gibberish, Frances. I didn't raise you to be a dupe.* 'There's a rat in your grain,' she added.

I wondered momentarily if Weston had spilled my secrets and was getting a cut of the woman's takings.

She smoothed her apron and I noticed for the first time that she had very fine hands, smooth like ivory. 'I won't normally cast black spells, for they can produce unforeseen consequences, but this will need a strong force.'

'I'm not having any part of it.' I made to stand. 'I'm sorry to have wasted your time, Mistress Woods. If you'd just return my ring . . .'

'Wait,' she said, putting one of those beautiful hands on my shoulder. She was stronger than she looked. 'I didn't mean to frighten you.'

I met her eye directly. 'I'm *not* frightened.'

Her mouth curled at one corner. Something happened then. She began to shake as if she'd been taken in a seizure and her eyes popped open wide. 'He's dead. The prince is dead.' We all stared at her, aghast, and could hear then the slow chime of the Whitehall bell ringing to announce a royal death. I was trying to remember if the bell had begun to toll before her fit or after, when she said, 'Poisoned!'

At once I recalled the Queen accusing Thomas Overbury of such a crime. I'd thought her hysterical at the time.

'You can't scare me, Mistress Woods. I'm made of sterner stuff than you think.' I stepped towards her to take back the ring but she folded it tightly into her fist. 'Weston!' I expected him to intervene but he continued to stand motionless in the doorway.

My only thought was escape – damn the ring. 'Get out of my way!' Weston refused to budge. 'I'll have you punished for this.' I would have shouted for help but I remembered the inquisitive neighbour and knew it would be reckless to draw attention to my situation, as it would surely be misconstrued.

When I turned back hopelessly to the room Mary Woods was standing over the fire where a pan hung, stirring and muttering something unintelligible.

'Do something! Help me stop her!' I cried.

Anne wore a wan expression, seemed paralysed, rooted to her chair. Weston, unperturbed, was cleaning his nails with the tip of his penknife, watching me.

A foul smell surged through the space. I felt light-headed,

yet my body was heavy and immobile as I tried to cross the room to stop the woman. The more I tried to move towards her, the more distant I felt and was only able to look on in revulsion, as she took a fold of paper, opened it, then plucked something up between her fingers. It looked like the carcass of a large, iridescent beetle. She dropped it into the mixture and suddenly, as if doused by an invisible splash of water, the fire died, causing Anne to scream.

'It will take effect within the week. You shall have the man's desire returned to you a thousand-fold.' Mary Woods paused. 'So I hope it is really what you want.' She had begun to tidy away her paraphernalia nonchalantly, as if clearing a dinner table.

'It's not what I want. I want no part of this.' My nails bit into my skin where my fists were gripped. She merely raised her eyebrows as if to say she didn't believe a word I'd said. 'Now give me my ring.'

'With pleasure.' She smiled. 'Once you've paid me ten shillings for my services.'

'I have no intention of giving you payment for something I didn't request.' I was so angry I might have hit her.

'I'm more than happy to hold on to this,' she held up the wretched trinket, 'until you send back your servant with the money.'

'That man is nothing to do with *me*,' I snapped, waving my hand towards Weston.

'That's none of my business.' She smiled again, slowly opening and closing her bovine eyes, head tilted, as if flames wouldn't burn her.

I knew there was nothing to do but leave.

She bade us a good day. Weston and Anne filed out – Anne couldn't look at me, aware, no doubt, that she would meet the full force of my anger for having compromised me so. I was following them when Mary Woods held me back by the arm, saying, 'Why are you afraid of water?'

'I don't know what you mean.' I tried to keep steady but was barely able to breathe. Cold liquid lapped at my neck, rising, filling my mouth, my nose.

She still had my wrist. 'Beware. Danger runs close to you. Very close.'

I shook myself out of her grip and ran towards the stairs.

Him

James's eyes were hollow and rheumy, like open oysters. Our footsteps echoed through the hush as we approached the chapel. The prince looked as if he might be asleep, though up close I could see that the warm colour in his cheeks was painted on. A fine dark down on his upper lip made me want to weep – they say even when the body dies the hair goes on growing for a time. I had a sudden memory of Frances reading his palm, her expression of horror and the way she had dropped his hand as if it had burned her. Had she seen his death there?

Princess Elizabeth peeled away to kneel beside her dead sibling. She sobbed silently, thin shoulders heaving. Prince Charles looked at a loss. His older brother had had all the natural allure, and obstinate little Charles would be compared and found lacking. James was stiff as a guardsman with only those raw eyes revealing something of his state of mind. He'd always professed, in confidence, to dislike his elder son. But I knew his feeling was born of fear – fear that his boy would grow strong enough to topple him and that he would be powerless to prevent it. He hadn't wanted to talk of his loss, not even privately, with me.

I pressed Frances's pearl hard into the flesh of my palm until it hurt. Our separation had created empty inner places in me, where a new intense loathing for Thomas welled. I was ashamed that thoughts of her drew me away from fully mourning the prince. Inappropriate erotic thoughts swilled through my mind without warning, mingling with the agonized longing that had tortured me for days, a force so strong I knew I would never resist it.

Perhaps the astringent presence of death was having its effect on me. The sudden demise of a man so young and full of promise concentrated my thoughts on the shortness of life. The chance of true love is so small that when it is offered it is surely too precious to refuse, whatever the price.

I still believe that. I still roll that pearl between my fingers and long for her.

Out in the anteroom I lingered while condolences were made to the royal family. A group of the prince's closest companions had gathered there, at a loss with their champion gone. But that negates their grief unfairly, for they were devastated, all dressed in black, like a parliament of jackdaws.

Essex caught my eye with a venomous glare. He seemed so callow and inconsequential, yet I couldn't help thinking of the terrible temper Frances had described. He whispered in a huddle with Southampton. Pembroke turned and cast a frown over me through a cloud of pipe smoke, like the devil in a play. I held his gaze for a long moment. I had the trump card, and he knew it.

The prince's collection of bronzes, displayed on a table nearby, offered an excuse to turn my back. There was the little shepherd on his plinth. I picked it up and was struck once more by the thought that it would make an effective weapon; its weight and the sharpness of the shepherd's staff could do damage. Feeling a pang of shame to have such a thought, given the solemnity of the occasion, I looked to the door, glad to see our party was making to leave.

And there she was, as if I'd cast her with my own thoughts – but love is a spell, isn't it, the greatest spell? She was with Northampton, her parents and a collection of Howard siblings and cousins. The sober jackdaws couldn't hide their disapproval as that glittering tribe entered.

They had worn their best in respect to the prince, and presented a sea of colour. She, in crimson, her slipped halo leaking gold on to her skin, stood beside the surprised-looking sister who was once proposed for me. Her sad eyes flicked my way for the smallest moment. I felt my legs weaken and imagined collapsing on to the black and white marble floor, my head cracking open to spill my deepest, most secret, shameful thoughts.

I felt a touch on my arm, firm. It was James. I looked back. Northampton was holding her hand and she brought two fingers to her lips, kissing, blowing, with such subtlety that no onlooker would have thought she was doing more than biting off a hangnail. Northampton nodded to me, a single slow movement, and I decided in that moment that I would seek him out later. Between us we would find a solution, for I might as well be dead without the hope of Frances.

I made my way through the crowds of mourners towards Northampton House, a maelstrom of grim thoughts twisting through me. I knew I would have to divulge the facts about Thomas holding me to ransom and the political secrets he threatened to reveal. My greatest fear was Northampton's response, that he might suggest silencing my friend permanently. His enemies said he'd stop at nothing to achieve his aims.

I hoped I might find Frances with him but he was alone in his book-lined study and rose as I entered. 'I'm glad you've come, dear boy. I was hoping you would.'

The endearment made me feel drawn into the great Howard family, embraced as one of theirs. It was true, I was the King's creature, but for my entire childhood I'd been passed round, like a parcel, never quite belonging anywhere – that is the fate of orphans. I suppose it had marked me with a weakness for those who offered a permanent place in their affections.

He sat me down and said he hoped I had come for the reason he thought I had. I told him of Thomas's threat and he surprised me, saying he knew of it already, had seen my letter to Frances.

I felt exposed, a step behind. 'I've been a fool,' I said. 'A fool to involve Overbury in so much state business.'

'The fault doesn't lie with you.' His sympathetic tone reassured me. 'You can't have expected to take on so many responsibilities without help. Salisbury had an army of secretaries and clerks. This is a lesson in misplaced trust.' He paused. 'And with Overbury being such a dear friend, well, you must feel doubly betrayed. What *exactly* did he threaten to reveal?'

'Sometimes I sent papers to him without opening them myself. I trusted him implicitly.' I didn't mention what Thomas had seen at Royston. I wasn't so foolish as to lay open *that* secret. But I told him of the covert dealings with Spain. Then Northampton's demeanour seemed to change: he became distant, his eyes hard as gemstones, and thoughts of hired assassins circled my head.

'I don't want him hurt but I *must* have this marriage.' I tried to sound measured and unsentimental, as if this was not about love and death, but about politics and protecting the King.

His tone was softer than his expression as he said, 'There *will* be a way, there always is. You care for her deeply, don't you?'

I nodded. I'd clearly failed to hide my feelings effectively and I had the sense that my love was visible to all, as if I'd ingested one of the poisons that makes blood seep out through your skin.

He was looking at me. I felt stripped bare under his inspection, with those terrible thoughts still teeming. 'I know Frances wants this marriage too. I can't think of a better match for her. And, well . . .' he exhaled slowly, seeming in that moment very, very old and exhausted '. . . I find I can't refuse her. I'm like clay in her fingers. You know she's more to me than a daughter?'

I nodded again, unsure how to respond. I would have liked to ask what he meant by that, but didn't.

'And you're fond of this Overbury fellow, despite his threats?'

'I am. He's been a kind of mentor – no *more* than that.'

'I understand. A boy who's lost his parents will often seek guidance from someone a little older.' His perceptive words made me feel understood. 'A bond of affection such as that is something to respect.' He stood to shut the window as the wind was up and making it rattle. 'We need to negotiate his silence without resorting to desperate measures.' He sat again and steepled his fingers. 'Can you suggest anything?'

'I don't think he'd be open to bribery. He feels so strongly –'

'Everyone has his price,' he interjected.

'Could *you* speak to him?' I felt sure that Northampton would be able to reassure Thomas, bring him round better than I. To Thomas, I would always be the callow youth in his wake, rather than the man others saw me as.

'I already have.'

That surprised me. 'You have? Where? What did he say?'

'It's of no consequence. I was merely sounding him out – getting a sense of him. You see, our paths have never properly crossed before.'

He wasn't answering my question. 'I hope you didn't threaten him.' I was firm, made it clear I wouldn't tolerate such an approach.

'Dear boy, what do you take me for? I'm not a monster.' He was insulted. 'I merely tried to convince him of the benefits of your marriage to my great-niece, benefits that might extend to him.'

His slender greyhound, which had been asleep on the floor, uncoiled and approached the table, nudging his nose into Northampton's hand, insisting on some affection. He scratched behind the dog's ears, causing it to arch its neck in pleasure. 'I find this animal such a comfort. Do you have any pets?'

'No, not really. But I'm fond of my falcon.'

'Funny you should say that. I was in the mews the other day and the falconer was talking about her. Said she'd caught an adder. Raptors are such efficient killers, wouldn't you agree? However tame we make them, that blood lust is in their nature. Can't be erased.'

I was confused by the turn the conversation had taken. But when I looked at him, his expression was as amiable as ever. He was just a man talking about hawking.

'There is *something* we could do about your friend,' he said, as if an idea had come to him from nowhere. 'We need to send an embassy – a trade delegation, a little diplomacy, some currying of favour in high places – to Moscow. Perhaps your Overbury would like the honour of leading it. Someone has to go, and it's far enough to keep him away until we have our annulment and . . .' he took something from his pocket and fed it to the dog '. . . our marriage.'

'Thank God,' I said, only realizing then how great my fears had been that he might suggest something altogether darker. 'Moscow.' I was laughing inwardly with relief. 'Moscow.' I repeated it like an idiot.

A blast of wind whipped up, slamming into the window. Northampton leaned down to take up the poker and prod the fire, which responded instantly, cracking as it threw up licks of flame.

'He won't be able to travel until the worst of the winter is over. But say he left during Lent. That would give ample time for the church commission to do what is necessary to release Frances from her marriage. He'll be gone several months.'

'He'd be honoured, I'm sure.'

'Yes, for a man such as he' – Northampton's distaste was apparent in his pursed lips – 'it would be no small thing to lead an embassy. I think you should propose it to the King. He may take a little persuading. Overbury is hardly of high rank. What do you think?'

'I don't foresee any problems.' James would be as keen as I, once I divulged to him what was at risk.

'You seem confident. That's good. You see, if the King offers this ambassadorial role, Overbury will be *compelled* to accept it.' The greyhound rested its muzzle in Northampton's lap.

'And if he refuses?'

'If he refuses, it will be a serious breach of the law. He might end up in prison for a time.'

'I'm sure he won't refuse it.' I *was* sure, absolutely so. Thomas was ambitious enough to grasp at such an opportunity.

As I made my way back to Whitehall I felt infused with new optimism. Thomas would go to Moscow, the church commission would give Frances her annulment and we would have our marriage.

And when I explained the circumstances to James, he said, 'Have the papers drawn up.' I'd expected him to make more of it. 'I'll send the blasted creature to Moscow and that had better be the end of it.'

It was all so easy, as if he knew of the plan already – too easy, perhaps.

Her

Nelly is rocking the wicker cradle with a foot. It rasps out a repetitive creak, *ad infinitum*. Frances would like to throw it out of the window.

'It scares me,' says Nelly, 'that life can be snatched from you like –' She clicks her fingers. They have been talking about the prince's death.

'Give me your hand.' Frances reaches forward, but the girl is reluctant, wants to know why. 'I can tell you how long you'll live.'

Nelly's eyes are wide with disbelief but she holds out her hand nonetheless. Frances traces her lifeline all the way round to the root of her thumb. 'You'll reach an old age. That much is clear. Only . . .' She tilts her head, moving Nelly's hand towards the candle.

'Only what?'

'You have an important choice ahead of you – a life-changing choice.' Nelly looks enthralled. 'See here, this cross.' Frances points to the place. 'You must choose between betrayal or loyalty.'

This seems to make a great impression on the girl, who asks her to explain but Frances can't, so turns back to the prince. 'It was a truly terrible loss. Everyone at court was beside themselves. Apart from Uncle, that is.'

'I don't understand.' Nelly is still looking at her palm, as if it is her first encounter with her own hand.

'It made the Essex crowd a spent force overnight. Prince Henry was their great hope, you see. For years they'd been positioning themselves for the moment he came to the throne.' Though there is no one to hear, she lowers her voice. 'I shouldn't be saying this, but when I look back on it, Nelly, I can see how it all worked in Uncle's favour, all his enemies receding into the background. He always had everything under control.' Frances feels disloyal casting aspersions about him, even vague ones. Loyalty was the first lesson for the Howards, and God forbid anyone transgressed it.

'Luck was on his side, then.'

Frances replies, without thinking, 'Luck had nothing to do with it.'

'What are you saying?'

'I'm not saying anything.' Frances remembers that lesson in loyalty being taught to her and suddenly begins to cough, as if her windpipe is waterlogged. Nelly jumps up to pat her on the back, and when the coughing stops, Frances adds, 'It was God, not luck, who must have been smiling on Uncle.'

'God wasn't smiling on *you*, being separated from the man you loved.'

Frances feels a surge of sentiment for the girl, jumping to her defence no matter what. 'But I knew the moment I saw Robert at St James's Palace, from the look he wore, that he'd come back to me, one way or another. Of course, Anne Turner said it was Mary Woods's spell doing its work. I knew better. It was love – that was all.'

The baby begins to whimper. Frances wants to cover her ears.

∞

A trio of Howards waited at Northampton House: Uncle, Father and my brother Harry. Uncle ran a finger down my scrubbed face. 'As close as you'll ever be to ordinary.' I had been instructed to dress as plainly as I could and to cover my

169

hair as Essex was coming with his advisers to discuss our annulment.

Mother had lent me her pearls. Harry tugged at them. 'They make you look like someone's maiden aunt.' He seemed amused by his new dull sister.

Master Larkin's portraits were finished, and made an impressive display along the length of one wall. I wondered what the collective noun for Howards might be: a 'shrewd-ness', perhaps, or a 'threat'. We could hear the visitors mounting the stairs and I found myself suddenly awash with trepidation. They entered, a solemn crew, Southampton, Pembroke and Essex, unbuckling their swords to leave to one side.

Essex appeared tense, a frown scored into his forehead. I hadn't seen him in months and felt a little sorry for him: he was as much a victim of the situation as I. He wouldn't look my way, hanging back behind Southampton. People said Southampton had been very dashing in his youth. But there was no evidence of his former charm in the man who stood before us with his ruddy complexion and the bitter twist to his mouth. I wondered if having been constantly overlooked for promotion had made him lose his looks.

Pembroke stared at me as if I were a work of art he wasn't sure he liked. His face was strangely smooth for a middle-aged man, his beard tamed into a sharp point, and he clutched a small ivory pipe between his lips. I was careful not to meet anyone's eye, keeping my gaze down, like the docile creature they all suspected I wasn't.

The atmosphere was painfully polite as Uncle offered everyone a seat, though I saw my brother Harry and Essex swap noxious looks. I loved Harry for his reckless streak – he would have done anything to protect me – but I willed him not to cause trouble.

Uncle placed a companionable hand on Southampton's

shoulder and said how deeply sorry he was about the prince. 'I know how close you were to him. It must have been an even greater shock for you than it was for the rest of us.'

My father was speculating with Pembroke as to whether Princess Elizabeth's wedding would go ahead as planned in the light of her brother's death. 'I think the English people would like a joyous occasion to take their minds off their grief.' Pembroke emitted a stream of smoke from his nose. 'And the princess seems genuinely fond of the boy.' He sounded quite caught up in the romance but I knew that he'd championed the marriage as a Protestant alliance. In our world there was nothing that wasn't infected with politics.

I sat to one side, not at the table. I wasn't there to say any-thing, just to appear meek and dumb while the men discussed my future. Essex sat in silence, wearing the look of extreme intractability that I knew only too well, and I couldn't imag-ine these men, with their excruciating false courtesy, finding a way to persuade him to release me from my ties.

But as soon as Uncle suggested they get down to the mat-ter, Southampton announced, 'I firmly believe we will be able to come to an agreement that is acceptable to both parties.'

My spirits lifted a little.

'Yes,' Pembroke added, 'it is of the utmost importance that there be no stain of humiliation for Lord Essex. If he is deemed to have an impediment to proper consummation, it will impair his chance of a happy union in the future. Obvi-ously, he would like to produce a family and I happen to know, as does Lord Southampton – indeed we have seen it with our own eyes – that Lord Essex is entirely capable of performing the act.' He spoke as if it pained him to use the phrase, shifting his focus to stuffing the bowl of his pipe. Essex had turned puce with embarrassment, and I wondered if he might burst into one of his tempers for all to see.

'We can testify before the church commission to Lord Essex's . . .' he seemed to fumble for the correct word '. . . *virility*.'

I was trying to avoid my brother's eye, as I knew we'd succumb to laughter at the idea of quite how they had been witnesses to Essex's 'virility', and imagined it being explained to the bishops on the bench.

'That's entirely reasonable,' said Uncle. 'But I must insist that Lady Frances does not suffer any implication of physical impairment.' None of them seemed to react to the fact that he hadn't called me 'Lady Essex'. 'I think we all know what I'm getting at.'

I stared at my hands as they discussed me and set my mind on Robert. He wasn't to be mentioned. My husband wouldn't be so keen to give me my liberty if he knew I was to be pinned together with the King's favourite the minute I was free. But, no matter how discreet we'd been, some people had got wind of it, thanks to Overbury's loose mouth.

I had seen the man walking in the gardens. The way was narrow and I girded myself, staking my claim on the centre of the path, so he would have to step back against the hedge when I passed. I stared beyond him but as he neared I caught a whiff of bergamot and encountered his eye long enough to recognize that contemptuous look, remembered the hand pressed over my mouth and the force of his warning. So, he had been working against me longer than I'd known.

'I hear you're bound for Moscow,' I said, blocking his path. He mumbled something about it being undecided. 'You'd better pack warm clothes. I've heard of people dying from the cold there.' His polite mask fell away fleetingly, and he looked shaken. I hadn't mentioned to Uncle that I'd identified my assailant — too much had happened since.

Southampton's fingers, thrumming on the table, drew me

back to the room. 'What we propose,' he glanced towards Pembroke, who nodded his assent, 'is that Lord Essex will swear to being able to achieve relations only with women *other* than his wife. That it is simply a case of physical incompatibility between the couple specifically.'

'*Insurmountable* physical incompatibility,' affirmed Pembroke, going on to list various legal precedents.

I wanted to cheer. At last my future came into vivid focus. Overbury would be in Moscow, my marriage would be undone, then Robert Carr and I would be united. It was all I wanted. My scheming family could play their power games without me.

'I think that seems eminently satisfactory to all parties,' said Father, who found a rare smile. Hands were shaken on it, promises signed, and the visitors eventually filed out. Essex hadn't looked at me once.

'Well,' said Uncle, once they had gone. 'It seems they are more desperate to undo this thing than I'd thought.'

Father laughed in a sudden burst. 'They face a decade in the political wilderness. The King can't abide them, their champion is dead, and our girl will be in the bed of the King's closest companion. I think we should drink to our triumph.'

I found his gloating ugly. 'You shouldn't talk of the prince's death as an advantage. It's disres—'

'Don't get high and mighty with me, girl.' He raised a hand to slap me, but Uncle stepped between us. 'Just remember you can be pulled down faster than raised up.'

'Now, now.' Uncle was calm and firm. 'Harry, would you pass that jug?' My brother handed round glasses, throwing me a smile. 'Let's drink to the smooth untying of our girl's vows.'

I drained my glass, unwound Mother's pearls from my neck, slung them on to the table and left without a word.

Him

At Thomas's lodgings a young servant opened the door. He seemed familiar to me, and when I asked how I knew him, he said, 'I'm the boy you rescued from a beating a while back. Lawrence Davies.'

'You've grown!' The day came back to me – Thomas's rudeness to the Queen that had precipitated his expulsion from court. The boy had matured in the two intervening years, had filled out and become quite handsome in a placid sort of way. I wondered what his back looked like and supposed it was striated with silver scars. His face was oval, still smooth with youth, like his hands, but his fingernails were bitten to the quick. 'How is he?'

'He's in a terrible state. I don't know what to do with him.'

'You mustn't upset yourself over it.' I tried to sound untroubled. 'I'll make sure this business is sorted out.'

He didn't seem reassured as he showed me in and I wished I had a little more confidence myself. Thomas was slumped over the table, amid piles of detritus, an empty flagon tipped up on the floor beside him. I'd rarely ever seen him so much as merry but that day he was dead drunk.

'What dragged you out of Northampton's arse, Robert Carr . . . *Lord* Rochester, or have you been given a new title yet?' He was slurring, had a black eye and his coat was torn.

I had come directly from the celebrations for the departing Princess Elizabeth, who was leaving for Heidelberg with her new husband, and was head to toe in embroidered silks. Jewelled pompoms, the size of cabbages, bounced on my shoes and my dress sword, polished to a high shine, swung on my hip. I wished I'd changed, as the outfit was frivolous and inappropriate for my task. I was concerned it might make Thomas remember what he was missing.

'What happened?' I stepped towards him, my finger hovering near his bruised eye socket.

'Go away. I've nothing to say to you.' He dropped his head into his arms on the table, hiding his face.

I opened the window to let in some fresh air, beginning to clear a few things into piles. I called Davies in, asking him to bring a plate of bread and ham and an infusion of ginger, while Thomas continued playing dead. Eventually, once Davies had returned with the food and drink, Thomas sat up and looked at me. 'So why are you here?'

'Just eat something.' I pushed the plate towards him. 'And drink the infusion. It'll settle your stomach.' He did as he was told, sullen as an infant. I was struck by the reversal of roles. He had done the same for me many times in the past. 'Listen. I'm here as your friend.'

He glared at me. 'If I remember rightly, the last time I saw you, you slapped my face and as good as said I was dead to you.'

'It's hardly surprising, Tom. You'd threatened me – and the King. But the situation has changed. I'm here to mend things.'

'I wasn't born yesterday,' he snapped. 'You're here to persuade me to take the embassy to Moscow. I'm not going. They've been here twice.' He indicated his bruised eye. 'I've already told them I won't go. I mean *Moscow*, for God's sake.' He pinched his brow, screwing up his eyes, seeming in pain. 'Just so you can have that little bitch in your bed.'

'Please don't call her that.' I kept my calm. 'You're going to have to face it. She and I will be wed as soon as she's free.' I tried to take his hand but he wouldn't allow it. 'I truly wish you would accept it and we could have our friendship back.'

'People like you don't have friends, only those you can use. You're just like her – made for each other.'

His words cut to the bone and it must have been evident in my involuntary wince, for he added, 'I didn't mean that. You are one of the few at court who's not –' He stopped and rubbed his eyes, taking a sip of his drink. 'Christ, Robin, didn't you learn anything from me? Those Howards have you dancing to their tune. They're *using* you to get to the King. They've pimped that girl to you and you've fallen for it.'

'You've always loathed the Howards.' My irritation flared but I kept it in check. 'It's nothing to do with her family.'

He made a sardonic snort.

'Don't,' I said, standing and turning my back, looking out of the window into a courtyard. It was an oasis of peace with the hubbub of the market just visible through the arch beyond. Two maids sat in a splash of spring sun. One was spinning, the other combing wool, and the light spilled from the brick wall bathing them in a pinkish glow. I had a sudden memory of watching my mother spinning – a fragment from deep in my past, for my mother was dead before I'd even learned to speak.

'For God's sake, take the embassy. If you refuse it there's nothing I can do to help you.' I returned to the table. 'Think of what it'll do for your career – I mean, an ambassador of the English King. You'll return and he'll ennoble you. I'll make sure of it.' I was babbling. 'Baron Overbury – come on.' I gave his shoulder a little shove. 'Sounds rather good, don't you think?'

'Stop it,' he barked. 'Just stop.'

'If you don't go, they'll throw you in the Tower.'

'You're one of them, Robin. Can't you see that?' His voice

was flecked with despair, and shame clouded me. 'If I'm locked up in the Tower it will have been you who put me there.' I began to protest but he shouted me down. 'You can't go on playing the innocent. You want me out of the way as much as Northampton and the rest of his clan, as much as the King –'

'The King *does not* want you out of the way.'

'If you believe that you're more of a fool than I thought. The King is terrified that I'll spill his secrets.'

'So, rescind your threat – promise him your silence. Write it down and I'll take it to him myself.' I knew, as he did, that once words have been said there is no unsaying them.

We sat in silence for some time. He had picked up a pen-knife and was carving patterns into the table-top. Davies began to clear away the dishes, moving discreetly so as not to interfere.

'It's an honour, the embassy,' I said eventually. 'An honour.'

He exhaled deeply, like a man who has given up on life. 'I'm frightened.'

'Frightened?' Thomas was never really afraid. He was always so sure of himself, such conviction, such confidence. 'Of what?'

'That I won't make it to Moscow. That our party will happen upon trouble of one kind or another somewhere *en route*, and the English ambassador to Moscow will just happen to be killed in the skirmish. "What a terrible misfortune," they will all say. "Sir Thomas had a great career ahead of him." Will you weep at my funeral, Robin? You'd like to weep now. I can tell. I know you better than them all.'

He was right. I was barely able to hold my tears, tears of guilt, and felt embroiled so deeply I'd never find a way out. 'Don't go,' I blurted.

'Then what?'

'You will go to the Tower and I will find a way to get you out.' Davies poured a drink for me. It was cool as it slipped down my throat. 'But you must stop this mission to prevent my marriage. If I can assure the King of your silence – he trusts me and I trust you. I do, really.' I tugged at his sleeve, like a beggar.

'You have to promise to protect me.' I could see he doubted I was able to. 'You're the only one who cares, Robin. Even my supposed friends have abandoned me. I hadn't fully understood, until this' – he opened his palms and shrugged with a hollow look – 'how greatly I am disliked by everyone.'

'Not by me.' I meant it. I truly did. 'And I promise – I *promise* to protect you.'

He laughed bitterly, took my hand and held me with dead eyes. 'I wish we could go back to the beginning. Just you and me.'

I wanted to say that I did too, but I couldn't: it wasn't true. Frances was whispering in my ear: *the sweetest pain*.

It was the last time I saw him alive.

Her

'Your Mistress Turner sounds like trouble to me.' The baby is asleep and Nelly is dealing the cards. 'I'd have sent her packing.'

'I had it in mind to do that, once I was married and out of my great-uncle's house. He governed all our lives, really.' Frances doesn't pick up her cards, just stares blankly at them on the table. 'But you're right. Anne Turner's bad judgement compromised me greatly. It's easy to be wise with hindsight.'

∞

Approaching my rooms on the upper floor of Northampton House, I became aware of a caustic reek in the air and thought I could hear an incantation that seemed to be emanating from behind the door. I opened it a crack to see Anne, her back to me, kneeling on the floor, swaying and making strange gesticulations. The chanting was coming from her. My stomach knotted. I crept in, careful not to make a sound, though she seemed entirely absorbed in whatever she was doing.

The smell was stronger inside, making my nostrils burn. She took a pinch of powder from a small jar and trickled it into the flame of a candle. It fizzed and crackled, throwing out a halo of blue sparks.

'What are you doing, Anne?'

She turned to me with a gasp, making a fumbling attempt

to hide the jar beneath her clothes. 'I spilled the salt. It's bad luck if you don't throw a pinch over your shoulder for the devil.' She was not a good liar.

'Have you lost your mind? You must know how easy it is to be called a witch. A rumour starts and the next thing you know you're on the ducking stool.' I remembered only too well what had become of Essex's unfortunate mistress. In spite of all the trouble Anne had caused me, she'd cared for me in childhood and I didn't want her to face a similar fate. 'Whatever all this is, get rid of it.'

I wrenched the jar from her and threw it into the fire where it shattered, causing, as she shouted, '*No!*' a small, vivid explosion, like a firework. We jumped back, stunned into silence, as the room filled with the smell of sulphur.

'What *is* that stuff?' Gaining my composure, I blew out the candle. 'In fact, don't tell me. I don't want to know.'

'Listen,' she said. 'There's a problem. Weston can't find Mary Woods and she still has your ring. He says her lodgings are empty. It's as if she was never there.'

My own stupidity mortified me. 'I was a fool to follow you to that place. I don't know why I persist in our friendship – I hope I don't regret that too.' But even if I had tried to cast her off, I suspected Uncle would have prevented it.

She looked distraught and began to wring her hands, apologizing profusely, making me feel unkind as she'd only been trying, in her misguided way, to help me.

'I told Weston he must find her.'

I curbed my exasperation. My starched collar was pressing at my throat. I unpinned it, throwing it to the floor. 'Let's put it behind us. After all, everything is turning our way.'

I sounded light and optimistic but, much as I wanted to believe Mary Woods a fraud, I couldn't shake her words from my head: *Beware. Danger runs close to you. Very close.*

Him

'Goodness, dear boy, you really are in a terrible state.' I was shaking like a drunk when I arrived at Northampton House.

'What have we done?' My tone was desperate. Thomas had been locked away for three weeks. All I'd had was a brief note, smuggled out, describing his cell, and scrawled below, this: 'A tear dries quickly when it is shed for the woes of others.'

I'd gone to Northampton because I didn't know to whom else I could turn. I'd realized that, for the host of acquaintances I had, Thomas was my only true friend. James wouldn't even have his name mentioned. It was as if he was dead. Of anyone, James held a grudge the longest.

'I know you're fond of the man,' Northampton was saying. He stood behind me and began to rub my shoulders, pressing into my painfully knotted muscles. 'We'll make sure he's well looked after. I've been laying plans, arranged for someone trustworthy to stand as his gaoler. A Master Weston – he's well known to Mistress Turner, worked for her for many years, and he's run errands for me in the past too, so we can trust him implicitly. Weston will look after your Thomas Overbury.'

'I need to be sure he's well treated.' I tried to sound authoritative but it wasn't convincing. It had all seemed to make so much sense in theory – Thomas in the Tower for a while until the annulment was resolved – but once the wheels had begun to turn I saw how little influence I would have on how he was treated in there. 'He's not a nobleman so he won't have any privileges.'

'I've made arrangements for him to be housed in the room above the watergate. It's one of the best there is.'

'Thomas didn't mention such a room, far from it. He said he was in a damp chamber half below ground, with only a grille a few inches wide to let the light in. You must arrange for him to be moved.' I was insistent.

Northampton stopped kneading, pulling up a chair to sit beside me, and my mind filled unexpectedly with all the things his detractors said of him – his ruthlessness, his cunning, his cruelty. I was unravelling, wondering if I could trust the man I'd followed so blindly.

'He'll be moved – as soon as he cooperates.' He paused and I studied him closely. Suspicion continued to press at me. 'You're still shaking. You really must stop worrying.' He got up and crossed the room to pour a measure of something, then stood over me, like a nurse administering a tonic, as I gulped back the liquid. 'That'll sort you out.'

It was pungent and made my throat smart.

'Better?' he asked, with a smile. I nodded. 'Now, what can I do to allay your worries? What if we made sure someone we trust is installed as lieutenant at the Tower? Someone like Gervase Elwes – he owes me several favours. I think he'd be the man.'

He seemed benign now, not the monster I'd feared him to be. 'But how?'

'I don't think you understand quite how much influence you have. If you petition the council they'll be sure to do your bidding. I've heard the present lieutenant has been rather lax with security. You could mention that.'

'This is all a mistake. We must have him released.'

'But he's there on the King's order. You could try to convince the King, I suppose.'

But Northampton wasn't party to the event at Royston.

Even if Thomas made his peace with the Howards and apologized to Frances, I would still have to convince James he was no longer a threat. I was tangled in it all, unable to escape and muddleheaded with drink.

'Once Elwes is in place you'll feel much better,' he continued. 'Elwes will make sure we can get correspondence in and out more easily. And your friend will be properly watched over.'

'I'll petition the council tomorrow.' My head began to swim and it all seemed to matter much less.

I noticed the portraits that were half finished on my previous visit had been hung – a regiment of Howards appraising me with painted eyes, following me, moving as I moved. Each one wore the confidence in their demeanour that came from the knowledge they belonged to something powerful and unbreakable. However many times the Howards had tumbled and lost everything – an execution in each generation, sometimes two – they always rose again.

Wed to Frances, I would belong to them. My children would wear that unassailable look. Frances's likeness shone, the apotheosis of them all.

Northampton refilled my cup and must have noticed me looking at her, as he said, 'Do you want to see her?'

'I thought she was in the country.' I felt tricked. We had been exchanging letters but she hadn't mentioned she was returning to court and I wondered why he hadn't said anything until that moment. 'You didn't tell me.'

'She had to come back. The church commission want to see her. You look so worried. It's nothing she can't cope with. I'll call her down.'

He rang a bell and a servant arrived, who was sent to fetch her. 'We must be cautious about these meetings until after the hearing. But you know that, and I don't see why it should harm anything for you to have a few moments together.'

She came almost instantly. The portrait, which only a minute before had seemed perfection itself, diminished in the face of the real woman. In her presence everything made sense, even the scurrilous treatment of Thomas.

'Look at you,' she said, gliding towards me. 'You're here. I thought I would die of pining.'

'He's worried about his friend in the Tower,' said Northampton. 'I hoped you might reassure him.'

'It must be terrible for you – I can't imagine how terrible.' Her velvet voice soothed me. 'I know how devoted you are to him.'

Northampton sidled away, saying, 'Just a quarter-hour.'

She leaned herself against the table and I began to undo her, exposing her sharp white clavicles and the smooth upper mounds of her breasts. I let my mouth skim over the cool, firm flesh.

'I need to feel close. Touch me,' she breathed. 'Down there.' Her skirts murmured as she guided my hand under them.

My finger slid between her, into that warm place. Her breath shook. I untucked a nipple, drawing it into my mouth. I glanced up. Her mouth was open, tongue tip to her upper teeth. Her sudden exhalation was the loudest thing in the room. 'Tell me you love me.'

'You know it, my angel.' I drew my hand out.

There was that smile again. She grabbed my wrist and, lifting my fingers to her nose, inhaled her own scent with her eyes half shut, emitting a little moan.

'You're wicked as sin,' I said.

'A moment ago, I was an angel. Which is it?'

'Both,' I said. 'Both.' I undid my laces, pushing her gently to her knees. 'But, right now, I want you wicked.'

Her kiss was light as a moth and she slid her tongue the length of me. I looked at her portrait in disbelief that Frances

Howard was on her knees with my prick in her mouth. A gargled sound escaped my throat.

She got to her feet, wiping her mouth with the back of her hand. 'I'd do anything for you, Robert. I can't bear to see you upset over your friend, can't bear the thought of you suffering. I'm going to make sure I do everything I can to make him comfortable.'

She became business-like. 'Uncle tells me he has arranged for your friend to be well housed. And I'm going to prepare food for him, nice things, jellies and confections, and I'll send in some good linens and a featherbed. He'll live like an emperor. And it'll be for just a few weeks until this awful hearing is done with.' Her sweetness struck me, made me feel unworthy of her. Her expression clouded. 'People are starting to say such dreadful things about me.'

I would have torn all their tongues out, each one of those vile gossips. 'They don't know who you are, Frances. We'll make them regret it, once we're married.'

'Hold me! Please.' She riveted herself to me. 'I need you – so much.'

If it was possible I loved her even more then, knowing she craved my protection. I had never been needed as a protector before and it made me feel like a man.

Eventually looking up, she asked, 'What does he like, your friend? Crab apple? Redcurrant? Does he like tarts? Does he have a sweet tooth?'

'He does have a fondness for sugar. You would do that, Frances? For someone you don't know, who has never done anything but wish you ill?'

'Of course.' A small furrow appeared between her eyes. 'If *you* care for him, then I do too. We are the same person, Robert, you and I.'

Her words made my heart expand.

It had never occurred to me until then that all those I was fond of called me by a different name: Robert, Robbie, Robin. Perhaps I was someone different for each of them.

There was a cough beyond the door and we hastily straightened our clothing. But Northampton seemed, thankfully, too preoccupied to notice anything much. He was talking of the whereabouts of a ring belonging to Frances, asking where it was and had she lost it.

I saw something flash over her face – something resembling fear. But as quick as it came it was gone.

As I was leaving Northampton said, 'I have a letter for you.' He pressed a fold of paper into my hand. 'It was rather difficult to obtain. If you want to reply, it can be easily arranged through Elwes, once he is installed – so the sooner you convince the council the better. You see,' he slapped me on the shoulder, 'no need for you to worry so much, dear boy.'

I opened the letter while waiting in the yard for my horse to be brought round. *You must help me*, he pleaded. *I'm desperate. I have to get out of this hell-hole. Send me powders, an emetic to make me sicken, and then the King will take pity and let me go. He surely would not want a seriously ailing man in his custody.*

I replied immediately, with news of the comfortable rooms above the watergate where he would be moved, once he had made amends with the Howards. I told him that Frances would send him everything he needed for his comfort. *You see*, I wrote, *she is not what you think. She has a heart of gold.* But I couldn't agree to his request for powders. *What if the dose is wrong*, I asked, *if it is stronger than you think? It might have an unintended effect and there would be no one to come to your aid.*

Her

'Your ring, Frances,' Uncle was saying, 'the diamond given you by Essex. Where is it?' I shrank under his cool glare.

He hustled Robert out with a whispered conversation. I wanted to ask what secrets they were sharing, but as soon as the door was shut he turned the full force of his disdain on me: 'What in Hell's name do you think you were doing?'

'What do you mean?' I kept my voice steady. I had no intention of showing Uncle the alarm that fermented beneath my surface.

'Don't play the innocent with me.' He slapped his fisted right hand into the palm of his left. 'I've just been informed that a woman has been to the authorities saying,' he prodded a finger at me repeatedly as he spoke, 'you gave her your ring as payment for the murder of your husband. A slow-acting poison is what she says you requested, "that will kill a man in a matter of days rather than instantly".' He was seething. 'You'd better explain yourself.'

'Uncle, what do you take me for? How could you think – of course the woman is lying.' I was horrified – horrified that he might think me capable of such a thing. If I'd dared, I would have reminded him that I wasn't like him. His life's project had been to form me in his image.

'So, tell me how she comes to have your ring?'

'I went to Mary Woods – Anne took me there.' I was stumbling over my words, racking my brains for a plausible story to explain the visit. I knew he wouldn't believe the truth – that I'd been duped. It would only exacerbate his anger. 'It – it must be at least four months . . .' I counted back in my head '. . . no, five months ago.'

'God knows, Frances, if you've jeopardized by your stupidity all we have carefully worked for just as the hearing is beginning . . .' A threat hung unspoken.

'No, of course I haven't,' I blathered. 'The woman's a laundress. Anne wanted to see her about an improved formula for yellow starch. One that would hold its colour better, not rub off on things as the other does.' Uncle looked exasperated, rolling his eyes. 'I gave her the ring for safekeeping, as I was going straight to the festivities for the princess's wedding and I feared I would lose it while dancing. Young men will try to slip your rings off.' I was tying myself in knots, barely drawing breath. I knew that a lie must be credible to be believed and the story I was telling had become increasingly far-fetched.

'Do you expect me to believe that?'

I don't know why I didn't come clean then but I was enmeshed in my lie. 'It was loose. The ring was too big. I've become thin with worry lately.' I held out my arms to show him how loose my cuffs were, and made a silent prayer for forgiveness of my lie.

His brows were raised in doubt. 'Well, the matter is being investigated and we will have to explain how your ring came to be in the possession of that woman, so you'd better get your story straight. Is that what you want me to tell them – that you gave her the ring for safekeeping?' His tone was scathing, and I had the sudden dread that, if things went wrong, he would abandon me in an instant.

I nodded. 'No one will take her word over mine, will they?' The gravity of what Mary Woods was saying only fully dawned on me then – that I'd sought to murder my husband. 'They won't believe her, surely.'

I was flailing inside. I wanted him to take me in his arms and tell me that he would make everything all right, but he didn't. He looked at me without a shred of sympathy and said, 'You'd better hope they don't.'

∞

'It was a terrible time, Nelly. We'd all expected the annulment hearing would be over in a few days but it dragged on and on all summer. The bishops couldn't come to an agreement. Robert's poor friend was festering in the Tower and he was eaten away with guilt at having put him there. On top of that the accursed business with Mary Woods simmered on. I truly thought I'd lose my mind with worry.'

Nelly is feeding the baby again. It is growing fast and is out of its swaddling, more than four months old already.

Frances crosses the room, stretching, beginning to pace up and down like her father. Her hair is too tightly pinned, giving her a headache, so she undoes it, imagining the relief of hacking it all off. Still restless, she looks out of the window into the night, but there is nothing to see, only the vague outlines of the buildings and the occasional flit of a shadow. She imagines Robert looking simultaneously on the same barren scene from wherever he is kept in this Godforsaken place.

She won't look out on the other side where the river runs, tries to forget it is there, but its sliding, watery presence makes itself felt. She shivers. She can just make out the guards in the gatehouse, passing a pipe back and forth, its glow a hovering firefly.

She finds herself awash with hopelessness that it has all come to this, her life steeped in uncertainty and disgrace. She momentarily considers flinging herself out. But she can picture, with pitiless clarity, her sordid broken corpse on the cobbles, and cannot contemplate that it should all have been for nothing.

'That Mary Woods – I've come across her sort,' says Nelly.

'They saw through my lie about her. Discovered she was no laundress. But it didn't matter because she discredited herself by changing her story.' Frances turns to watch the baby feed, eyes shut, fat cheeks pumping like bellows. 'Silly woman. If you're going to lie there's no point in having a change of heart and not seeing it through.'

'How do you mean, changed her story?' Nelly can't hide her curiosity.

'She said I'd not wanted to have my husband murdered after all. Claimed I'd only gone to her to have my future read, which was the truth. It turned out she'd tried the same trick before, cast similar aspersions over other women. One day Uncle came to me and tossed the ring into my lap, saying, "It's been dealt with." That was the last we heard of Mary Woods.'

'It's clear to me what he meant.' The girl is appalled.

Frances shrugs. There's nothing she can say to that.

Going to her chest in the corner, she rummages, finding the small casket where she keeps her jewels. 'Look, this is it – the ring that caused all the trouble.'

'Can I try it on?' Nelly holds out her hand.

Frances slips it on to her finger. 'Keep it.'

'I couldn't. Things like this aren't for people like me.' She pulls it off and begins to roll it back and forth over her knuckles, so fast it seems liquid. Then it is gone. Nelly snickers with laughter as it reappears on the finger of her other hand. She removes it, placing it on the table. 'I couldn't.'

'You'd be surprised, Nelly. Scratch the surface and all those well-born women at court are not so unlike you, only you have more integrity than the lot of them.'

'Integrity?'

Frances sometimes forgets Nelly's lack of education. 'It means you're a better person, more honest. More loyal.'

She presses the ring into the girl's palm and strokes the tip of her finger over the little cross in her lifeline.

'Betrayal or loyalty,' whispers Nelly.

Frances kisses her head, as she might a child's. She smells slightly of nutmeg, reminding Frances of the hot milk Anne Turner used to bring her at bedtime when she was a girl. 'Please keep it. You've been good to me when there was nothing to be gained from it. I want to repay your kindness. It could be a nest egg for you, and I'm sure it will bring you more luck than it has me.'

Nelly holds the ring up to the candle. The diamond flares in the light.

'I wouldn't wear it, though,' Frances adds. 'Put it somewhere safe or people will assume you've stolen it.'

Nelly puts the baby back in the cradle and tucks the ring away in her pocket. 'You're a good person.'

'Not everyone would agree.' Frances meets the girl's eye. 'It is likely those investigating the murder will want to ask you about me. You mustn't be afraid to tell them whatever you want. Don't worry about it, or refuse to speak or anything like that, because they will think you have something to hide and make it difficult for you.'

'I understand.' Nelly nods. She must know that 'making it difficult' is a great understatement. Frances cannot tell if the girl is afraid or not.

All the candles in the room have burned down to their nubs and are sputtering. The two women replace them. Nelly fits them into the lamps and Frances sets the taper to their wicks, deriving a simple satisfaction from the task.

'I won't say you lay with your husband before you were wed, though. That is a promise.'

Frances laughs. 'I don't suppose it really matters if you do. Everyone suspected I'd been with him anyway. There was so much gossip, I had to stay away from court and the hearing was taking an age. Towards the end of the summer it had to be adjourned because the bishops couldn't arrive at a decision, and then my brother got himself into trouble with Essex. Harry accused him of not being a real man – well, he was a little more vulgar than that – and Essex challenged him to a duel.' Nelly smirks. '*That* had to be dealt with. It was extremely hot that August and tempers were running very high.

'The pair of them had got halfway to France, away from English soil, and had to be brought back. Uncle was furious, of course. And all the time Anne and I were trying to make poor Thomas Overbury as comfortable as possible. I felt many conflicting things, Nelly.

'If I'm completely honest, part of me wished him ill. I suppose it was guilt for my bad thoughts that drove me to do all that – to send in all the luxuries. I sent him a featherbed and a set of velvet cushions from my own chamber. Given he'd been locked up on my account, it was the very least I could do. Would you believe Anne and I even made the jellies and tarts ourselves?'

∞

'You two look like butchers,' said Uncle. Our aprons were stained with raspberry juice and Anne's lips were red from all the berries she'd eaten. Every surface was cluttered with dirty pans and utensils, making the potboy sullen with all the extra work. He muttered under his breath that he didn't know why we couldn't tell the cooks to do the work for us.

We'd been dealing with a laundry maid who was beside

herself. She'd found the mouser with her six kittens stone dead in the courtyard that morning and was in a seemingly endless crying jag. We'd barely managed to get one of the lads to remove the carcasses, calm the poor girl down and get back to our cooking when Uncle arrived.

He'd been with Robert, he said. The two of them were hand in glove all through that summer, constantly exchanging letters and having little meetings. I must confess to being jealous of their closeness, of feeling rather left out, as I was kept away from Robert until the hearing was over.

We were making a batch of tarts to send to the Tower and the big kettle was on the heat with a mixture of berries and sugar. We'd gathered the fruit in the kitchen garden the previous day.

The bushes were taller than I and heavy with their bright harvest. I took particular pleasure in the simple act of picking the raspberries. Enjoyed the fragile touch of the flesh beneath my fingers, the way if I pinched them gently on either side they would slip away from their stems without protest.

There were several gardeners employed at that time of year and the comings and goings were frequent. But I was surprised to see, in a shady corner close to the orchard gate, that Anne was talking to the strange crook-backed Master Franklin, the one she'd lied to me about. Curious, I approached them. Anne had her back to me and jumped when I put my hand on her shoulder. 'I didn't hear you coming.'

He greeted me, removing his cap. Close up I saw how horribly ravaged his face was, his nose all but eaten away, poor fellow, and I tried not to stare.

'What brings you to Northampton House?' I asked.

'I had a gift for Mistress Turner. At Caritas House they told me I'd find her here.'

'A gift?' I was becoming increasingly puzzled.

'A birthday gift,' he said, as if stating the obvious.

'I didn't know it was your birthday, Anne. You should have reminded me.' I'd thought her birthday was in the autumn.

Anne seemed embarrassed, saying she didn't want any fuss and that, at her age, being a year older was hardly something to celebrate.

'I'd best be going,' he announced. 'Business to attend to.'

'What is it you do for a living?' I tried to make it sound like casual politeness, but I truly wanted to know how a man who looked as he did might find employment.

'I am set up as an apothecary,' he said, then added, 'more or less.'

We said goodbye and made our way back to the house. 'I wasn't aware that you were quite so friendly with him.'

'I feel sorry for him, that's all,' said Anne.

'He must frighten everyone. I suppose it's a lonely existence if you look like that.' We walked on in silence until I asked, 'What did he give you?'

'Give me?' She seemed confused.

'Your birthday gift.'

'Oh.' She laughed. 'I'd quite forgotten.' She began to fumble in her sleeve and pulled out a square of lace, handing it to me. It was creased and looked to me as if it had been in her sleeve for some time, making me wonder why they would lie to me.

'I thought your birthday was later in the year,' I said.

She hesitated. 'He was mistaken and I didn't have the heart to put him right.'

'Surely he didn't give you that creased old thing.'

She stuffed the handkerchief away, out of sight. 'Sad, isn't it?'

I still felt something wasn't quite right.

When Uncle appeared in the kitchens, I was rolling pastry, up to my elbows in flour. He stood watching me. 'You shouldn't be wearing that,' he said under his breath, pointing at my diamond ring. 'For pity's sake, put it away.' I asked why, and he said, 'Don't play the fool with me.' But I truly didn't know.

Once he was satisfied that the ring was out of sight, he wandered about as if he'd never set foot in the kitchens before, picking up utensils and putting them down again, inspecting them as if they were rare artefacts. He peered into the large pan where the fruits were simmering, giving its contents a stir. He asked whether it was for Overbury, and told us to let him know when we were finished, as he wanted to conceal some private correspondence in the parcel going to the Tower.

'He *is* being properly looked after in there?' I asked.

'Absolutely! The last thing we want is any harm to befall him. If the bishops would give us our annulment he could be released.' He continued stirring the jam. 'Elwes is making sure he's comfortable. When you send these tarts in, Frances, write a note to Elwes warning him they have letters concealed in them. We wouldn't want them going to the wrong inmate by mistake, would we? We certainly wouldn't want some heinous felon profiting from the fruits of your labours.'

He dropped the wooden spoon he'd been stirring with and a little of the hot liquid spattered his white stocking. He made a great bother about it, insisting it was doused with water and thoroughly blotted, though the mark was almost too small to see.

Once the fuss was over I noticed him catch Anne's eye, saying quietly, 'A word outside,' nodding towards the door.

She gave me a shrug of bewilderment as she left. On her return she seemed shifty, hovering silently over the pan, giving it an occasional stir. I began to cut the pastry to make the tarts. 'What did he want?'

'He wanted to offer me a paid position in your household, once you are married.' She was stirring slowly, not looking at me. 'As your companion.'

'I don't know what business it is of his.' I was annoyed that Uncle felt it his right to employ my servants without consulting me, and more so, as when I married I'd hoped to distance Anne and all the trouble that followed her.

'Do you not want me?' She was clearly upset but trying to hide it.

'Don't be silly.' I smiled but she was on the brink of tears, turning back to the pan.

'What's the matter?' I could see her shoulders heaving. 'What's going on, Anne?' I asked. 'Is there something you're not telling me?'

'I don't know what you mean.' She lifted her head and threw me a dimpled smile. She was flushed and her fair hair was plastered to the edges of her face. 'I think this is ready to cool.' She heaved the pan off the heat, thumping it on to the table.

The potboy peered in at it. 'Looks like a bucket of blood,' he said, with a murderous leer.

'Go away,' said Anne. 'Haven't you work to do?' He scuttled off into the yard.

I lowered a finger towards the crimson liquid. 'Stop!' she cried, slapping me sharply over the knuckles. I looked up, shocked. 'I'm so sorry,' she said. 'I was afraid you'd scald yourself.'

'There was no need to strike me.' I showed her the red mark on my smarting hand.

'I don't know what came over me. I'm so sorry.'

I had rarely seen her so flustered over something so small. 'What is it?'

'I'm sorry,' she said again, as she covered the pan with a

length of muslin, tying it tightly, and began to help me with the pastry.

I saw a droplet run down her cheek. 'You're crying,' I said.

'Just perspiration – it's hot in here.' She wiped her face with her apron, smearing herself red, which made her look as if she'd been in a fight.

'Has Uncle threatened you in some way?' She recoiled, vehemently denying that anything was amiss.

'You need to tell me what's going on. Is it to do with that man Franklin – or with Mary Woods?'

She hid her face in her hands, shaking her head. 'I can't.'

I knew it was futile to try to tease anything out of her, not if Uncle had demanded her silence. The risk was too great.

∞

'We were all at sixes and sevens that summer, Nelly. There was so much to worry about, but had we known then that our troubles had barely started, I don't know if we'd have coped at all.'

Him

A loud thudding penetrated my sleep. It was an airless night and I woke bathed in sweat. Someone was at the door. The banging stopped. The bolts shot back. I could hear my servant protesting that I was asleep and that whoever it was should come back in the morning. But the visitor sounded insistent.

It was Lidcote, Thomas's brother-in-law, whom I hardly knew. He had written to me the week before, registering concern for Thomas's health. I hadn't replied. He stood in the hall, still in his outdoor clothes, hands on hips, legs apart. A film of sweat made his face glow ghoulishly in the dim light. His was not the stance of grief but of hostility.

He brushed off my greeting and refused to remove his coat. 'You have to do something. He's in an appalling state. I fear for his life.' His voice was charged with accusation.

'You've seen him?'

He nodded, smearing back straggles of hair that had fallen forward.

I wanted to ask how when Thomas was not permitted visitors. 'Dr Mayerne –' I began, but he interrupted me.

'That quack's remedies are making him worse.'

'But the King himself ordered Mayerne to treat Thomas. He's the best in the country.'

'How do you explain his condition, then?' He was barely able to contain himself. 'More than four months he's been in that place. Shouldn't be there at all.'

'I was under the impression he'd rallied.' Thomas had

written to me repeatedly in early summer, telling of his symptoms: the terrible thirst, the weight loss, the vomiting, the strange smells rising from his body. I had confronted James about it but he remained unmoved. He didn't want to know – even when Lieutenant Elwes had sent word in late July that he feared for Thomas's life.

Correspondence had flown back and forth, between myself, Northampton and Elwes, detailing Thomas's condition and the remedies prescribed to cure him. Then, all at once, he was better. But that had been at least a month before.

'I'm telling you, he needs help.' Lidcote took a step forward, raising an arm. I thought he might strike me and instinctively stepped out of his reach.

The song of a lone bird cut through the quiet. It must have been almost dawn.

'I'll deal with it.' I managed to sound firm and hustled him out, but just after sunrise another visitor arrived.

It was old Master Overbury, Thomas's father, hobbling in on a pair of sticks, grey with worry and swollen-eyed, as if he hadn't slept in months. He'd known me from before – when I was a nobody – and I remembered how kind and hospitable he'd been and the friendship he'd offered. I'd neglected to maintain contact, had become too caught up in the excitement of court and my own meteoric rise. I regretted it then as he stood before me, an old man devastated by his son's circumstances.

I couldn't look him in the eye. He ranted, asking repeatedly how it was possible that the mere refusal of an embassy could result in such a pitiless punishment. I explained that Thomas had contravened the King's specific order.

'In that case I will petition His Majesty myself.' He fell into a fit of coughing. I offered him a chair but he refused to sit. 'I haven't come for your hospitality.' His loathing was plain to see, and I wished Lidcote *had* struck me earlier. I deserved it.

'Let *me* convey your concerns to the King,' I told him. He looked sceptical. 'You *mustn't* approach him yourself.' I sounded overly harsh but I couldn't risk James's anger being provoked further.

'Are you forbidding it?' His tone abraded me.

'No, no, not at all.' I could see the doubt etched into him. 'It's just that it wouldn't be a good idea.'

'My son's life hangs in the balance.'

'Listen.' I lost control, was almost shouting. 'I'll deal with it. Now, go!' He reeled back in shock. I tempered my tone. 'I think you'd better go.'

He shuffled towards the door and left without a word. I was furious with myself for having lost my temper but Thomas was my primary concern, not his father.

Mayerne was an angular man with short hair and a very long beard. His house was spacious and appointed with fine French furniture, which made me conclude he was charging a fortune for his services.

He began speaking to me in French, and I had to explain that I didn't understand. He gave me a disdainful look and opened the window, complaining of the heat. 'No sign of this weather improving.' His accent was pronounced and littered with French words, as if he couldn't bring himself to succumb to the vulgarities of our language.

There was a newssheet on the desk with a sordid image of a woman in a state of undress. It was supposed to represent Frances. There had been a proliferation of such things since the annulment proceedings had begun. I turned it face down. Meyerne seemed amused, smiling behind his beard.

'We would benefit from an *orage*.' It was true we needed a

storm, the air was thick as treacle. 'But you did not come for to talk about the weather, like an Englishman.'

'No,' I said. 'It's your patient, Sir Thomas Overbury, I'm here to discuss. His brother-in-law said he found him in a terrible state.' Mayerne asked me to repeat myself more slowly, picking up the newssheet to fan himself. 'Lidcote was complaining that your remedies were making Overbury worse.'

'Worse?' Mayerne mimicked my pronunciation with a baffled expression, distorting the word out of all recognition. 'Ah, you mean *pire*.' He shifted in his chair and fixed his gaze on me. 'You must understand, my lord, that it is usually the bitterest remedies that are most *efficace*.'

'Most effective. Yes, I see.' I was remembering the controversy over Mayerne's unusual treatments for the prince before he died. But James seemed to have the utmost faith in the man. It was *he* who'd ordered Mayerne to treat Thomas.

'Often a patient must become worse' – he tussled with the word again – 'before he becomes better. But you are correct to be concerned.' He stopped fanning himself for a moment and met my gaze. That image of Frances stared from the page. 'This patient is very important to me.' I suspected he was thinking of his own reputation rather than Thomas's welfare. 'It may be that the other remedies my patient is prescribed do not mix well with mine.'

'*Other* remedies? I'm not aware of another doctor charged with his care at present.' The only other remedies I knew of were the powders Thomas had requested from me months before to induce sickness in the hope of provoking the King's mercy. I'd struggled with my conscience over that matter – it had seemed like madness. But his pleas were so very pitiful.

If you understood the way I'm suffering in this hellhole . . . I fear I will lose my sanity and do harm to myself. I beg of you, Robin, if you have even a shred of mercy . . .

The memory was horribly vivid, casting me back in time: I am almost in tears as I make my way to Killigrew. The little bell chimes in the bowels of the shop as I open the door and am engulfed in a heady herbal smell. My eyes take time to adjust to the gloom. He shuffles out, asking what I want.

'A powder. Something to make a person have the appearance of illness – an emetic.' I sound as if I am up to no good.

'This is most unusual.' He prods at me with a pair of filmy eyes and I feel he can see right into my black soul. But my distress must move him as he relents, asking questions: 'What is the patient's weight and constitution? Is it a man or woman? What is the preferred method of administering?'

I answer as best I can. 'Make it very weak.' He breaks the buds from a plant I don't recognize, dropping them into a mortar. 'Just a minuscule quantity of whatever harmful ingredient you intend to use.'

'You'd likely be as well served by powdered chalk,' he tells me, holding his pestle aloft. 'It can sometimes have the desired effect. I have occasionally even cured people with it, when they believe it to be something else.' He shrugs. 'I have no idea why.'

Relief soaks into me. I want to hug the man. 'Yes! Give me some of that.' I tip my purse out. I would have paid a hundred pounds for that powdered chalk.

But a few days later I had another letter from Thomas, saying the remedy had had no effect, demanding stronger. I ignored his request. He'd fallen ill anyway, weeks later, desperately so. But I had no knowledge of anyone other than Mayerne treating him, come the dregs of August.

I began to wonder what else I didn't know about. Had the Howards sent in another of their doctors? Surely Northampton would have mentioned it – we were corresponding daily. Perhaps Lidcote had requested a second opinion but surely he would have mentioned it when he'd confronted me that night.

'Not a *doctor*.' Mayerne seemed offended. 'No. My apothecary, Master de Loubell, whom I trust *implicitement*,' he threw me a look as if to dare me not also to trust de Loubell, 'has seen various *treatments*' – the way he said it made it quite clear that he didn't regard them as treatments at all – 'in the patient's rooms.'

'He has seen *Aurum potabile*,' Mayerne continued. 'It is a concoction by a man I happen to know is not a doctor at all.' His mouth curled into a scowl. 'This *Aurum potabile* may *se mêler avec* . . .' He hesitated. 'How do you say? Interfering, with my remedies.'

'Might render them ineffective?' I asked. 'What are *you* prescribing him?'

He launched into an exhaustive listing of Thomas's ailments and his treatments: 'I have diagnosed a distemper produced in the liver and wrought in the spleen. To allow the issue of bad humours, I have made between the *omoplates*' – he lifted an arm to point at his back between the shoulder blades – 'an incision. De Loubell is instructed to apply to it daily a balsam and to administer an emetic of *Crocus metallorum* to remove from his body the filth . . .'

When I left I was confused with worry for Thomas. A few days later a letter arrived from him, more desperate than any I had yet received. It was a pitiful entreaty to be released, saying he feared he was on the brink of death. It was drastically different in tone from the missives he had sent a month before: a series of thinly veiled threats, the worst of which stated, *I'm sure there are many who would be interested to know what I saw with my own eyes at Royston.*

That one had arrived when I was with James. I'd attempted to hide it from him but he became suspicious, snatching it out of my hand to read.

'If I could have that miscreant silenced for good!' he ranted, tearing the letter to pieces. He didn't mean it. We were all frustrated because the annulment commission had reached a deadlock.

'It's my fault. I created this.' My burden of guilt had become so heavy as to be almost unbearable.

He turned to me, as he flung the remnants of the letter into the fire. 'Overbury's swollen arrogance is his own undoing. I don't blame you for this, Robbie.' I didn't entirely believe him.

But that letter in the final days of August was different. It was written in a feeble scrawl: *I believe I am dying here. I fear I will not last the week. Would you have that on your conscience, Robin?*

I went immediately to James, ignoring any fears of rousing his temper. 'I am begging you,' I got on my knees to plead, 'set him free. He's been there more than four months. Surely that is punishment enough. I truly fear for his life.'

James's exasperation was evident in his terse tone. 'He's already receiving the best possible care. His lodgings are comfortable. It would make no difference to his health if he were at home. Indeed, he is likely better off where there is always someone to keep an eye on him.'

My attempts were futile. It was clear the King wouldn't be moved. He was exhausted, his eye flickering manically. 'I have more on my mind than that wretch.' He waved towards his desk piled high with papers. 'Best would be if the man was to disappear.' I could almost taste his bitterness. 'They call me a wise fool, Robbie. What do you think they mean by that?'

I didn't say it was because, despite his great intellect, he seemed unable to curb his profligacy and it was drawing him into alliances that might be disastrous for England. For all his wisdom James was blind to his own flaws.

I tried to appease him but he brushed me off with a serrated look. He couldn't hide his resentment, despite what he had said about not blaming me. I had visited the problem of Thomas Overbury on him when I should have been there to relieve his burden of concerns, rather than add to it. I felt toxic to those who loved me, for they all met misfortune: the King, Thomas, Frances – oh, how Frances was suffering, just to be my wife.

I begged his forgiveness and he pulled my head down on to his shoulder, stroking my hair, which only made me feel worse. I wanted him to rage at me, felt it was what I deserved. 'The sooner this business is done with and you are wed, the better. I've called in two more bishops to sit on the annulment commission. We simply must break the impasse and these two will do as I say.'

I suppose it had become a matter of principle for him that his favourite should have his chosen bride. Neither was I oblivious to the fact that my marriage didn't create a bond only for me with the Howards but for him too. Even kings must make alliances with their subjects. We were silent for a time until he said, 'I plan to make you Earl of Somerset.'

'You've given me enough.' It was true. I felt in such great deficit to him that I couldn't stomach the idea of a larger debt.

'It elevates you sufficiently to be an appropriate match for the daughter of an earl and makes sense politically. Gives you more influence abroad. You'd be doing me a service by accepting.'

I met his gaze. 'If it will help you.' I may be judged devious but I meant it.

'You will be Earl of Somerset and you will have a splendid week of wedding celebrations at court.' He sounded calm but his eye was still quivering. 'There will be no more skulking about for us, as if we are guilty of something. One thing I do know is the value of making an impression. We need only the bishops' ruling and all will be set. They have said they will request a physical examination of the lady. Once that is done it will be over and –'

'They can't!' I spoke too abruptly.

'Why?' His expression was rigid. 'Is there something you haven't owned up to? Have *you* had her?'

Despair was taking hold in me and I envisaged the whole thing crumbling away. 'No, of course not.' I don't know why I lied. Had I told the truth, he might have put a stop to the examination but I wasn't thinking clearly. 'It's only that I don't want Frances to suffer such humiliation.'

'Don't worry.' He poked me with a smutty look. 'If the girl wants you enough she'll do what's necessary.'

He patted me on the head as if I were a favourite dog. He was relishing it, pleased that Frances would have to pay a high price for a piece of me when I belonged to him.

Her

Frances is startled out of her thoughts by a loud knocking. The guard enters.

'This was pushed under the outside door. It bears your name.' He holds out a fold of paper. 'I'm not meant to allow you to receive any correspondence, but . . .'

'But what, William?' Frances aims a beam at him.

He looks pleased that she has used his given name, returns her smile. Perhaps he is remembering, as she is, the downpour drenching them both. 'I thought if you were happy for me to look at it first, to make sure it is innocent, I could . . .'

'Of course.' Frances feels safe in that no one would send anything worth keeping secret by such obvious means. 'You are unusually kind.'

The compliment makes him blush, but as he reads the colour falls away and he crushes the paper in his fist.

'What does it say?'

'I – I don't – I don't think – I can't.' He doesn't know what to do, can't look at her.

It's Nelly who snatches it from his hand, smooths it open and passes it to her. On it are four lines of verse:

> A page, a knight, a viscount and an earl
> All four were wedded to one lustful girl.
> A match well made, for she was likewise four,
> A wife, a witch, a murderer, and a whore.

'Don't worry, William,' Frances says steadily. 'It's not something I haven't heard before.'

Nelly picks up the letter. Frances hadn't known the girl could read but evidently she can, as she mutters the final line of the verse aloud before throwing it on the fire with an angry huff.

'Leave us now,' she orders the boy, opening the door, hustling him out. Frances notices the caustic look that passes between them, igniting her suspicion, making her wonder what has made the girl dislike him so much.

'There was no need to be so brusque with him, Nelly. I have few enough friends here.'

'How can you be sure he's your friend?' She is defiant, her lips pressed tightly together. 'Just because he's handsome and blushes when he speaks to you.'

Frances resists the urge to rebuke her for her insolence. 'Do you have reason to believe he can't be trusted?'

'I hear them all talking about you.'

'Him? You hear him talking about me?'

'Not him, no, but a group of them. None of them can be trusted.'

'Saying what?' Frances feels her moorings loosen, is afraid she has lost her instinct for sniffing out dishonesty.

'They say you're as much of a witch as that Anne Turner. I tell them to mind their mouths. I'd throttle them all, given half a chance. Put it this way, I wouldn't be surprised if he wrote that poem himself, just to rile you.'

Frances cannot tell if Nelly's outrage is genuine. 'Where did you learn to read?' She manages to keep the tremor out of her voice. Her aim is to find a solid fact, however small, to secure herself to, so she isn't carried off into unknown waters. But she is painfully aware she has no way of knowing whether the girl will tell her the truth.

'My pa taught me – he wasn't all bad, see. Not like your great-uncle. Such a monster. It's all *his* fault. If it wasn't for him . . .' The anger fizzes out of her. She would have to be an accomplished actor to make it so convincing '. . . you would not be . . .' It is clear what she means: that Frances would not be on trial for murder. 'You must hate him.'

'No point hating the dead.' Frances's hand is gripping the arm of her chair. She unclasps it to see the imprint of the carvings embossed into her palm.

'When he said people would attack you, it was true.' Nelly points towards the fire, where the ball of paper is no more. Then she takes a taper, dips it into the flames, then touches it to the candles on the table. Light bleeds into the room rendering the damp on the far wall visible. It is growing, its black fingers reaching out over the stones.

Frances pinches the skin of her wrist between her fingernails. The pain settles her. 'It was different back then, though. It was the enemies of my family who thought the Howards were becoming too powerful. They spread rumours to get back at us, thinking I would buckle.'

Nelly discharges a sardonic grunt. 'They can't have known you very well.' Her face is lit from beneath, strange shadows making her unrecognizable.

And *you* don't know me as well as you assume, thinks Frances, as she forces a smile and agrees that they didn't know her very well. 'It was just gossip, but out there,' she points vaguely towards the door, 'they'd lynch me, given half a chance.'

She makes it sound light but at night she often wakes in a cold sweat, the mob having infiltrated her dreams, a thousand hands tearing at her clothes, then at her limbs.

'They'd have to get past me first.' The girl wears an opaque smirk and begins to rock the cradle with her foot. Creak, creak, creak. The baby is fast becoming too big for that crib.

Frances is overwhelmed with the thought of time gushing by, dragging her under. It knocks the breath right out of her.

∞

A bank of eyes, thorny with reproach, followed our progress as we walked the length of the gallery. Mother's fist was firmly clenched around my elbow, as if to prevent my escape, making me thankful for the light touch of Lizzie's hand at the small of my back. Even my sister's gentle presence couldn't protect me from the poisonous comments that hung in the air.

I knew what was said of me. I'd read the pamphlets that were whisked out of sight to the hiss of whispers when their readers saw me approaching. I knew them all, those people. I'd played cards with them, dandled their infants on my lap, visited them when they were sick, provided alibis for their trysts, and there they were, dressed in their sanctimony.

We progressed at a funereal pace. Lizzie murmured encouragements and I kept my eyes fixed on the door at the end. All those assembled must have relished the idea of my humiliation, my private parts being laid open to inspection by strangers, but I had no intention of displaying any frailty.

My dress was unbearably heavy. Mother had insisted I wear something impressive. 'Don't let them think you are humbling yourself,' she had said, as she and Lizzie tied me into the unyielding garment. 'You're a Howard.' No matter how imposing my outfit, it couldn't return my virginity to me and I had no plan, only the vain hope that the inspectors' knowledge of anatomy would be poor. Still, I didn't regret that single, glorious afternoon at Paternoster Row.

Helping me dress, Mother managed to jab me with a pin,

sucking her teeth to see a smear of blood defiling the fabric. My laces were drawn tight, pressing my stomach into my throat. 'It's been agreed that you can wear a veil for modesty's sake'. She draped a length of dense lace over her arm.

'I don't see how a veil will help,' I'd said.

'You don't need to worry about a thing.' Lizzie's tone was softer. Sensible Lizzie, who had all Mother's beauty but none of her hardness, was too kind-hearted to be a Howard.

'You don't understand,' I blurted. 'I'm not intact.'

I expected her anger but Mother barely looked at me, and said, with practised insouciance, 'Really, Frances, do you take me for a fool? I know what you've been up to.'

'How? How do you know?' I felt turned inside out, the holes in my lining on show. 'Did Anne tell you?'

'It's all in hand.' She didn't answer my question and I knew there was no use in pushing her. I assumed someone must have been bribed, or something like it, and felt heavy with the weight of all the untruths. If it all came toppling down it would be my loss, mine and Robert's – no one else's.

A woman I'd thought a friend pushed forward to stand in our way. 'It's witchcraft that makes a man impotent with one and not others.' She looked around the gathering for support and a few mumbled their agreement. I could have slapped her.

'Ignore her,' said Lizzie, and we marched on, giving the woman no choice but to stand aside.

Once out of earshot, Mother said, 'In a month they'll all be paying homage to you – eating their words – and we will have our revenge.'

My mother's vindictiveness was ugly. Revenge was the last thing on my mind. All I wanted was Robert. I held him firm in my thoughts to bolster me against all those pursed mouths and narrowed eyes. They might judge me but they wouldn't break me.

At the door I felt my resolve slip and stopped a moment, resisting the impulse to flee, girding myself before following Mother and Lizzie inside. It was gloomy, just a sharp blade of light slicing through the room from a gap in the curtains. A bank of six matrons hovered around a large canopied bed. One or two of them I knew, like Lady Tyrwhitt, others I had never seen before. I wondered if their pockets were heavy with their enticement – filthy coins that would stain those fingers that would soon be probing me. The mood was sober. None of them could quite look me in the eye, and I wondered if they'd agreed to my wearing a veil to preserve them from embarrassment rather than myself.

Mother, as ever, was haughty and unapproachable and I was relieved that Lizzie took control with her light, easy manner, which lifted the awkward atmosphere for them, if not for me. Two more women arrived, introduced as midwives. They, contrarily, were rather jolly and undaunted, saying things like, 'Let's get this over and done with, shall we?'

I felt unsure of myself. Was I to lay myself open there and then on that bed? My dress was unbearably tight and I doubted I'd even be able to sit unaided. But one of the midwives said to Lizzie, 'Why don't you take your sister in there, dear, and help her get ready?' She pointed at a low door in the corner that I hadn't noticed.

Lizzie took my hand and we entered a small space, not much wider than a corridor, designed, I supposed, as a wardrobe. Lizzie peeled back a curtain at the far end, revealing another, smaller, door, which she opened and in walked a girl. Confused, I saw that she was almost my duplicate, exactly my build and colouring and wearing identical petticoats to the ones beneath my own dress.

'She's to take my place?' Lizzie hushed me, nodding, and

it dawned on me then that everything had been thought of: the chamber with its convenient anteroom and secret door, and the girl, my mirror image. Wherever had they found her? So, there had been no need of a bribe.

'Why wasn't I told of this?'

'You know what Uncle's like. He insisted. Even I didn't know until an hour ago.'

It occurred to me that perhaps Uncle enjoyed the idea of me agitating over the humiliation. It was so like him, wanting to control us all.

I cast my eyes over the girl again. She wouldn't look directly at me. She was a child, really, couldn't have been much more than twelve or thirteen, a good half-dozen years my junior, though she was quite well developed and could easily pass for me veiled in that shadowy room.

It was only then that I remembered where I'd seen her. It was at Paternoster Row: she had served us drinks. I supposed that Uncle had asked Anne to procure her for this purpose, but Anne hadn't mentioned it. The whole business stank of some quiet plot between the two of them from which I was excluded. Imagining them cooking up their ruse together, I felt steeped in bitterness and had to keep my attention firmly adhered to the fact that the aim of the piece of shady theatre was to unite me with Robert. Perhaps I'd been kept in the dark for my own protection.

Lizzie set to work, removing my jewels and clasping them round the girl's neck and wrists, pushing my rings on to her thin fingers. 'I'm so sorry,' I said, thinking of the humiliation she was to suffer on my behalf, all those matrons tutting over her privates. She lifted one shoulder minutely in response as my sister draped the veil over her head.

'You wait through there,' whispered Lizzie, indicating the far door. 'We won't be long.'

Behind the door was a set of steps, which must have led to one of the back courtyards, or even, it occurred to me, the underground corridor to Northampton House. I would have sat on the top step but my dress wouldn't allow it so I leaned against the wall and tried not to think about what the girl was going through on my behalf.

Soon Lizzie returned with her. The jewels were unclipped and the veil removed. She was red-eyed, clearly distraught. 'I'm sorry,' I said once more, but she turned away to look at the floor.

'If you go down the stairs,' Lizzie whispered, as she helped her into her dress, 'someone will be there to take you home.' She pressed a purse into her small hand. It all seemed so sordid.

I took off a bracelet, holding it out for her. It was unusual and quite valuable, a long string that wrapped several times round the wrist, threaded with seed pearls and rubies. She seemed in two minds, her hand floating. I could hear the chapel bell ringing below. Eventually she snatched it, folding it into her tight little fist, still unable to look me in the eye.

I was whisked back to thank the matrons for their trouble. The shutters had been opened wide, bright light bleaching the hangings pale, and the atmosphere had lifted. The women seemed relieved it was over, smiling and chattering quietly as they took turns to wash their hands at a copper basin. Lady Tyrwhitt turned to me with a serious look. 'I'm speaking for all of us when I say there's no doubt in our minds that you are still intact. I'm only sorry you had to be put through such an ordeal.' She seemed genuinely sympathetic and completely unaware of the sleight of hand that had just been perpetrated.

'I'm very glad you now know I have nothing to hide.' The

untruth felt like a stone in my shoe. I sensed God listening and shame crept into my bones.

∞

Nelly is clearly amused. 'I'm picturing those embarrassed matrons. I won't breathe a word of that either.'

'It probably wouldn't matter if you did.' Cozening a nullity commission is a small offence beside a charge of murder, and it will make no difference now if anyone discovers she slept with Robert before they were married.

'What became of the girl – the child?'

'I've no idea. Poor sweet, it must have been an awful trial for her.'

'She will have liked the money.' Most girls would put themselves in the child's shoes, feel her humiliation, but not Nelly. Nothing in Nelly's world is complicated by problematic morality. It makes Frances wonder, not for the first time, what price would buy Nelly and who might pay it.

'I expect she did,' Frances says.

'So, then you were married.'

'Eventually, yes.'

'Hallelujah to that!' Nelly claps her hands together, startling the baby out of its sleep, making it cry.

The sound burrows beneath Frances's skin, like a maggot into an apple, its damage invisible. Nelly picks the infant up, walking about, jigging her until she is quiet.

'And what about Overbury?' Frances is caught off guard by the directness of the question. 'Was he dead by the time of your wedding?' Nelly's back is turned and Frances can't tell if she means anything by it.

'He died a few days before the nullity was granted.' Frances coughs, feeling the dead man in the air.

'And then you had your wedding.' It sounds, for a moment, like an accusation, but then she adds, 'Your great-uncle, I hope he's burning in Hell.'

The two women are silent, and Frances is thinking about the confession she made to Bacon, doubting the wisdom of it once more.

Nelly offers the baby for her to take; Frances shakes her head. The idea of holding her child is intolerable.

The girl sits down, cradling it, cooing and gurning. 'Why can't you love her?'

'I suppose I'm loath to become too attached. My future is so uncertain.' Frances tastes blood in her mouth.

'I hadn't thought.' Nelly looks apologetic.

'You see, I wanted him dead. I wished him dead.' Frances seems to overflow with distress, words streaming out of her. 'He'd been imprisoned on my account, so deep in my heart I believed that I'd done it to him. That it was my fault.' Frances fixes Nelly with a desperate look.

Nelly starts to speak and Frances knows what she'll say: *But wishing someone dead and actually killing them is not the same thing.*

She holds up a hand to silence the girl.

She can't begin to explain how it is or how she feels about it.

Him

The look of the river on the morning I learned of Thomas's death is branded on my memory. It was not long after dawn and the moon was still visible, a pale sliver in a violet sky, and the water, flat and livid as a slate floor, was part shrouded in mist.

I whistled down a sculler and clambered into his small boat only half listening to his chatter. He told me how much he liked being out early, when no one was around, how it got him out of the house, which was swarming with children and never a moment's peace to be had. How I envied his ordinary life. He talked of a monstrous fish, which had beached at Deptford the day before, and how the locals had tried to haul it back into the water with ropes but that it had died and no one dared eat its flesh in case it had been sent by the devil.

I watched the sky, its colour leaching away as day began to assert itself, the fact of Thomas's death a spillage of darkness in my mind. It was a terrible shock, though not a surprise. Mayerne had warned me a few days before that he didn't think his patient would last the week. I'd wanted to visit him then, and I'd tried, but Elwes hadn't allowed me in. He was sympathetic enough but said he feared punishment if he contravened his orders.

I tried to envisage what would happen next, dreaded the thought of encountering the Howards in case they were jubilant. Frances wouldn't be. I knew that. She had taken so much care to make sure Thomas was comfortable and well fed. In the few snatched moments we had had together she confessed to me how terrible she felt about his incarceration. Her concern touched me deeply. That she was facing public humiliation yet still had sympathy for a man who had loathed her made me feel small and grubby in the face of her love.

On arrival, I was shown into Elwes's chambers to wait. Thomas's servant, Lawrence Davies, was there, seeming confused and very young, like a boy who's witnessed his house burning to the ground. We exchanged a few bland condolences. 'I don't know what to do with myself,' he said, and he hit his head with the heel of his hand several times as if to knock the grief out of it. I was reminded that Thomas had been his saviour. That day came tumbling back to me, Davies's shredded back and Thomas's kindness. It struck me then – the brutal finality of death.

Elwes appeared soon after. He attempted a smile, more of a grimace, exposing a huddle of yellow teeth. He was dishevelled and agitated, grasping a fistful of letters, which he deposited between the pages of a book on his desk among a mess of other papers and dockets. 'This is not a good occasion,' he said, to no one in particular. 'I feared it would come to this.' We stood facing each other, floundering in a moment of silence. Then he fitted a cap carefully over his thinning hair and straightened his rumpled outfit, saying, 'I'll take you over there.'

Leaving Davies, we walked across the green where the birds were chattering, flitting in and about the vegetation; a dog-rose, heavy with bright clusters of hips, climbed over a nearby wall. The scene was incongruously pretty. As we entered a building we passed a man whose appearance was so grotesque – bent-backed, his nose rotted almost to the bone from the pox – that the sight of him made my stomach turn. He seemed the outward manifestation of my inner state, and I thought how much more appropriate that hideous fellow was to the occasion than the pretty gardens.

Elwes stopped and said a few words to the creature before we continued down a short flight of steps and into a dark corridor. Master Weston was there, a big brute of a man whom I half recognized: he had occasionally brought letters to me from Frances. I remembered the white scar, like a stitched seam, running from his cheekbone to the corner of his mouth that had made me wonder what kind of trouble lay in his past.

He greeted me, saying how sorry he was and that he knew how dear a friend Thomas had been to me. His accent was coarse but he was well turned out. 'Terrible business,' he kept saying, shaking his head and shuffling his huge, rough hands.

'There's no need for you to stay down here, Weston,' said Elwes. 'It's not as if –' He stopped himself. *It's not as if the prisoner needs guarding now.* 'Though don't leave the Tower just yet in case the coroner has any questions for you.' Weston went, leaving a key with Elwes, who used it to open the heavy door. Before we entered he suggested I tie a handkerchief around my mouth and nose in case of infection.

Even so the stench took me by surprise, making me gag. It was not the pleasant room above the watergate where I'd believed Thomas to have been housed but a small hostile chamber, half underground. One wall was slimed green with damp and there was a single, very small window that looked out on to an inner yard at ground level, so all Thomas could have had was a view of people's feet and the dung heap across the way.

He was in the corner laid out on a bed of sorts. An array of magnificent cushions surrounded him, and beneath him the soft puff of a featherbed was visible. The sight of that displaced luxury, sent by Frances, I supposed, made me feel choked once more with tears.

I crouched down. Thomas's hands, which someone had crossed over his chest, looked raw. Glass eyes stared out from sunken sockets. His lips were blue and scattered with sores and his mouth hung open so I could see that several of his teeth were missing. He'd always been so proud of them. Somehow those missing teeth touched me more profoundly than anything else I saw that day.

My hand hovered over him. I wanted to coax him awake, to tell him I'd make him better. Elwes pulled me back sharply. 'I wouldn't. Not without gloves. We don't yet know the cause and he might be infectious.'

'I'd like to take him out of here, give him a proper burial – some dignity.' Even saying it I knew there was no dignity in death, not that kind of death – the worst kind.

'The coroner will have to look at him first, with witnesses.'

I hated the idea of a stranger picking over him, cutting him open, no secret left unexposed. I knelt to pray but felt the weight of God's judgement. It was too late for His intervention anyway, so I got back to my feet. 'I'll stay to witness the post-mortem.'

'It'll be a grim business. Are you sure you want –'

'I am.' I sounded more assertive than I felt but I was compelled to be there while he suffered that final indignity. It was the least I could do.

We went in silence to Elwes's lodgings to wait. Lawrence Davies was still there, hunched on a bench, cradling his head in his hands. Elwes suggested he go home.

He deliberately bumped me with his shoulder as he made for the door, saying under his breath, 'If it wasn't for you he'd still be alive.'

The sickening accuracy of his statement jolted me. I saw

he wanted someone to blame and tried to placate him, but he told me he had no use for my sympathy. 'If you want to help me, find me work. Nothing will bring Sir Thomas back, but the means to put food on my table and a roof over my head . . .' He paused. 'Someone like you could never understand what it is to be stalked by destitution.'

I heard Thomas in his words; it pulled me up. I hadn't even considered that the boy had lost his livelihood. 'Of course,' I promised. 'I'll find you a position.'

He looked me full in the eye, then went on past me and out of the door.

'What was that about?' asked Elwes.

'Poor lad's beside himself with grief. Overbury was something of a father figure to him, you see.' Elwes was happy with my explanation but I was left with the feeling that Davies had been coercing me – with what I wasn't quite sure. Grief had addled me too.

It wasn't long before the coroner arrived. Elwes gathered six of the Tower guards to stand witness and before long we were all crammed into that stinking charnel house of a room.

The coroner came with an assistant – a young lad who might have been his son, for they both had the same dark hair and sallow skin. He was asking questions of Elwes and carefully noting the answers. He opened a large bag to reveal the instruments of his trade: long-bladed shears and clamps, and a set of knives buckled to the lid in order of size. He asked what Elwes knew of the treatments that had been given to Thomas. He called him 'the deceased'.

'For God's sake, use his name,' I shouted, without thinking, and everyone turned to stare at me as if I was a lunatic. I couldn't stop. 'Sir Thomas, that's what he's called. Sir Thomas.'

Those near me took a step away but Elwes clapped a hand

to my back. 'It's the legal term, that's all. No disrespect is meant.' He turned back to the coroner. 'Sir Thomas was bled regularly and, as far as I know, an enema was administered several hours before he expired.'

Weston was called in to tell what he knew. I couldn't listen any longer for the despair thudding through me.

The coroner and his boy efficiently removed Thomas's shirt with gloved hands and slid all the bedding from under him, until he lay naked on the hard bench beneath. The whole thing was half dragged, half lifted, to the window to make the most of the small ration of light. The witnesses shifted uncomfortably, not looking at each other and hardly able to look at Thomas either.

He was pathetically thin, the deep valley of his stomach covered with pustules. The coroner made more notes and gave instructions to the boy who, with docile nonchalance, lifted Thomas's skeletal arms to look in his pits, then inspected his mouth and his pitiable genitals for lesions. They found an issue in his arm, which must have been a conduit for bleeding him. It was held open with a small gold bead, plucked out with tweezers and dropped, with a plink, into a dish.

'We'll turn him over,' the coroner said to his boy and together they rolled him on to his side, exposing his back. The entire company, coroner included, gasped in unison. Thomas's skin from nape to buttocks was dark brown, the colour of Madeira wine, and the movement had released a new pungent odour of decomposition. I heard one of the witnesses whisper to another that it must be the pox.

I stepped towards the man. 'Keep your filthy speculation out if it.' Though it was said quietly, it came out with force and he was cowed, mumbling an apology.

A plaster was removed and beneath it lay a deep black

abscess an inch in diameter. I remembered Mayerne telling me of the incision between his shoulder blades to be anointed daily with a balsam. I had imagined a small clean carefully tended wound designed to allow the bad humours to escape, but this was a putrefying crater.

The room had become unbearably hot and sweat flared beneath my clothes. Someone retched. Most looked away but not me. I'd turned away from Thomas in life and was determined to give him my full attention in death, though it took all the will-power I could muster. I suppose it was a kind of self-imposed penance to force myself to face the unendurable truth.

The coroner picked up several of the phials and bottles that were on a small table to one side, examining their labels and jotting down his findings. 'Natural causes. I see no foul play here,' he announced, looking around the company, who seemed to accept his pronouncement.

I doubted a single man among us could have coped with another moment in that foul chamber, and the idea of the body being opened was too much for anyone to bear. Elwes, hovering half in and half out of the door with a hand clamped to his forehead, uttered a great sigh of relief.

As the coroner was leaving, Lidcote arrived with old Master Overbury, labouring on his sticks. They looked straight through me as they passed to enter Thomas's cell. I stood outside in the curdling heat. It was too hot for the time of year, as if the seasons were muddled, too, by Thomas's death. A blacksmith was shoeing a horse nearby and the sound of his hammer rang through my head, like a punishment, the blighted image of Thomas's corpse more deeply engraved with each strike.

When they returned to the yard old Master Overbury gave me a look that could have soured milk, but he couldn't make me feel guiltier than I already did. He was asking that the body be released, so his family could bury Thomas at Compton Scorpion where he'd been born and where his relatives lay. Lidcote, by the look of him, would have plunged his sword into my heart, given the chance. I couldn't blame him.

'I don't think it will be possible,' said Elwes. He turned to me to uphold his refusal and wore a strange expression I couldn't read. I supposed the whole episode happening on his watch had rattled him greatly.

'For goodness' sake,' I said. 'Release his remains. Give him a little respect in death at the very least.' Elwes looked doubtful so I added, firmly, 'Just do as I say.'

A messenger interrupted us, panting and puce-faced, handing a letter to Elwes. He excused himself and half turned his back to read it, folding it and stuffing it away before calling for writing materials to scrawl a reply.

'I'm very sorry,' he said, addressing old Master Overbury, 'but with the heat at the moment and the condition of the body – you saw it for yourselves – we will need to bury your son without delay in the chapel here. We'll make sure it is done properly.'

'What's going on, Elwes?' I pulled him aside. 'I told you to release the remains to the family.'

'With respect,' he seemed unsure of himself, '*I* have the jurisdiction here in the Tower.' He looked at his shoes. They were scuffed.

'You didn't have the jurisdiction to let me see him when he was still alive.' He still didn't meet my eye. I turned to Master Overbury. 'I'll ensure your son is returned to you.'

'As the lieutenant says' – the air was sharp with hostility – 'in this heat . . .' His words trailed off.

'As you wish.' I had no choice but to let it go.

Back at his lodgings, Elwes discarded his coat, slinging it

over a bench in the outer corridor, and led Master Overbury on. Seeing the letter forgotten, peeping up from his inner pocket, I lingered, on the pretext of wanting a smoke, and made a point of asking for a candle to light my pipe.

Once I was sure I was alone I slipped the letter out, recognizing instantly Northampton's distinctive looping hand: *When the coroner has seen it, bury it as soon as you possibly can.* 'Him,' I muttered under my breath. 'Not "it", him!' *We don't want to provoke scandal and in this heat keeping it above ground might give more offence to the deceased than honour* . . .

A floorboard creaked. I turned to see Elwes in the doorway. 'What are you doing, reading my private correspondence?'

His letter hung from my hand. I took a stride towards him, exhaling a lungful of smoke. 'The question that needs answering is why the rush to get Sir Thomas underground? This doesn't smell right, Elwes. What does Northampton want hidden?'

'We all want to see Sir Thomas treated with respect.' He sounded surprisingly unruffled and gave me a sympathetic smile. 'The shock has put us all on edge. It must be so distressing for you, particularly.'

I was disarmed by his kindness. He took the letter – 'Let's get rid of this, shall we?' – and touched its corner to the candle. It flared up and he dropped it in the empty hearth.

Thomas was buried within the hour and all his secrets with him.

Her

Thin sunlight dapples the floor of the room above the water-gate. It is four months since Frances made her confession. Bacon came yesterday to question her again but she had nothing to add that he didn't know already. It is May, yet still no date has been set for the trial. She wonders how her husband has fared under interrogation.

Her heart feels loose and worn, its petals falling. Time creeps in the Tower, yet she has the incongruous sense that her life is disappearing too fast, like water into a drain.

The baby sits upright on Nelly's lap. It has a fine fluff of hair, so fine that a bald patch, like a tonsure, has appeared at the back where it has rubbed against the pillow. Nelly is making small objects disappear – thimbles and hairpins – causing waves of astonished chuckling from the child. Frances can hardly bear to listen, not when the past is winding itself around her until she cannot move.

She wonders where Nelly went during the long hours Bacon was here. 'Nowhere much,' is what she said when asked. Just after he'd left Frances had seen her with him, deep in conversation.

'I saw you talking to him.'

'He wanted to know –'

'What? *What* did he want to know?' Frances feels her moorings loosen.

'If you were well in yourself. He was worried about you.'

'There's nothing wrong with me.' The words snap out of her. She doesn't believe the girl. Something grazes her face, and her head is thick with the stench of bergamot. It is suffocatingly sweet. Her arms wave frantically, batting it away. A guttural cry escapes from her throat. 'What's that?'

'There isn't anything.' Nelly leans across and gently takes Frances's hands, holding them in both of hers.

'That terrible smell.'

Nelly, with a strange look, tucks a long strand of fallen hair behind Frances's ear. 'Bergamot?'

'You can smell it too?' Frances is sniffing at things – a cup, a cloth, her cuff. Her eyes are black and round.

'It's the hair oil. Don't you remember? There was no more lavender so I used that pot of bergamot I found.'

'Oh, God!' Frances sinks backwards into her chair, with a short burst of manic laughter.

'This place is wearing you down. Here, why don't you tell me about your wedding? That'll take your mind off it all.'

∞

I was back at the heart of things, had almost forgotten what it had been like to be the subject of adulation and relished it more than I should have.

My wedding day passed in a glittering whirl. All those who had vilified me in the previous months were determined to make amends and I knelt at the altar filled with gratitude for my good fortune. The celebrations went on for ten days. It was a wild blur of pleasure and indulgence that culminated in a lavish performance at the Inns of Court, hosted at great expense by Francis Bacon. I only tell you that detail because it seems to me an irony that he is now determined to send me to my doom.

The day of the marriage was the most extravagant, and Uncle's delight at the whole occasion was apparent. At one point, he whispered triumphantly, 'We did it, Frances, against the odds. All your life I've been preparing you for a moment like this.'

I remembered him saying the same thing eight years before at my first wedding, but didn't remind him – he wouldn't have liked that.

'Now we are as close to the King as it is possible to be,' he added. Uncle liked to believe he had made me ruthless, with the drive to power my greatest attribute. I let him believe it. It would have disappointed him greatly to know that, whatever his intentions for me, I'd married for something as banal as love.

We had a few minutes alone in my chamber before the ceremony. 'Only *you*'d dare be married with your hair down, considering the circumstances,' he'd said.

'Since we went to such a bother to prove me a virgin I might as well dress accordingly.' He laughed, but I still felt uncomfortable with the deception. And yet I reconciled myself with the knowledge that God saw all and, given my good fortune, must have chosen to pardon me.

Uncle asked if he might comb my hair, as he'd sometimes liked to do when I was a child. He did so in a trance, smoothing it through his fingers, and lifting it to his face to smell, murmuring, 'Goodness, he is a lucky man.' There was something else in his voice – not happiness.

'You sound envious?' I said.

He launched a look at me, like a stone from a catapult. 'I couldn't be more delighted. We've achieved the impossible. We Howards are unassailable now.'

Father was waiting for us on the steps when we went down. He flicked a brief look over me before continuing some kind of squabble with the groom about the team of horses hitched to the carriage. I might have been upset but I was accustomed to Father's coldness.

Uncle, too, became quite heated about those horses, hissing to Father, 'We can't let them accept.' It was a magnificent team that I'd never seen before, all identical thoroughbreds, jet black with white socks and brushed to shine like polished leather.

'We can hardly send them back to Winwood. It's too late now, and she can't exactly *walk* to her wedding. All the other horses are in use. And, anyway, we've none even half as good as these.' They talked of me as if I was absent.

'Who accepted them?'

One of the grooms was attaching white ostrich plumes to the horses' headstalls and another was arranging their manes, which had been threaded with gold beads.

'Carr, of course.'

'Didn't you have words with him?'

'He was insistent – said Winwood was an old friend of his.'

'He must know that Winwood is on the wrong side. He can't have dealings with those kinds of people now.' Uncle expelled an exasperated sigh. 'You know what Winwood's after with this *generosity*: secretary of state.'

I stood on the steps, waiting for them to finish their hushed conversation. It had rained earlier, which had made the cobbles slick and dark. A line of white birds pecking at the ground made a perfect diagonal line, like a strip of lace running from the stores to the stables. There must have been a hole in a sack of grain. Watching the birds, I was only half listening. From nowhere one of the greyhounds came bounding into the courtyard, causing the birds to take flight, up and up, until they became dark against the bright sky, turning from white to black in an instant.

In the carriage, Uncle said to me, 'You must work on Carr to promote our choice of secretary.'

I protested, reminding them it was my wedding day.

'Surely you haven't forgotten what this is for, Frances.' Father's tone was frigid.

'She knows. She's a Howard first.'

I was thinking, a thrill catching in my throat, that in a matter of hours I would no longer be a Howard but a Carr. Uncle had picked up a hank of my hair and was stroking it absently.

Robert was captivated by my hair too, winding tendrils of it through his fingers during the celebrations. By nightfall, I was impatient to be alone with him, but when we finally left, the King insisted on accompanying us. We were all the worse for drink but he was more so, lolling on the bed and stumbling over his words. He seemed delighted with me, as if I were a new toy. I was surprised as I'd anticipated his resentment. Perhaps he hadn't thought it possible that Robert might love me.

He proposed we play a game. I suppose he wanted to prolong the moment before he had to leave us. It occurred to me that being king might be a lonely business. 'This is what we will do.' He fumbled in his pocket for a pair of dice. 'Each of you throws in turn and the loser must remove something from their body.'

'I don't think –' Robert looked dismayed.

'Has marriage made you dull already, Robbie?'

'Humour him,' I whispered. 'It can't hurt.'

Robert and I were sprawled on the floor. He lost the first three rounds and was undressed down to his bare torso. I saw the King's gaze fix on his exposed flesh. I'd always known I would have to share Robert but witnessing that look made me understand the extent to which my position was dependent on the King's goodwill.

I lost the next round, removing my necklace, clipping it around the King's neck, which amused him, as had been my intention. I continued to lose, as if the die was weighted, each time unpinning another Howard jewel from my dress.

The King light-heartedly accused me of cheating: 'Clothes, I meant clothes.'

'Would you have me parade naked for you, Your Majesty?'

He was laughing raucously by then, swigging from his glass, ordering us to continue. I lost again and removed a shoe. My foot throbbed. A burst blister had soaked blood through my stocking. I had worn five different pairs that day, each less comfortable and more lavish than its predecessor. I kicked off the other.

'That's two items,' slurred the King. 'Such eagerness.' Robert was staring in horror at my bloody feet. 'You might be labelled a whore.'

It was meant in jest but Robert was riled. 'That's enough.' He took the King's drink from his hand, pulling him to his feet. 'You need to go to bed.'

He staggered, almost tripping over a discarded shirt. 'You're a killjoy, Robbie. I might end up liking her more than you.'

Robert propped him up and got him to the door where he was poured into the arms of a waiting servant and we were alone at last.

It had been my first encounter with the King in private and I asked if he often behaved in such a way.

'Very rarely.' He was unlacing my dress and kissing the nape of my neck, running his fingers round my throat.

'It must have been hard for him seeing you wed.'

'He wanted it. He consented.' His voice rasped. My skirt fell to the floor.

'Even so, you need to take care he never feels he has lost you, or –'

He pressed a hand over my mouth. 'I don't want to think

about him.' He was tugging off my underclothes, pulling me on to the bed.

Afterwards we lay in quiet exhaustion, he leaning up against the pillows with my head on his chest. I sensed he was brooding, felt the air around him thicken, and asked him what was wrong.

He sighed slowly. 'My happiness was bought with Thomas's death. The thought plagues me. I can't shake off the feeling that it will blight us.'

I could see the grief stamped into him. 'He was very dear to you but we mustn't make his death all for nothing by being miserable.' I felt suddenly overwhelmed by the sense that everything between us had to be laid bare, no hidden cankers. I wanted a *tabula rasa*. 'There's something I must confess to you.'

He recoiled minutely. 'What is it?'

'It is my fault your friend met his death.'

'What are you talking about, Frances?' He shifted. The patterns of candlelight on his face made him impossibly beautiful and I balked a moment, fearing I'd lose him. 'Tell me.'

I hesitated, had to find the right words from the confusion in my head, but when I finally said it, it came bald and unembellished, the sickening fact: 'That woman, Mary Woods – she made a spell.'

'I don't understand.' He was looking at me, right in the eye, right into my soul.

'When Overbury made those – those threats.' I was stumbling over my words. He went to speak but I asked him to let me finish. 'When he made those threats and you – you discarded me, I was desperate, Robert. Utterly desperate. I went to her in the vain hope that she could see a future in which you loved me once more. Not knowing was unendurable.'

'God, Frances!' he said, as if he were trying to prevent me from throwing myself off a cliff. 'How can you think that I ever stopped loving you?'

'Anne took me there with that servant of hers. She told me the woman was a fortune-teller, but she was a witch. I was duped.' Tears were coursing down my face. 'Such a fool . . . I was such a fool. She took my ring, refused to return it and made a spell, against my wishes. I should have stopped her. I tried but . . .' I felt Robert recoil from me. 'But – but now I see that your friend's life was the price for your love.'

'That woman was proved a fraud.' He was almost shouting, or so it seemed in the entombed space of our bed. 'You fell for her ruse. There's no shame in that. She robbed you of your ring and would have had more if she could have got away with it.'

No matter how much I wanted to believe him, no matter how much I rejected the idea of some supernatural force conjured up as nothing but plain deception, I couldn't quite accept my innocence. 'I craved him dead so I could have you.'

'No, Frances. No!' He knelt up, holding my upper arms, not quite shaking me. 'If anyone is to blame it is *me*.' He let me go, twisting his hands together as if squeezing liquid from a cloth. 'I shouldn't have allowed it to go so far. You're entirely blameless. That whole business was corrupt. Your great-uncle's scheming – oh, God.' He shivered then, as if someone had walked over his grave. 'I'm the guilty one, Frances. It was me. I killed my friend.'

∞

'You see, Nelly, I knew that and chose to do nothing. That's why I have a black heart.'

233

The girl has been hanging on to every word and is shaking her head. 'That's not true.'

The fire is almost dead and Frances's fingers are white with cold. She prepares for bed in silence, stuffing her hair into a cap so she cannot smell the bergamot in it, and slides under the covers almost fully clothed. Sometimes she thinks it would be better not to wake up.

Him

We left the Privy Council meeting. James intended, finally, to appoint a secretary of state, and tempers had flared over the matter, making for an atmosphere of stiff politeness as we filed out. Northampton was limping badly, leaning on me. He looked derelict, his skin sallow, eyes discoloured. It seemed to me that his smooth surface was rusting in places, making visible the years of hidden corruption – the secrets and lies.

Nine months had passed since Thomas's death and no one spoke of him but he was on my mind constantly. I had confronted Northampton about the haste in which he'd been buried.

'Dear boy!' he'd said, his insincerity like a smack to the face. 'It was the only way to give your poor friend the dignity he deserved in death.' He made the sign of the cross. 'Awful business.'

'You didn't think to consult me?' I stood my ground, holding his cold, hard gaze.

'You were grieving. Such a terrible loss.' I began to see he had an answer for everything and felt a fool for ever having trusted him. All the rumours I'd dismissed about his iniquity began to haunt me. But I was chained to him. It felt like a pact with the devil.

We were the last to exit the council chamber, making slow progress. Loitering outside in the melée of the hall were three men I'd been trying to avoid for some months. I'd accepted favours from them all in return for appointments that I hadn't yet fulfilled. On becoming Earl of Somerset I'd been beset by an endless stream of requests for patronage and had accepted the gifts on offer – some might call them bribes – making assurances without proper consideration. I was fast gaining a reputation as someone who promised much but delivered little.

I avoided eye contact but one of the men was bullish and stood in our path. Northampton gave him short shrift. 'If you want to speak to the earl, then make an appointment through the proper channels. Stand aside, or I'll call the guard.' Despite his enfeebled state, he was as intimidating as ever. The man slunk off, throwing me a poisonous glare, and the others melted away with him. Keeping at bay all those to whom I was indebted was proving problematic.

We shuffled along. He talked of Frances, asking how I was finding married life. Frances was my world, and it was a world I guarded jealously, so I glibly joked that she was making a man of me, but would never have shared the depth of intimacy I felt. If people know what you love most, it is a fault line they can exploit to break you.

Once the gallery was empty he pulled me into an alcove. 'Listen, dear boy, I'm relying on you to make sure *our* man is installed as secretary. He's the one to help us achieve the alliance we want.' He looked at me directly. 'It'll resolve the King's debt. You want to help the King, don't you? Have a word with him.'

It was not the first occasion Northampton had mentioned this but it was clear he hadn't considered the possibility that I might not do his bidding. He was oblivious to the fact that I had already promised the position to Winwood, who had paid me a very large sum of money. It was Thomas who had championed Winwood and it became a point of personal honour that I fulfil his wish, even posthumously. It would be a signal to Northampton, too, that I wouldn't be manipulated.

It was Frances who had encouraged me to show him that I was my own man. 'He'll respect you all the more if you make it clear you are not simply the instrument of his will. I know Uncle very well,' she had said. 'I know how his mind works. If you always do exactly as he asks, you will never gain his admiration.'

She was lying on her front, completely naked, on the floor beside the fire. Her narrow-hipped shape and long, slender limbs made her seem like an adolescent boy. Stripped bare like that, unencumbered by the trickery of clothes and disarmingly at ease with her nakedness, she was at her most perfect.

She rolled over, transforming suddenly from boy to woman, and began to run her finger absently over her belly. I was that finger, traversing the undulating landscape of skin and muscle, skimming the edge of her pubic hair and up, round her navel, circling. 'Uncle hates a lapdog.'

Northampton was waiting for my response.

I said firmly: 'I'm afraid I can't promote a man I don't know.'

I felt him tense but he maintained his surface calm. 'He's sympathetic to us.'

I was fast coming to understand that what he meant by sympathetic was a shared open-mindedness in religious matters and a willingness to turn a blind eye. I imagined Thomas turning in his grave. I knew by then that Northampton planned to convert privately to Catholicism, which caused me to wonder if he thought he was dying. People tend to make amends with their faith when they feel their life is coming to an end. I am ashamed to say it had crossed my mind that his demise would be a relief.

My response was noncommittal: 'I'm sure he is.'

Northampton fixed me with a menacing look. 'I don't think you fully understand the advantages of being one of us.'

I found Frances with James, playing cards. They were laughing at something. I watched them unseen for a while. Watched the abandon of her laughter, measuring it, comparing it to how she laughed with me. Before my wedding, I had worried that James might not take to my wife. As a rule he didn't like women. But I should have known that she would work her magic on him. He took to her – of course he did: she was perfect and seemed to have an innate understanding of what would please him.

It was as if the pair of us belonged to him, and we did, I suppose, though I resented the nights I had to spend with him. Frances was adamant that I do my duty, and when I quizzed her as to whether she minded, she said, 'If half of you is all I can have then I am happy with half of you.' But I wanted her to want all of me. I wanted her jealous and angry, as I was, about those lost nights, and came to see that there was an innate coolness to Frances, which made my desire burn even more ferociously.

I stepped out of the shadows. 'Thank goodness you're here,' James said, waving his hand of cards. 'I'm in deficit, three shillings, to your wife. I need your help, come.' He shuffled along to make a space for me to sit and continued playing but even with my help he didn't win. Frances was simply too canny.

'It's only luck,' she said.

'I have a riddle,' said James. 'I wound the heart and please the eye. Tell me what I am, by and by.' He was looking at me. 'Come on, Robbie, don't you know?'

'I loathe word games.'

'I'm sure your wife has the answer.' I hated him in that moment and the thought blasted through my mind of some violent accident befalling him, a piece of the plasterwork crashing from the ceiling, knocking him dead.

'I came to tell you about the council meeting.'

'Wound the heart and please the eye,' repeated Frances. 'It's beauty, of course!'

'Sharp as a pin,' oozed James. They shared a smile.

I began to list the potential candidates for secretary – who on the council was backing whom. James had deliberately remained absent to see if he could flush out the true opinions of his councillors.

He sighed pointedly. 'If you're determined to ruin our pleasure, why don't you tell me who *you* think I should appoint?'

'Winwood.'

'Winwood!' said Frances. 'Is that a good idea?'

The tic in James's eye began to judder. He turned towards her. 'This is men's business.' Frances was seething, but part of me was pleased to see their friendly bond fractured. 'Why Winwood?' He had turned back to me, shutting her out. 'You don't find him intransigent?'

'He can be stubborn, it's true, but I think that might be a good thing. It means he knows his own mind.'

'Perhaps.' James seemed doubtful. 'He's rather more fervently religious than I'd like ideally . . . I suppose *you* could continue handling the more delicate foreign business. We wouldn't want Winwood disrupting things. You know what I mean.' What he meant was, it wouldn't be wise to let Winwood get in the way of his hoped-for Spanish deal.

I noticed that Frances was still simmering, her expression rigid. 'It might appease the Essex crowd,' I added, 'to have someone with such obvious Protestant sympathies appointed. If they become too disenfranchised they may seek new ways to cause problems.'

'You've thought of everything.' He was impressed and I felt the glow of his approval.

Frances had begun to gather up the cards, putting them back in their box. She caught me then with a look of displeasure that cut me to the quick.

'Well, you'd better call Winwood in to see me,' said James. 'The sooner the better.'

Once we had left, Frances said, 'Why in Heaven's name did you do that?'

'Not here,' I hissed. We walked in silence through the crowded corridor until we arrived at our rooms.

The minute the door was shut she turned to me. 'When I suggested you stand up to Uncle, I didn't expect you to do something as reckless as favour a Howard enemy.'

'I don't think you understand —'

She snapped back, 'Don't patronize me, like *he* does. I understand everything — everything.' She was staring strangely into the fire. 'I've seen it. Seen how it all unfolds.'

'Whatever do you mean, you've seen it?'

She took my hand, opening the palm. 'I saw it here.' She half turned. 'When we first met.' The flames scintillated in her eyes. She folded my fingers into a fist, lifting it to kiss the knuckles, hooking her gaze into me, whispering, 'Please, Robert, I beg you, don't let that appointment go through. That man will come back and bite you.'

The air seemed alive, and an image infiltrated my mind's eye of Thomas, so vivid it was as if time had folded back on itself. I could hear him, clearly, as if he was in the room with me: *You owe me, Robin, and this would be a way . . .* It was Winwood he talked of and I knew I couldn't refuse him, even in the face of Frances's pleading. His gelding broke into a canter, leaving me behind, watching his back, so straight – he always looked fine in the saddle, better than anyone. Then he turned and flashed me that rare lightning smile.

I want to remember you like that, Tom, not the image that haunts me: your glass stare from sunken sockets and your mouth, flaccid and bruised. Was it painful, Tom, or did you slip into sleep and never wake up?

Her

The windows are open allowing the outside in: the distinct scent of fresh-cut grass and birdsong mingles with the calls of the men on the river. But there are the other sounds, the sounds you wouldn't know a human could make unless you had been in a place like this.

Frances hums to keep those noises at bay while she practises Nelly's card trick. The cards are succumbing to her will at last, when the lieutenant arrives wearing a grave expression, his rodent eyes flicking about as if he is guilty of something.

'Are you here to tell me a date has been set for my trial?'

'I'm so very sorry.' He seems devastated to have to impart the news. 'You have a week –' He stumbles slightly over his words and his small hands pick at his gloves.

She looks at Nelly to see her reaction. Perhaps she knew of this already – Heaven knows what she is party to. Nelly is on the brink of tears. In the five months since Frances arrived in this place she has never seen the girl cry.

∞

He didn't know I was awake and watching him through slitted eyes. He was perched on the edge of the bed gazing at my husband. In his nightclothes he looked quite ordinary, like the man who lays the fire or the one who tacks up the horses. But the way he looked at Robert wasn't ordinary: it was the exact look that Robert had when he looked at me.

I wondered if the King regretted giving me his lover. There were signs that the novelty of his beloved favourite having a female plaything seemed to be fading. I lay still as a corpse. Robert made a little groan, beginning to wake and they kissed, tongues writhing like fish in a net. Robert shifted, releasing the smell of our mingled bodies that had been trapped in the bed. I felt hot, too hot, but couldn't throw off the covers without drawing attention to myself.

'Not now,' whispered Robert.

The King made a noise of resignation as he pulled away. 'Any news?'

Each morning he asked this. He was more desperate than either of us to know whether I was carrying a child. I wasn't. I was glad. Some happy alchemy occurred when Robert and I were together, making ours a charmed existence that I feared a baby might fracture. We were courted by everyone. No one could touch us, except perhaps the King. Even Uncle was satisfied.

A soft tap at the door catapulted the King to stand by the window. Robert nudged me, thinking I was asleep. I clambered from the bed, dragging on my robe and turning my back so he wouldn't look at me, with that hungry longing, and would give the King his attention instead. It was Anne at the door with news that Uncle had taken a turn for the worse.

Father was there when Anne and I arrived, pacing the hall, restless, barking orders to the servants. 'He's been asking for you.' He sounded brittle and vindictive. As a child I'd learned to avoid him in that mood, but on that day, there was no choice. 'Over here first!'

He yanked me to one side, handling me roughly. 'I've learned that it was *your husband*,' he spat, as if he couldn't bear to say Robert's name, 'who recommended the appointment of Winwood.' He had my finger bent back. I shook off his hold. 'Explain to me how that happened.' His face was pushed up close to mine. 'I thought we could trust you.'

'I did everything in my power to stop him, but he wouldn't listen.' I was up against the panelling and turned my face so I didn't have to look at him. I often wondered if Father's dislike of me stemmed from Uncle's fondness. He must have known of the rumours, the doubts about my paternity.

'Let's hope he doesn't become a fly in our ointment.' His mouth was a pinched line but, for all his posturing, Father had never really had Uncle's talent for intimidation. 'In future keep your husband in line.'

My retort was sharp: 'Or what?'

His lip curled but Anne's small cough made his eyes flick up to the stairs where she was on the half-landing, looking down on us. 'Just do as you're told.'

Uncle's room was quiet as a church and the scent of incense hung in the air, only half masking the stench of decay. Dr Mayerne was with him, which puzzled me, for Uncle had always seemed to disapprove of what he called Mayerne's 'unconventional methods'. Methods, he'd always maintained, that had brought on the prince's death. The doctor stepped aside as Anne and I approached, going to the far end of the chamber where Uncle's greyhound was curled in the only small patch of sun that penetrated the heavily curtained space.

Uncle seemed small and feeble, dwarfed by the expanse of bed and acres of spotless linen emblazoned with the Howard arms. In a weak and ponderous voice, he told us he'd recently heard mass. 'The priest will still be loitering, no doubt, waiting to come back and give me extreme unction.' Shock rendered me dumb.

Though he had been deteriorating for some months, I hadn't fully registered the extent of his physical diminishment until that moment. His bony wrists poked from the crisp, bright cuffs of his nightshirt, and his face was grey with pain, eyes opaque. I did my best to hide my response but Uncle knew me too well. 'It's monstrous what the march of death does to us, isn't it, Frances?'

I didn't answer. I couldn't patronize him with a lie, and silently asked God to give me strength. Anne hovered half in and half out of the door. 'Is that Mistress Turner?' he asked. 'Come here. Let me see you properly.' Anne approached to stand beside the bed. 'Time has been kind to you, my dear.'

She leaned forward to place a hand over his. 'I will pray for you.' I could see she was holding back tears.

'And I for you.' He began to reminisce, talking of when he'd first known her and employed her to take care of me as a child.

I was reminded that Anne had known Uncle long before she had known me, that they had a separate connection to each other that I had no part in. I didn't want to think about it – didn't want to poison the moment with my suspicions. 'Now, if you wouldn't mind, dear, I'd like a little time alone with my great-niece. And would you kindly also ask the doctor to wait with you in the hall.'

As they were leaving he said, 'Mayerne has some very odd ideas but he has a talent for finding remedies to relieve my pain. They make me a little muddleheaded but have helped me feel more comfortable. It became excruciating, you see.' He rasped as he spoke, like an ancient pair of bellows. 'I find my belief a great source of succour. I'm profoundly thankful that I embraced the true faith before it was too late.' I knew he was going to allude to my own faith, for he always did. 'I'd like to think you might follow my lead. I sense that young husband of yours is opening to our ways. Perhaps he will persuade you once I'm gone.'

I felt myself teetering on the edge of an abyss. 'I don't know, Uncle. I feel too deeply mired in sin.'

'In sin?' He held my forearm with his big claw of a hand and drew me close to speak in my ear. 'In the true faith you can be forgiven if you confess. I've felt it as my salvation to be able to leave my sins behind on this earth. There's no such comfort for Protestants. They must carry their sins for eternity.'

I could feel panic slicing through me, bringing a desperate desire to stop time. I wanted to ask what he meant by leaving his sins behind. I believed I was the receptacle for all that wrongdoing.

'I don't want to see you upset, Frances. I don't want weakness to be the last impression I have of you.'

'Of course not, Uncle.' I was fragmenting, crumbling to dust.

'I want to think of you carrying the banner for the Howards when I'm gone. You have been the culmination of my life's work, my greatest legacy.' I expected him to rail about my failure over Winwood but he didn't mention it. 'And you've been magnificent lately. You've not been married half a year and yet you have the King's confidence. I know you'll help him to forge our alliance. England will find herself again.'

I didn't want to say what I really thought, that he was wrong, that England wouldn't want a Spaniard as queen, that the people would rise up to prevent it, that even I was against it. His great vision was nothing but a delusion.

'I'll be watching you when I'm gone.' He seemed to find some strength from somewhere as he still had hold of my hand, tourniquet tight, as if he might drag a vital part of me out of the world with him.

'Please don't talk of that.' I shook my head.

'Frances, it's not like you to shy away from the truth.'

∞

The day after the lieutenant's visit someone else arrives. He is a young man with a pronounced under bite who looks at Frances with a mixture of fear and contempt, as if she is leprous. He gets down on his knee, but reluctantly so. Normally Frances would say there is no need for such formality but she doesn't because of the scorn he takes no trouble to conceal.

Nelly watches the visitor carefully as she plays peekaboo with the baby.

'What's your business?' Frances asks, and he tells her he's come on the King's orders. She is glad there is no matting between his knee and the cold stone floor.

'I am to deliver your infant into the care of Lady Knollys.' He is speaking to her feet. He dares not meet her eye while telling her she is to be separated from her baby. It makes her think less of him than she already does.

'I'm sure she will be well looked after by my sister.' This means the trial really is to go ahead. Nervousness threads through her but she'd rather die than let it show.

'The wet-nurse is to go with the infant, until other arrangements are made.'

Frances wonders what he means by this: until someone more suitable can be employed, probably. She sits at the table and pens a letter to Lizzie, recommending the girl.

'Why don't you get up off the floor?' Her tone makes it seem as if it is the young man's own fault he is still kneeling. He stands, looking unsure of what to do with himself, until she tells him to wait outside while they prepare the baby.

Frances folds and seals the letter. Nelly mumbles her

gratitude. Her lower lip wobbles. 'Don't cry, for goodness' sake,' Frances tells her firmly. 'Here, give the baby to me, while you get your things ready.'

Its small hand grips the edge of her dress, and she wonders why she doesn't feel more. She has seen mothers who suffered at having to hand their babies to a nurse for an afternoon. She is not like those women. She never was. She is Uncle's unsentimental creation. The child smiles, a wide gummy beam. Frances remains unmoved. She cannot allow herself to indulge in emotion – it might engulf her.

Nelly has gathered her paltry belongings and tucked them in with the baby's things. Frances rummages in the box that houses her few valuables, pulling out her purse to give Nelly a few crowns. 'This should see you all right for a while in case my sister doesn't take to you.' A beaded string slithers to the floor without Frances noticing and the girl crouches to retrieve it, holding it out for her.

But then, with a small pant, Nelly draws her hand back to inspect the pearls and rubies, wrapping it around her wrist, unwrapping it, looking hard at Frances. 'You described exactly this bracelet. It's the one you gave to that girl – the child that stood in for you.'

'It was one of a pair.' Frances takes it from her with a firm smile, stuffing it back into the box, then holding out the coins.

'You never said what happened to that girl.' Nelly is concentrating on Frances, as if she is a sum that needs to be calculated.

'That's because I never knew.' Nelly seems to be weighing up whether to believe her or not. Frances places the coins in her palm. 'I don't know how I can ever repay you for your kindness to me.'

Nelly stares at the coins as if they might burn her. For an

endless moment, she appears to deliberate. Then she pours them into her apron pocket and, looking up, says, 'I've never seen so much money in one place.'

'Mind you keep it safe.' The baby is becoming restless on Frances's hip.

'You've been very kind to me too.' Nelly sounds choked.

'Let's not get mawkish. Now remember,' Frances drops her voice, 'it is highly likely you will be questioned about me. They will want to know anything I might have told you to help their investigation. You won't hold back trying to protect me, will you, Nelly? I don't want to think of you being *forced* to speak.'

Nelly pales and seems suddenly very young. She must be thinking of the terrified howls they hear at night. 'What'll they do to you?'

'Most likely hang me,' Frances says, in a matter-of-fact way, holding out the baby.

'But you've done nothing wrong.' Nelly looks aghast.

'It's not what actually happened but how it looks that counts.' Frances hands her the child. 'Do you know what the punishment for poisoning was in the old King Henry's day?'

Nelly shakes her head.

'Boiling alive!'

The girl almost loses her grip on the infant, and Frances thinks she may have gone too far with that last comment.

'I doubt they'd do that to me. Not to the Countess of Somerset.' She pauses while the girl pulls herself together. 'Perhaps they will hear what *you* have to say and I'll be set free.'

'I'll tell them that you've done nothing – nothing at all but obey your great-uncle.' Nelly seems invested with new purpose. 'He's the one deserves boiling alive – and your husband isn't much better. The pair of them deserve to burn in –'

'That's enough, Nelly.' Frances senses everything falling

249

beautifully into place. She has strung the instrument and is wielding the bow, playing it to her own harmony, everyone dancing to it. 'All you have to do is tell the truth.'

She laughs inwardly and thinks of something she once said to Uncle: *There's no such thing as the truth.*

A couple of lads come in to take the luggage, balancing the wicker cradle on top of it. Frances will be glad to see the last of that creaking thing.

They stand opposite each other. 'I wish you all the very best, Nelly. I'm grateful to you for all you've done and for judging me kindly. Most wouldn't have, you know.'

Frances is relieved to see that the girl's eyes are dry. Nelly fumbles in the folds of her apron, pulling out her treasured pack of cards. 'Here, have these.' Frances is touched and thanks her warmly.

'I . . .' she begins, and Frances expects her to say she'll pray for her but she doesn't. 'I wish you luck,' is what she says.

Oh, luck has nothing to do with it, Frances thinks, as she watches them leave. She goes to the window and can see the lads loading the trunk. They drop the cradle, breaking one of the rockers, and it is left abandoned beside the gutter. Nelly climbs up into the cart. It is high but she refuses to hand over the baby to make it easier for herself.

Frances shuts the window and turns to regard the empty room, imagining the girl being questioned and convincing them all of Frances Howard's innocence, rendering her confession null and void.

A victor's smile moves over her face. There is always another truth – another Frances Howard.

The Other Frances Howard

Her

Uncle still clung to Frances's hand, as if she were the only thing left to moor him to the world.

'The truth? There's no such thing as the truth.' Her tone was bald. 'Is there?' He looked as if he had been slapped. 'Is there?' she repeated.

'I don't know what you mean.' His voice was a rattle.

'Oh, you do.' She puffs out a disdainful snort. 'You won't be watching me. Not from where you're going.'

'Frances?' He was horror struck – confused. 'Who are you?'

'Don't you know me, Uncle? You made me. You wanted a device to do your bidding so you created *me*.' She offered him a frost-bitten smile. 'I was your instrument to gain power but now I have my own instrument: the man you matched me with, the man who has the King's ear. Does your invention frighten you, Uncle?'

'Frighten?' His breath was coming in short, urgent bursts.

'The difference between you and me is that you care about it all so much. That's your weakness. Your pretty speech about me being your legacy – oh dear, do you think *your* legacy means anything to *me*?'

'But I love you. I've always loved you as if you were my own daughter.'

'*Your own daughter?* You've never behaved as a father to me, *have you*?' She gave him a moment to consider that, to remember. 'But if you say something often enough to yourself, I imagine you must end up believing it.'

'I beg your forgiveness, my dearest, dearest girl.' He brought his hands together. His eyes were soupy with tears. She was disgusted. 'What I did, I did for love.'

'Love?' Her bitterness rings through the room. 'I predict the next thing you ask of me is to call your Catholic priest, so you can have your deathbed absolution. Poor Uncle, all those wicked deeds will be too heavy for you to carry up to Paradise. No! You shall plummet to the other place.'

'Sins.' He could hardly rasp the word out. 'I *have* sinned. None of us is free of sin.' He then appeared completely lucid, clutching at her with his damp gaze. 'But not murder – never murder.'

'*I* know that. You never had the courage to deal with things properly. Never the strength to look someone in the eye as you extinguished their life.' A frisson of pleasure runs through her body as she remembers the feeling of omnipotence. It had been a shame to dispatch one so innocent, but she had known too much. The girl was so like herself, Frances thought, almost a mirror image. It was as if she were doing away with the last vestiges of her own virtue.

'But who else will believe it,' she continued, 'when everything points to you? You always thought yourself a step ahead. It's not how things are but how they seem that matters: that was your great lesson to me. See how well I have learned it.' She had her face right up to his, close enough to smell the death-stench hanging over him. He turned his head away. 'Do I frighten you?'

'Frances, please.' His breath whistled and laboured, and she had the satisfaction of seeing his terror – his eyes shot through with it, his face collapsing.

She placed the point of her elbow on his sternum, pressing all her weight down. She didn't want to cover his face, not if it wasn't necessary. She wanted to watch.

He began to cough and flail, as if his body was trying to expel the devil. For an instant, she slipped back into childhood with his big hand pushing her face into the water, sputtering, drowning, panicking. 'You trained me well.'

He croaked, 'Father, Father.'

'You'll need to call louder if the priest's going to hear you.' She watched his terror crystallize as he recognized the blunt fact of what lay ahead.

'I beg of you, Frances. I beg of you.'

She stood back as a seizure took hold in him, violent spasms tossing his body. And then he was still. She'd expected more of a struggle.

His greyhound stood, stretched, and ambled over to the bed, resting the tip of its chin on the pillow with a sigh. She felt for a pulse, held her palm close to his open mouth to see if she could feel his breath. There was nothing.

She opened the door, descended to the half-landing and, arranging her expression into one of distress, said very quietly to the gathered company below, 'He's asked for the priest.'

Him

Thomas came to me in a dream. He stood before me laughing, then turned to reveal the flesh of his back, blackened, suppurating, decomposed so his scapulae poked through, like the wings of an avenging angel. I couldn't shake the image out of my mind.

He was there in my study, floating behind Winwood, who was trying to restrain himself. 'I can't respond to these without having the full picture of our foreign policy.' He was waving a sheaf of papers. His eyes bulged with rage and his face was flushed. 'I feel as if I'm working with one hand tied behind my back.'

'Sit, why don't you?' I didn't try to hide my impatience. It was not the first such outburst.

He huffed down into the chair opposite. His suit was a bilious shade of green that made his face seem redder, and he was bleating on about being kept in the dark about foreign policy.

'Ah, that, yes.' Thomas would have known how to appease Winwood without damaging his pride. I could feel his hand on my shoulder, had his voice in my head: *You betrayed me, Robin.* 'His Majesty is keen to keep foreign and domestic affairs separate.'

'If everything goes wrong the blame will be placed at *my* door.' Winwood held his hands firmly in his lap and sat very straight and still, as if any sudden movement and he might burst. 'I simply can't work under these conditions –'

'Be assured,' I interrupted him, with a smile, 'I won't allow any blame to fall on you. Now, I'm sure you have things to do.' He cleared his throat and began to complain about another matter, so I stood, making it clear he was dismissed.

When he was almost out in the corridor, I heard him mutter under his breath, 'You are not invincible, Robert Carr.'

I suppose, looking back, that is exactly what I believed myself to be. Northampton was gone, my misgivings buried with him, and Frances and I were at the pinnacle of the court. We were the charmed couple, at the height of our power, gilded with the King's adoration and, if I am honest with myself, my head had been turned.

My father-in-law had been given Northampton's post of lord treasurer and I was made lord chamberlain. The Howards had all the top positions: I'd a brother-in-law as treasurer of the Household and another as the captain of the King's guard, not to mention those on the Privy Council. I was beginning to understand what it meant to be one of them.

Thomas loomed, his toothless grimace mocking my vanity.

The universal flattery that came with such privilege masked a good deal of envy and loathing. It sat uncomfortably with me – I hadn't been raised to it like my wife. 'Sometimes, Robert,' she said of it, 'when you hold high office you have to do things that are unpopular. It is better to be respected than to be liked, don't you think?' Frances was always right. But it went against my grain. I wanted people to like me – Thomas always said so. Perhaps that was a weakness.

After Winwood's departure I stood at the window awhile, watching the comings and goings on the river. I rarely looked at the Thames without remembering that grief-ridden trip to the Tower almost a year and a half before.

I saw Winwood below, crossing the yard towards the river steps, unmistakable in his livid green suit. He climbed into a barge. Even at a distance I was able to see Essex seated in the back beside Pembroke. And Southampton was taking Winwood's hand to help him aboard.

The Essex crowd had been scarcely at court in recent months. As my father-in-law liked to put it, they had been cast into the 'political wilderness', and I'd supposed them to be licking their wounds. I'd certainly never thought Winwood particularly close to them. He hadn't been their candidate. I watched the boat set off in the direction of Essex House. Something was askew. Thomas whispered: *You reap what you sow, Robin.* I wondered if Winwood knew more about our foreign policy than he was letting on, began to suspect that trouble was being concocted on that barge – trouble for me.

My servant came to tell me that someone was waiting outside. It was Lawrence Davies. He looked gaunt, his clothes were shiny with wear, and I couldn't meet his eye. I hadn't found him the promised position and he took no pains to conceal his resentment. It would have been easy to give him a post in my own household but I didn't. I made a vague excuse. I don't know why. That boatful of enemies had disturbed me and perhaps I didn't want Davies about the place as a further reminder of my dead friend.

I rummaged for a handful of shillings, which I held out, suggesting he return another time. He refused the coins, saying it was a job he was after rather than charity.

'I thought you would be more like him,' he said, as he left.

I hope you are ashamed, whispered Thomas.

Her

Robert burst in, ugly with rage, slamming the door. An angry vein pulsated in his forehead. 'That snake! He's *knighted* the bastard.' He grabbed a candlestick, violently hacking at the table with it, splintering the polished oak surface. 'He can't do that.' The candlestick flew across the room crashing against the far wall.

Frances watched with chilled calm, recalling, with a sliver of disgust, her first husband flinging a glass once in a similar petulant fit and their rage-fuelled coupling in the aftermath.

A crack was forming. This husband was collecting enemies. The snake he referred to was George Villiers, a young man to whom the King had taken a shine lately. Another object whistled past, shattering on the skirting. He reached for a precious alabaster vessel that belonged to her.

'Leave it!' She spoke as if to a dog, stepping towards him and grasping his wrist, prising the object from him. He was shaking. 'Take hold of yourself.'

'But he's an impostor. It's a plot to push me out and James is giving him . . .' He slumped. 'You don't understand.'

'I understand perfectly, Robert. You must be able to see that this is your own doing. You neglected the King.' Robert's infatuation with her had increased to the level of mania. It was becoming a problem. He was becoming a problem.

'James can't stop talking about how wonderful he is. "Such a fine horseman, Robbie. Have you seen him in the saddle? An accomplished linguist . . . have you seen what a beauty he is?" and now a knighthood. Give it a month and he'll be lord something or other and telling me what to do.' The vein continued to throb as he ranted. 'I'm going to tell him he's making a mistake.' He tried to shake off her grip but she held him firmly.

'You'll do nothing of the sort. Do you want to make a bad situation worse?' Frances had been aware that George Villiers was being groomed by their enemies to supplant her husband. She'd been keeping an eye on the situation. 'You should befriend him.'

'Befriend him? I'd rather cut my own arm off.'

'Yes – get close enough to discover his weaknesses. Find a way to discredit him.'

'I'll make James send the bastard away.'

She would have liked to knock some guile into her husband. 'Don't. It's not as if his rise is your loss.' Not yet, she was thinking. 'You'll only push the King into Villiers's arms.'

Frances went instead.

She cut across the courtyard. It was deserted and there was no moon. The only light came from a brazier next to the stable arch. She could hear two cats squalling on a nearby wall and one dropped suddenly into her path, startling her before slithering off into the shadows. Her mind churned on Villiers. It wouldn't be impossible to make him disappear, though risky. But the obstacle was Robert. As long as he continued to neglect his duties, there would always be some young thing ready to step into his shoes.

Villiers was with the King, making to leave as she arrived. There was no doubt about his physical charms: bright, inquisitive eyes and a complexion that left most women boiling with envy, teamed with a languid poise, surprising in one so new to court. His suit was cut tight to the body and the breeches short, to make the best of his lean, muscular legs, which unfurled gracefully as he stood.

She touched his sleeve. 'Beautiful, this.' She happened to know Pembroke had funded that suit of clothes. Villiers was as poor as a church mouse. 'Who's your tailor?'

She'd intended to embarrass him a little, hoping to measure his willingness to tell a lie, but he thanked her with a straightforward smile. 'It was a gift.'

His calm self-possession made it difficult for her to assess what kind of adversary he would make. Beside that dewy boy, the king looked dog-eared. It was vanity on his part to think a young favourite would make him seem anything other than an old fool.

Once Villiers had left, she sat, a little closer than was correct. 'I'm worried about Robert.'

'He's not ill, is he?'

She registered the King's genuine expression of concern. It gave her confidence that her husband had not drifted too far from his affections. 'No, it's nothing like that. You know what he's like. Driven by his passions. And he's got a bee in his bonnet that you don't care for him any more. He's eaten away with jealousy, you see.' She stopped, allowing her words to sink in. 'He's very much in love with you.'

'Jealous of?' He nodded towards the door, through which Villiers had recently left. She saw the slight smile and felt her message hit its mark.

'He's afraid he's losing you.' She placed a hand carefully on his arm.

'And after everything I've given him —'

She interrupted: 'He doesn't care about any of that. He only cares about you.'

His features hardened. 'Well, he has a strange way of showing it. I've barely seen him lately.' The sceptical look he wore made her understand that this would not be as straightforward as she'd hoped.

261

'He's . . . Oh, never mind. Shall we play something? Remember the game we played on my wedding night?' She ran her finger lightly across her neckline, leaning back with a breathless little laugh. He seemed amused by the memory, just as she'd hoped. 'That was fun. Life can become so serious, can't it?'

'What would you like to play?' There was a flash of mischief in his eyes.

She ran her hand down on to his, turning it palm up. 'I could read your fortune.'

He laughed. 'I've heard about you and your soothsaying games.'

'Oh, but they're not games.' She began to inspect the creases with studied concentration. 'This is your head line and this your heart line.' She allowed her breath to deepen. 'I can hear someone.' Tipping her head back, she rolled her eyes, half closing them, lids flickering, and whispered, 'What are you telling me? Who are you?' She could feel the force of his fascination. 'What is your message?'

Jolting suddenly with a loud gasp, her eyes flew open and she dropped his hand with a terrified expression.

'What is it?'

'No, no.' She frowned. 'I can't.'

'I order you.'

'It's a warning!' She wiped the back of her hand over her brow. 'I see destruction. There's an untrustworthy person newly in your orbit. Someone who seeks to take from you rather than give.'

She hadn't expected his great guffaw of laughter. 'I don't need your soothsaying game to tell me that. You describe most of my court.'

She suspected then that he might be impervious to her but, rather than feeling quashed, she rose to the challenge. 'It is your choice to disbelieve.'

'If it's not a game' – he drilled into her with a stony look – 'I should have you burned as a witch.' He paused in a charged silence, then laughed again.

'You're making fun of me.' She feigned amusement. 'Divination is not witchcraft.'

'Most can't see the difference.' He was smirking.

'But *you* can.' She tilted her head, keeping her tone light.

'There's a good deal I can see that most can't,' he said, 'such as all those who take rather than give.'

It was abundantly clear to Frances that he would not be manipulated. Of course, he, like she, had been raised to trust no one. 'My husband doesn't fit that description.'

'Ah, Robbie.' He gave a wistful sigh. 'That's true. He's not a taker. It's what made me want to be so generous with him.' She noticed that he was talking of his generosity in the past tense. 'He mustn't neglect me, though.' There it is, she thought, the real warning, hidden by a smile. 'And what about you, Frances, are you a giver or a taker?'

'I do as I'm told.'

He laughed again, as if she'd made a joke. 'If you seek to give me something' – he was pointed – 'then let it be his child.'

Frances felt her way back across the courtyard through the dense night. She could sense her hard-won power slipping through her fingers. Two men in a shadowy huddle to one side fell silent as she passed. Picking up her pace, she stumbled on a loose cobble. A hand reached out to steady her. 'Take care.' His coat smelt strongly of tobacco smoke. It was Pembroke, and the other man, hidden in the gloom, she suspected was Villiers. Had she imagined it, or were Pembroke's words weighted with a double meaning?

'Thank you.' Her response was perfunctory and she continued up the steps to the side door, unease swilling inside her.

It was clear that if it came to it, and Robert fell from power, her family would detach themselves from him. It meant she, too, Howard or not, would be cast adrift, for there would be no denying her marriage a second time.

'Only death will get you out of this one,' her brother Harry had said to her on her wedding day. It was meant as a joke. But things had changed and Frances was determined she would not be swept into oblivion with a fallen favourite. Better to be a widow. And she would always be a Howard.

Him

I stood unseen on the threshold, watching. The room was hot, the windows misted, making it impossible to imagine the February chill outside. Frances was draped in a fine, almost transparent, linen shift and was seated with her bare feet in Anne Turner's lap. Anne was paring her toenails with a small blade. I was transfixed by the intimacy of the scene, its secret femaleness, as if I was witnessing something forbidden. She held a mirror close to her face and seemed to inspect some small blemish but must have seen my reflection there as she turned, saying, 'What are you doing lurking in the shadows like a thief?'

Anne got up and slipped away, leaving us alone. I'd quickly warmed to my wife's companion, had sensed instantly her deep care for Frances. I felt she was a kind of saintly presence in our lives with her angelic looks and gentle disposition. How strange it is that sometimes people are not what they most appear to be.

'What are you doing here? Shouldn't you be with the King? Hasn't he asked for you?' Frances was blunt as a club and I felt my desire flare.

I began to pour out my fears, fears that Villiers was supplanting me and that Winwood was hatching something against me. She lifted one leg up, bending it so her foot was in her own lap and took the little knife to her nails. Her hair fell forward like a flow of treacle so I couldn't see her face as she spoke. 'Will you never learn that if you have the best of things there will always be someone who wants to take them from you? Rise above it. And you'll be giving it all away if you don't spend any time with the King.'

I reached out to touch her hair and a sharp jolt forced my arm to recoil, an invisible charge of power. It was as if beneath her skin she might not be human at all but something that came from the heavens, brought to life by the force of lightning.

'I'll go to him shortly. He hasn't called for me yet.'

She passed me her comb. 'I may as well put you to good use if you insist on staying.' She ran her tongue over her teeth, standing, turning her back. 'You shouldn't wait until he calls for you. It'll annoy him.'

'You have a heart of stone, Frances.'

She knew I didn't mean it but still replied, 'I'm only acting in *our* interests. One of us must.'

'I know, my darling. I know.' The comb slid through her hair, where I buried my face to breathe the clean dry scent. I lifted her shift over her head. She stood, as ever entirely at ease unclothed – a prelapsarian Eve – and I continued combing, crouching to reach the full length of that extraordinary mane, listening to the faint crackle of the teeth separating its strands.

The backs of her knees, exposed where her hair thinned towards the ends, strangely enthralled me, a place usually hidden beneath layers of stocking and skirt. It was impossible to believe that after more than a year of marriage there were still territories of Frances's body that remained undiscovered to me. While I'd accepted that her mind would always be just out of reach – that enigma was the seat of her powerful allure – I'd believed her physical self entirely knowable. But in that moment I understood how wrong I'd been. Nothing was knowable about Frances.

Boyish, her knees curved out only slightly from the slender

adolescent shape of her long thighs and in again before giving way to the slight swell of her calves. Where they folded at the back, each knee was decorated with a filigree of blue veins visible through her transparent skin and marked with a definite H shape, as if God had branded her a Howard.

I dropped to my own knees as if in worship. That fragile part made her seem so friable and human and transient, and I was struck profoundly by the fear of her loss, like panic, as if time were running out. I never wanted her more than in that moment and never more clearly understood the impossibility of truly possessing her. It made me want to snatch up that sharp little knife, nick one of those veins, and suck the blood from her.

A rap at the door interrupted me. I jumped to my feet, sickened by myself, feeling I'd been caught with blood around my mouth, like a monster. She, though completely naked, didn't move to cover herself, just called out, 'Who is it?'

'I come from the King. He is expecting the Earl of Somerset in his chambers.'

'Understood,' she replied. 'You can tell His Majesty the earl is on his way.' She sounded so business-like, bolted through with pragmatism, while I was being pulled hither and thither on waves of desire, unable to think of anything but her. 'You have to go,' she said.

'I'll make an excuse.' I put my arms round her, running my fingers down the small articulations of her spine – down, down to the soft bulge and cleft of her buttocks. 'He can't deny me time with my wife.'

'You'll upset him. He's upset already.' Her whisper was almost too much for me.

'Think of *me*, Frances, how upset *I*'ll be.' I knew how unattractive my petulance must be but I couldn't help myself, and her sheer calm flustered me. I wanted her to beg me to stay but it was the very fact that she would never do such a thing that kept me captive to her.

'I *am* thinking of you, Robert.' She skimmed my cheek with the tips of her fingers, running them over my lips. 'If you continue to offend him our lives will become very difficult. We'll lose his favour and that boy will step into your shoes before you know it. Then what?'

'I don't care.' It was unimaginable to think of leaving her and going to him.

'Well, you *should*. Everything he's given he could just as easily take away.'

'Don't you ever feel jealous?' I asked, desperate for her to tell me she was eaten away by it.

'Should I be?'

'What he wants usually from me is affection and friendship.' I feared the truth would repulse her, feared most that she would stop loving me.

'*Usually?*' She laughed baldly. 'You look as if you wish the floor would swallow you. I understand my part of the bargain.' She stroked my head, taking a lock of hair, tugging it sharply. 'There has long been speculation about the exact nature of your relationship with the King. The depravity.'

'What do you mean?' I felt my hackles rise as if I'd been threatened. She laughed again. In that instant, she became something monstrous. Grabbing her by the hair, I spat, 'Don't laugh at me!' I could sniff the fear on her.

She spoke softly. 'Oh, my love, I didn't mean to suggest . . . It's nothing. But people like to imagine things. That's all. Nobody really believes that it's less than pure, what you have with him.'

I let her go, horrified by myself, distraught, apologizing repeatedly.

'It's all right, Robert. I understand.' She took my hand and kissed each of its fingers. 'Nothing you could do or have done could make me love you less.'

I was aghast that I'd cast her as my enemy, even for a moment. 'Once there might have been more to tell but there was an incident that changed things.' I found myself telling her about how Thomas had come upon us at Royston and how it was never the same between the King and me after that. 'It felt as if something innocent had been sullied.'

'So, Overbury tried to blackmail the King.' The word 'blackmail' rolled off her tongue in the way a thief might talk of diamonds.

'I didn't say that.'

'You didn't need to.' We were silent for a moment, and I hoped she wouldn't press me further for details, but she simply said, 'Well, he's gone now, God rest his soul.' She tried to pull herself out of my arms. 'You'd better be off.'

But I held her. 'What he wants most is for us to have a child. You said it yourself. If I spend all my time with him and none with you —'

She made a small sound that was half sigh, half moan and pressed her mouth over mine. Her tongue tasted of aniseed. We crumpled to the floor and with the efficiency of a surgeon she unlaced me.

When she was done, I wanted to linger, to bask a while in the aftermath, hold her in my arms, but she pulled herself back together with brutal swiftness and returned to the paring of her toenails.

Her

The early-morning bustle had started in the yard and she could hear the servants padding along the corridor. Frances pulled back the curtains so light flooded over the bed. Robert lay in a tangle of sheets looking as if he hadn't slept for a month. Dark smudges ringed his eyes. Frances was ebullient. Fortune was smiling on her, or perhaps it was a darker force that had taken her part and swung the wheel to her advantage. She didn't care which.

'I've decided.' Robert was wrapped up in his own small world, oblivious to her good mood. 'I'm going to offer the King the money Winwood gave me for his appointment.'

'What – *all* of it? Whatever for?' The idea was preposterous. No one gave money to the King. It simply wasn't how things worked.

'I was put in charge of delivering the Spanish marriage and I've failed abysmally.'

'I don't see why that has anything to do with Winwood's money.'

'James is desperately short of funds. He was counting on the dowry.' He paused. 'I want to make amends.'

She wanted to shake him – shake the kindness out of him, tell him it made him weak. 'You should have come to me.' She was annoyed with herself for not being aware of the situation. Villiers's rise had been distracting her, but now she had a trump to play.

He began to whine about his failure, saying how he wished her great-uncle were still alive as he'd have surely had more success. Uncle had been gone almost a year.

Frances didn't miss him.

Robert looked downcast. 'I thought I could show James my talent for diplomacy in the face of that upstart Villiers.'

She forced a smile and took his hand. It was clammy. 'I thoroughly approve of your proposed donation.' Preposterous as it had initially seemed, the gesture would certainly remind the King that Robert was a 'giver' not a 'taker'. That conversation of a month ago remained at the forefront of her mind.

'There are people who wish me ill. They watch my every move.' His fingers clenched around hers. 'I fear someone will try to read something sinister into my Spanish dealings.'

His weakness repulsed her but she tried to reassure him by saying that the accrual of enemies was a sign of his success and that he'd have plenty of opportunity to impress the King with his loyalty on the coming royal progress.

He still looked stricken with worry. 'Someone might try to construe it that I was negotiating for personal reasons – spreading papism. It was all done under such secrecy, you see.'

'I shouldn't worry about that.' She hardly recognized him. Familiarity had made his beauty commonplace, muting the desire she'd once felt so fiercely. He began to talk of his enemies, how they might levy a charge of treason against him without the King's knowledge.

He wrapped himself around her, too tightly. Nausea ground through her gut. She pulled away, getting up to open the window, taking a few deep breaths of fresh air, watching one of the grooms trying to control a nervous young horse in the paddock. He whispered gently close to its ear and the creature fell instantly into his thrall. She knew she must shore herself up against potential disaster, with or without her husband.

'And if that happened, James would have no choice but to see me tried.' He was still gnawing at his fingers.

'Ask the King for a general pardon,' she said. A refreshing draught penetrated the thin fabric of her nightgown. 'So if there's any trouble you will have recourse directly to him, no matter what. I'm sure he won't refuse you that. It's not unusual.'

'A pardon?' Robert looked at her in wonder. 'Of course. I don't know why I didn't think of it.'

'It'll give you peace of mind, at least. Not that you've really done much wrong.' But she was thinking that a person doesn't need to have done anything wrong to be found guilty. She explained that all he had to do was make the request, the King would order it, and the lord chancellor would ratify it. '*Et voilà!*' She opened her hands, like a magician who has made a dove disappear.

'I don't know what I'd do without you.' She noticed a new cloud pass over his face. 'But what if he refuses?'

'I shouldn't worry about *that*. He'll be more than willing, I'm sure, when he hears your news.'

'What news?'

'We're going to have a baby.'

His face transformed, a little of his old allure restored. 'When?'

'Not until December. It's still very early. I wasn't going to say yet, in case. But you seemed so desolate.'

'A Christmas infant.' He was looking at her as if she were a miracle. He had waited such a long time for this baby – they all had. She was relieved to see him cheerful once more. No one, least of all the King, wanted to be confronted by his pitiful long face. 'But are you sick with it, my darling?'

'Not a bit.' She *had* been, horribly so, but she had no intention of admitting to the same weakness other women complained of. 'Go and tell him. What are you waiting for?'

He wanted her to go with him but she refused. 'This is

your moment.' She imagined the scene: Villiers being shoved down to make space for Robert to sit beside the King, toasts drunk for the baby. 'And use your advantage to ask for the pardon.'

He had only been gone a short while when Anne appeared, looking ashen.

'Franklin's here,' she said, under her breath, pointing to the door that led to the antechamber.

'I hope to God he hasn't been seen. What does he want?'

'Money. He's still owed money from —' Anne didn't say it. She didn't need to. Her eyes were scudding back and forth.

'How much?' Frances had barely given Thomas Overbury a thought since he'd been buried almost three years before, and felt annoyed that he should infringe upon her content-ment from beyond the grave in such a way.

'He says five hundred.'

'That's a fortune. Uncle promised him that much? Typical that he should leave me to clear up his mess.' She looked at Anne to see if she would contradict her, but she didn't. Frances had been very careful to give her the impression that Uncle had pulled the strings.

'He says it's owed him.' Anne was wringing her hands.

'I can't imagine why he thinks I'd keep that kind of sum lying around here. You'd better show him in.' She hurriedly threw a gown over her nightclothes. Time was pressing. If Robert returned and found Franklin in her rooms it would be difficult to explain.

He limped in like a ghoul. Frances had forgotten how grotesque-looking he was. Anne was wavering near the door, clearly perturbed. Frances told her to wait outside and head off any of the servants, then turned to her unwelcome guest. 'Have you lost your mind, coming here in broad daylight?'

'A debt's a debt,' he said bluntly. 'You owe me –'

'It is not I who owes you, Master Franklin. If you remember, the debt was my great-uncle's and should have died with him.' Thinking of Uncle, the terror on his dying face, gave her an unexpected frisson of power. 'But I intend to honour his debt.' She looked him right in the eye. 'Even if it was accrued for wicked purpose.'

'With respect, it was you who ordered the . . .' he hesitated '. . . the final batch of – of substances. The dose that did him in.'

'I think you'll find you are mistaken.' She smiled. 'It was a long time ago, wasn't it? It's no wonder you've forgotten.' He gripped his hands together and brought the knuckles up to cover the lower part of his face. She could see the seed of doubt germinating in him: it was written in his frown and the confusion in his eyes. 'I was merely the one who conveyed my great-uncle's letter to you. Don't you remember? When you read it you were so agitated you spilled a bottle of ink down your front. You *must* remember that.'

He pinched the fabric of his shirt, looking at it, frowning. 'I do. Yes, I do. Ruined a good shirt.' He seemed glad to have a hard memory to hang on to. 'Of course.'

He *had* spilled the ink but there had been no letter. 'Indeed,' she said. 'I was nothing but the messenger, never knew of the letter's contents. Not until Anne told me. Terrible business – that poor, poor man. I don't know why you let yourself become embroiled in it, procuring poisons. I hope you destroyed that letter. These things always have a way of resurfacing.'

She rummaged for her purse, handing it to him. 'This is all I have on me. You'll have to wait for the rest.' He inspected the little pouch, knowing from its weight that it came nowhere near to repaying the debt. His hand was shaking slightly and she knew she had him exactly where she wanted.

'Listen.' She patted his shoulder lightly. He flinched, and it occurred to her that, looking as he did, he must rarely have been touched by anyone. 'Your secret's safe with me. No point digging all that up now, is there?'

Him

The going was painfully slow in the July heat with the ground unforgiving as granite. We were on the coast road and still a fair way from our destination at Lulworth when my mare lost a shoe. The royal party continued, Villiers up front beside James, leaving me on edge, contemplating the flat expanse of sea, while my groom went to find a blacksmith.

As Frances had predicted, news of the baby had worked like a magic elixir and I was reinstated in James's affections. But it was not as it once had been. Villiers nipped at my heels and I suspected James enjoyed watching us vie for his favour. A rumour had been circulating that he might be made master of the horse, a position James knew I coveted. Apparently, people were laying bets on us.

The court's divisions were laid bare, each faction seeking a way to score points against the other, as if our lives were a game of chess: my baby was a point in our favour, as was the granting of my general pardon, but the refusal to ratify it was a point scored to them. Villiers and I stood facing each other across the board wearing counterfeit smiles, James the amused invigilator. I found myself wishing Northampton were still alive. He would have had no qualms about dealing with the upstart.

The luggage carts lumbered past, followed by the stragglers, and I was surprised to see, beyond, Winwood's carriage hurtling my way. Winwood was meant to be answerable to me and as far as I knew he was more than a hundred miles away at Whitehall. Something was not right. I waved him down.

As the carriage drew to a halt, I flung the door open, abandoning formalities: 'Why wasn't I informed of your visit?'

'There wasn't time. A matter's come up that needs urgent attention.' He seemed furtive, fidgeting with his treasured timepiece and shading his eyes from the sun – but also from me. I supposed he was regretting his infringement of protocol. 'I thought it best I get immediately on the road.'

'So what is this urgent matter?' I was wondering why he hadn't sent a messenger and it occurred to me, sickeningly, that he might have happened on something he shouldn't have seen.

Winwood rubbed a finger slowly over his nose. 'For His Majesty's ears only.' He smiled. I'd never seen him smile before. His two front teeth were large and grey, like a pair of gravestones. He didn't attempt to hide his air of self-satisfaction, continuing to swivel the lid of his timepiece. I longed to snatch it from him and fling it into the sea.

'Just tell me what it's about and I'll deal with it.' I'd meant to sound authoritative rather than exasperated, but unease was weaving through me. 'The King won't want to be disturbed with state matters after his journey.'

'With respect' – he looked quite triumphant – 'this is a matter for the King alone.' He patted the seat beside him. 'Would you care to travel with me?'

I didn't relish the idea of spending a couple of hours cooped up with the man and made an excuse about wanting to be sure my horse was properly shod.

'As you wish.' He rapped the roof of the carriage and they rumbled away.

I immediately regretted my decision, realizing I shouldn't have let Winwood and his shady matter out of my sight. As I waited an interminable time for my groom to return, I became increasingly apprehensive, believing that Winwood's surprise visit in some way involved me.

The luggage carts were still being unloaded when I finally arrived. Harry Howard was waiting for me in the yard, reminding me, with a jolt of longing, of my wife. Lulworth was their brother's house and I was glad at least to be on Howard territory where my enemies would be at a disadvantage.

'Where's the King?' I said, before he had a chance to greet me, making my way up the steps into the house.

He tugged me back by my coat. 'What's the hurry? Shouldn't you wash and change first?'

I looked down at my clothes. I was filthy, covered with a film of dust, my fingernails black. 'Never mind that. I need to see him.'

'You can't!' His face screwed up in sympathy. 'He's said he's not to be disturbed.'

'Where's Winwood? Where's Villiers?'

'Not with him. He's alone.'

That at least was a small relief. 'Something's going on, Harry. Have you heard anything?'

He shrugged, seeming evasive. 'Let me show you to your room. You can settle in and see him later.' He led me up the stairs to the back of the house and a spacious, light-filled room that smelt faintly of sage. My belongings were already there and unpacked but there was no sign of Copinger, my servant.

The large bed was hung with finely embroidered curtains and strewn with fat pillows. The plasterwork ceiling was beautifully wrought in a pattern of ivy, which spilled on to the wall above the hearth, winding about the Howard arms in relief at its centre. Beneath it were inscribed the words: *sola virtus invicta* – courage alone is invincible. I could have done with some of the Howard courage rubbing off on me.

From the window, there was a view over a courtyard where a boy was beating a length of matting, making a rhythmic thwacking sound. Through an arch, I could see the fishponds and, far beyond, a range of hills, purple in the evening light. I wished Frances were with me. The thought of our baby taking shape inside her was soothing and pushed my worries into the background.

'Not what you're used to, I'm afraid,' said Harry, dragging me from my thoughts.

'But it's lovely. King's rooms through there?' I asked, pointing to a second door.

He shook his head and looked to the floor. 'His Majesty's at the front of the house.'

'But he always insists I'm adjacent –' A new wave of disquiet sluiced through me. 'Villiers? He's put bloody Villiers next to him, hasn't he? What in Hell's name's going on, Harry?' I grabbed him roughly by the shoulders. 'Tell me!'

He pushed me away. 'Look, I'm on your side. I don't know what's going on but, whatever it is, I'm sure we can handle it.' He sounded reassuring but couldn't look at me. 'I'm sorry. Listen, my brother's going to make sure you're beside the King at supper. You can talk to him then.'

At supper, though, I was seated at a distance. James appeared distracted and Villiers was where I should have been, next to him. I felt the company retract slightly from me, weighing up whether the balance of power had shifted permanently. I barely ate, fuming silently through the courses. Once the tables were cleared Villiers approached, all long legs and winsome smile, offering ingratiating compliments about the fit of my suit and what fine shoes I was wearing. He wore a jewel that the King had offered me not long before. I had refused it, told him he wasn't to give me expensive presents, given the state of his finances. And there it was, pinned to the breast of my adversary. I wanted to rip it off him, stab him in the eye with the pin.

'His Majesty would like to see you in private.' He seemed so mild and sincere, and I hated him for inspiring such extremes of emotion in me. I knew it wasn't his fault, that he was just a pawn in someone else's game. But it didn't make me hate him any the less. 'I'll take you up there.'

'I can find it perfectly well myself.' My retort couldn't have been more lacking in grace but Villiers didn't respond, which was just as well as I might have hit him.

James couldn't hide his agitation: the twitch in his eye was pronounced, his right leg jigging frantically. He dismissed everyone and we were entirely alone for the first time in months. He didn't offer me a seat, not even the low stool beside him, and I was obliged to remain on my knees while he lolled back in his chair.

'The secretary of state has heard a rumour.' He hesitated, scratching at his beard. 'Well, more than a rumour, really.' The eye twitched on.

'Winwood can't be trusted.' My voice was clipped. It was all I could do to maintain an unruffled surface.

'Do you think I don't know that?' he snapped, almost shouting. '*No one* can be trusted.' It was unusual for him to display his anger so overtly, which made it more menacing. 'Even you!' I blanched, attempting to defend myself but he continued. '*You* were the one who petitioned me to install him as secretary, Robbie.'

'But I believed he was upright. He was a friend of –' I stopped myself before blurting out Thomas's name.

But James said it for me: 'A friend of Thomas Overbury.' He had calmed but looked forlorn and said, very quietly, 'Winwood says that the deathbed testimony of some apothecary's boy has come to light. The boy said that Overbury was deliberately poisoned, claimed he was witness to it.' He brought his hands up to cradle his forehead with a great sad exhalation, repeating, 'Deliberately poisoned.'

I couldn't speak. My entire being was filled with that image of Thomas's corpse and I was struck to the heart with regret – regret and sorrow over the whole sordid business.

'I have no choice but to demand an investigation.' He tapped a finger repeatedly on the arm of his chair, looking around shiftily, lowering his voice. 'It can't touch me. You know that. He was imprisoned on my order. If even a whiff of suspicion alights on me . . .' He paused. 'If it's found to be murder . . .'

'But you're the King – anointed.' Thomas was murmuring urgently in my ear, trying to tell me something, but I couldn't make it out.

'A smear of oil on my mother's forehead didn't save *her*. Be realistic, Robbie. Even a king can't get away with murder. Well, not one as unpopular as I am, at least.'

'*Get away with murder!* How can you say that? Nobody could ever accuse –'

'It's a figure of speech,' he snapped.

I was still on the floor but leaned forward to put my hands on his knees. 'It wasn't murder. Tom died of neglect and for that we are both guilty.'

'You have to consider how things might seem. Whatever the truth is, people jump to conclusions and there are quite a number who'd be happy to see the back of me if they could find even half a reason . . .' He was silent a moment and I was shot with a bolt of realization.

'You want *me* to take the blame?' My suspicion began to spin out of control. I fixed on his eyes – that twitch: was it a sign of guilt? – asking myself if he had more to hide than I knew about, remembering it was *he* who had employed Mayerne.

'Goodness, no. I merely want the truth to be uncovered.' He patted the back of my hand. It was a cool gesture, patronizing. 'I'm going to have to cut you loose, Robbie.' I felt the floor fall away beneath me. 'You'll leave for Whitehall tomorrow. You can continue to carry out your offices but you will keep your distance from me. Just until the investigation's over. Unless, of course –'

'You think *I* killed him!' Dismay stared me in the face.

'Don't be ridiculous. I know you couldn't harm a fly. But Winwood says your name came up –'

'Oh, God!' I was thinking about the powders I'd sent in. Had they been more harmful than I'd thought? It couldn't be that as I'd sent them in May and he'd died in September and, anyway, Killigrew had assured me they were made up of chalk, nothing else – but if somebody wanted it to look a certain way . . . I couldn't line up my thoughts properly. They were spinning out of my reach. 'Winwood's telling lies. It's a conspiracy. My enemies want to get rid of me. You must know there's nothing in it.' My voice was shrill.

'Everything will become clear in the investigation.'

He sounded stone hard and alarm was taking hold in me. I blurted, 'If anyone killed him it was Northampton.' That man would have been capable of anything. 'He set it all up, put Weston and Elwes in there to do his bidding.'

Horror frothed in my gut. *Oh, God, Tom, what did I allow to happen?*

'Well, Coke will get to the bottom of it.' I couldn't remember if Chief Justice Coke was a friend of the Howards. I thought perhaps he was. 'And you're innocent, so there's nothing to worry about, is there?' His brow was corrugated and I couldn't tell if it was with concern or disbelief.

'You said it yourself. It's how it seems that matters. If people want me . . .' My voice cracked. I was hollowed out with remorse. *Forgive me, Tom, I beg you.*

'You know it's impossible that I do nothing.' He held out a hand. 'For goodness' sake, what are you doing on your knees, soft lad? Sit here.' He indicated the chair beside him. I was relieved to hear the endearment on his lips.

'Look,' he continued, putting an arm over my shoulders. His leg was still jigging. 'Make your peace with the boy.' I was confused, didn't know immediately whom he meant. 'I can't have that kind of tension, not in the light of all this. His elevation doesn't have to diminish your position. You know that, don't you? I'm fond of you, even if you've been impossible lately.' He lifted my fingers to kiss them. His mouth was wet. 'But I'm fond of *him*, too. You have your Frances and I have my George. See?'

I was in turmoil. I wanted to say that it wasn't the same, that Frances didn't visit humiliation on him, as George Villiers's preferment did to me – everyone gleefully hoping it was the first sign of my fall.

'I'll send him to you before you leave and you make your peace. Is that clear?' It was an order but spoken with firm tenderness, as if he was my father, and I felt a little reassured.

I nodded and mumbled a garbled apology. I meant it. I was sorry, very, very sorry for everything. Thomas emerged, toothless and putrid, following me towards the door.

As I left James said: 'Go back to your wife. See that baby born and, before you know it, everything will be back to normal.' I didn't believe him.

I couldn't face my bed, was too disturbed, and sought out

Harry, going from room to room trying to ignore the turned shoulders. Unable to find him, or any other friendly face, I went outside, Thomas still clamped to my back. The weather was balmy, though it was well past ten o'clock, and the moon was up, casting a steely glow over the walls and giving life to inanimate objects in the shadows. I lit my pipe from a nearby torch and took the path through the arch to where the fish-ponds lay.

I slumped on to a bench, inhaling deeply, trying to forget, for a moment at least, the surplus of worries that had begun to silt in me. The night was still and full of sounds: the wet plop as a frog took to the water, the faint crackle of something creeping through the undergrowth, the crunch of footsteps on the path. A figure was approaching, the orange glow of another pipe wavering against a dark shape, short and broad, unmistakable.

'Winwood?' I said.

'Ah, it *is* you. I thought as much. Do you mind if I join you?' Not waiting for my response, he sank on to the bench beside me with a rasping exhalation. 'Peaceful out here. It's chaos upstairs. I'm bedding down with three other fellows. No more room here, and your brother-in-law wasn't expecting me, you see.' He talked on about missing the comforts of home. 'Long time since you lodged at my London house. You were just a boy.'

I wondered why, in the light of the reason he was at Lulworth, he was being so companionable. It set me on my guard, questioning if he had an ulterior motive for bringing up his past generosity.

'Dear Thomas,' he continued, 'you were his protégé then. Strange how Fate works.' He sucked on his pipe. The tobacco fizzled.

'What in God's name do you think you're doing bringing

your trumped-up accusations to the King?' I had meant to keep my cool but found I wasn't able.

'Not *my* accusations.' He was firm. 'You must understand, I was duty-bound to report the allegations.'

'You should have come to me first.' I sounded riled, but not as riled as I felt. 'I was the one who had you installed as secretary.'

'Then you should be pleased I'm fulfilling my duties with such diligence.'

'Listen to me,' I spat. 'If there's been foul play then I'm the first person to want it exposed.'

He remained completely calm. 'I must say, the testament of the apothecary's boy is most compelling. He seems to have been employed by a man named Franklin.'

'Should I know of him?' I was telling the truth but I could sense him listening carefully for a flaw in my voice. 'The only apothecary I know who visited Thomas was Mayerne's man, de Loubell.' As I said it I remembered Mayerne complaining about Thomas having taken remedies he hadn't prescribed.

We fell to silence. A mosquito was whining in the air. I felt it bite my wrist and slapped it dead.

Her

Frances arrived to find the Whitehall apartments silent as the grave. The place smelt of stale tobacco smoke, ash spilled out of the dead fire, and the remains of a rudimentary meal were scattered over the table, as if someone had left in a hurry. She threw her coat over a chair, raising a cloud of dust.

She'd stayed away for as long as she could but eventually it was Harry who insisted she return. Robert needed managing, he'd written:

> *He's out of control, assaulted Villiers, of all people. Villiers had gone to him in friendship but Robert became violent and threatened to break his neck. The King is incensed. Everyone is talking about it. I tried reasoning with Robert, told him the investigation was all founded on rumour and speculation, said they didn't have any tangible evidence and it would all come to nothing. It didn't help and now he's gone to ground, won't see sense. He's even dismissed most of the servants, says they can't be trusted. You need to come back and keep an eye on him before he does us any more damage.*

The only evidence of Robert was a pair of his boots abandoned in the middle of the floor. She called his name, her voice echoing back through the silence, and lumbered through to the bedroom. The growing baby sapped her of strength, rendering her body gross and unwieldy, making her resentful.

She found him lying on the bed, hands folded over his chest, eyes bruised with exhaustion, cheeks pallid. It shocked her to think of the monstrous force of desire she had once felt, the lengths to which she had gone to possess him. For a joyous instant, she thought he might be dead until she noticed the barely discernible rise and fall of his abdomen.

Her immediate thought was how easy it would be to extinguish that breath. But with Uncle gone the finger might point too easily at her. Besides, Robert might yet salvage his reputation. Stranger things had happened. If it came to the worst she would find a way to cut the ties from him, and she still had some dry ammunition: she knew the King's secret. What a fool he'd been to confide in her, but that was Robert: too guileless for her world.

She said his name. His eyes popped open and he made a small cry, as if in terror, before waking fully to see her. 'Thank God you're here. I've been going half mad with worry.' He pawed at her. She resisted the urge to push his hand away. 'They're trying to make it appear that I killed Tom.' He swallowed as if his words were stuck in his throat. 'I don't know what to do.'

'You do nothing. Go about your business in the usual way until it blows over. Your duties as lord chamberlain must be seen to and the Privy Council – you can't just abandon everything. It makes you look like a man with something to hide.'

She could hear Anne in the other room, instructing the servants where to leave the luggage. Anne, too, had been in a state of almost permanent agitation since she'd heard of the investigation. Frances had had to pull her into line more than once. Looking at her husband with counterfeit shock, she exclaimed, '*Have* you something to hide? What is it you're hiding?'

'How could you even ask me that?' He was strung with distress. She wanted to slap him, tell him to be a man. 'You can't think I did it?'

'No, of course not,' she said. He lowered his head against her breast. She stroked his hair, careful to mask the revulsion his weakness induced in her. The baby moved – something trapped inside. 'You must make your peace with Villiers. Apologize, disarm him with friendship.'

'I fear it's too late for that,' he whimpered into her neck.

She paused, tempering her tone. 'Remember, Robert, you still hold high office. You are the Earl of Somerset. You are lord privy seal. Lord high chamberlain.' She wanted him to sit up, to find his fight. 'If it's too late for reconciliation with that fop Villiers, then show the King that you're indispensable. You're still the one he trusts with state duties. He clearly has some residue of fondness for you. Love cannot be blown out like a candle.' But that wasn't true. 'The embers are still burning. Rekindle it.'

They didn't speak for a while, until she added, 'For the sake of our baby.'

He seemed a little renewed by the thought, began to talk about what they would name the child, when Anne appeared.

'What is it?' Frances asked.

'I need you to come.' She looked ashen.

Robert began to get up but Anne met Frances's eye with a minuscule shake of the head.

'Women's problems,' she said, planting a kiss on her husband's head. 'I'll be back shortly.'

'Whatever's the matter?' Frances asked, once they were in the corridor.

'Franklin's here again.'

'I suppose he wants the rest of his money. Get rid of him, Anne. Tell him I'll have it sent.'

'No, it's not that, it's – it's – it's –' Anne was falling to pieces, and Frances had to use all her self-restraint not to lose patience with her.

'Where is he? I hope no one saw him.'

They crossed the hall. Ugly little carved faces looked down from the beams and her husband's portrait followed them with its eyes. Larkin had spotted Robert's failing: his yearning to be liked. It was in the dog-like hopefulness of his painted expression.

They entered the music room, a small, rarely used chamber off the hall. Franklin was inside, slumped on a stool. The room smelt strongly of the beeswax used to polish the instruments. He stood as the women entered, taking a step towards them. He was wearing a moulded leather mask over his rotten nose, which, rather than improving his looks, made him seem more menacing. Anne locked the door.

'What do you think you're doing coming here?' Frances was firm. His stance told her it was a matter of importance. She hadn't believed it possible for a man like Franklin to appear scared but his eyes flitted restlessly as flies and he worried at a button on his waistcoat until it came off in his hand.

'I wasn't seen,' he said.

Someone coughed beyond the door. A floorboard creaked, followed by the quiet shuffle of footsteps. Frances put her index finger over her lips to indicate silence and sat down at the set of virginals that had been a gift from the King in better days.

As she lifted the lid a small gold moth flew out, fluttering aimlessly before alighting on the wall where she stamped her thumb on it, smearing its dusty remains down the panelling.

She began to play, explaining quietly that the music would mask their conversation, saying to Franklin, 'If anyone sees you when you leave, you're the tuner. Now, tell me why you're here?'

'Weston's been arrested.'

Her playing faltered but she forced herself to continue. It

was an unremittingly jolly tune, the sort of thing a child might play. Anne, across the room, was rocking back and forth with vacant eyes. Frances pictured Weston, his bulk and broad shoulders and the white scar that embroidered his face. He was the sort that could withstand anything.

She pasted a look of confusion on to her face. 'What – the man Uncle employed as Overbury's guard? Wasn't he *your* servant before that, Anne?' Frances imagined rolling the ball and them all tumbling like skittles. 'What do you know?' she asked Franklin.

'He was questioned by Coke and can't have given much away because Secretary Winwood and two others went in this morning to question him again.'

She quizzed him as to how he knew this and he told her – with a slight air of smugness, she thought – that he had a connection with Winwood's page, who had been present while the interrogation was taking place. Frances was impressed by his resourcefulness but didn't allow it to show. 'What else did this page tell you?'

'That Weston held out. He maintained that Overbury caught a chill, sitting too long in the window, and that was what did for him.'

Her fingers continued to dance, repeating the simple refrain over and over. 'That's good.' The mention of Overbury had caused Anne to whimper.

'But they broke him down,' continued Franklin. 'Weston eventually told them about a phial of poison and that Mistress Turner had instructed him to administer it.' Anne made a groan and clapped her hands to her head.

'Did he mention my great-uncle?' asked Frances. Franklin shook his head. 'But they must have asked who was giving instructions. No one could possibly think Anne was acting on her own.' She paused the music, making a brief silence for her words to sink in, then added, as if it was something she'd just thought of, 'I hope to goodness you destroyed that letter he wrote you, Franklin.' She watched as mention of the letter that had never existed caused a twinge of panic on his face.

'After I saw you last I searched for it. Couldn't find it.'

'I expect you got rid of it at the time.' She felt heady with it all, as if she had climbed inside his head and stolen his memories, replacing them with lies. 'You can't have wanted to keep something like that lying around.'

'Of course I did!' He was indignant, as if she'd called him a fool to his face, his pride getting the better of him.

'What else did Weston say?'

'Nothing more.'

Frances imagined what they might have done to Weston, wondered if they'd beaten him or stretched him yet. She'd heard of a knotted rope that interrogators tied around the temples and tightened. A new thought was forming, making her heart palpitate, as her fingers trotted out the chorus once more, a plan that might solve everything.

She saw then, with absolute clarity, what she would do. The idea had been lurking for some time but indistinctly, like pond life seen in glimpses through surface ripples. Now the water was still, revealing the drifting masses of cloudy spawn, the golden flit of fish threading through tangled weed and, in the very depths, the shifty slink of the eels.

She plastered concern over her face and turned to Franklin. 'My *husband*'s name didn't come up when Weston was questioned, as far as you know, did it?'

'No.' Franklin seemed surprised. 'Why?'

'I was worried about something he wrote to me at the time. When Overbury had already been incarcerated for a while. It's been playing on my mind.' She held her hands still, as if too distressed to continue playing. 'He was very close

291

with my great-uncle, you see. And he wrote something in a letter that I didn't fully understand.' She began to play again, slower, more awkwardly, occasionally striking a wrong key. 'No, it can't have been anything sinister . . .' Frances watched Franklin's interest ignite. He thought he was the canniest person in the room. It made her want to laugh and crush his pride, just as she'd crushed that moth.

'What did he write?' asked Franklin, all ears.

'No, it's not important.' She allowed the silence to hang, tantalizing him.

'Tell me.'

As if it had been squeezed from her, she mumbled, 'He wrote that he couldn't believe the business had not yet been dispatched. That word, *dispatched*, seems suspicious in the light of . . . Oh, you know.' She wiped her hand slowly over her brow, saying, 'It was innocent, *I'm sure*,' inflecting the words with a questioning upward lift. 'Like the dispatch of a letter, or some other harmless thing, don't you think? It couldn't be anything more, could it?' She momentarily stopped playing again to place a hand over her mouth, as if something terrible had just occurred to her.

'Your *husband* wrote such a thing?'

Nodding slowly, she allowed the information to percolate in Franklin's mind, then said, 'I can't believe he has any stain of guilt on him – not Robert.' She was a perfect, besotted wife, unable to see even the slightest flaw in her spouse. Franklin's eyebrows rose minutely, giving away his disbelief. He was as easy to play as the instrument beneath her fingers.

'They'll want to talk to both of you.' She changed the subject abruptly. 'You must admit nothing.'

Anne still had her head buried in her hands. 'Anne, look at me. I need to know that you've heard. I'll do my best to clear up this mess that Uncle has left you with, but you *have* to cooperate.' Anne lifted her eyes then, regarding Frances with a dead expression. 'If you don't, they might hang *me* – you wouldn't want that on your conscience, would you? I will *not* be made to pay for Uncle's deeds.'

Anne looked horrified, Franklin too, and Frances was glad that her great-uncle was no longer there to refute what she had said.

'No.' Anne was suddenly animated. 'It's *me* who'll hang. I was the one . . .'

'It was Uncle who forced you into it, Anne. You must explain it to them when you're questioned. They'll understand – you had no choice.'

From the side of her eye Frances watched her words register in Franklin's expression, as she played a final verse, the notes marching like an armed guard through the room.

A blessed silence descended and she took Anne's hands, meeting her distressed gaze, saying in a whisper, 'Hold your nerve. Uncle got you into this and *I'm* going to get you out of it.' She tightened her grip. 'Do you trust me?' Anne mumbled that she did, of course she did, that she'd known Frances since she was a child, how could she not?

Frances released her and began to play again, a different tune, more dirge-like to go with the atmosphere. How credulous people were, how easily convinced. It had been the same when she had made Anne believe all the orders had come from Uncle: notes written in his looping hand, initialled 'H.N.' for Henry Northampton, requesting Anne to acquire poisons from Franklin: a drop of this and a drop of that to send to Weston, or to add to the jam. *Frances mustn't ever know*, the notes always insisted. It had been almost child's play.

The thought of it made her feel vast and invincible, as if she held enough power to harness the winds.

Him

Frances's return was like a salve, smoothing over my despair. She began to undress, asking me to help her. I untied her laces and her clothes came away, layer by layer, until she was in nothing but her undergarments.

'Here!' She took hold of my hand, lifted her shift to bare the great moon of her belly and placed it there. 'It's moving.'

To feel that blessed life, a form unfolding, beneath her surface and know it to be our baby quietened the bicker of dread that had been my constant companion. I covered her with a blanket. Winter was settling in.

'Only a couple more months and December will be on us.'

She was referring to the birth, but thinking of the future made all my fears into a cacophony once more. 'I hope to God I'll still be here.'

'You have to stop thinking like this.'

'But there are so many things – things that could be construed to make me seem guilty.'

In the flicker of the candle I saw Thomas's disembodied face, grim with contempt. *You could have saved me.* I blew it out.

In the dark, it seemed easier to talk. 'There's something you need to know, Frances.' I felt her tense, as if afraid of what I was about to divulge. 'I don't know what to do. Will you hear me out without judgement?'

She said of course she would, and I began to tell her of the powders I had sent in to Overbury. 'He asked for them. To make him sicken, in the hope of provoking the King's sympathy, so he might be released. I didn't at first – I thought it a terrible idea.'

'What on God's earth made you do that?' She half sat up, shifting away from me.

'I didn't want to.' I sounded desperate, feeling intensely the space opening up between us. 'But eventually I relented. What I sent wouldn't have had the power to harm a mouse, but it looks bad.' It was a relief to confess, like a boil lanced.

She began to speak but I was determined she would hear what I had to say in its entirety so, finding some dregs of assertiveness from the maelstrom in my head, I told her I hadn't finished. 'And there is a great deal of correspondence between Northampton and myself. In some of the letters we discussed Thomas's imprisonment, how we meant to prolong it deliberately until the nullity was dealt with. And there are others from Thomas in which he described the state of his health. To be honest, I can't remember what was in them all and I'm worried they might contain things that could be misconstrued.'

Her hand reached back across the space to me. I held it tight. 'Where are they, these letters?'

'That's the trouble. I gave them to Sir Robert Cotton for safekeeping.' I'd been such a fool for not holding on to them.

'You trust this Cotton? Who is he?'

'As much as I trust anyone. He's responsible for organizing most of my correspondence.'

'Tell him to burn them.'

'*Burn them?* All of them?'

'I suppose –' I heard her head shift on the pillow. 'No, forget that.'

'What? Tell me what you suppose.' I was desperate to know what idea she was so reluctant to share. Frances always had the answer to everything.

'You could see if Cotton, or someone, might keep one or two of the letters. For example, those in which Overbury speaks of his condition. If there are any in which he remarked that his health was improving, you might ask Cotton . . .' She paused. 'No, I never said that. It's a bad idea.'

'Let me be the judge. Finish what you were saying, Frances – please.'

'You could ask Cotton to have the dates altered, to make it absolutely clear that Overbury was feeling better after you sent him those powders.'

'It's the truth. Tom *was* feeling better.'

'Well, then, it wouldn't even be subterfuge to change one or two dates by a few weeks. But it must be done properly – by an expert. I think Uncle knew of a man – I'll try to remember his name. That way, if it ever comes to it – which I very much doubt it will but if it does – then nothing can be misinterpreted.'

'My God, Frances, you never cease to amaze me.' She had dragged me back from the abyss.

'I've done nothing. It's all you.'

'We'll come through this stronger.' I felt it already, her potent efficiency pouring into me, making me newly resilient.

'It goes without saying that any letters casting doubt on Uncle's motives should be kept. I know he's no longer here to defend himself but . . .' She left her words hanging.

'What do you mean, his *motives*?' She had as good as confirmed my long-held suspicions about that monstrous man.

'What did you think, Robert?' She clutched her hand around my back, coiling herself into me. 'He put Overbury in the Tower, as far as I can tell. I'm not having *you* taking the blame for him. The idea of having to live without you is . . . is . . .' Her voice was trembling. 'It's inconceivable.'

'My poor, poor Frances. Don't cry.' I knew then that I could stand up to every last one of my enemies. 'He's gone now, and we have each other, my darling.'

Her

They arrived just before dawn, two weeks after Franklin's visit. Frances was lying awake, listening to the song of a lone blackbird when she heard the horses. She slipped from the bed, quietly pulling on her clothes. For a moment, she thought they might have come to arrest her and had to remind herself that she wasn't under suspicion. Robert half woke, groggy and confused. She told him to go back to sleep, slipping down to the hall before they began banging on the door and woke the whole household.

Four men entered, all armed. They seemed embarrassed that the pregnant lady of the house had answered the door, making effusive apologies for having disturbed her. They had come for Anne. Frances offered them her most beguiling smile, asking if they would mind waiting a few minutes, to spare Anne the indignity of being arrested in her nightgown.

Anne was still asleep, in peaceful ignorance, her pale hair spread on the pillow. Frances shook her gently. She sat up, startled, tensing as she remembered her situation. 'Why are you here?' It was clear, from the fear daubed over her face, that she knew why.

Frances opened the curtains. It was barely light and the windows were frosted with an intricate pattern of icy stars. She prodded the embers of the fire and tipped on some kindling to combat the chill before sitting and taking Anne's hand. 'I need you to stay calm.'

'They've come for me, haven't they?'

'You mustn't worry. It'll just be a few questions. That's all.' Anne's nails dug into her flesh. 'I'm going to make sure you want for nothing and that they don't hold you for longer than is absolutely necessary. I'll put up the bond for your release.'

'I'm frightened.' She looked blighted – green with fear. 'Frightened of what they'll do to me if I deny all knowledge.'

'They won't torture a woman.' She felt Anne flinch.

Frances got her up and began to dress her. She was reminded of all the times Anne had dressed and attended to her in childhood, treated her as if she was her own child.

'What if I have to lie? They'll see right through me.' The eye-rolling and hand-wringing made her look quite mad.

'Listen to me.' Frances reined in the urge to shake her and held her firmly with a look. 'This is important. If you *must* lie, then give something small away. A nugget of truth – something that compromises you only in an insignificant way. Then they will be more likely to believe anything else you have to say. Disguise your deceit with a veneer of truth. Do you hear me?'

Anne nodded meekly, like a child awaiting a beating.

'Now,' Frances continued, 'I want you looking splendid.' She pulled a saffron ruff from the shelf and began to tie it around Anne's neck.

But she tugged at it. 'Won't they think me brazen in this? Shouldn't I wear a plain collar?'

'No.' Frances was insistent, tying the tapes tightly into a double bow. 'You must look like a woman of breeding. I won't have you put in a commoner's cell. I'm going to get you something. Wait here while I fetch it.'

Frances rummaged in her jewel box for the diamond ring, the one that had caused all the trouble with Mary Woods. She threaded a length of tape through its shank before returning to find Anne scrutinizing her own upturned palm, as if she might find an answer there to what was happening. 'Can you see anything?' She held her hand out to Frances. 'I can't see my future any more.'

'Don't be silly.' Frances pulled her to her feet to comb her hair back under a cap. 'Remember not to hang your head. You mustn't seem ashamed. You must appear as if you have nothing to hide. And whatever they threaten, say nothing. Say you know nothing.'

'You don't understand,' Anne said. 'I don't have your courage.'

'I'll be with you in spirit. When you feel yourself weaken, remember that. And there's this.' She tied the ring round Anne's neck, tucking it out of sight beneath her clothes before Anne was able to see what it was. 'It's a ring, if you need funds.' Anne tried to protest but Frances wouldn't allow it.

Finally, she stood back. Anne looked perfect, but her expression was blurred with fear, like a painting finished to the finest detail save for the face.

'I curse the day I ever set eyes on your great-uncle.' Her voice was barely audible.

'I know. And we are left to mop up his sins.' Frances led her to the door. 'Now you must eat something. I won't allow you to go anywhere on an empty stomach.'

The kitchen was deserted, the servants still not up, and Frances forced her to drink a cup of milk and eat a little of yesterday's bread. It was there that Anne told her about a box of letters that she feared might incriminate her.

'How do you know of it?'

'Franklin told me yesterday. It came out when Weston was questioned. I didn't know he'd kept them.' Her voice shook. 'He offered them as a makeweight for lenience.'

'So much for your loyal servant Weston, dragging you into this to save his own skin.' Frances took a gulp of milk. It was unpleasantly sharp, on the turn. 'What can the letters possibly say that is so bad?' She mustered all her reserves of patience in the face of Anne's fragmented composure.

'I fear they are the notes I sent him with the – the –' Anne seemed incapable of saying the word 'poisons' and eventually said 'remedies' in its place. 'The directions of what exactly they were and how they were to be administered. My handwriting is so distinctive, I can't deny I wrote them.'

'Oh, Anne! Why ever weren't they burned? Uncle has left a hellish chaos in his wake.' Frances controlled her exasperation to ask coolly, 'What else was discussed in those letters? We need to be sure of your safety.'

'Nothing, I think. Nothing of importance.' She was feverishly rolling a morsel of bread in her fingers.

'No mention of me?' Frances tossed it in as if it were barely significant enough to mention.

'Only in passing, I think.' Anne's breath was thin.

'In passing?'

The ball of bread was grey from her kneading. 'I can't remember, really.'

Frances could hear the soft pump of blood in her ears. 'And where are these letters?'

'At Weston's house. I went there last night, as soon as I heard of it, but his son wouldn't admit me.'

'You went there? You should have told me.' Frances wondered how many more such letters there were in existence and exactly what Anne had meant by, *Only in passing, I think.* It didn't inspire confidence. She would have to get her hands on those letters before Winwood and Coke. 'I'll see to it that they're destroyed. Is there anything else that proves your involvement?'

Tears ran silently down Anne's face. 'What if Franklin speaks out?'

'If he does he's a dead man.' Frances noticed that the edge of Anne's cuff had dipped in her cup of milk and imagined how rancid it would smell in a few hours. 'He provided all the poisons, didn't he?'

'I curse the day you first led me to that Dr Forman and his vile assistant.' She lifted her eyes. They were bloodshot.

Frances leaned over the table, taking both the other woman's hands, speaking softly, 'You're not remembering, Anne. Distress has muddled you and you need to recall everything clearly if you are to be questioned. I didn't take you there. It was *you* who sought out Forman.'

'But . . .' Anne seemed unable to find her words.

'Don't you remember? You wanted Arthur to propose to you. I only went along with you for support.' Anne was shaking her head but Frances could see she was beginning to doubt her memory. Fear had addled her. 'It's not surprising you're confused. Such a terrible business – Forman's death. And you were so close to him.'

Anne was rubbing her eyes. 'I'm in such a mess.'

'I know, I know.' Frances's tone was soothing. 'Just stay silent on the matter. No one needs to know you consulted Forman, or Franklin, or anyone else of their ilk. And if Franklin starts to sing, who will believe *him* over you?' Anne was puffing out short, shallow breaths. 'Hold yourself together. I'll make sure you're home to see the birth of this one.' Frances patted her belly. 'Trust me.'

'They'll hang me, Frances.'

'Of course they won't.' She met Anne's distress with a smile. 'Listen, Weston's a lost cause now and Franklin can be sacrificed, if need be.' In response to Anne's look of shock she saw she'd gone too far and added, 'Desperate times call for desperate measures. Don't you understand? It's either *you* or *him*.'

Anne had begun to quake. Frances held her firmly by the shoulders. 'Listen to me, Weston's already tried to implicate you and don't imagine that monster Franklin will do you any favours either – he's a man who trades in poison, for God's sake. Open your eyes, Anne. This is about *your* survival now.'

'But I *am* guilty. I did everything your great-uncle asked of me without question.' She was racked with sobs. 'I'm going to Hell.'

Frances waited, before saying, 'Uncle was a wicked man who coerced you. You only did as he said. You were terrified of him. We all were.'

Anne calmed down eventually and Frances led her from the kitchen into the hall, where the guards took hold of her, shoving her towards the door.

'Let her go,' Frances barked. 'You should be ashamed of yourselves, treating a woman in such a way. Mistress Turner will go with you without a fuss.' They obeyed her command without hesitation.

Anne went in silence, but as she passed through the door she glanced back at Frances with a look of sheer terror.

It was the identical look that Frances's little mirror image had worn when she was pleading for her life to be spared.

Him

'Wake up. Wake up, Robert.' Frances was shaking me urgently. I had a vague memory of having already been disturbed that morning. 'Something's happened.' I pulled myself up, dazed with sleep. She placed my writing box on my lap, drawing the bed curtains wide so the light streamed in, temporarily blinding me. 'I need you to sign a warrant permitting a search of Weston's house. I've called for Harry to witness it.'

'I don't understand?' I was still fuzzy with sleep. 'Why?' She took out a sheet of paper and a pen, dipping it and holding it out for me to take. Black spots dripped on the sheets.

'Weston's being held and now Anne's been arrested.'

In my head, I was running through the several Annes we knew. 'You mean your Anne?'

'Of course my Anne!'

'But whatever for?'

'I don't know, Robert. She thinks there might be letters at Weston's house that make it seem as if she was involved.'

'Involved in what?' I couldn't make sense of what she was saying.

'Thomas Overbury's death, of course.' She sounded impatient, annoyed by my sluggish understanding, but I supposed her distressed by events. She and Anne Turner were as close as sisters. The whole business was encroaching on our world, creeping in through the cracks, like a noxious smoke.

'*Was* she involved?'

'*No.*' Frances seemed appalled by my question. 'But Weston worked for Anne, before – before . . . You know.'

I did know. Before Northampton had employed him as Thomas's gaoler. I was beginning to see the web of connections around Thomas's death that had previously been invisible to me. I knew that Northampton had employed Anne Turner years before, as Frances's nurse, and – it struck me like a jab to the gut – also much more recently, as her companion. It was becoming increasingly clear that, as I had suspected, Northampton was the spider at the heart of the web – a wider web than I'd ever believed. All the threads ended with him. 'What exactly is in the letters?'

She threw up her hands. 'I'm as confused as you, Robert. But Anne insisted that those letters will send her to the gallows.' She looked at me, her eyes glossy with distress. 'We can't let that happen. I don't *care* if she's guilty. I have to do everything I can to save her.'

It seemed impossible to think of the angelic Anne Turner being involved in such a heinous deed. 'Even if she is' – thoughts were still forming in my mind – 'then surely she can only be guilty of acting on another's orders.' I didn't feel I could mention Northampton by name. Frances might have broken down altogether if I'd suggested her great-uncle was guilty of more than merely ensuring Thomas's incarceration.

'Please just write it, I'm begging you. We can't lose any time. We can't risk the investigators getting their hands on them. I can't lose Anne.' She was pawing at my shoulder. I found myself strangely renewed. Beside my wife, who was normally so contained and resourceful, needing – desperately needing – me to take the reins, I felt in control.

'I don't know about this.' My pen hovered above the paper. A concern was nagging at me.

'You don't know about what?' She sounded on the brink of despair.

'If there's a warrant with my seal on it, it may reflect badly on me – make it seem that I have something to hide.'

'I don't see why.' She had calmed down and was running her hand over my back. I could feel the firm curve of her swollen belly against my shoulder and thought of the life growing there. 'As a Privy Council member, you must sign warrants all the time. Such things are part of your official responsibilities, aren't they? And my brother as a witness. It'll be quite correct.'

She was right. But still I hesitated.

'You're behaving like a guilty man, Robert.' She jumped back, snatching her hands away from me, looking at me, seemingly horrified. 'I don't want to believe you were involved. Not *you*. Not my Robert.'

'No.' It was not the first time she had looked on me with doubt in recent weeks. 'Of course not.'

'I'm sorry. It's just I'm mad with worry.' She slumped against my shoulder. 'Robert, I *need* you.'

The way she said it, as if her very existence depended on me, touched me more profoundly than anything she had ever said or done before. I felt an inner rage boil for the man who had broken her. If he hadn't been dead already, I would have marched then and there to Northampton House and run my sword through his ribs right to the hilt.

'I need you,' she repeated, in a whisper.

'I know, my darling, I know.' I imagined Northampton's warm blood soaking into my cuff. I wrote out the warrant, signed my name, and she heated the wax, dripping it over the paper for me to push my seal into it.

'Dress yourself. I can hear Harry arriving.'

I pulled on some clothes. She opened the window to tell her brother she was coming down, then whipped away the paper and rushed out of the door with it while I struggled to get my boots on.

Harry was already countersigning the warrant when I arrived in the hall, sealing it with his arms beside my own. I'd always known, from the way he looked at her and hung on her words, that Harry Howard idolized his sister. He smiled – a copy of her smile – rose and pressed me into a hug, patting my back, saying, 'We're going to have to make haste to Royston.'

'To Royston?' I was confused and listening with one ear to Frances, who was briefing two of the servants to go and search Weston's house.

'Any letters, any written matter at all, bring it back to me,' she was saying, as she bundled them out of the door. 'Quick as you can.'

Harry was explaining: 'I've just heard that Coke left for Royston yesterday. He's gone to ask the King if he can appoint the lord chancellor for help with the investigation. Ellesmere is an enemy of the Howards. It's clear what's going on.'

I wished it were as clear to me as it was to Harry. 'I don't understand.'

'Can't you see?' he snapped. 'They're trying to bring us all down – starting with you. We've got to stop them. You must persuade the King not to sanction Ellesmere's appointment.'

'Why would he listen to me? I doubt he'd even let me see him.'

'You can say you've come to make amends. Think, it's what he wants – to have you back in the fold. Get on your knee, tell him you'll apologize to Villiers. It'll make him happy.'

'But it's a full day's ride to Royston.' The fall of the Howards was being masterfully orchestrated, all Northampton's people under arrest, another enemy brought in to investigate and me at the heart of it. Fear churned through me.

'Coke left yesterday by carriage and he'll certainly have

stopped for the night. It's not yet eight. If we make haste we might even get there before him.' He was already striding towards the door. 'I have horses waiting ready in the yard.'

I turned to Frances, a forlorn figure standing beneath my portrait, loath to leave her in such a state of distress and so heavily pregnant. But she insisted I go. 'Don't worry about me, my love. This is far more important. I can manage without you for a day or so.' My wife had hidden reserves of stoicism I could only dream of.

We arrived at Royston, exhausted. I had some trouble gaining admittance and was left loitering in the hall while a message was sent up to James. Once I was allowed in I found him with Villiers, laughing together at some private joke. They were both in their riding clothes, spattered head to toe in mud. On seeing me, Villiers stood, dipping his head in respect. His pointed politeness was an irritant but I tried not to let myself be distracted from my mission by my festering animosity.

'Give us a moment, would you, George?' the King said, and Villiers obediently left by the door to the bedchamber that used to be mine – that same room into which Thomas had burst four years before. Images from that encounter were swirling through my head and I wondered whether, had that not happened, Fate might have followed a different path. A fire roared in the hearth. I was still frozen from the journey and my fingers began to thaw painfully.

'You look terrible, Robbie.' The affection in his voice gave me a trickle of hope. 'Now, what can I do for you?'

'Your Majesty –'

He held up his hand to silence me. 'Come now, there's no need for that formality. We are alone. I think you can call me by my given name, don't you?'

I wanted to burst out in tears of relief. He poured a cup of something, holding it out for me to take.

'I know I have not been a good servant to you and I want to make amends.' I sounded pathetic, pleading. 'I intend to reform myself. I want to apologize to Villiers.' I sipped the drink. It was warm and sweet.

He was calm, without the tics and jitters he displayed when he was anxious or overburdened. I should have been glad but I assumed his contentment was derived from the company of George Villiers. 'I'm glad you've come to your senses, Robbie – very glad.' He probed me with a look. 'Is there something else?'

'I believe Chief Justice Coke has been to see you.'

'Yes, only this afternoon. His visit prevented me changing out of my dirty clothes and now you are here, so I am still covered in filth.' He laughed but I had the impression that he was annoyed by all the disturbances.

'I understand he is seeking to appoint Ellesmere to the investigatory commission.' I tried to make myself sound staunch.

'That's correct. There has been a plethora of revelations about your friend's death and the case is becoming far too complex for Coke to manage alone. It's of the utmost importance it is all looked into properly. Now it's been set in motion, I can't be seen to be preventing the correct course of justice. I'm sure you agree.'

I realized I knew very little about the revelations he talked of and feared greatly all the aspersions that must have been cast my way. The blame would be forced on me and I would have no way to defend myself.

'Coke has made inroads,' he continued, 'talked to a great many people. I'm told that Overbury's servant, I forget his name, had some very interesting things to say about you.' He was running a finger slowly back and forth over his bottom lip. I couldn't read him as I used to.

'Lawrence Davies? What can he possibly have said about me?' My voice came out high-pitched, like a child telling a lie.

'He said that it was *you* who advised Overbury to refuse the embassy to Moscow.'

My head was thrown into a spin. I was back in Thomas's lodgings on the last occasion I saw him alive. He was in despair and terrified that misfortune would befall him on his journey to Russia. I remembered then that Davies was in and out, serving us drinks and clearing plates while we talked. I racked my brains for what I'd said, but it was all a blur.

As if he could read my mind, the King spoke: 'The fellow told Coke that you said of the embassy, "Don't go. Go to the Tower and we will get you out." Is that what you said?'

'Yes, something to that effect. But it's been taken out of context.' I was trying not to sound as desperate as I felt. 'I had gone to Overbury to persuade him to *accept* the embassy.' I was reminded that I'd promised Davies a position and done nothing about it, so there would be no goodwill towards me from that quarter.

I felt off kilter, as if I might collapse. I wondered if Davies had more – letters, perhaps, written evidence – that could throw me in a shady light and made a mental note to contact him, offer him something to mitigate his bad opinion of me. 'You know' – I wanted to use James's name, but something in his expression told me not to, despite what he'd said earlier – 'we both wanted Overbury out of the country before he spilled any secrets.'

'If you speak for *me* then you are mistaken.' His tone was imperious as he shot me a frozen look, and I had to use all the will-power I could muster to hold myself together.

'I didn't mean to offend you. I humbly beg your pardon – shouldn't have put words into your mouth.'

'Oh, Robbie, what has happened to you?' His face softened and I wondered if I'd imagined that frosty glare.

'This was all Northampton's doing,' I blurted. 'Your investigators will discover that he's the one with Thomas's blood on his hands.'

'I think we both know that the whole business is more complicated than that.' He smiled, as if I was a child, or an idiot. 'Now, tell me why Ellesmere should not be appointed to the inquiry.'

I was glad the conversation had turned to the topic I had come to discuss. 'I fear he will attempt to skew it unnecessarily. Ellesmere is known to have a great antipathy for the Howards – and for me in particular.'

'I know him to be exceedingly reliable.' James was nodding thoughtfully.

'The Howards will feel alienated if Ellesmere's appointed. They're your most loyal servants and wield such great power.'

'Are you telling me who I should trust now? Do you think my judgement skewed?'

I felt myself slipping out of his orbit. 'I beg you to reconsider. I will feel I have lost your favour and –'

He interrupted me, saying that nothing had been decided yet, refusing to talk further on the matter. He began to describe the hunt in detail and it felt like it always had before, which allayed my worries a little, until he told me he had made Villiers his master of the horse.

'So, the rumours are true.' I lost my self-control, blurting out, 'Can't you see what's happening? My enemies have dealt Villiers up to you. They want me ousted, and you've fallen for it.' It was spilling from me. 'At least when you chose *me* it was a free choice.' I was almost shouting. 'There was no faction pulling *my* strings. I truly cared, as if – as if . . .' My words died. I couldn't say, *As if you were my father.* He didn't want to think that my love for him had sprung not from passion but from an orphan's need for paternal care.

I was surprised to see he was smiling and concluded that he must have enjoyed my jealousy. 'Don't sulk, Robbie. Haven't I given you enough? I gave you Frances Howard, and goodness knows how much trouble that's caused. I gave you a multitude of honours. I privileged you above all others.' He tweaked me under the chin, scraping me with the sharp edge of his ring.

When I opened the door to leave, Villiers stepped back as if he'd been listening. He had his back against the wall and I stood close enough to make him uncomfortable. 'Hear anything interesting?'

All his careful manners fell away as he grabbed me roughly by the arm. 'Leave us alone. Nobody wants you here.'

I laughed. 'Oh, you're full of yourself now, but you won't last.'

He loosened his grip slightly. 'Why don't you go back to your whore?'

With my free hand, I punched him sharply under the ribs making him double over with a groan. 'Seems you're a better dancer than a fighter,' I said, as I walked away, quite confident he'd keep quiet about our little exchange, that he'd be afraid to look a coward.

It was too late to begin our return journey so Harry and I stayed the night. In the morning, when we were readying to leave James was affectionate, kissing both my cheeks. Villiers had made himself scarce, I noticed, feeling a little twinge of victory.

James's last words to me were, 'I'll send news about my decision on Ellesmere soon but' – and he looked me in the eye as he said it – 'there's no need to worry about a thing.'

Consequently, Harry and I were jubilant on the road home. But we had barely been back at Whitehall an hour when a messenger arrived with a letter. It bore the King's seal. Frances and Harry watched – two pairs of matching eyes – as I opened and read it.

I felt the blood drop from my face and had to sit.

'What is it?' asked Harry. 'What does it say?'

I couldn't find a way to tell them. The King must have had the letter written even when he was making the performance of bidding me goodbye, kissing me, looking me in the eye and telling me I hadn't a thing to worry about. It had all been an act to be rid of me without a scene.

'Let me read it.' Frances took the letter, scanning it. 'He thinks you should be happy to have someone as thorough as Ellesmere investigating. "If you are innocent" – what's he insinuating? *If you are innocent.* Oh, and he says,' she began to read aloud, '*You are not behaving like a man who wants an honest trial of the facts.* He's as good as accusing you.'

She passed the letter to Harry. 'What do *you* think?' It was done with a genuine desire for her brother's opinion but to me it felt like an infringement of my privacy, as if I myself were being opened and inspected. I insisted he hand it back to me.

He shrugged. 'I'm not the enemy, Robert.'

One of the servants interrupted us with a note for Frances. 'Oh, God.' She thrust a hand to her head. 'Franklin's been arrested now.'

'Who?' I asked.

She looked at me without saying anything for a moment, as if confused. 'I'm not entirely sure who he is either, but he's some connection of Anne's.'

Frances was suddenly as white as bone. 'We've got to get Anne out of there.' Her look made me think she must have been envisaging her friend on the gallows, which put an image of it in my mind too – that angelic-looking woman with a noose about her neck.

'Was the box of letters found?' I asked, remembering how anxious Frances had been for me to sign the warrant on the previous morning – it seemed a lifetime ago.

She nodded. 'I burned them.' She was pointing to the fire. 'But if Weston testifies to what they contained Anne will hardly be better off. Can't we at least put up a bond to bail her out?'

'Leave it to me,' said Harry.

'I'll see to it,' I snapped.

'I'm only trying to help.' He scowled, turning away dismissively.

'Don't be like that, Harry.' Frances's tone was firm and she took hold of my elbow in a gesture of solidarity. 'Don't forget Robert's one of us.'

It dawned on me in that moment that I was only one of the Howards while it remained convenient for them. I wondered when they would start to regard Frances and me as a spent force and cut us adrift. The thought made me feel sick. But with my wife by my side, I could withstand anything.

Her

Frances couldn't concentrate on the play. It was one of Webster's so she knew it would end with pigs' blood all over the floor. Her mind was too busy and her baby too restless. It had grown so large, a parasite, pushing upward, giving her heartburn, and prodding painfully at her liver. She longed for it to be out of her. Robert, though, would gaze in wonder at the vast protrusion, stretched tight as a drum. He liked to sing it lullabies. It seemed to be the only pastime that relieved his almost permanent anxiety.

Looking around she noticed there wasn't an inch of yellow lace in sight. It was only a matter of months since they'd been falling over themselves to get their hands on one of Anne Turner's saffron ruffs. Robert hadn't managed to secure her release. Frances had been confident of this and sure, too, that his attempts would seem suspicious.

Anne had been surprisingly stalwart and kept tight-lipped even after a month of incarceration but Frances knew it was only a matter of time before she succumbed. There were already rumblings of witchcraft surrounding her. Once those took hold Anne would be doomed, of that Frances had no doubt. Would they hang her, she wondered, or burn her?

The men had shown none of Anne's fortitude. Some servant or other was always happy to take a shilling in return for a little information, and in this way Harry had managed to glean snippets of what was being revealed in the interrogations. He told her that Franklin, in particular, had sung like a canary in a bid to save himself.

'He's no good, that Franklin – divulged something about your husband,' Harry had told her only the previous evening, in a whispered conversation. 'Said that Robert had written a letter, when Overbury was in the Tower. It said –'

Frances finished his sentence for him. 'That he "wondered how long before the business would be dispatched".' She laughed inwardly. That man monster, who'd believed himself so resourceful, had played right into her hands.

'How do you know that?' Harry was surprised.

Frances raised her eyebrows. 'I might have been the recipient of that letter.'

'Is that so?' He seemed impressed by his sister's calm.

'Don't tell Robert. He'll only fret about it and I'm sure it can be explained away.' Her husband's slow unravelling gave her a sense of her own power, as if his loss was her gain.

The sound of rain was heavy on the roof, making it difficult to hear the players speak their lines from the back of the hall where Frances was sitting. A current of air passed over her and she turned to see the door was slightly open. No one else seemed to notice her sister Lizzie standing there, out of breath and soaked to the skin, beckoning her with some urgency.

Frances slid from her seat, and as she tiptoed towards her sister, a hiatus in the downpour allowed her to hear:

> *Other sins only speak; murder shrieks out.*
> *The element of water moistens the earth*
> *But blood flies upwards, and bedews the heavens.*

It occurred to her that the staging of that particular play might have been a deliberate attempt to unsettle her. It was true, she had been surprised at the invitation, given the circumstances. But if the Queen wanted to unsettle her she would have to do more than that.

315

Lizzie grabbed her hand, pulling her out of the door. Frances asked what the matter was but all she said was 'Not here,' and dragged her through the corridors until they arrived at her private apartments. Two of her maids gawped as they entered, with Lizzie soaked to the skin. Frances dismissed them.

'You're to be put under house arrest. You and Robert.' Lizzie looked petrified.

'For goodness' sake, calm yourself,' Frances told her. 'It's hardly a surprise.'

'How can you be so cool-headed?'

'I've no concerns for myself.' She touched her sister's shoulder. It was saturated. 'Let's get something to dry you with.' Frances walked towards the inner door. 'It's poor Anne Turner I'm worried about. She's been meddling with things she shouldn't. I found her making spells at Northampton House once. If a sniff of witchcraft comes out at her trial, it'll be the end of her.'

She pulled open the door sharply, to find the two maids jumping back. 'Do you know what happens to snoops?' They squirmed. 'You're completely transparent, the pair of you. Whatever you might have heard, keep it to yourselves. Anne Turner's a decent woman who's made mistakes, that's all. Now, go and fetch a towel and some dry clothing before my sister catches her death.'

Frances knew they wouldn't hold out for five minutes if anyone came asking questions. As they scurried off, she turned back to Lizzie. 'Am I to be held here?'

'No, you're to stay at our house. I wanted to warn you.'

One of the maids reappeared with a towel and a dry gown. She sent the girl away and helped her sister out of her wet clothes, then sat her by the hearth to rub her hair dry.

'Did he pull some strings then, your husband, so I could remain among family?'

'I don't know how you can be so composed.' Lizzie was still unable to comprehend her sister's coolness. 'It's a *murder* they're investigating.' She was twisting her handkerchief.

'I'm not accused of anything and, besides, I am all taken up by the imminent arrival. They won't hang a pregnant woman.'

Lizzie was clearly horrified.

'I'm joking,' Frances said. 'It won't come to that. You don't think I'm actually guilty of anything, do you?'

'Of *course* I don't. But I'm worried for you.'

Frances took her sister's hand. It was cold and damp. 'There's no need, really. Nothing will happen to me. Just think, you'll be there to help deliver my baby.' Frances was glad that she'd have the solid presence of her sensible older sister for the birth. She'd been trying not to think about it.

The door opened and Robert appeared, wearing a hunted look. 'I've been or-ordered to remain here.' He was tripping over his words. 'I had to walk through the palace with an accompaniment of guards. They're outside the door now.'

Frances took him with both hands, giving him a firm shake. 'Pull yourself together, for God's sake. You look guilty as sin.'

'Everyone believes I am.'

Lizzie was watching them. She had shredded her handkerchief, leaving tufts of lint on her lap.

'Well, you aren't.' Frances held him firmly with her gaze for some moments. 'Are you?'

'Oh, God, Frances. *You* don't think . . .' His voice trailed off and a tear slid down his face, causing repugnance to well in her.

'Don't be silly.' She painted on a smile and wiped the tear away with her thumb.

'You didn't answer me.'

His whining grated. 'I said, you're being silly.' She pressed his chest. 'Where's your composure? Don't let them beat you. We're under house arrest. We're not being *tried*, and we won't be. They can't find you guilty if you're innocent.'

'You know that's not true. Innocent people are condemned all the time.' He looked waxen, as if he was already dead. 'If I hang, it will make you a widow. Oh, God, Frances, I couldn't cope with the thought of you having to . . .' He brought both hands to her distended abdomen.

She remembered the Robert she had first encountered, that reckless spirit, the raw charisma: so much unfulfilled potential. He had had all the power he could have wanted – *she* could have wanted – yet he'd thrown it away for something as commonplace as love.

'How will you manage without me?'

She had to resist laughing. 'I'll only be a hundred yards away. I'm to be housed with the Knollys', aren't I, Lizzie?'

Lizzie nodded. 'She'll be safe with us. You mustn't worry about her.'

'*You*'re to be held too?' He clutched his head, either side of his temples, railing, 'I can't bear it,' and kicked out at the panelling. 'That monster Northampton – this is all his doing.'

Lizzie cowered in her chair.

'Listen to me,' said Frances. 'First, I won't have Uncle slandered. Whatever you may think, he's not here to defend himself.' Robert muttered an apology.

She pulled him into the corner, near the inner door, where she was sure those girls were still listening, and said, 'You need to keep control of yourself. Just remember, if it comes to it, and you are charged,' he winced, 'which it *won't* . . .' she paused '. . . but if it does, you *must* maintain your innocence. Do you understand?' He nodded, like an admonished child. 'Even if they offer you a pardon for saying you're guilty, you must not under any circumstances accept it, because they will be trying to trick you. You must maintain your innocence,' she reiterated, 'or you will *lose your head*.'

He made a kind of strangled sound and dropped into a chair. Frances noted how diminished he appeared, every last glimmer of gilding gone. It was impossible to see the man he had once been or feel the attraction he had once ignited in her.

'Remember who you are,' she continued. 'You are lord privy seal and lord high chamberlain. Look.' She picked up the white staff of office that was propped in a corner, handing it to him. 'You haven't been stripped of your offices.' She took the Garter jewel he wore around his neck between her finger and thumb, giving it a tug. 'And *this* proves you are one of His Majesty's most intimate companions. None of this is being taken from you.'

'But you – *you*'re being taken from me.'

She couldn't look at him: he would have seen the derision in her face.

Him

I had been deprived of visitors and correspondence for three weeks, with only Copinger to bring me my meals and prevent me falling to filth.

Thomas would appear, his flesh almost eaten away, to remind me of things so unpalatable I feared I would choke on them. I contemplated escape. He mocked me. *You can never escape yourself, never escape me. There's nowhere to go.* He was right. *You'd have to abandon the woman I died to make way for.* His eyes were gone, just empty sockets, yet still I felt watched. *You yearn for her. Now you know how it feels to be deprived of love.*

The jangle of keys and the scrape of bolts made him dissolve into thin air. Words were exchanged between the guards, one laughed, and then came a rap at the inner door. It swung open to reveal the King's steward and my mood lifted in an instant. Surely he'd been sent to release me. I straightened my clothes, standing to greet him. He wore an apologetic expression – ruffled brow, lips pinched together. He wasn't a man I knew well. He seemed uncomfortable, unsure of what he should say, and my hope began to disintegrate.

He cleared his throat. 'I – I – I . . .' Time was suspended as I waited for him to overcome his stutter. Two unfamiliar men in royal livery had followed him in and were leaning against the panelling by the door. One was very large, the other smaller and younger but muscular and tight as a spring. 'I – I have been sent to – to collect –' Both henchmen were armed with swords and the large one had a firearm attached to his belt. He sniffed repeatedly, wiping his nose on his sleeve. It is strange how one can recall insignificant details with great clarity when things of importance disappear into the air. 'To collect your seals of office.'

A wave of nausea broke over me as Frances's voice echoed in my mind: *You've not been stripped of your offices . . . None of this is being taken from you.*

'I'm so very sorry,' he was saying. He sounded as if he was a long way off, an echo. I looked about the chamber, remembering the elation of first discovering, some years before, that I had been allotted the best rooms in the palace. All my magnificent things, the priceless set of tapestries that had been given to me by someone who wanted a favour; the chairs carved by a master craftsman, given in lieu of a debt; my desk, exquisitely inlaid with marquetry, a gift from the King. The only thing I'd paid for myself was my portrait, looking down at me from the wall.

Larkin had invested my expression with just the correct combination of gravitas and humour. Perhaps it wasn't apparent to all but I saw written there, too, the tell-tale lack of self-possession derived from never quite feeling I belonged with the best. It was that which made me mould myself to others' approval. I had had time to understand much about my shortcomings during my incarceration.

The steward was awaiting my response and I found myself unable to muster a single sound from my throat. It was clogged with a concoction of regret and self-reproach. I pointed to a coffer that sat on the shelves to one side. He took it, placing it on my desk, remarking on the beauty of the marquetry work as he turned the small key in its lock. Even that coffer had been the receptacle for a bribe from someone once. I couldn't look but heard the shuffle and clink of things being unwrapped and inspected. The large man at the door blew his nose loudly.

The steward was on his feet and I expected him to leave but noticed his gaze had rested on the lord high chamberlain's white staff, which was propped up in the far corner. 'I'm afraid,' he said, blanching a little, 'protocol dictates that you must hand it to me freely. I haven't the right to take it otherwise.'

I traversed the chamber, each step heavier than the last, picked up the staff and walked back to him. The younger guard snorted slightly. In my mind, I struck him with the staff, until blood poured from his ears.

I handed it over and the steward apologized again. At last I found my voice and begged him for news of my wife. 'As far as I know she is in good health. More than that I cannot say.' I managed to thank him for his dignity in performing a task he clearly found distasteful.

He made to leave, booty tucked under his arm, still wearing that apologetic expression. In the doorway he turned and, with the look of a child being made to take a foul-tasting medicine, said, 'I hate to be the bringer of bad tidings, my lord, but you are to be removed to the Tower. They will be coming to fetch you before the hour is up.'

I closed my eyes and pinched the bridge of my nose, imagining throwing myself to the floor, weeping and begging for mercy, but thankfully my composure remained intact. A performance like that would have been round the palace like wildfire. Villiers would have been snickering about it by dinnertime. God forbid that Frances would have known of it.

I went to my desk and slumped into the chair, noticing only then my Garter jewel splayed across the surface. I hung it around my neck, feeling the threat of tears for this small concession. The jewel, an effigy of St George, became my only reminder that I had once been dear enough to the King for him to make me a knight of the Garter. I would cling to it in my most hopeless hours, remembering the solemn ceremony in which it was bestowed and harbouring a small, vain hope that it might save me.

Her

'Robert's to be taken to the Tower.' Harry grimaced.

'The Tower!' Frances dropped her face into her hands, to hide her triumph. Strictly speaking, she wasn't supposed to receive visitors at the Knollys' but no one would deny her the company of her brother.

'I'm sure it's just a formality.'

'What else?' She looked up, tempering her expression.

'Overbury's guard was hanged.'

'They must be getting to the bottom of this bloody business, then.' She was reminded that it had been Weston who had procured the meeting with Mary Woods, which had caused her such trouble. Mary Woods had had to be dealt with. It made her glad Weston was dead.

Putting his arm over her shoulders, he said, 'Don't be frightened, Francey.' He hadn't used that name since childhood.

'I'm not – not in the slightest.' It was true, as long she didn't allow herself to ponder on it.

'You were never afraid of anything,' he went on. 'Except water. Do you remember what Uncle –'

'Don't bring that up now, Harry.' She didn't want to be reminded of the cold shock, her lungs threatening to explode: *Teaching you a lesson, my girl.* 'Just tell me what was said at Weston's trial.'

'Coke called you a rotten and corrupt branch of our family. I could have throttled him.'

She snorted derisively. 'He'd better not underestimate me.'

'At his peril.' Harry tried to sound composed but he was biting his bottom lip and jigging his leg nervously as he recounted the evidence that had been presented. 'An apothecary, name of Franklin, took the stand – good God, he's a grisly-looking beast.'

'He's a friend of Anne Turner's. Heaven knows where she came across someone like that.' An image of Franklin loomed in her mind. He *was* a grisly beast, a grisly beast whom she believed was wrapped tightly enough around her finger not to cause any trouble.

'He said he hoped they'd not make a net to catch the little birds and let the great ones go.'

'I suppose by "great ones" he meant Robert and me. If he intends to drag us down with him, he won't get very far.' She hoped Franklin wouldn't become a problem. Her shoulders felt tight so she stretched her arms out and back until her joints clicked but the discomfort wasn't relieved.

'And Weston testified that he carried messages and arranged secret meetings between you and Robert before you were married.'

'Well, that much is true. But no one hangs for being a lovers' go-between.' The baby was kicking, distracting her. 'What was said of the poisoning?'

'It all came spilling out. He told of a phial of liquid, which was confiscated by Lieutenant Elwes. Then mentioned some tarts he thought were contaminated but claimed they never got to Overbury anyway. Then an enema – mercury, if I remember rightly, or perhaps it was arsenic. It was supposedly the enema that did for him in the end.'

'Someone really wanted rid of Overbury.' She met her brother's look directly and had the fleeting impression of gazing at herself in the glass.

'There was confusion about the tarts. More than a single

batch. And some that went bad apparently, so Elwes ordered his cook to make fresh.'

'Uncle sometimes sent letters in with the tarts I made.'

'*You* made tarts?' She saw alarm flit across her brother's face.

'What are you thinking?' Frances gave the impression of being aghast. 'You said yourself there was more than one batch. Robert sent him some too.'

'*Robert?*'

'We were all trying to make sure the poor man was fed properly and had a few comforts – I sent him my own feath-erbed as well. Nothing wrong with that.'

They sat in silence for some moments. Frances allowed her thoughts to drift. Her brother watched her intently as she pulled the pins from her hair, each one making a little chink as she dropped it into a bowl. Then she unravelled her plaits and separated the tresses with her fingers. 'I wonder if things would have been different if Uncle hadn't died.' She gave the impression of thinking aloud. 'Do you think *he* would be under arrest too?'

'I doubt it. Nothing ever stuck to Uncle. He was too clever for everyone.' She noticed a flash of hate in Harry's eyes as he spoke of their great-uncle. Not too clever for me, she was thinking.

'Do you miss him?'

He looked surprised by her question. 'Not really. He had his favourites and I was never one of them. But, somehow, we Howards seemed a greater force with him at the helm. Father's different – weaker, more impetuous.'

They fell back to silence. Frances liked Harry's company, liked the way he didn't need to fill the quiet with words. The baby's foot was wedged painfully against the base of her ribcage. She stood, walking up and down in the hope it would shift. 'Have you seen Robert?'

'No, it's impossible to get to him. They're being much more lax with you.'

'That's because they know I'm innocent.' She smiled, tilting her head. 'This is just for show.' She swept her arm in an arc, indicating the four walls.

'Let's hope so.'

She laughed at his grave expression. 'Don't worry, you won't lose your favourite sister.' Touching her belly, she added, 'Unless this thing kills me on its way out.'

'Stop it!'

She shrugged. 'Is it true that Lieutenant Elwes has been arrested? I overheard something.'

Harry nodded.

'So, they all come tumbling down.'

All of a sudden Harry looked like a hound with a whiff of its prey. 'Did *Robert* have a hand in it?'

'The only thing I can be sure of is that *I* didn't do it.'

Harry looked at her with an intensity that suggested he was putting things together in his head.

Him

The journey downriver to the Tower reminded me of that earlier journey I'd made, choked with grief, but this time Thomas was with me, a shadow in the corner of my eye. There was a grim symmetry to it all. It was not dawn but a sunless midday, overhung by a glowering blanket of cloud. An army had come to stare, pasty October faces gazing in silent reproach as I was marched through the palace to the river steps. I lacked the courage to look at those who had come out to witness my humiliation but thought I saw Pembroke and Southampton lurking near the back entrance. I supposed them jubilant. It was ever their wish to see me fall.

As I was about to embark, Harry Howard came running down, pushing past the guards. 'How is she?' I cried.

'Bearing up.' He came close enough to speak in my ear. 'She sends you word to remember not to make an admission under any circumstances, whatever they offer –' He was hustled away before he had a chance to finish.

At the Tower I was greeted not by Elwes – he had been arrested, too, and lost his post, I was to learn – but by the new lieutenant, a diminutive man with pointed features named Sir George More. He seemed to believe we had met before. I didn't remember. It was entirely possible that he was one of those to whom I'd promised preferment and carelessly forgotten – goodness knows there were so many of them, and all baying for my blood, I didn't doubt.

I was led to a round chamber, with small, curved windows and a door leading to a crenellated walkway where I was told I would have permission to take the air under supervision, twice a day. One of my windows offered a view of Tower Hill. I realized, with a jolt, that it would likely be the site of my demise. I was allowed my own servant, Copinger, a comfort that did little to assuage my churning dread.

More's obsequious courtesy seemed too pedantic, with his tight little smile, to be genuine. He informed me that he regretted I would not be permitted ink or quills, and that the sending and receiving of correspondence was strictly prohibited, but I would be allowed books to read and my Bible. I was glad when he left, so Copinger could unpack my things and make the room at least a little comfortable. My furniture was delivered including, somewhat absurdly, my marquetry desk and carved chairs, which looked utterly forlorn in that grim setting.

Copinger set to making the bed and hanging my tapestries, though they were too long for the room and dragged in the dust on the floor. It occurred to me that if I was to be executed my effects would fall into More's possession – that was the rule – and I supposed he must have been rubbing his small hands as he watched my priceless furnishings being unloaded from the cart.

Despite Copinger's protestations I helped him with his work, afraid that without anything to keep me busy I would fall to pieces. 'What must you think of me?' I said.

'Others might, but I don't judge you,' was his answer. It brought me a splinter of comfort.

Her

Lizzie crept in. Frances was lying on the bed, feigning sleep. She felt in a permanent state of exhausted torpor, as if the baby had sucked all the life out of her. Every time she tried to rest it would start its vindictive kicking, making her resent its possession of her body.

'Frances,' she was whispering.

'I'm awake, just thinking.' She stretched herself but nothing would relieve her discomfort.

'The chief justice is here to talk to you.' Lizzie's face was taut with worry. 'But there is something I must tell you before you see him.'

'Coke can wait.' Frances heaved herself up to sitting. She was wondering if Coke had questioned Robert yet and whether he'd begun to dig his own grave a spoonful at a time. 'What do you need to tell me?'

'It's about Anne Turner. She's been . . .' Lizzie seemed unable to say anything more, just handed her sister a small package. It contained her diamond ring, returned again, like a bad penny. 'They didn't understand how it came to be on her person. They assumed she had connections to the woman who stole it from you.'

'Mary Woods – how strange,' Frances said, holding the ring up to the light. She felt invested with power, like Athena in the Trojan War, controlling events invisibly. 'Have they hanged Anne?'

Lizzie looked at her sister, nodding slowly, seeming unable

to comprehend how Frances could appear so unaffected by the news.

'It was bound to happen. She was up to her neck in this business. Did she make a good death? Were you there?'

'Of course not.' Lizzie had the appalled look that her sister should have worn. 'You know I can't bear hangings.'

'A sensitive soul, aren't you?' Frances took her hand; it was cold and damp.

'Harry went. He was at her trial, too, and there are things he wanted me to make you aware of before the chief justice talks to you. He's worried Coke will try to make it seem as if you had something to do with it.'

Frances was thinking that she was more than a match for Chief Justice Coke but didn't say so. 'What did Harry want me to know?'

'He said Anne Turner was made to remove her yellow lace in court. Coke thought it inappropriate apparently.' Frances had that feeling, again, of invisible power at her fingertips. 'At her hanging, she wore all black up to her chin and begged forgiveness. She prayed for *you* on the scaffold, Frances.' A big wobbling tear hung in the corner of her sister's eye.

'For me?' Frances was surprised to feel a stab of something like sorrow but it was short-lived.

'They made terrible accusations at her trial. She was too distressed to speak for herself. It's hard to believe she really was as wicked as they said.' Lizzie seemed not to want to continue but Frances gave her a nod of encouragement. 'They said she embodied the seven deadly sins.' She began to count them off on her fingers, as if it were a memory test. 'A whore, a bawd, a sorcerer, a witch.' She hesitated, repeating the list to jog her memory. 'Oh, yes, a papist. Was she really a papist?'

'Probably. I don't know,' said Frances, with a shrug. 'We never really talked of those things.'

'A papist, a felon and a murderer.'

'Oh dear, poor Anne. What else?'

'Oh, all sorts about witchcraft. Apparently, she used to make spells at Northampton House – imagine that, right under Uncle's nose.'

'Imagine!' Frances suppressed a smile.

'A wax doll was produced, as well as a picture of a man and a woman . . .' Lizzie blushed beetroot.

'A picture of what? A man and a woman coupling? They must have raided Dr Forman's house.'

Lizzie nodded. 'They made a good deal about the connection with Forman, apparently. There was parchment, too, with human skin attached, which bore the names of devils. And when these things were brought out, the scaffold where the crowd stood cracked and half collapsed.' Lizzie looked petrified. 'Do you suppose she really was a witch, Frances?'

'Anything's possible. Don't you remember those stories she used to terrify us with when we were children?' Frances continued to hold that smile at bay. It was all unfolding beautifully.

'Coke kept saying that poison and adultery go together. They produced the doctor's list of all the adulterous ladies at court and the men they loved. Harry said Coke took one look and confiscated it. Everyone was saying he must have seen his own wife's name there.'

Frances snorted. 'The old fool.'

'Anne eventually confessed in private to procuring poisons from Franklin and sending them to the Tower. I don't know how Harry found out what she said but she condemned Uncle – said she acted on his orders.'

'Well, he's not able to defend himself now, is he?'

'But there's worse.' Lizzie had grabbed hold of her arm. 'She said that her love of *you* brought her to a dog's death. I don't like what she implied with that. Do you think that's why Coke's here?'

'Don't look so worried. Anne could have meant anything by it. Coke's here because he wants to build a picture of what happened, that's all.' Lizzie looked on the brink of falling apart. 'I suppose I'd better not keep him waiting any longer.'

As she entered the hall Coke began to heave his bulk out of the chair but she told him not to trouble himself, so he sank down again with a grunt. He had brought a clerk with him. He was young with limpid brown eyes and ink spots on his hands.

'Are you not going to introduce your clerk?'

'Oh, him, he's nobody.'

'He doesn't have a name?' She gave the boy a little smile and rolled her eyes, nudging her head towards Coke. He was tall and slender and embarrassed, if the flush on his throat and cheeks was anything to go by. 'What do they call you?'

'I'm Henry. Henry Crowther.'

'My favourite brother's a Henry. We call him Harry, though.' Frances could sense Coke's irritation at the attention she was paying the boy. 'Do your friends call you Harry?' He nodded. His eyes were rather beautiful, she decided. 'Why don't you sit at the table?' He did so, unpacking his ink and pens, lining them up carefully.

Finally, she returned her attention to Coke, who swiftly wiped away his disgruntled expression, asking if she would also sit, but she explained that in her condition sitting was extremely uncomfortable. Her aim was to have the advantage that standing over him offered. She placed a hand on her abdomen. 'This infant may well surprise us and arrive early.' He looked somewhat distressed at the thought, which had been her intention.

'Another beautiful bud on the tree of the Howards. An infant is truly a great blessing –'

She put up a hand to stop him. 'Really, Chief Justice, surely you are aware that I know what you think. What was it exactly? *A rotten and corrupt branch of my family.* Isn't that what you said of me?' He looked chastened. He was revolting with his swollen red nose and the redundant yellowing tuft on his chin. 'I see you like the arboreal metaphor. I find it a little overused.' She glanced towards the clerk, who was stifling a smirk.

She waited for Coke's response but he seemed lost for words.

'Are you here to accuse me of something specific?'

'Just a talk.' He smothered his face with a disingenuous smile. 'To clarify a few things.'

'I doubt I'll be able to clarify very much for you. I seem to have been in the dark about everything. But ask what you will and I shall attempt to answer.'

'Am I right in thinking you made visits to Dr Forman?' He wrung his hands, which she noticed only then were disproportionately small for his size.

Frances could see what he was doing by phrasing it in such a way but she knew that there was no hard evidence attaching her to Forman. Their correspondence had been destroyed after his death; Anne had seen to it. 'Most of the women at court were seeing that charlatan,' she said. 'The fools. I wouldn't have dreamed of wasting my money on his quackery. He had no right to call himself a doctor.' She imagined Coke was an insect and she was pulling its limbs off one by one.

'I see.' He regarded her with gluey, old man's eyes. 'Did

you send any foodstuffs to Overbury while he was in the Tower?'

'I don't know why you insist on asking when everyone knows that I sent tarts and other dishes to him.' She held her hands palms up, as if to indicate she had nothing to hide. 'Scores of them. I made them myself. If you must know, I felt sorry for the fellow, shut away like that. It seemed so unfair on him. I thought some nice things to eat would make him feel better. He was such a dear friend to my husband, you see.'

'With respect, might it be that some of your tarts were less than wholesome?'

'That wouldn't be for me to judge. I am not accustomed to making tarts, so I doubt they were as good as any my cook might have made. But it's the thought, isn't it?' She knew what he was intimating and could see the frustration in his quivering mouth.

'It is generally believed that you disliked Overbury.'

'We had our differences. He was in love with my husband, you see.' She waited for that to sink in. 'He made some very public insults regarding me, much like some of the insults you yourself have made, Chief Justice, but it doesn't mean I wish you ill.' He shifted uncomfortably in his seat. 'Doesn't the Lord ask us to turn the other cheek?' In the quiet she could hear the clerk's breath stutter and thought he might be trying to keep himself from laughing.

Coke seemed undeterred, meeting her gaze directly. 'Is it not the case that you offered to pay Sir David Forest to pick a quarrel with Overbury in the hope that he would be killed in the ensuing fight?'

Frances laughed, tossing her head back. 'For goodness' sake, where's your sense of humour? It was said in jest. That man Forest loathed Overbury. He wouldn't have needed my encouragement to pick a fight with him.' How like Forest to come crawling out of the woodwork, she thought. In truth, he'd been horrified by her suggestion. 'If I'd truly wanted rid of the fellow, I hardly think I'd have gone about it in such a way.'

'How *would* you have gone about it?'

'I *wouldn't* have gone about it.' She brought both hands to her belly, to remind him of her condition. 'Really, Chief Justice, don't try to trick me like you tricked all those poor people you had executed.'

'I'm merely seeking the truth.'

'Of course.' She offered him a chilly smile. 'But I've told you all I know and I'm feeling rather weary now.' She slid her hands behind her waist, tilting her body backwards with a slight groan. 'So, I'm afraid your search for the truth will have to continue at another time.'

With that, ignoring his protestations, she bade him a perfunctory goodbye and left the room.

Him

Chief Justice Coke appeared very early on the morning after I arrived at the Tower. Increasingly vivid visitations from Thomas had kept me from sleep, leaving me dull-headed and in no fit state for an interrogation. I knew Coke vaguely from court: he was friendly, commenting on the weather and the splendour of my furnishings, but we both knew why he was there. So I cut short the niceties and insisted he get straight to the point.

'You may as well tell the truth,' was his opening gambit. His nose was bulbous and red-veined and he was clean-shaven, apart from a greasy, once-white tuft that sprang from beneath his lower lip. I focused on that rather than having to meet his unkind eyes. 'I have the testimonies of a great many people, not least the woman Anne Turner, and the so-called apothecary, Franklin, though what the fellow's qualifications are, I have little idea. Perhaps you can elucidate.'

I told him I had never met Franklin, which was true, though of course I knew of him, as I remembered Frances being so distressed by his arrest. I assumed him an accomplice of Anne Turner, another of those in the pay of Northampton, but I was damned if I was going to say more. Coke tilted his head as if to indicate that he didn't believe my denial. I reiterated it but wondered if I seemed the more guilty for doing so. I was painfully aware that, never having attended an interrogation I had little experience of the techniques and potential pitfalls.

'And Weston,' Coke said, inspecting me for a reaction to

the name. 'Well, he told a few *most* interesting stories before he was . . .' He performed the action of tugging at a noose, letting his head drop to the side and lolling his tongue. I was horrified, which was surely the intention of his crude mime.

For a moment I lost my voice, thinking of Weston, remembering him there at the Tower outside Thomas's rooms. His face was a blur. Only that neat scar and his big hands were distinct in my mind. 'I didn't know Weston, either.' I wondered if my fib was obvious to him. After all, he had accrued a lifetime's experience at detecting such things. 'I know only Mistress Turner, as she serves my wife.'

'Serves no more. Mistress Turner has gone the way of Weston.' He made that awful gesture again. 'Along with Elwes. All dead – and Franklin will follow them, as soon as he's spilled everything he knows.'

I feared I might vomit there on his shoes to hear of all those deaths, and couldn't bear to think of how poor Frances would suffer when she learned the news of Anne Turner. Coke shifted in his seat with a wheezing sigh. He looked at me with something like amusement, as if he thought it was all a joke. 'You say you *didn't* know Weston? That is most interesting, as Weston was adamant that he knew you.'

I had already wandered unwittingly into one of those pitfalls. 'On reflection, I *did* encounter him once, *after* Overbury's death. I don't believe we exchanged words beyond a greeting.'

'Ah. Your memory is jogged, then.'

There was a slight smile on his lips. I realized, with a sinking feeling, that as I had already shown an inconsistency in my account, others would be teased from me without much persuasion, and he knew it. 'Lieutenant Elwes had some very interesting details to divulge before he met his end.'

It dawned on me then that Elwes, too, had been one of

Northampton's appointments. I said as much, but Coke rightly pointed out that it had been I who petitioned the Council to appoint Elwes. 'But I did so on behalf of Northampton.' I heard the unwitting shrillness in my voice, which made me sound desperate and guilty. 'You must be able to see that Northampton was behind this whole sordid business.'

'Is that so?' He paused. My heart throbbed too fast. 'I have found no firm evidence of that.'

'But I have letters from him that prove –' I stopped, cursing myself inwardly for having had those letters destroyed. I'd thought they could only serve to make me seem guilty. It hadn't occurred that the opposite might be true. I'd never really believed I would have to prove my innocence.

'I should be interested to see them.'

'They may be mislaid,' was all I could think to say.

'*May* be or *are* mislaid?'

'Are,' I mumbled.

'Not burned then?' I flailed for a response but could find none. 'Sir Robert Cotton – he worked for you, I believe.' Coke waited for me to indicate that this was the case. I nodded. The air in the room seemed suddenly thin and the walls close. 'He told me you demanded he burn most of your correspondence. What was left is now in my possession.'

I gripped my hands firmly together for fear he would see they were trembling. 'Yes, I believe that is the case. But there are one or two letters from Overbury to me that will prove my innocence.'

'We shall see.' He said he would enquire about them, but clearly wasn't convinced.

'This fellow Franklin, of whom you claim to have no knowledge, said he hoped we would not make a net for all the little birds and let the great ones go. Rather a nice turn of phrase for a common apothecary, I thought. What do you think he meant by such a statement?'

'I think it could be interpreted in many ways.' I was pleased with my ambiguous response and felt slightly buoyed up.

'I wonder whom he meant by "great ones"?' He scrutinized me for what seemed an age, then stated, 'Weston testified that you sent powders to Overbury.'

I was completely unprepared for the change in tack, felt stunned as if I'd suffered a blow to the head, and denied all knowledge of any powders. Why I denied it, I don't know, and the more emphatically I claimed no knowledge of those powders the more transparent I felt.

'Elwes also testified that you sent powders.'

I blurted: 'He asked for them. Thomas requested powders to make him sicken enough to – to –' I had begun to stammer. 'Enough to raise the King's sympathy so he would be released. It was done in good faith. It was only chalk powder.' I was blathering.

'Chalk powder!' His eyebrows were raised, as if he thought I was having him on. 'You must understand how this appears.' He was serious again, deathly so. My last residue of hope leaked away. 'It was in your interests that Overbury remain incarcerated until your wife's nullity case was decided. In the light of that, it appears strange that you would go along with a plan to have him released.'

'But it wasn't how it seems.' I sounded pathetic, like an infant begging its nurse to believe it hadn't eaten a plum when the juice was dribbling down its chin.

Her

News of Franklin's execution came as Frances went into labour. She had never experienced pain like it, as if her body was being torn in two, but she was determined not to succumb to it.

'I've never known a mother so quiet during a birth,' said the midwife, once it was over. 'They usually screech loud enough to raise the devil.'

Lizzie gave the woman a glare, as if in saying the word she had invited the devil in to possess the new arrival. She handed Frances the bundle, with the words 'A little girl. Never mind, at least she's healthy.'

Frances gazed at her baby. It was purple and angry-looking, with tight-squeezed eyes and mucus clinging to a slick of black hair. She felt suddenly overwhelmed at having brought a creature into the world that would always want something of her. It would want her to love it. The thought made her uncomfortable. It began to cry, a searing, desperate sound, like foxes at night. It became clear to her then that while the baby had been inside her she was protected, but that was no longer the case.

The midwife took it, swaddling it into a tight bundle. 'The wet-nurse will be here soon, but would you like to give her a feed in the meantime?'

Frances felt unexpected revulsion at the idea of the infant sucking at her breast and wondered if other women felt so after giving birth. Resentment welled in her for the excruciating pain it had caused. Thoughts of all those executions seeped through to her, the violence of it all. It was creeping too close and the birth had made her weak.

The wet-nurse arrived eventually, a great fat woman with pendulous breasts who sat in the rocker, feeding. Frances drifted off, but in her sleep she was on the gallows with Anne Turner, watching the naked bodies of Franklin and Weston slung on to a cart, like butchered livestock. She looked at Anne, her face a vast, open, howling mouth. A noose was put round her neck, the coarse hemp chafing. Her head spun. Anne was whimpering. Frances was silent but buffeted by nausea. Anne began to cry then, a persistent, desperate wailing. She felt the pressure of the rope on her throat, the surface shift beneath her feet. She looked towards the executioner. He turned. It was Thomas Overbury, mouth set in a snarl, eyes red with rage, the stench of bergamot hanging in the air. She woke with a jolt to the sound of the baby crying.

The following day Harry came. He barely glanced at the infant as he dismissed the wet-nurse and took off his coat, flinging it on a chair. 'God, Frances, how can you bear it in here? It's hellishly dark.' He threw a log on the fire, prodding it with the poker until it flared up. Then he pulled back the curtains. 'You look exhausted.'

'Hardly surprising. Come and sit a moment.' He did as she asked and she leaned against his shoulder. He brought both arms tightly around her and they stayed like that without talking for some time. She hadn't realized how she'd craved the contact of another human being, proper physical contact. Lizzie's bird-like embraces were too brief and stuttering to offer real satisfaction. The thought struck her that she might never see Harry again, gouging her out. She held him more tightly.

'I was at Franklin's trial.' His voice was muffled in her shoulder. 'It's not good.'

She pulled out of the embrace. 'Tell me!'

Harry was pale, his eyes darting about and his voice tightly strung. 'He claimed seven different types of poison had been administered to the prisoner over time.'

'Well, he would have known, wouldn't he, since he procured them all?' She kept her tone light, though she felt leaden. 'Did he mention they were all ordered by Uncle?'

Harry nodded slowly. 'But he said more.' He stalled. 'Oh, Francey.' His voice cracked. 'The bastard said that it was you who ordered the final dose – the dose that killed him.' He looked at her, desperate for her to refute the accusation.

'How low of him,' she managed to hide the wobble in her voice, 'lying to save his own skin.' So, Franklin hadn't been as easily manipulated as she'd believed. 'But it didn't work, did it? He hanged like the rest of them.'

She managed a smile and smoothed a hand over his. 'You mustn't worry, Harry. The truth will come out in the end.'

'They're going to move you to the Tower, Francey.' She'd never seen Harry so upset. Harry was a Howard, not like Robert, who'd weep over a lost button. 'I won't be able to visit you there.'

'When?' She was falling, losing control.

'Not yet. After Christmas, once you've recovered.' She'd forgotten all about Christmas. They said nothing for a while, just sat with their thoughts. The Tower loomed in her mind and she was forced to accept that the outcome of her situation was at best uncertain.

Harry broke the silence. 'I hate to say this but I think Robert was involved in it all.' With a sickened expression, he told her how sorry he was.

'Nothing would surprise me any more.' She had an image of her husband making his scaffold speech but couldn't help also seeing herself there, facing her own end.

343

'Oh, God, I almost forgot!' Harry thumped his head with the heel of his hand. 'The King wants to see the baby. He asked me to arrange for him to come here. But no one must know. He can't be seen to –'

'Can't be seen to associate with a whore like me?' She laughed bitterly. 'I'd never have believed him so sentimental.'

But Frances wasn't thinking about the King. She was thinking about Franklin and regretting not having dealt with him properly. She had always believed herself untouchable but now she was not so sure.

Him

My world was reduced to a circular chamber ten paces in diameter. I would walk from one window to the other as time eked away, taking in the small square of river on one side, watching the boats pass by. The water, the essential mutability of its liquid state, began to represent freedom in my mind. I watched the birds for hours, wheeling above it. But then it froze for a full month – skaters dashing across its surface – and I understood that its freedom was an illusion, that even the river was enslaved to the weather. Incarceration was making a philosopher of me.

I had witnessed Elwes's execution at Tower Hill from the opposite window. It was a brutal sight even at a distance – the visceral shock as he dropped, his body twitching sickeningly for endless moments and subsiding to stillness as the crowd roared, hungry for retribution. I hadn't meant to look but found myself unable to drag my eyes away, casting myself in his place. His death seemed so profoundly unjust. As far as I knew, Elwes had done no more than obey Northampton's orders. But obedience is not always moral, I have learned. We had all obeyed that monster one way or another.

Since Elwes's execution I had asked Copinger to help me move the tapestry so it covered that window. Living thereafter in the half-light, I waited in a grim state of ignorance for events to unfold, for more questions, for a trial, for something, anything to happen. I only felt grateful for the company of Copinger, who would try to distract me with games of cards and chess, or accompany me to plod those few paces back and forth, back and forth, along the walkway twice a day, no matter the weather.

I tried to find comfort in my few books but found none there. The only book I wanted, *Troilus and Criseyde*, had not been among the things delivered to me at the Tower. I tried to remember its verses but my memory failed me and I resorted to the Bible, which made me certain I was headed for Hell.

A moment of joy cut through my despair when Copinger told me Frances had safely given birth to a baby girl. I imagined my infant, a duplicate of her mother, wearing the look that all the Howards wore, of unquestioned belonging, of absolute dignity. The thought of my daughter with that look in her eyes made my heart soar, then crash to earth on the realization that I might never know my own child.

I asked him for writing materials so I could send word to Frances. I was with Copinger so much I had learned to interpret all his little gestures, and his hesitation – the clearing of his throat – when he said he would try made it clear he was unsure. But he must have seen my desperation, for the next day he brought me a single sheet of paper, a small pot of ink and a quill, all concealed beneath his clothes.

The paper was creased. I smoothed it carefully over the table and brought the ink to my nose, breathing in its cheap vinegar stench as if it were precious as myrrh. Dipping my quill, I sat holding it over the paper, unable to think of what to write. But once I'd made the first mark the words came in a torrent and I bared my soul, telling her that only she and no one else had given meaning to my existence; the mere awareness that she had borne my child gave me the strength to face what I must. *I am profoundly sorry, my dearest, that you are suffering for my misdemeanours and I promise to right all those wrongs* . . . I scribbled on until both sides of the paper were dense with text.

Her

An idea began to form in Frances's mind as she waited for the King's visit. The wailing creature she'd produced had a new function. It had revealed a weakness she could exploit, was luring power to her door.

By the time he arrived, via the back stairs and dressed in the kind of innocuous mud-coloured wool that the servants wore, Frances was sitting up with her baby in her arms, the picture of perfect motherhood.

He swooped in for the child with a delighted beam, saying, 'So like Robbie, don't you think?' He licked his lips as if about to eat it.

She agreed, though it was not what she thought. The baby was hideous, nothing like her beautiful father. 'You're still fond of him,' she said. 'He thought he'd lost your love. It made him desperately sad.'

'Of course I'm still fond of him. Robbie's never lost my love, but this whole affair, it's made a terrible mess of everything.' He continued to gaze at the sleeping baby. 'You understand I have no choice.'

'He told me *everything*. I wish he hadn't.' She looked down and away, as if the burden of that knowledge was too much to bear. Robert didn't understand the power of secrets, and to have shared such a weapon with her was the height of imprudence. But Robert was an innocent. She was the only person alive, apart from the two involved, who knew why the King so desperately wanted Overbury out of the way. His Majesty's dirty little secret, volatile as gunpowder.

'Everything?' There was a long pause before he added, 'What exactly?'

She spoke very quietly and slowly, as if it was being teased from her. 'Oh, the business at Royston and – and . . .' She still kept her eyes down but sensed him beginning to fret. She had played her card at exactly the right moment.

'Royston?' She watched the dismay spread over him as her words – her velvet-wrapped threat, made to look like nothing more than a distraught revelation – sank in.

'Everything, and the rest of it after – with . . .' She wanted to laugh in his face and tell him it was love that had sapped his power.

'With Overbury?' His voice was high-pitched with shock. 'His death?'

She nodded. 'I'm so sorry.'

He was appalled, the guts knocked out of him.

'It's not you who should be sorry.' He looked at the baby again and back at Frances, suddenly seeming ancient and exhausted, and she knew, at last, his resistance was overcome and she had him in the palm of her hand. 'What exactly?' he asked again.

But she didn't answer, just said, 'I think I can help you save him.'

'Save Robbie?' His exhausted eyes filled with hope.

'If I make a confession and throw myself on your mercy, that should satisfy the investigators and those who seek justice.' She rubbed tears into her eyes. 'I know it would mean time spent under lock and key.'

'You would do such a thing – make such a sacrifice?'

'For him – and you, yes.' Her words hung in the silence. 'If, once it is all done with, you would award me a pardon. After a reasonable time, when the dust has settled and I have demonstrated my contrition, I could be released.'

'That goes without saying.' He placed his hand on his heart. 'You have my solemn promise.' She would have liked to persuade him to sit at the table, write it and stamp it with his seal as proof, but she knew that might raise his suspicion.

He lifted the baby up to look at it again, his expression crumpling, and she felt omnipotent, reading his thoughts, where the seed of doubt she had sown about his beloved Robbie was rooting.

Him

Lieutenant More visited, accompanied by a man I didn't know. He had a disconcerting trait, an eye that wandered independently of its twin. More announced that this man was to be Copinger's replacement. He told me that my servant had contravened the rules of my incarceration, refusing to elucidate, but I knew it must have been the letter.

The thought of More reading my most private intimacies, articulated in that thin ink for Frances's eyes only, made me feel horribly violated and I hated him deeply for it, despite the obvious pity he felt for me. He informed me, with an apologetic shrug, that Copinger was under lock and key. I begged him not to punish my servant for my own transgression but he was impervious to my pleas, saying more than once: 'The choice is not mine.'

'Tell me at least how my wife fares. Is she still safe at the Knollys'?' He shook his head minutely. 'She is freed?' A bubble of elation swelled in my heart. But he shook his head once more. 'Where is she?'

'I'm not able to say.' He was looking at the floor.

'Is she here?'

From his expression, his mouth pursed and his thick silence, I knew that she was. My elation burst.

'You cannot prevent me from making an entreaty to the King.' I stood as I said it, as if to show him I would not be cowed. More was a small man and I hoped to make him feel smaller. He seemed to hesitate, about to refuse me, I thought, so I added, 'When I am proved innocent, the King will not be best pleased to know that you denied me such a request.'

It was a small victory that brought little satisfaction. He sent my new cock-eyed man out for writing materials and stood over me as I wrote. I implored that Frances not be tried, that she be released to live quietly somewhere away from court with our daughter. *She is the most innocent of us all.*

I flattered James and reminded him of the moments of joy we had once shared, how I loved him like a son and a subject. I tried and failed to cast out thoughts of Villiers standing at his shoulder, as James read, stifling laughter at my desperation. Even the memory of the hard punch I'd given him was no consolation.

Her

Frances's nose was running with the cold but her handkerchief was not in her sleeve. With a jolt, she remembered it that morning, bobbing on the water like a white bird and then the gob of spit, launched from that snarling mouth in the throng of other faces, all distorted with rage. They would all rejoice if she was hanged.

It was a good hour since Bacon and Coke had departed, leaving her alone with her thoughts in that empty room above the watergate. She was having doubts about the confession she'd made to them, wondered if she had played the wrong card, whether the King's word was good, whether he was playing his own game. Unfamiliar doubt stitched itself through her. She knew that a king's promise, spoken rather than written, was easily retracted.

But Frances retained her secret deterrent: King James's dirty little secret. He knew she knew. That gave her power but she was only too conscious that people who make threats can be killed for their silence. She knew to keep that particular powder dry for the direst of circumstances.

There was a noise beyond the door and the sound of bolts being pulled back. A gust of air caused the fire to stir and two men entered, holding either end of a large chest. Frances recognized it as the one she had taken with her to the Knollys' and supposed her maid must have packed it with her effects. Balanced on top was a wicker cradle she had never seen before. They set the trunk down and lifted the cradle, which creaked like a laundry basket, asking her where she would like it.

Frances was lost for words, dreading the possibility that she might be left on her own with her baby. They must have thought her witless as she simply stared at them, mouth half open. Lieutenant More returned, giving instructions to the men. He appraised her with his rodent eyes and tried to make conversation. She told him firmly that she would rather be alone.

The workmen also left, returning a few minutes later with a bed, which they began to put together. Other pieces of furniture arrived. Someone who didn't know her must have been sent to collect her belongings. The items they had chosen were not hers but from one of the spare bedchambers, where she had consigned all the things her husband owned that she didn't like.

A set of German bed hangings, depicting the life of John the Baptist, was spread on the floor, waiting to be hung. They were ugly but would keep out the January draughts. Frances expected that whoever had selected those curtains from her husband's things had done so deliberately to communicate some kind of moral lesson to her. There was Salome holding her platter. She imagined it was Robert's head spilling gore. That was not the lesson they'd intended.

The men worked quietly, whispering instructions to each other so as not to disturb her. She sat staring blankly at the fire so she didn't have to look at the wicker cradle, which had been placed beside the bed.

She must have fallen asleep for a while, as she half woke to find the men gone and the fire almost dead. It was bitterly cold, the air was saturated and her body ached. Since the birth six weeks before she had felt the bones of her ribcage and hips drawing back together where they had opened to accommodate the baby.

She stood, stretching and rubbing her eyes with her fists.

A small cough jolted her and, looking round, she saw she was not alone. There was a girl with a pinched face and stringy hair standing in the shadows beside the bed.

'I didn't mean to startle you.' She took a diffident step forward. Her dress was drab. It had had several previous owners, as Frances could see the marks where it had been altered, and the fabric was almost bald in places.

'Who on earth are *you*?' Frances noticed the girl was shivering, either with cold or fear.

'I've been sent to wet-nurse your baby.' She pointed to the cradle where Frances then saw her baby was sleeping.

'You?' She looked so underfed she didn't seem capable of nursing a cat, let alone an infant. Frances thought of the fat woman with the great pendulous breasts. 'I suppose they had trouble finding anyone willing to put themselves in this dreadful place. Have you even any milk?'

'I fed her once already, while you were asleep.'

Her lips were tinged blue or perhaps it was just the grimy light. 'Come closer to the fire.' Frances stirred the embers with her foot, noticing the absence of a poker. Too much like a weapon, she supposed. 'What are you called?'

'Oh, yes, of course. I'm Nelly.' She smiled, revealing a haphazard jumble of teeth.

'Well, Nelly, I hope you're good at cards, for we shall be bored out of our minds shut up in this place.'

'I am that. I can do a three-card trick.' Her eyes gleamed.

Frances was glad that this odd girl had been employed. Her apparent absence of affectation was a welcome distraction from contemplating her uncertain future, and Frances was sure she'd be better company than the dismal kind of well-bred young woman she might have expected. 'You'll have to show me.'

A guard arrived with wood and began to build up the fire.

'Surely that's not a job *you* should be doing. Isn't there a serv-ant assigned to me?'

'I don't know about a servant but I didn't want you left in the cold.'

'You and I will get along very well, I think.' Frances gave him the full force of her attention and watched him respond. She thought she might, one day, need a favour from him. She sat up so her breasts, still swollen from pregnancy, bulged slightly over her dress, watching his eyes glance over them.

She asked his name, skimming the back of his hand with the tips of her fingers as if by mistake. He was a big lad, good-looking, dark and young with curved eyebrows and a cleft in his chin. He said his name was William. She could see he was already her captive.

'Look,' said Nelly. Both Frances and William turned to see she had produced a dog-eared pack of cards from some-where and had placed three of them face down on the table. She turned them up: two black kings with an ace of hearts. 'Follow the heart.' She flipped them back down. 'Don't take your eyes off it.'

She began to swap them round, sliding them swiftly over the surface of the table. Her hands were red, as if they'd recently been scrubbed with a hard brush, and her nails were short and very clean. When she stopped, she asked them to point to the heart. They both indicated the middle card. They were right. This happened again and Frances told the girl she was not very impressed.

'I'm gaining your confidence,' piped Nelly, undaunted by Frances's frank sneer. 'You see, if you were actually laying down bets, you'd think you'd be sure to win now.'

Her expression was puckish and she repeated the process, moving the cards more slowly. Frances was sure she had the right card that time but when Nelly turned it over it was one of the kings. She laughed, glad of the distraction, and imagined the girl fleecing passers-by in the marketplace with her card trick.

'I'm supposed to be guarding the door,' said William. 'I'll get myself into trouble.'

As he left, the door clanged, waking the baby, who began to wail. The noise tugged at Frances as if twin fishhooks had lodged themselves in her breasts, pulling her by some invisible force.

She went to the window and pressed her forehead against the cool glass, imagining it shattering. She could see the courtyard below, busy with people, and looked at the buildings opposite, the round towers with their arched windows, like hooded eyes. Robert was trapped behind one, and she wondered whether he'd been offered lenience for a confession, sure he must have refused. She'd planted her warning too deeply in his head for him not to take heed of it.

She could hear the creak of that basket cradle as Nelly lifted the baby out. When Frances turned, the girl was unlacing her bodice and deftly positioned it to feed. The wailing subsided, replaced by quiet snuffling sounds. Frances crossed her arms tightly over her own front to stop the sharp tugging sensation. 'So how did you come to be wet-nursing – a girl your age?'

Nelly fell into a long, drawn-out story about how she found herself pregnant without being wed and was cast out by her family but that when the baby came it was stillborn.

'When did you have this baby, Nelly?'

'A few days ago.'

Frances was shocked, thinking of her own six weeks of pampered recuperation, impressed by how this scrawny little creature had recovered so quickly and with an apparent absence of self-pity.

'I have a cousin took me in for the birth and she is a laundress for the lieutenant here. I don't quite know how it came about, but here I am.'

Who are you with your clever tricks? thought Frances, as she watched the girl flicking through her cards with her free hand. But once she'd finished feeding she laid the baby on the bed cooing and clucking: 'Is that a smile for your nursey, is it? Are you a perfect little poppet, are you?' And Frances felt silly for imagining she was more than she said she was.

They were well into their second week in the Tower when Nelly said, 'I hope you don't mind me asking,' as she settled the baby for her morning feed. Frances balked. That phrase usually hailed a question she didn't want to answer, and she would have liked to say that this wasn't how their relationship worked, that she didn't answer questions. 'But how is it you came to be here, you being a countess and all?'

Frances cut the conversation dead, but Nelly persevered with dogged determination. A thought took her by surprise. She could use this girl to undermine her confession, at the very least, cast some ambiguity on it in the eyes of her prosecutors. They would surely want to have a few words with Nelly at some point, to see if she might inadvertently spill any incriminating confidences from the murderous Countess of Somerset.

Frances would offer the girl her story, a version of it that would cast her confession as an act of sacrifice made to save a beloved husband – a husband who couldn't prove his innocence, a husband who wasn't innocent. How could they hang her then? But *he* would hang and make her a widow.

What was it Anne had said once of widows? *The best of all worlds.* There was appeal in the idea of belonging only to herself. She sensed a perfect symmetry to her plan, felt as if she had once more taken up the reins.

So, a story began to unfurl, winding right back to the first marriage of a girl called Frances Howard, an imagined Frances Howard who was wed seven years yet remained a virgin, right back to Essex's grim Staffordshire house and playing Blind Man's Buff.

'I pulled the short straw. Uncle took his silk kerchief and wrapped it around my eyes. We were all playing . . .'

Him

I am waiting for the attorney general. More had come to warn me of his imminent arrival and I sensed a fragment of hope as Bacon was once a friend. But some of that hope was doused when More also gave news that my request to James for Frances's freedom was not to be granted.

Bacon arrives with a clerk. The stony look on his face instantly dissolves any vestiges of optimism I may have harboured. He removes his hat and I can see he has combed his hair in such a way as to disguise that it is thinning. It is russet in tone, like his beard, and I wonder if he colours it. He arranges his cloak very carefully over the back of a chair, balancing the hat on top, and comments vaguely on the weather. I cannot stand to think that it is spring outside and things are growing while I shrivel.

He runs his eyes over me and I recall that once he tried to seduce me, long ago, before I belonged to the King. I rebuffed him. I suppose that won't help my case. He is polite enough not to register any surprise at my appearance. Though I have tried to make sure I am well dressed and my clothes properly laundered, nothing can disguise my sallow skin and the black beneath my eyes, which I see reflected in the glass when I can bear to look.

I notice the clerk's curious glances. I suppose he thinks me a murderer too. Once seated, Bacon places both hands carefully flat on the table with the word 'So.'

The clerk lays out his papers. I try to see what is written there, but cannot. I ask Bacon where Coke is, if he remains in charge of the investigation, but he dodges my question with one of his own.

'Am I right in thinking that you are in receipt of an annual pension from Spain?' It is asked in a matter-of-fact way.

He's caught me unawares. I'd expected questions directly related to the case. 'Absolutely not.' My response is essentially true and I have no intention of telling Bacon that the Spanish ambassador had promised me an annuity but that it hadn't yet been arranged.

'Northampton had one.' I don't know if it is a question. Bacon seems quite sure that it is the case. *I* certainly know it to be true. 'Northampton had rather more dealings with Spain than people thought.'

He seems to wait for an answer but I say nothing. I know Bacon is clever, much too clever for me, and this could well be a trap. I try to remember what I said to Coke but it was months ago now and my memory is foggy.

'Have you had many dealings with Spain?' He says it lightly, as if asking whether I had ham for dinner.

'Only when the King asked me to make enquiries into a betrothal for Prince Charles.'

'But it came to nothing, didn't it?'

'The King was not prepared to accept the Spaniards' conditions.'

'So, you negotiated badly.'

'I don't see what this has to do with –' I fear I sound petulant and I stop because I can see what he's doing in trying to make me irate. 'Perhaps that is so.'

My silent cock-eyed servant brings us some bread and cheese and a jug of beer, which Bacon serves as if he is the host. My throat is dry from nerves. The beer soothes it a little. He digs further on the Spanish pension and I am forced to deny it vehemently several times. He brings up

Northampton again and all sorts of queries about matters that seem irrelevant. I manage, in the main, to slide by with noncommittal answers. It is unclear what he wants from this line of questioning and he continues to come over as rather cordial, making it seem as if this is truly just a conversation.

But without warning he changes the subject. 'Were you aware of your wife's antipathy towards Thomas Overbury?'

I am completely unprepared, had been lulled into a false sense of security, and flail for a response. 'I wouldn't have put it like that.'

He looks at me intently, with one eyebrow slightly raised, as if he can see right into my confusion of thoughts. His moustache prevents me reading his expression accurately. 'How *would* you have put it?'

'Frances isn't like that.' I wish I sounded more assertive. 'She was naturally upset by the things Overbury said of her. It was more a case of *him* not liking *her*.'

'Ah.' Bacon taps the table with his index finger. 'Then your friend was doing everything he could, to prevent you marrying a woman he loathed.'

'I suppose so.' I realize too late that I have walked into his trap and try to retract my statement. 'Not exactly. It was . . . it was not straightforward.'

Bacon echoes me. 'Not straightforward?'

A long pause follows. I don't know where to look but am conscious that my darting eyes must make me seem shifty.

'Overbury's death delivered what you desired.'

'No!' It came out as a kind of cry.

'You say "no" but it certainly appears like that.'

'I'm innocent!' I exclaim, too loudly.

'Your wife said you'd say that.'

I can feel my anger rise, fast as milk on the boil, at the thought of this man questioning Frances – my broken Frances. My hate for him sucks the air from the room.

'My wife said I'd say that because it is the truth.' Frances walks into my mind. Where is she? But I can't think of her, not now, or I will lose my composure completely.

The light is going, evening has appeared from nowhere, and Bacon sends his clerk in search of someone to light the candles. He gets up and walks about the chamber, picking things up and putting them down again. It is all I can do to prevent myself forcing him to stop.

He is lifting the tapestry from the window. 'You have a view of Tower Hill.'

'Deliberate, I suspect.' I find myself telling him that I saw Elwes executed from there.

'He made a noble death,' Bacon says. I wish now I hadn't mentioned Elwes, who has fixed himself in my mind wearing a yellow-toothed grimace. 'Not like Franklin. *He* made a dreadful fuss.'

'I didn't know Franklin,' I say. Now the four who have been executed are hanging in my mind.

The clerk has returned with a handful of candles, which I take from him for something to do. I place them in the holders, light them, then fill my pipe, touching it to a flame, drawing in the hot smoke. Almost immediately I regret doing so, as my hand is on display, trembling visibly.

'Franklin had all sorts of things to say. I suppose you know a cat was given poison at Northampton House, as a test to see if it would kill her? Enough to kill twenty men, if Franklin is to be believed.'

'I don't know what you're talking about.' I sound defensive but it's true: I don't know of any dead cat. 'I was rarely at Northampton House.'

'Mistress Turner said you were there often. She believed you were in league with Northampton.'

I try to explain that I was only friendly with Northampton because I was to marry his great-niece but I can tell he doesn't believe a word of it. He mentions that some at court thought Northampton was a mentor, of sorts, to me. I cannot deny that. Then he says, '*And* Franklin said he had dealings with you.'

'He's a liar. I never met Franklin.' I know I sound desperate and sit back down at the table. My heart thrums and I am struck by the irony that the effect of love on the heart is identical to that of fear.

'Franklin said your poor friend Overbury was served up so much poison it's a miracle he lived as long as he did.' He stops, leaving silence to well a moment. 'He seemed quite sure you had a hand in it.'

'Why would I have wanted Thomas dead? He was my dearest friend, my closest –' I have grabbed Bacon's arm and, realizing what I am doing, drop it as if burned. 'I didn't want him dead. I loved him.'

The gold embroidery on Bacon's sleeves catches the light. We are sitting in a flickering yellow pool with a sea of darkness around us.

He looks at his arm, at the place where I had hold of him, then back at me. 'Don't be disingenuous.'

'I know it looks that way.' I am sweating.

'Now, about these powders you sent in to Overbury.'

'I explained all that to Coke. Thomas *requested* them. They were harmless.' I try to remember exactly what I'd said to Coke on the matter, fearing some small inconsistency might cast doubt on the truth.

'You must understand how it looks.'

'I know how it looks.' Bacon is scrutinizing me. 'But it is

not so.' My voice is suddenly wet, as if I might burst into tears. I'm in confusion. The four who have already hanged are still swinging through my mind and I am trying not to think of my own fate or that of my wife. 'Have you not yet seen the letters I received from Overbury at the time, saying how much better he felt? Cotton has them.'

'Yes, Cotton handed them to us,' Bacon says, steepling his fingers. 'They prove nothing as their dates have been altered.'

'That's not possible.' My insides shrink and I inwardly curse Cotton for not doing the job properly.

Bacon regards me down his nose. He doesn't believe a word I say. 'Some have suggested Overbury knew things that might have caused trouble for the King.'

'That's not true,' I blurt. My heart is beating even faster now. I know I seem guilty as sin.

'Coke believes in a wider conspiracy.' Bacon's calm is chiselling away at me.

'What do you mean?' He is watching my shaky hand.

'He believes the prince's death was suspicious too. Surely you heard that at the time. But Coke suspects you invented a plot to do away with *all* the Stuarts. I am inclined to believe him wrong. I don't think you have the imagination for a great conspiracy, unless you were the pawn of Northampton.' He pauses, receding into the darkness a moment.

This sudden change in him has wrong-footed me. 'What do you mean? I didn't –'

'I know. I know.' He smiles but in the dim light it looks more like a scowl. The sweat is cold beneath my clothes, though the chamber is warm. 'I think you did it for love. Such a trivial reason to kill a man – about your level.'

I jump up and jab my finger at him. 'I told you, I didn't do it. Look to Northampton if you want the culprit.'

Bacon doesn't try to hide the fact that he thinks I am lying

364

and remains in his seat, absolutely composed, while I continue to rave and prod, professing my innocence.

'There is sworn testimony that you advised Overbury not to take the Moscow embassy.'

Eventually I claw back some restraint and slump into my chair, saying, 'I *did* want Overbury out of the way. I *did* want him detained but for his reformation, not his ruin. I didn't want him dead. I loved him dearly.'

'But not as much as you love your wife.'

I have given in to my tears now, head in hands, sniffing and heaving, repeating, 'I'm innocent,' over and over again until the words seem senseless. All I want is the comfort of my beloved Frances – the only friend I have left. The clerk clears his throat. I had forgotten he was here at the edge of our small pool of grubby light, recording my shameful tears for posterity.

I feel Bacon's eyes boring through me, watching until I have calmed myself. Then he says, 'Your wife confessed.'

Her

Frances waits alone. Her story is told, the story of that other Frances Howard. She imagines it out in the world, spreading from mouth to ear, working her revenge, planting the blame elsewhere and setting her free.

She was glad when Nelly left but now she misses her company. Over and over she practises the card trick but, without a witness, has no idea if her sleight of hand is improving. She even vaguely misses the baby and thinks of it at Lizzie's house in a proper mahogany cradle, tucked into crisp linens with its big round black eyes, like mirrors.

She waits for something to happen. There is a new maid, timid as a field mouse. Her name is Lalage. She is plump and milky, and comes from a good family. Lalage is scared of Frances and does what she is charged to do with quivering befuddlement. Frances supposes she must believe all the stories of witchcraft. Perhaps she was at Anne Turner's trial when the scaffold cracked as the evidence was produced.

She waits in limbo for her trial, wants it to be over, but the single week plays its own sleight of hand, stretching itself out interminably. In her mind, she goes over what she said to Bacon and Coke when they questioned her, remembering how she'd thrown them with her confession. They had been back, of course, on the day after Nelly's departure, for the details.

They'd asked if her husband had also sent tarts and jellies to Overbury. *Of course*, she'd replied. *We both did. But he never let me into his private dealings with my great-uncle — they were very close.* That, funnily enough, was the truth. They asked whether

Robert knew Franklin. *I don't know who you mean,* Frances had replied. *What did he look like?* When Bacon described his features – the crook-back, the rotten nose – she'd clapped a hand over her mouth in false shock: *I have seen this man. I saw him with my great-uncle and with Mistress Turner and –* She'd stopped, only eventually stuttering out: *With Robert once? What was he doing with such a man?*

Bacon had struggled to hide the upward flick of his lips when she'd said that. *But Robert's innocent,* she'd added.

I'm sure he is, Bacon had replied, his voice replete with sarcasm, and she wondered if they had already squeezed her story, like juice from a lemon, out of Nelly before they came. Strangely, they didn't think to ask her about the final lethal enema, procured from Franklin, which had seen the job done.

She shuffles the cards. Lalage comes in with a basket of clean linen and begins to make the bed. A fresh scent wafts through the thick, damp air.

'Come here,' she says to the girl. 'I want to show you something.'

Lalage's eyes are wide set and long-lashed.

'I won't eat you.'

The girl approaches diffidently.

Frances lays out the three cards face up. 'Follow the heart.' She flips them over and begins to move them around, faster and faster. Lalage watches as if her life depends on it. 'Which is the heart? The girl points to the left-hand card. Frances turns it up. It is the king of spades.

Lalage gasps and murmurs, 'The devil.'

'It's only a trick. Look.' Frances demonstrates how to hold two cards together making them appear as one. 'See?'

'May I be excused?' Her voice is small.

'For pity's sake, I'm no witch. Witchcraft is just something people invent to explain things they don't understand or to make others do as they want.' Frances can see that her words are not making any difference. 'Go on, then. You may as well.'

The girl slips away, and Frances is alone once more with her thoughts and the sound of the spring rain. She runs through the possible outcomes of her trial. There is a chance that Nelly has not been questioned, that the story of that other – spotless – Frances Howard will never be told. She will not allow herself to consider the possibility of her royal pardon being worthless, but the thought is there, like a small, hot flame in her head that will not be stamped out. The King's dark little secret is all that prevents it flaring up and catching hold. Surely, she reasons, he wouldn't take the risk that she might spill it. But she failed once to manipulate the King. She remembers his derision: *I don't need your soothsaying game to tell me that.*

Desperate for a distraction, she goes to the door, tapping gently. It opens slightly and William's eager cleft-chinned smile appears. 'Come in,' she mouths, sliding the tip of her tongue over her lips. She pulls him through the door, leaning against it to press it shut and pushes his head down on to her breasts, dragging her dress down so they are fully exposed. He is hard.

But when he has gone the vortex of fear returns. The more she thinks of it, the more aware she is that there are many possible permutations of her future. There is nothing more she can do to influence the situation, and it remains to be seen whether she has done enough. It is out of her hands – perilously.

She fans her cards, selecting one and saying to herself: *If this is a heart I will be tried and pardoned, Robert will be executed and I will be free.* She flips the card: it is the two of spades. *Best of three.*

She is a Howard, after all, and the Howards always get what they want.

Him

In a month it will be five years since Frances Howard read my palm and saw love engraved there. In that time I have risen as high as it is possible to rise and plunged to the depths, dragging her with me. There is only one place lower in life: the gallows – and I cannot bear to consider what lies beyond. I beseech God to spare my wife but fear He no longer listens.

A dog howls and scratches pitifully at a nearby door. I refuse to accept that Frances has confessed – not her. I'm no fool. Bacon lied to me in the hope that I would incriminate myself. But my mind plumbs the shadows, where thoughts of Northampton dwell. I can't deny his influence over her, the way she was blind to his silk-clad malice and her unfailing faith in God's forgiveness. I am accosted by the fate of her parrot, can feel the terrified jabber of its pulse in my fingertips. Perhaps she has been brought so low she would rather die than live. I know I would rather be dead than live without her.

On my small rampart I can feel the warmth in the air and hear the birds singing to their mates. It makes me want to weep. Then it rains for three days without letting up. My neglected poetry books mock me from their shelf, the pining lovers imprisoned for eternity between their covers.

I rack my mind for things that might help my case when it comes to trial. I try to see a pattern, an organizing principle of fate, but can see only that I have tripped haplessly through life from one experience to another. There is no map of the past, only a tangle of half-remembered events, and I have no pen or paper to make sense of them.

Through my muddle of recollections, a single forgotten letter emerges. Overbury had sent it to me from the Tower. I can see now, with forensic clarity, Thomas's precise hand asking for a stronger powder, saying the one I'd sent had had no effect. In the margin he had drawn a crude image of a heart in flames, which had touched me and made me want to keep it. I put it between the pages of *Troilus and Criseyde*. The verse it marked spills into my thoughts:

> *What is this wondrous malady that fills me*
> *With fire of ice and ice of fire, and kills me?*

His image and that couplet belonged together.

The remembering renews me. Thomas's own words will help prove my innocence. But my optimism falters as I realize I have no way of laying my hands on that letter and I fall to questioning the point of proving my innocence anyway, if Frances is doomed.

I listen to the incessant sad chorus of that howling dog as it rains on and on, with Thomas hovering, the stench of his putrefying flesh hanging in the air.

On the day the rain stops, leaving the eaves dripping and gurgling, Harry Howard comes to visit. He has a letter of dispensation from the King to see me alone. More, who arrives with him, seems annoyed when Harry politely asks him to leave.

Harry is so like Frances it pulls me up, makes me want to kiss him full on the mouth. My imagination escapes, running wild, and I'm shocked to feel myself stir.

'You look frightful, Robert,' is the first thing he says. 'The sooner you're out of here the better.'

I allow myself to believe I am still one of the Howards and

that they have the power to secure my release, but before I can ask him if this is the case he adds, 'Your trial will be the day after tomorrow.'

'Two days?' He nods. I make an inadvertent choking noise. 'What about Frances?'

'She confessed to the murder.'

I struggle for breath. To hear it from two different sources surely makes it true. 'My Frances. Such a heinous deed.' But even knowing it, perversely, I have already forgiven her. She did it for me – for love of me. 'My Frances.' I'm confused, gibbering, staring despair in the face. I feel faint and can barely get my question out. 'Will they execute her?'

He doesn't answer, just shrugs, saying, 'Her trial's tomorrow. With a guilty plea, it will be short.'

'I'm telling you, she's not a murderer.' There are no other words in me.

'Of course she's not.' He says it as if it is obvious and I am an ass for not realizing.

'But why did she confess?'

'How should I know?' He is upset, almost shouting. 'Coerced, perhaps. God knows.'

The blood is rushing through my ears, making it hard to hear what he is saying. 'She *didn't* do it?' Thomas, just a disembodied voice in my ear now, says: *How can you be so sure?*

Harry's face stiffens suddenly with rage. 'What do you think she is, a monster? How could you ask such a thing? Or perhaps she's sacrificing herself for *you*.' His eyes are boring through me.

'You know that's not true.' A great anguished roar comes out of me. I sound barely human.

'You need to find some self-control.' He is filled with disdain, as if my weakness is repulsive. 'You can't let yourself fall apart.'

371

I see now that to be one of the Howards I would need to be hard and sharp as an executioner's blade and I am not. That look they have is one of absolute resilience. They are born with it – it cannot be acquired, but I already know that.

'The reason I'm here' – I had altogether forgotten he was visiting me on the King's business – 'is that His Majesty wants you, too, to make a confession.'

'A confession – me?'

'He thinks it's not enough that the servants have been executed. Says the public must be given more, or *he* will pay the price. He doesn't want any further investigations and a solid confession provides an end to the matter. I suppose he has something to hide. *You*'d know better than me, what the King has to hide.' He looks at me as if I am an idiot. 'Put on a show of remorse in the dock and he promises your life will be spared. Then, once the fuss has all died down, he will give you a full pardon. Or so he says.' Something seems to occur to him. He slaps the side of his head. 'Why didn't I think of it? Is it possible my sister made such an agreement with the King?'

I have my wife's words spinning about my head: *Even if they offer you a pardon for saying you are guilty . . . You must maintain your innocence or you will lose your head.*

'No. It's impossible. She'd never have done that.' It all comes clear. The Howards are casting us adrift – Frances and me. I begin to doubt once more whether my wife has truly made a confession, or if Harry Howard is deceiving me, like Bacon was. 'I won't.' My voice is firm and I feel my resilience return.

'For pity's sake, if nothing else, do it for your daughter. Do you want her growing up in the shadow of a father executed for murder?'

That poor dog starts up its howling once more.

My focus sharpens and I can see that I had been wrong all along. The look, the Howard poise I wished my daughter to inherit, is the look of pure corruption. The Howards are rotten to the core, the lot of them. Only my Frances is free of it. I look at him and can see now that his resemblance to his sister is only superficial. Harry Howard is a sham. His eyes lack the warm intensity of hers and his smile has none of her beguiling sweetness. 'Where are your parents?' I ask. I am sure now that *they* are the source of this mission, rather than the King.

'At Audley End. They scuttled back there until this business is all over.' He looks angry again, which confuses me.

'They'd abandon their daughter.' My poor Frances, even her own mother has left her to her fate. 'Why would they do such a thing?'

'To avoid becoming mired in her scandal. I tried to stop them going.' He wipes a glaze of sweat from his forehead. 'I beg you, come to your senses, Robert. Do as the King asks. Your confession could save my sister.' He omits to say how this could be and I know better.

I am certain Frances has not confessed and that her trial will be a mere formality to demonstrate her innocence.

'In a year or two you may be living with your wife and daughter.' He gesticulates expansively. He is convincing. He could earn his living at the playhouse. 'You will probably have a new infant on the way. You will retain your lands, your respect. It will be a good life.'

He thinks I can't see through him. A thought rises to my surface, like a forgotten splinter – something that will save me.

I tell him I will think about confessing. He looks pleased, triumphant even, perhaps. Harry Howard cannot see that I have no intention of falling into his trap, that far from making a confession I am determined to prove my innocence.

'Would you do something for me, Harry? There's a book I need from my Whitehall apartments.' I explain what I want of him. 'It must be possible to conceal a single book among my linens.'

He tells me he will do his best. I don't know if he can be trusted but I have no other choice.

I am newly spurred with the thought that, rather than being cast adrift, I will find a way to save my wife from the poisoned claws of her flesh and blood.

Her

The barge pushes on up the Thames. It is a perfect day, clear blue sky and a gentle breeze. The river is crowded with craft and choppy for it. Frances holds on to the side so tightly her knuckles are white. She is more afraid of the water than the trial she is about to face.

The oarsmen swerve to avoid a boat that has come alongside theirs, picking up the rhythm to leave it in their wake, but not before Frances is hailed with a volley of insults. She doesn't need to look at them to know the expressions they wear, like a pack of hounds at the kill. Lalage is petrified, gasping and stammering. Frances pretends she can't hear and puts on a show of chatting pleasantly, refusing to display any weakness, biting down hard on her inner cheek until sharp iron floods her mouth.

Thankfully the Westminster steps are cordoned off and the crowds kept well away, but the roar as Frances disembarks is thunderous. Guards surround her for her own protection. They walk in an unwieldy group towards Westminster Hall and in through the side court. The door is open. She halts on the threshold to gather herself and for her eyes to adjust to the gloom after the bright sunlight.

She removes her cape, handing it to Lalage, who is shrinking into the wall. Someone leads the girl away and Frances steps forward. She looks around, remembering all the occasions she danced in this room, closing her eyes a moment so she can hear the music and the rhythmic thump of feet. The place is filled to the rafters. A great banked scaffold has been constructed to accommodate the crowd.

She tells herself that it is nothing more than a performance and they are her audience. She is sure she sees Essex, almost hidden, twitching in a distant pew, and has an abrupt memory of their first night together – his swollen, fumbling desire and her own, assaulting her perversely from nowhere. They coupled like dogs, despite their distaste for each other. The lie about that became fact: *There is no such thing as the truth.*

Harry sits at the front. He meets her eye with a smile of encouragement. Lizzie is beside him, looking at the crumpled handkerchief twisted round her fingers. Frances seeks out her parents but they are nowhere to be seen.

Fear crashes over her, as sudden and unexpected as a summer storm, and with it the doubts about her pardon return. But she holds herself upright and walks across the floor. The peers who will try her are seated in ranks to her right. Most of the men she once danced with are here. None will look at her. Opposite them are the legal men who will judge her.

She takes a deep breath. As she steps forward the place falls to a hush. A single cry of '*Whore*' comes from the scaffold, followed by a scuffle presumably as the culprit is ejected. She stands at a lectern on which there is a Bible and she is guided through what she must say to make her oath. She stoops to kiss the leather binding, and when she speaks, she makes her voice so soft she can barely hear it herself.

She is led to a seat and listens while all that brute Weston's wrongdoings are read out and it is suggested he was acting on her orders. She mustn't think of Weston now or she will lose her composure, for in her mind he is with Anne and Franklin and Elwes, suspended from a gibbet. She is horrified to feel a real warm tear roll down her cheek, berating herself inwardly for letting her emotions show, then realizing it is to her advantage to put on a display of weakness and remorse.

She stands to make her plea. It is as if the chamber itself holds its breath when she admits her guilt. Her words have to be repeated by the clerk of the court because those on the bench complain she can't be heard. Harry, at the front, holds both hands to his face. Lizzie begins to sob.

Bacon stands to address the lords and she cannot interpret whether the brief look he gives her is benevolent or otherwise. He begins by praising her for her honesty. 'Unlike those tried before for this crime, the countess has made a full confession. I know your lordships cannot look on her without compassion.' Her fear begins to drain away. 'Many things may move you: her youth, her person, her sex, her noble family, yes, her provocations, but chiefly you must be moved by her penitence. I will enforce nothing against a penitent . . .' She can smell victory. He is laying the way for her pardon. She will not need to spill the King's dirty secret, then.

The clerk asks her if she has anything to say before sentence is passed and she keeps her voice small. 'I desire mercy and beg that the noble lords will intercede for me to the King.'

The lord chancellor stands to pronounce the sentence. While he is stating that she will hang by the neck until she is stark dead, Frances is thinking about the card trick she has been perfecting. His tone of voice is infused with compassion and there is no doubt in her mind that she has won. The dumb show is over and her sentence will be transmuted.

She makes a meek curtsy to her judges before she is led away. As they walk back towards the river the crowd that was baying for her blood a mere hour ago is completely silent. They are satisfied that justice has been done. The blood they want now is her husband's. It is all she can do to prevent herself jumping and whooping.

She turns to the head guard and, with affected confusion, says, 'Is it over? Am I to be returned to the Tower now?'

When he replies that it is, she cries, 'No, that can't be so. I have not had the opportunity to tell the lords of my husband's innocence.' She even manages to generate a few more distressed tears. 'Let me go back. I *must* tell them.'

She flails at the guard with her fists and he very gently takes her by the forearms, saying, 'I'm so very sorry.' His pity is apparent. 'It is over – there's nothing more to be done.' He very carefully helps her into the barge as if she is made of finest crystal.

The boat sways beneath her. She collapses on to the bench at the back. The water is dark. It wants to swallow her. She begins to shake uncontrollably. They will all assume it is the looming thought of the gallows that has made her so afraid.

Him

I stand before the court, eyes down, clutching my prayer book. It conceals the letter that will prove my innocence. Harry's word was good — it seems he, of the Howards, is friend rather than foe — for he sent me the book and the forgotten letter was between its pages, as I'd remembered. It is written in Thomas's hand, beside that inflamed heart: *The remedy you sent has had no effect. You must send me stronger.*

Westminster Hall is heaving with life. I can feel every pair of eyes burning through me, can sense the impatience to see me brought to my knees. More takes a seat close behind me, whispering his encouragement. This diminutive man, my gaoler, is my only friend here and I hardly know him at all. I think of Frances standing on this spot only a few hours ago, but I am a fool if I think comfort can be had in reminding myself of her ordeal.

Finally, I lift my eyes from the floor to find, right in my line of sight, Essex, wearing a smirk of triumph. The scarring on his face pulls his eye out of shape, as if his skin might peel away to reveal someone else beneath. He mouths something, I can't make out what, but I can imagine. He is starched through with bitterness. I see Pembroke nearby, whispering something to Southampton, and there is Winwood, wearing a self-satisfied sneer. Frances had been right about him: *That man will come back and bite you.* I mustn't think of Frances, or I will fall apart. I realize the place is filled with my enemies, and I feel as if I am a condemned man before I have even been tried.

My Garter jewel hangs from my neck, my reminder that I was chosen by the King. I touch my fingers to it as if it has the power to bring me good fortune. But I feel the heft of judgement in the room and see myself, suddenly, as the court sees me: the jumped-up, orphaned son of a minor Scottish nobleman, who gained all he has by dint of his pretty face, like a woman. The only blessing is that the King is not here to witness this and neither is my replacement. The instant I think of Villiers I regret it, for it reminds me of the stark truth of my situation and dread upends me.

A hush takes hold and I am sworn in before the clerk stands to read out the evidence. He is a long-faced man who speaks as if his tongue is too big for his mouth and tells in detail the many ways in which Weston, supposedly on my orders, administered poison to my friend Thomas. 'There was barely a morsel that passed the victim's mouth that was not in one way or another adulterated. It is a wonder he survived as long as he did.'

The room is swimming and I'm finding it hard to concentrate on what is being said because Thomas is growling in my ear: *You think you are innocent but you are as much responsible for my death, in your abandonment of me, as those who administered the deadly dose.*

'The Earl of Somerset, here before you, stirred up, moved, commanded, abetted, aided, hired, counselled' – the clerk is clearly enjoying himself – 'and assisted Weston in the execution hereof and is therefore indicted as an accessory before the fact of the murder of Sir Thomas Overbury.'

I turn to More behind, whispering, 'This is all wrong. It's not true.' He tries to reassure me that I will be given a chance to defend myself against the accusations. 'Or . . .' he pauses, imploring with his eyes '. . . you could still confess and fall on the King's mercy.'

I do not reply. I can barely hear for Thomas's rumbling.

Then the clerk addresses me directly. He asks me how I plead. When I say, 'Not guilty,' I sense the tension tighten in the chamber, like the air before a storm. He asks me then how I will be tried. I search for the correct protocol. 'By God and the country.'

The clerk shakes his long face minutely and whispers, 'My peers – by God and my peers.' His mollusc tongue emerges and withdraws. A wave of nausea catches me unawares.

I correct my mistake and hear a ruffle of suppressed laughter. I am like a man set in trembling aspic and I fear I will forget everything, so I beg the clerk for pen and paper. 'This is most unusual,' he informs me, before consulting with Ellesmere – another enemy – and Bacon. Is he also an enemy? I don't know. He wasn't once, but everything is different now.

My request is granted and writing materials are procured. I hope this is a good sign. A fuss is made about finding a stool on which to place the ink as the lectern slopes too steeply to hold it. If I could sit it would all be much easier, but I do not have leave to do so. I am ham-fisted as I try to organize myself. Thomas, with his invisible hand, pushes the paper all on to the floor in a cascade so I am forced to bend to gather it up. I dip the pen. Thomas grabs my hand, shaking it, so ink drips on my breeches. I am thankful they are black.

Ellesmere says his piece. He has the air, with his fluff of white beard, of a benevolent grandfather. But his tone is bereft of even an iota of compassion when he reminds the lords that an instigator is more heinous by far than one who simply acts on orders. Essex watches him with a smug expression. Ellesmere was a great friend of his father. Then he turns, fixing me with a look of utter disdain. 'To deny the truth is an affront to God.'

Bacon speaks next, standing with a flourish of papers and

making an assessment of the room, before speaking: 'Murder is the most grave of crimes, and of all its methods, poisoning is the most odious. It is a silent killer, a vile deceit that creeps up stealthily on its oblivious victim.' He looks round to ensure his words are meeting their mark. Bacon has the appearance, with his pointed russet beard and unswerving gaze, of a fox. I imagine I can see his tail bushing out at his back.

'The fact that the victim was incarcerated at the time of his poisoning makes it all the more abhorrent an act.' He is enjoying his speech, delighting in his selection of adjectives, moving his paws in a dance to emphasize his point. He certainly has his audience captivated. 'My esteemed lords, it is not necessary to deliberate on the manner, the actual mechanics' – he pinches together his index finger and thumb, holding them aloft – 'of the unfortunate victim's death, as it is already proven that Weston committed the deed, for which he, and his accomplices, have paid with their lives. What must be decided is whether the Earl of Somerset,' he slides his eyes towards me, 'did seek to procure the victim's death in any way . . .'

He talks and talks, of Thomas and me, of how our friendship was turned to loathing by our dispute over my wife. On and on he talks. I am trying to concentrate, I know my life depends on it, but I can't follow. I attempt to scribble notes, but they seem to make no sense either. Thomas has a hold of my pen, is writing gibberish. Bacon talks of 'an unholy alliance, a deadly triumvirate' of myself, Frances and Northampton, 'dedicated to securing Overbury's downfall'.

On and on '. . . poison in salts, poison in meats, poison in tarts, poison in medicines . . . such a quantity of poison was administered to the unwitting victim that its force was blunted on him . . .' On and on '. . . there grew a root of bitterness, a mortal malice . . .'

On and on and on '. . . over and above his motive and the obvious acrimony between him and his victim, the accused's subsequent behaviour . . .'

My paper is a mess of scribbles. People are being called to give evidence. Some man named Forest is saying that Frances offered him money to ambush and kill Thomas on my orders. I want to stop his lies with my fist. Someone must have paid him to say those things.

Thomas is in my head, making my thoughts spin.

A witness is called. He is saying I had many meetings with Weston, though I have denied knowing the man. The truth is that I remember him as Thomas's guard and only vaguely as someone who conveyed letters between Frances and me before we were married – in my mind that is not 'knowing'. Other witnesses are called and a tangled web of evidence is knitted around me from my unravelled threads. I cling to the thought of the letter lying between the pages of my prayer book as the only tool to free myself.

And then old Master Overbury hobbles up on his sticks. My heart lists. He looks shattered with grief. He tells the court that I forbade him to petition the King for his son's release. His words hammer a nail into me. I am guilty of that – saturated in remorse. I want to prostrate myself before him and beg his forgiveness.

Here comes Lidcote now, the brother-in-law, talking of how Thomas believed I was deceiving him. He trains his eyes my way, like twin cannons. Another nail. Then it is Lawrence Davies's turn, the loyal boy we rescued from a beating once, to whom I promised a position. What nail will sweet, placid Lawrence Davies pound into me to add to all this incriminating testimony?

'I overheard the earl say, when he was discussing the Moscow embassy with Overbury, "Don't go." I am sure I was not mistaken.' Bang, bang, bang. He was *not* mistaken, it is true, but I want to scream out that it was not meant as it sounds.

I turn to More. He must read my distress, as he seems very sorry for me – deep creases cut across his brow.

Lawrence continues. Hammer, hammer, hammer. 'Overbury became very sick in the wake of receiving a letter from the earl, which contained white powders.'

I lean back, whispering to More, 'But I told them – I told them about those powders, that they were nothing but chalk.' The man behind him titters in disbelief. I cling to my prayer book for fear Thomas will spirit it away. My letter will prove this point false at least, and so cast doubt on all the other accusations against me. I dare to believe this – it is all I have.

More pats my arm. 'In good time. You will have your chance to refute it all.' His hand is small as a child's.

Bacon is back on song, recounting to the lords how Northampton and I inveigled to commit Thomas to solitary confinement and ply him with poisons, and that I was constantly asking for news of his health. 'There was one thing pretended and another thing intended.'

He talks of the testimony of some wet-nurse I have never heard of, saying she was sure of my guilt and that I confessed it to my wife on my wedding night. I want to shout that they are twisting the facts – it was not like that.

I am staggered to see how easy it is to make something seem like incontrovertible fact when it is all lies.

A hush falls and I feel myself unbearably heavy, sinking down and down. Ellesmere, with his cuckoo-spit beard, asks if I want to change my plea. 'No,' I say. My voice is a croak. 'No, I do not.' All I have to cling to is the truth. He shakes his head, as if he thinks me a fool.

An interval is announced. I have no idea of the time. More is kind enough to let me take his chair for a few minutes.

He is the only one present who feels the remotest sympathy for me.

I am offered bread and cheese. I cannot eat and my throat is parched but all there is to drink is wine. I long for something weaker but gulp it back all the same and am glad of it, not for quenching my thirst but for the way it tempers my fear and the blessed befuddlement it brings.

Her

Frances dozes in a pool of sunlight. The door to her room, a new room – bright and clean and away from the river – is wide open and the day spills in. She can hear, vaguely through her half-sleep, the sound of laughter from the guards playing dice in the courtyard. There is a vase of yellow-eyed forget-me-nots on the table. She picks flowers every day in the gardens. Beside the vase is her full pardon, which arrived this morning, on vellum bearing the royal seal, thick and red, like a clot of blood.

Earlier, from her window at a distance, she had watched her husband walk to the waiting barge, his gait reluctant and his posture desolate. She is no longer confined to her rooms. She can come and go as she pleases within the environs of the Tower and could have gone down and caused a scene with his guards, insisting upon the opportunity to send him on his way with a kiss from his wife. But she didn't.

Someone somewhere is playing music, and plangent notes thread through her half-sleep. A tap on wood draws her out of her languor and, opening her eyes, she sees her sister's face appear round the door.

'Darling Frances,' says Lizzie, her voice thin with apprehension.

'This came.' Frances hands her the King's pardon.

She needs only to read the first line to see what it is. 'Thank the Lord for that. I've been –' Lizzie looks as if she might burst into tears of relief. 'I've been half mad with worry. So, what will happen? You'll be housed here for a while?'

'Until things settle down.' Frances pulls a chair up for her sister. 'Mother not with you?'

Lizzie looks apologetic, twisting her hands together. 'I'm sorry, but Mother and Father went back to Audley End more than a month ago.'

Frances snorts an indignant puff of air. 'How like them.'

'But I thought you'd want to see your daughter.' Lizzie goes to the door, saying, 'Come in.'

The pendulous-breasted wet-nurse lumbers in carrying the baby. Frances wonders what became of Nelly, thinks of her rolling that diamond ring, like quicksilver, over her knuckles. Nelly can look after herself but Frances is a little disappointed not to be able to show her how well she has mastered the sleight of hand.

Lizzie cuts through her thoughts. 'She's good as gold. A little dream.'

The nurse holds out the baby for her to take. It offers her a big gummy grin, and Frances can see the edge of a single tooth that must have appeared in the last week. It is wearing a little brocade dress and has a string of amber beads that it brings up to its mouth with a fat hand. She takes it on her lap.

'She's just like you,' says Lizzie.

A little fist grips Frances's finger. She feels herself momentarily captivated by the child who looks like her.

'Do you have news from Westminster Hall?' She tears her gaze away from her baby.

'We stopped there on the way and saw Harry. He said it's going on and on and Robert has yet to make an account of himself.' Frances can tell by her sister's taut expression that it is not going well.

'But what was his plea?'

'Oh, not guilty.'

'The fool,' says Frances, and, with a little moan, claps a

387

hand to her forehead in mock distress. 'If he'd only done as I did, he'd likely be back here already and sitting with us now.'

'I'm so sorry.' Lizzie is clearly upset at her sister's apparent suffering. 'But I fear you must prepare for the worst. There are too many who want to see him fall.'

'There may yet be a miracle.' Frances shapes her expression into one of forlorn hope but her sister remains grave.

Him

I don't know the lawyer who is speaking now. His eyesight is poor, and when he consults his notes he does so through a pair of glasses. '. . . I have not known, heard, or read of a felony more foul . . . He that dares to commit such an odious evil . . .'

I am glad of that slug of wine, as it makes his words skim over me like flat stones over a pond. But now he is talking of the white powder, saying that, according to Franklin, it was arsenic. Now he is reiterating what Lawrence Davies said about it. Now he is reading from Frances's deposition, telling of the poisoned tarts. My mind flaps and I am trying to note down all that is said, but Thomas will not give me back my pen.

He brings up Franklin, seems convinced I knew the man, is saying that he visited me at Whitehall in the wake of Weston's arrest.

I don't know what he's talking about. I wouldn't know Franklin if he were before me now, and I barely knew Weston, but he is making it seem as if we were a cabal of wickedness. Apparently his information comes directly from Frances. They are twisting her words. She would not say I knew Franklin when I did not. I am beginning to regret the wine for I am too muddleheaded to follow properly what is being said.

There is more: 'The accused ensured that a great number of the letters he wrote to Northampton were burned and –' He stops, tapping once more for effect. 'Letters from

Overbury, he had doctored with false dates. The destroying of evidence,' *tap*, 'in the burning and altering of letters,' *tap*, 'the signing of a warrant to search Weston's house,' *tap*, 'and that he sought a general pardon from the King,' *tap*. He is almost drooling, thinking he is in at the kill. 'These are not the actions of an innocent man.'

Put like that, I cannot imagine anyone who would not send me to the gallows. In my mind I run through all those things I did on Frances's advice – the burned letters, the search warrant, the royal pardon – and I have Frances's voice in my head: *It wouldn't even be subterfuge to change one or two dates by a few weeks. That way, if it ever comes to it – which I very much doubt it will but if it does – then nothing can be misinterpreted.* Oh, God, Frances, what have you done?

Several of my papers slide to the floor again. I retrieve them, tucking them beneath the inkpot, which Thomas tips so it spills in a pool over my scribbled notes. I could cry.

I can see Frances in my mind's eye, a hand on her swollen belly that houses the infant we made together, a crease on her brow, unbearably beautiful: *I need you, Robert.* And I know with certainty that any ill she has done was with the best, the most pure, of intentions.

All at once I am gripped by fear for her. It knocks the breath out of me, has an intensity that surpasses any fear I have yet felt for myself. I'd always believed her judgement so utterly sound and had turned to her for strength and direction. But if she has been so mistaken in her advice to me, then what kind of hazards must she have fallen into at her own trial? I imagine her in the Tower, half crazed with desperation and terror.

It is deep into evening by the time the prosecution has finished making its case. I am on the brink of collapse. My Garter jewel feels like a dead weight about my neck but it is all I have left of my dignity. Ellesmere asks me yet again whether I want to alter my plea. 'I feel sure the King will be merciful if you do so.'

I am paralysed with doubt. Do I follow Frances's advice or her example? She confessed and is condemned. My refusal is barely audible.

Another interval is announced and I am hustled into an anteroom, where, mercifully, at last I can sit for a half-hour. Kind More sits with me, neither of us saying a word. I cling to the letter cached in my prayer book – my last hope. He tries to make me eat some bread. It is like sawdust. I drink more wine. It is sharp as vinegar. The thought flits through my jumbled head that I could send word to the King, threatening to reveal our secrets. It shocks me deeply that I have become a man who would even consider such a low act. I am horrified by myself even as I dismiss the idea.

As we return to the hall More feigns brightness, reminding me that it is my turn to give my account of things. 'You will put it right.' I can see he thinks this is unlikely.

My hands are damp with sweat, my notes a jumble, and I try to recall each point but there was so much said, so many aspersions cast, my head swills with it all. When I find my voice, it is weak.

'I do confess that I wished for Overbury to be imprisoned.' I can feel the whole place prick its ears. 'But I never contrived that he should be killed.' I can feel the disappointment – they had been hoping for a confession.

'It is true Overbury and I argued often. We argued bitterly over my wife but he never did threaten me with blackmail.' Overbury's threat was to the King, not me, but all the same I am skimming the very edge of perjury with this.

I try to explain about the embassy, describe my efforts to convince him to take it. I keep fumbling through my illegible notes and attempt to address all the accusations.

'I did send Overbury tarts, but good ones. He was my friend. I wanted to make his time in the Tower less arduous with a few comforts.' Doubt is smeared through the room. 'Did Lieutenant Elwes not say in his testimony that the food I sent was good?'

I deny that I met Franklin, as my wife is supposed to have said. 'I didn't know him, have just heard him spoken of as some kind of apothecary. And neither did I know Weston then.'

One of the lawyers counters this, waving his papers. 'But I have it here that Weston was a go-between for you and the countess when you were not yet wed.'

I have dug a hole for myself. But rather than telling the truth and saying that may be the case, that I didn't 'know' the fellow, had never exchanged words with him, I say, 'He must have passed the letters to my servants to bring to me.' It sounds implausible and I realize I have cast even more doubt over my defence. So, when I tell of the chalk powders and how Thomas requested them himself, I can see that no one believes me.

But I have the letter – a spark of hope. I allow myself to imagine it as the catalyst to change all the minds in Westminster Hall.

I whip it out, flapping it. 'This letter here demonstrates incontrovertibly that the powders I sent were benign.' I feel the tide turn fractionally in my favour as I pass it to the clerk, who reads it out. Thomas's words fill the space: *The remedy you sent has had no effect. You must send me stronger.* I can feel Thomas is ready to forgive me: he has a hand on my shoulder. I can sense the atmosphere change as my accusers reassess their opinion. One or two flickering smiles and sympathetic looks are flung my way. My spark of hope becomes a steady flame.

The clerk passes the letter to the lawyer. Silence falls as he inspects it, slowly and thoroughly, through a magnifying glass.

Eventually he speaks. 'It looks to me as if the date has been altered on this letter.'

'No,' I wail. 'That's not true.' That steady flame wavers.

The lawyer passes it to Bacon, who also inspects it closely. 'It *has* been established that the accused has had other correspondence altered.'

'That one is untouched,' I say, but incredulity is carved into them. 'It has sat untouched in my apartments for three years.' It is God's truth but what use is the truth when no one can be made to believe it? Thomas's hand on my shoulder is heavy as lead.

'Why did you not produce it before now as evidence to support your case?' His voice seems tempered, or perhaps I am imagining it.

'I had forgotten about it.' I am aware of how unconvincing I sound.

'Is that so?' He has his fox's eyes on me and I can't tell what he is thinking.

Ellesmere is now inspecting the paper. He shakes his head firmly, saying, 'Inadmissible.'

And my flame is doused.

I am dog tired, can barely stay on my feet, but I continue nonetheless, tangling myself further and further into the trap that they have elaborately laid. Why did I burn Northampton's correspondence, why the warrant to search Anne Turner's house, why the doctored letters, why the request for a general pardon? They twist everything out of shape and my excuses ring hollow. 'That is not how it was.'

I know I am beaten and I wonder if Frances was reduced to this, for I, too, am on the brink of confessing. But I manage to cling to the truth – the truth is all I have left.

The lords withdraw and I am returned to the anteroom where I lift my Garter jewel over my head, handing it quietly to More. The humiliation of being publicly stripped of it would be too much for me to bear. With it go the final shreds of my dignity.

Out in the hall once more I try to hold on to my self-possession. I grip tightly to the lectern to prevent myself collapsing as the guilty verdict is announced and the sentence read out: *You are to be carried from hence to the Tower, and from thence to the place of execution where you are to be hanged until you are dead. And the Lord have mercy upon you.*

I cannot hear properly for Thomas's laughter is too loud, so loud I cannot hear my own thoughts.

Her

Frances has been walking with her brother in the gardens. Like children, they have made daisy chains and woven them through each other's hair. After she has waved him off at the gatehouse she returns across Tower Green towards her chambers, speculating on when they will erect the scaffold there or if Robert will be executed on the Hill. His trial was a month ago, so it is bound to be done soon.

More finds her there, picking sprigs of love-in-the-mist, so pretty now, but they will be dead by dusk. All the summer flowers here remind her of Forman's garden, that heady display of beauty with its hidden menace. More seems to have something pressing he wants to divulge. He twitches with it, and she can imagine rodent whiskers sprouting from his cheeks.

'What is it, More?' She hopes he is not about to announce that she has been allowed the charge of her infant.

She is preparing to convince him that the child would be much better off remaining with its cousins, when he says, 'Your husband has news.'

'What news?' She knows what the news is, and he knows she knows. She knots her brow, allowing her breath to stumble. 'It's not –' She points an unsteady hand towards Tower Green.

'I think it best he tells you himself.'

Robert's rooms are in one of the round towers, up a winding set of steps. She prepares what she will say. He will want her to cry. She will give him that, at least, allow him the delusion that he is still loved when he meets his end.

More remains outside and she finds Robert alone in the gloom. He seems to have dropped off in his chair with his head at an awkward angle, as if his neck is broken already. He looks gaunt with exhaustion. His eyes pop open and he must suspect he is dreaming when he sees her, as he looks confused, asking, 'Is it you?'

She flings back the hanging that covers the window and light floods the space. He shades his eyes with a hand, blinking. 'Frances?'

She watches his face break into a smile as it dawns on him that she is real. There is almost nothing left of the golden boy who ignited all the hungry animal desire in her. She misses that force of feeling a little but not enough for it to matter. There are always others to satisfy her needs. His shirt hangs open, revealing a hollow pigeon chest with a sparse smattering of pale fuzz. His skin is dry and his hair unkempt. She can see now that the abundant charisma he once had was a mere mirage, created by his proximity to the King, nothing more than a trick of the light.

He gets to his feet and she hopes he will not try to kiss her, as his lips are chapped and there is a residue of white matter in the corners of his mouth that makes her stomach turn. But he embraces her, burrowing his face into her neck. He is all skin and bone and smells musty. She feels nothing much and wishes he would let her go. There is wetness on her neck. He is crying.

She breaks apart from him, saying, 'I'm so sorry, Robert. So very sorry.' She has an image in her mind of him on the scaffold.

'It was terrible, Frances. Everything was twisted. I had no way to defend myself.' She wishes he sounded less defeated, more angry, more defiant. 'But you, what of you, my darling?'

'I have my pardon. My sentence is withdrawn.'

'You're saved! Oh, God, thank God.' He clasps her hands, holding them as if he will never let go.

'If you'd done as I did, Robert, you, too, would be facing freedom rather than –'

'My darling.' She waits for him to remind her, heaving with tragedy, that it was she who advised him not to confess. But his face lights up, confusing her, and she sees a glimmer of his old magnetism. It fails to move her. His breathless joy is making her uneasy. 'I heard from the King this morning. My sentence will not be carried out either. So, we live. Both of us. Together.' He opens his arms, as if he is Jesus performing a miracle.

'Together,' she repeats, lost for what to say.

'Look, you have daisies in your hair.' His banal delight is unfathomable. She touches her head, pulling them away, letting them fall. He reaches for her, kissing her throat and breast like a ravenous animal and fumbling with a hand to grope beneath her skirts.

'No.' She removes it, retreating a step. 'More is outside. He will hear.'

'What if he does? You are my wife, my darling wife. Do you remember our first time in those rooms at Paternoster Row?' His eyes are half shut in bliss as he presses those chapped lips to her mouth.

She turns her face away from him, stopping herself uttering the truth. This is not the moment to disabuse him of his belief that he took her virginity. She says instead, 'Has the King promised you a full pardon? The return of your estates? The reinstatement of your titles, your position on the Council?'

'What use are titles to us now? During my time in this place I have come to understand the emptiness of all those trappings. We have each other. What else matters?'

Uncertainty wraps itself about her. He is smiling like an idiot, talking about the quiet life they will lead when they are released – a life of purgatory.

'If!' she snaps. '*If* you are released.'

'Don't be afraid of that, my darling. He won't keep me in here for ever. Why would he do that? It's not as if I was tried for treason.'

All she can think of is that she wants to get as far away as she can from this grim little chamber and its inhabitant. 'I must go – not really meant to be here. Don't want to visit trouble on More.'

He grabs her hand, pulling her back to him, whispering, 'Together for ever.'

Him

More arrives in my rooms. I half expect – it is a hope, really – Frances to be with him, though he hasn't brought her in the several weeks since we had that tantalizing encounter, and he hasn't today. My disappointment is small. We have the rest of our lives to spend together and the afterlife, so a few weeks' wait will only make our eventual reunion all the more passionate.

More seems cheerful. He is holding something, which he places on the table with a knowing smile. It is my Garter jewel. The little St George on his rearing horse winks in a ray of evening sun. The tapestry covering the window has long been moved and my rooms are, consequently, light-filled and quite pleasant.

I look at More. 'What does this mean?'

'It means that I have word from His Majesty. He wants you to keep it.'

'So?' I feel my heart dilate, opening out as if it will burst from my ribcage.

'You continue to be a Garter knight.'

I spring from my chair, tempted to embrace his small form but he steps away, embarrassed.

'There is more,' he says. 'You are no longer to be kept as a close prisoner. You have the freedom of the Tower environs.'

'I can visit my wife?' Joy splits my face.

'Indeed you can.' He is smiling, too, and not the tight smile I am used to seeing on him but a broad, joyous beam.

'And I will have a full pardon?'

'Not exactly. The King says you may write to him and that he is prepared to reinstate a manor to you, which will provide a living. Eventually you will be released but you will not be permitted to return to court.' He looks apologetic and seems surprised by my ebullience.

'I have everything I need for my happiness,' I say, by way of an explanation. 'I have my wife, my life, my infant, the means to live, and I have not entirely lost the King's love. There is nothing more I could wish for.' Hearing myself say those things out loud, I am struck by the change in me. I think of the extent to which my younger self so desperately sought favour and status but now I see only emptiness there.

'Your wife is in the gardens.' More is looking out of the window.

'Can I join her?'

'Of course. There is no need to ask.'

I grab my Garter jewel, fling it round my neck and run from the room, taking the steps two at a time, bursting out of the door at the bottom into the bright heat of a July evening. All the torture of the past months slips away to nothing. I am galloping over the lawn, arms spread, calling her name. She turns, astonishment on her face, poppies in her hands. 'You,' she says, seeming lost for words.

'I am free,' I cry, as I reach her and draw her to me.

She fingers my Garter jewel. 'A full pardon, your offices reinstated?'

'Not exactly, but —'

'Then you are not free.' She pulls away.

'Don't be sad, my darling. We have all we need. I have the freedom of the Tower. We can live as man and wife.' I take her hand. 'Come and walk with me.' I guide her towards some steps that lead to a walkway overlooking the river.

Once up there we stand, completely alone and hidden from view, in our own private world. I lean over to look into the water below. I can feel her pearl in my pocket.

'Isn't the light beautiful where it catches the ripples? Imagine swimming in it.' I have a sudden image of Prince Henry vaulting on to the Greenwich pier and shaking his hair, droplets skimming the air like a crown of diamonds. I remember how I loathed him for his love of Frances, when I had secretly claimed her for myself.

'I can't swim,' she says, 'and I'm told the currents here are dangerous.' She looks at the already wilting bunch of poppies. 'I'm afraid of water.'

I had never thought her afraid of anything but knowing this small weakness makes my tenderness swell. 'You never need be afraid with me. I'll always protect you.'

We are silent for a while. I can't stop thinking of Northampton and all the harm he visited on his great-niece. How can someone wilfully break a person, a child, like that? It is incomprehensible. Were he still alive I would willingly choke the air from him with my bare hands. 'That man has much to answer for.' I don't really mean to say it aloud.

'Who do you mean?'

'Northampton. That man was a devil. The story you told me of your parrot – how he made you break its neck to teach you to overcome love.' I can feel the throbbing pulse, the frantic beat of feathers, the snap, as if the memory is my own. I remember the night she told me with acute clarity: the way the moonlight threw itself over her, the thrilling whisper of her voice, my deep shock at her revelation and how my love took form in the knowledge of her brokenness.

'Is that what I told you?' She turns to me and seems inexplicably on the brink of laughter. 'That's not how it went. It wasn't Uncle, it was me. *I* wanted to feel what it would be like to kill something I loved. Uncle had nothing to do with it.'

I don't know what to say. I don't recognize this woman wearing my wife's skin. The poppies watch me with their black eyes, just like hers. *Who are you?* I ask silently. *Who are you?*

'You didn't *believe* it, did you? That Uncle would be so evil. Uncle wasn't like that. How gullible you have been. I suppose you believed you had my virginity too.'

She is talking, telling me of her conquests: Essex, Prince Henry, others, a guard at the Tower even. I can't listen. Her words are a volley of shots to the heart. I am the broken one now. My thoughts whirr and clunk through the past, remembering all her advice to me: the general pardon, the burned letters, the warrant, the altered dates. What else? I wonder. *Even if they offer you a pardon for saying you are guilty, you must not under any circumstances accept it.* Whirr, clunk. It is the sound of everything falling into place.

The blunt truth confronts me: my wife designed my downfall.

'Did you imagine I'd be happy with an ordinary life? If we're going to be stuck with each other you may as well know the facts.' Her Howard smirk is torture.

Whirr, clunk.

I have that image of Thomas dead seared into my mind and I can hear him warning me about her: *For pity's sake, when are you going to wake up and see she's a base whore and her family are pimps?* I can feel the sting on my palm where I slapped him.

'Not *you?*'

She is still smiling at me, the indecipherable smile that hooked me in all that time ago in the prince's chambers. A new fear wells in my gut: a different fear, a fear born of finally grasping the truth. But the thing that frightens me most is that, despite everything, I can still feel her hook hauling me in.

'Why?' Thomas is in my head and my shame is fighting for sovereignty.

She cups her hand over my ear and whispers, 'Because I could. Because I wanted you.'

I wait for the old euphoria. 'And now ... what do you want now?' Why do I still want her to want me? But Thomas is telling me something: *You are nothing but an object to her, something to collect, like one of the prince's bronze figures.* His voice is indistinct.

He is leaving me.

He is leaving me with her.

'Oh, Robert,' she lets out a brittle laugh, 'when I use the term "want" it's not the same as what you mean when you say it.'

Those black-eyed poppies are mocking me.

Whirr, clunk.

I need to tell Thomas he was right. My anger swells. Thomas is gone and she is here.

A gentle shove would do it.

I look down at the water, black now, and take her pearl from my pocket. I let it drop. It vanishes instantly.

I will watch as the current pulls her slowly under, her waterlogged dress heavier and heavier, until all that is visible is a wisp of that remarkable hair, like a frond of vegetation drifting on the surface.

In a moment that too will disappear.

A cluster of bubbles.

Gone.

As if she never was.

Author's Note

The Poison Bed is, first and foremost, a work of fiction. It is, however, rooted in fact. Frances Howard confessed to the murder of Sir Thomas Overbury and was subsequently convicted for the crime along with her husband, the King's favourite. It was a scandal that rocked the Jacobean court and was one of the initial cracks that would eventually lead to the devastation of the Stuart monarchy. It also made of Frances Howard a living example of the wicked women so prevalent in the drama of the day.

Whether or not Robert Carr was James I's lover is disputed by historians because hard evidence is lacking. However, given that 'sodomy' was a capital offence, this is no surprise. James was famed for his close association with a string of beautiful men and there is no doubt that his relationship with Carr was intimate and that they loved one another – there are letters to support this. So it is not an audacious leap to suppose their closeness was consummated. James worked hard to convince Carr to make a plea bargain at his trial, which suggests he might have been anxious about something coming to light.

There has long been speculation about what really happened when an insignificant man died at the tail end of summer, 1613, in a gloomy cell in the Tower of London. It remains an enigma but there were many for whom Overbury's death was convenient and some, too, who wanted to see Robert Carr and his Howard wife fall. It is generally agreed that Frances's supremely powerful great-uncle had some part to play.

I make no pretence of uncovering any new or definitive

truths about the case, there are none to be had, and neither do I claim any veracity in my characters' intentions. My novel has instead been a way to explore the depths of an intriguing event, blurred by time and made murky by corruption, through the prism of an era in which the truth has become equally elusive.

Though often alluded to, few historians have tackled this episode of history head on, but for those interested in further reading Anne Somerset's *Unnatural Murder: Poison in the Court of James I* is a comprehensive and absorbing rendition.

Acknowledgements

Some novels slip easily into the world, while others arrive kicking and screaming. *The Poison Bed* is of the latter kind and, were it not for the skilled midwifery of three exceptional women, it might not have survived: Jane Gregory, hand-holder extraordinaire and titan among agents; Maxine Hitchcock, whose rare vision and commitment has kept me going even in the hopeless moments; and the indefatigable Jillian Taylor, who has worked ceaselessly to guide me through labyrinthine rewrites and whose razor-sharp editorial instinct has shaped this novel. I am indebted to you all for keeping my dream alive. I am hugely appreciative, too, of the teams at Michael Joseph, Penguin and Gregory and Company, who have done so much vital work on my behalf. Heartfelt thanks also to Mary Sandys and Katie Green for invaluable early input, Hazel Orme, for her seamless and sensitive fine-tuning, and Gill Heeley for an exquisite cover design – if this book is judged by its cover I will be very happy indeed.